ENDLESS

TERRORS

ALSO BY K.J. SUTTON

The Fortuna Sworn Series

Fortuna Sworn

Restless Slumber

Deadly Dreams

Beautiful Nightmares

Other titles

Straight On 'Til Morning

The Door at the End of the Stars

Summer in the Elevator

Content guidance for this title is listed at the back of the book.

ENDLESS TERRORS

K.J. SUTTON

1 3 5 7 9 10 8 6 4 2

Del Rey
20 Vauxhall Bridge Road
London SW1V 2SA

Del Rey is part of the Penguin Random House group of companies
whose addresses can be found at global.penguinrandomhouse.com

Penguin
Random House
UK

Line on p. 384 from *The Vampire Armand* by Anne Rice (Chatto & Windus, 1998)

First published in the UK by Del Rey in 2023

www.penguin.co.uk

A CIP catalogue record for this book is available from the British Library

Hardback ISBN 9781529909043
Trade paperback ISBN 9781529909050

Typeset in 10.5/14.75pt Iowan Old Style by Jouve (UK), Milton Keynes
Printed and bound in Great Britain by Clays Ltd, Elcograf S.p.A.

The authorised representative in the EEA is Penguin Random House Ireland,
Morrison Chambers, 32 Nassau Street, Dublin D02 YH68
www.greenpenguin.co.uk

MIX
Paper | Supporting
responsible forestry
FSC® C018179
FSC
www.fsc.org

Penguin Random House is committed to a
sustainable future for our business, our readers
and our planet. This book is made from Forest
Stewardship Council® certified paper.

Awake, arise or be for ever fall'n.

—John Milton

ENDLESS TERRORS

PROLOGUE

My breath sent plumes of air into the morning. Car doors slammed behind me, the sound stark, like someone clapping their hands in an empty room. We were all here, I noted distantly.

Well, everyone except for one.

As we made our way into the church, I tugged at the bottom of my gray dress. It was too short, but it was also the only one I owned that didn't seem like it should be worn by a faerie queen. I'd wanted to look nice.

After the service came to an end, I watched the casket get carried out.

My fault, I kept thinking. *My fault.*

CHAPTER ONE

*T*he door to Sugarland slammed behind me.

One of the icicles dangling from the roof broke from the force, and it shattered against the black concrete below. The sound must've disguised the door hinges whining again, because I wasn't prepared when a voice said from behind, "Hold it."

I spun and rose my arm in an instinctive movement, readying to block a weapon or a blow. My other hand was already reaching for the holy knife in my pocket. When I comprehended that it was only Leroy standing in the doorway, his earrings glinting from the yellow light above the door, I faltered. My gaze dropped to the wad of cash in his hand. *Oh.*

Recovering, I shoved my hands into my coat pockets and looked up at Leroy's dark, square face. He wore a thoughtful frown now. He'd seen something in my reaction. Something that revealed I was more than I was pretending to be.

"Table six?" I said casually, resisting the urge to wrinkle my nose with distaste. The man who sat there came every Tuesday and Thursday night, and he reminded me of Ian O'Connell with his intense eyes and arrogant familiarity. But his money was as green as everyone else's, and since no one in my family could use their credit cards

1

right now, we needed it. Desperately. I was sending half of what I earned to Emma and Damon, who used the extra funds for Matthew.

"Table six," Leroy confirmed.

"Thanks." I took the cash with my fingertips, careful as ever not to make physical contact, especially now that my gloves were in my backpack. I wore them during every shift as part of the look I'd created, and they had become my signature of sorts with the clientele and the other dancers. Laurie would be proud if he knew.

The thought caused a small pang in my chest.

With effort, I refocused on the human standing in front of me. Leroy's expression was impassive, but I suspected he hadn't missed my brief flare of emotion, either. He was perceptive, for a man. "Good night, Angel" was all he said.

I gave the bouncer a faint, fleeting smile—in spite of his tendency to see too much, Leroy was one of the few people in this place that I actually liked. His focus never wandered below my chin, and every time I slipped into the alley for a break, I always returned to find him on the other side of the door. "See you tomorrow," I said as I turned away.

I had no way of knowing if this was true. Eventually, it wouldn't be, because Finn, Gil, and I never stayed in one place longer than a few weeks. But it was part of the ruse. The ruse that my friends and I had created. Angel Jones, stripper by night, demon hunter by day.

Although, the demon hunter part wasn't going nearly as well. At least once a week, Lyari used her remaining connections at the Unseelie Court to obtain books, journals, and scrolls on the Dark Prince, and we pored over them in whatever dim motel room we were staying at. So far, none of us had found anything to help me kill an immortal from another dimension.

And we couldn't go home until Lucifer was dead.

Swallowing a discouraged sigh, I crossed the parking lot and began the long walk to my car. It was parked on a back road, away from prying eyes and men who hoped to catch me outside the club. It was an ancient Taurus I'd spotted in someone's yard a few weeks back, a faded FOR SALE sign on the windshield. We had needed a different vehicle, since mine was easy to recognize and it displayed Colorado plates. I only missed it when we were on a long drive and Finn wore his wolf form, taking up the entire backseat and filling the cab with his distinctly canine scent.

Not that I smelled much better. My skin reeked of beer, sweat, and men, made worse when I shoved my nose into the collar of my coat, desperately seeking warmth. Nightmare or not, it was the middle of the night, and temperatures were so low that I could see every breath. I reluctantly left the glow of the streetlights behind and headed into the trees, looking back to make sure no one had followed, just as Lyari had taught me.

Bringing Finn or Gil along on my shifts had started to draw too much attention, even when they'd waited outside, so now I sent frequent texts and never went anywhere without looking over my shoulder. It was a fantastic way to live. I suppressed yet another sigh and moved deeper into the darkness. Deeper into the cold.

The war between winter and spring was ferocious, especially in northern Wyoming, where we'd been for the past three weeks. The brown grass was still struggling to become more. Every morning, a curtain of frost hovered over the world, and birds did their best to coax the sun out with their high voices. But there was no sign of those birds now, and the moon was a faint crescent overhead. I gazed up at it, wondering if the people I loved were somewhere looking at the night sky, too.

Then a sound disturbed the stillness.

I stopped, hardly daring to breathe. I scanned the darkness and listened for any other noises. Nothing moved. A hush clung to the air. It was no different than the other nights I'd made this walk, but unease crept under my skin. I turned and kept walking, this time at a quicker pace. I pushed some branches out of the way, and that was when I heard it again. The sound. I imagined a shoe landing on a stick, snapping it in half. I spun around, but only dark, faceless trees stared back.

Lyari's name rose to my tongue, but I didn't want to summon

3

her unless it was an emergency. Unbidden, my mind went to the last conversation we'd had.

That night, we were somewhere in Utah. The harsh lights of a gas station shone down on the rows of pumps and the stained concrete. I stood alone, hands shoved in my coat pockets, staring at the climbing numbers in front of me. A tinny recording played overhead about a two-for-one special on doughnuts. Gil sat in the car, picking at the edges of his nails, and Finn was off in the darkness somewhere.

I fought the urge to fidget. We still had three hours of driving ahead, and I wanted to get it over with. Being crammed in a small space with Gil and Finn was like putting two chemicals in a vial and hoping it didn't explode. Most of the mythology about supernatural creatures was bullshit, but the humans had gotten one thing right—as a general rule, vampires and werewolves did not get along. My companions were no exception.

Suddenly, Gil's head jerked up. His eyes were narrow. I followed his gaze, my pulse already leaping as I shifted into survival mode. I'd half-positioned myself into a fighting stance when I saw Lyari. The tension seeped out of me in a rush, and I almost slumped from the weight of my relief. Lyari scanned the gas station, her mouth pressed into a thin line of distaste. It was still strange to see her without the armor of a Guardian. Tonight she wore jeans and a black turtleneck, her hair scraped back in a low ponytail. There was no visible makeup on her face and I didn't see any jewelry, either. I wasn't sure she even owned any.

"I looked over the motel," she said abruptly. Lyari tended not to bother with greetings. "The rooms didn't have any traces of magic or power. There's a vampire working the front desk, but he reeked of that plant Emma likes so much. I don't think he's in allegiance with anyone, much less an ancient evil from another dimension."

"Marijuana. The plant is called marijuana. You need to remember the names of human things, Ly. You'll blend in easier."

The look Lyari gave me communicated exactly how she felt about that. She'd been resistant to a lot of things since leaving the Unseelie Court, which included giving me any sort of information on where she lived or what she did during our time apart.

Suppressing a surge of frustration, I removed the nozzle from the tank and put it back in its holder. Just as Lyari's form began to shimmer, I remembered the other topic I'd been meaning to bring up with her. There was no time to wonder if I was about to make a huge mistake. "Have you spoken to Thuridan lately?" I blurted.

The question made her frown. "No, not since my banishment. Why?"

My jaw was clenched, my stomach tight. I couldn't bring myself to look at her, so I moved toward the car door and grasped the handle. "I'm sorry, I really am. I don't want to take that moment from you. I'd hoped Thuridan would say the words himself. But this is too important."

"What are you talking about, Your Majesty?" Lyari sounded exasperated.

I turned back to her, and my voice was hard as I forced myself to say, "Thuridan is in love with you, Lyari. I need you to use that in order to get close to him."

The faerie fell silent. She didn't tell me I was delusional. She didn't deny the truth I'd laid in front of her. Instead she said, her face carefully blank, "Why do you need me to get close to him?"

"I saw his memories on the night we broke Collith out. Jassin took a special interest in him, and I want to know why."

It wasn't enough that Jassin was dead. I wanted to confront his ghost, wrap my hands around its throat, and snuff whatever was left of him out of this world. And ever since that night, my instincts had been screaming. It's not over. Don't ignore this.

"Fine," Lyari said finally, the single word swirling through the frigid air between us.

Something about her response made me hesitate. I thought of everything Lyari had already lost because of her allegiance to me. If she did this—if she carried out my request and manipulated Thuridan to glean information from him—it would cost whatever future they might have together. I'd already considered this, of course, but seeing the shadow in Lyari's eyes was different than imagining it.

"You know what? Never mind. I can find another way," I decided.

"I said I would do it." Her voice was sharp now, and I fought the instinct to step back. For an instant, Lyari's face had changed. Her teeth had looked longer, her features more angular. Almost like . . . a goblin's.

I recovered quickly, but I must've flinched. I watched my friend's eyes flicker, and I knew that she'd seen my reaction. Shame filled my throat.

5

Before I could backtrack, Lyari sifted, and she was gone.

Even now, the memory made me wince. No, I definitely didn't want to contact Lyari unless I was out of other options. That left the two males waiting for me back at the motel room. A text to Finn was risky, considering he couldn't pick up his phone half the time. If I used the bond to contact Gil, he'd be here in a minute, but a lot could happen in a minute. Over the course of sixty seconds, people died, or made deals with demons, or overthrew kings.

Over the course of sixty seconds, everything could change.

All this time, we'd been trying to keep our heads down. Every time a man pawed at me, or a woman insulted me, or my skin brushed someone else's by accident, I tamped down the instinct to fight, snap back, feast. But not tonight. Not anymore. What good was staying under the radar if it got me killed?

I kept walking, slowly, my posture relaxed and unsuspecting. Like prey. Even when I heard the undeniable sound of more footsteps. Even when I sensed something coming up from behind. Then, just as Adam had taught me, I planted my heel and spun, bringing my arm around in an arc. Two seconds later, I had a knife to my stalker's throat and his back was against a tree.

"Any last words?" I hissed. Adrenaline pounded in my ears.

"Nice to see you too, honey," the stranger growled.

The sound of his voice opened a yawning hole inside of me. I stared up at him, disbelieving, and my voice was a hoarse whisper as I said, "Collith?"

He gazed back silently, and my mind struggled to accept it. This wasn't the Collith I knew. His appearance was . . . ragged. Several days' worth of stubble covered the lower half of his face. His button-up shirt was wrinkled. There were gray smudges beneath his eyes. His hair was tousled, wild, as if he'd been dragging his hand through it again and again. The cold, collected Unseelie King from my memories was gone, replaced with this weary figure.

The sight of him still made my heart ache.

When I didn't lower the knife, Collith's brows lowered. He frowned as he searched my gaze. "It's me, Fortuna."

6

Suspicion held my hand steady. I wanted to believe him, but my paranoia ran deep. "Prove it," I said flatly.

There was a beat of silence, and then Collith moved. Completely disregarding the knife—acting as if it wasn't there at all, in fact—he leaned down and kissed me.

I was so startled that I didn't react, at first. But the taste of him was achingly familiar. Within seconds, the knife slipped from my fingers and I crushed myself against Collith's hard body. I felt his palm skim my breast and his arousal press between my legs. I was still wearing a backpack, but both of us ignored it. I wrapped my arms around his neck and lost myself to his scent, his tongue, his hands. In the secret places in my head, I think I'd been expecting him, and even as the want consumed me, I felt a familiar prickle in my eyes. The sting of tears I didn't fully understand.

We ended the kiss at the same time, but neither of us pulled away. Not at first. Collith touched his forehead to mine, one of his hands buried in my hair and the other pressed against my waist, keeping me anchored to him. I breathed him in, still struggling to believe that he was real, he was here. It felt as if I was waking up after a long, terrible dream.

The thought was jarring, like the gong of a clock or the screech of brakes. Dreams. Nightmares. Danger. *You shouldn't have come.* The words stuck in my throat, because they felt like a lie. I shifted, stepping away from Collith at last. He stayed where he was, following my movement. His expression was unfathomable. I stared at him, breathing hard, battling the urge to throw myself back into his arms.

Instead, I snatched my knife from the ground and bolted.

Logically, I knew I wouldn't be able to outrun a creature who could vanish and reappear anywhere he wanted. I just knew that I had to move, get away, *away*. I didn't hear footsteps behind me or see Collith ahead, though. My shoes flew over dead leaves and sheets of ice. The car was visible through the trees now, and I burst into the clearing a few moments later, keys already in my hand. I shoved them into the lock, trying not to shake. Once it was open, I tossed my things inside—backpack first, knife second—and dropped into the driver's seat. I began to slam the door shut.

A pale hand moved in a blur. In an instant, Collith had forced the door right back open. He made a sound I'd never heard before and reached inside. White-hot pain shot down my arm at his unrelenting grip.

Without giving me a chance to react, Collith yanked my entire body back into the open. I stumbled and caught myself by flattening my palms against the closest tree. I whirled, my chest heaving in a mixture of fury and terror, and all at once I remembered what Collith had said to me when we first met. *The first thing you should understand is that I am not a man. I don't have human instincts or desires.*

He was a faerie, and a pissed one, at that.

"You've been missing"—Collith slammed the car door shut and came toward me—"for three months. No one knew where you were. What was I supposed to think, Fortuna?"

He'd never been so rough before, and something told me Lyari wasn't the only one struggling with the new, darker urges that came after being severed from a Court. My heart hammered in my ears. Collith could probably hear it, but I still tipped my head back and gave him a disdainful look. "You're not supposed to think anything. That's why I texted you. Or did you lose the ability to read during your time with Death Bringer?"

As soon as I said the words, I wanted to take them back. But I had to drive Collith away. I had to.

"You're scared," he said with that infuriating calm. His hazel eyes looked black as they bore into mine. "You're so scared you can't think straight. And before you lie, keep in mind that I can taste it. Your fear is like . . . sugar. Sweet. What are you running from, Fortuna?"

Ironic, I thought bitterly. It was so ironic that Collith was sensing my fear with the very power he'd taken from me. His question floated between us, and it almost felt visible, like the plumes of air leaving our mouths. But all my reasons were tucked away, hidden in the shadowy corners of my mind and available only to me.

"You think I could forget a little betrayal like that?" I said finally, shoving him away. My lip curled. "All I'm running from is the *smell* coming from you. How long has it been since you've showered?"

The insult bounced off Collith like a bead, skittering into the darkness. He stayed on my heels as I stormed back to the car. "I can help if you just *tell* me, goddamn it."

Lucifer's threats had gone too deep, a weed with long and numerous roots. I just shook my head. "No one can help."

Collith didn't stop me this time, but his voice stayed close, cutting through the night. "Tell me what you need, then. Forget the rest," he insisted.

I slowed, then turned. I raised my gaze back to his. I'd missed him. That was undeniable now. Looking at Collith made me feel a thousand things, all at once, everywhere. In that moment, I longed to trust him. To let someone else share the burden I'd been carrying since leaving home.

"I'm sorry," I whispered. Collith frowned, and I imagined my heart covered in a layer of steel plates as I continued, "I really am. But . . . I can't have you following me."

Before he could ask any more questions, I stabbed Collith in the gut. He cried out and doubled over, his face twisting in pain.

"You always forget about the one I keep in my shoe," I told him coldly. Then I yanked the knife back out and ran back to the car.

Collith's enraged shout echoed all around us. "Fortuna!"

I slammed the door at the same time I turned the key. The car started with a whine, and gravel spewed up from the tires. As I roared off into the night, my eyes flicked to the rearview mirror, searching the place I'd left Collith. But it was too dark. I couldn't make out anything. He'd heal, I reminded myself—my second knife hadn't been soaked in holy water. I kept reminding myself of it as I pulled my phone out and began a new text.

Burn it, I typed. *Burn it all.*

I pressed SEND and floored it.

Five minutes later, neither of them had responded to my message. They were supposed to confirm whenever they saw it. So much for our swift exit strategy.

Once I got to the motel, I killed the engine and stared out the window, clutching the steering wheel so hard my knuckles were white. My sense of urgency hadn't faded, but I needed a minute, just a minute, to regather my thoughts. It felt like they'd scattered and blown off in a hundred different directions.

The parking lot was dim and loud. A cluster of teenage boys lounged against a chain-link fence and music poured from one of the rooms. A woman stood in the open doorway, smoking a cigarette. Near the trash container, a stray dog shoved its snout into a bag that had split open, sending bottles clinking over the cracked pavement.

As I sat there, the neon sign above me flickered, a single word blinking in and out of existence. VACANCY. I gazed up at it, already dreading the next motel, the next sign. The three of us always stayed at this kind of place. Nobody asked any questions and everyone looked the other way if they saw something they shouldn't have. But that didn't mean we were safe, especially now that Collith might've drawn attention to me. We needed to keep moving.

The thought propelled me into motion. I got out of the car—the hinges moaned—and crossed the parking lot. Broken glass crunched under my shoes. All the rooms faced the lot; one door, one window each. I approached the door with the golden number 6 on it, twisted the key in the lock, and went in.

The TV was on. The sound of it filled the tiny room as I crossed the stained carpet and knelt by one of the beds. A form was huddled beneath the blankets, and all I could see of it was a tuft of dark hair. The transformation always drained my werewolf friend. No wonder he hadn't responded to the text. But where was Gil? He'd been the one to leave the TV on, no doubt. The vampire used it to block out noise that traveled through our thin walls.

"Finn." I pulled the covers down and touched his shoulder, reluctant to wake him. "Hey, we have to go."

He woke instantly. I couldn't see Finn's face, but I felt his body stiffen. I felt a flash of regret that I might've interrupted a good dream. The werewolf sat up, his eyes shining in the darkness. His voice was like gravel and thunder as he asked, "What's wrong?"

"I just finished a chat with the old Unseelie King." I was careful not to say his name. "He might've led you-know-who right to us. We have to go."

At that moment, the scene on the TV brightened, allowing me to see Finn's face. The werewolf's dark eyes dropped, probably following the scent he'd just picked up. His expression revealed nothing as he took note of the blood on my hands. I'd been trying not to think about it, but at the stark reminder, I moved toward the sink to wash the blue stickiness away. I heard the bed springs squeak behind me as Finn got up. He didn't ask me what had happened, and for the millionth time, I was grateful to have him at my side through all this. Finn's quiet strength felt like a port in a storm that had been raging for weeks. Months.

A minute later, my hands still slightly damp, I strode from one side of the room to the other and gathered my belongings. I packed what few things Gil had left out, too. Finn was even more careful when it came to keeping his bag ready. And just because I was constantly paranoid, I wiped every surface clean of prints. I didn't fully understand witches and their spells, but I wouldn't make it easy for them to find me.

Once I was done, I covered my fingers with the bottom of my shirt and turned off the TV. Silence filled my ears. Finn had grabbed our bags and gone to the door.

"The vampire is at a bar down the street. We can pick him up on the way," he said, looking up from his cell phone. The werewolf's tone was as calm as ever, but I still heard what he didn't say. Finn was more than willing to leave town without Gil. If I weren't so agitated from the encounter with Collith, I would've rolled my eyes.

Finn pocketed his burner, and seeing that sent a jolt of realization through me—I'd forgotten my phone. As he walked away, I whirled back toward the room, saying over my shoulder, "I'll meet you at the car."

Then I saw Laurie, and I froze.

While the sound of Finn's footsteps faded, neither of us moved. Laurie was leaning against the far wall, arms crossed, one booted foot propped up behind him. I stared, drinking in the sight of the Seelie King before turning my attention to the other faerie who'd appeared in the room. Collith sat on the bed I'd been sleeping in, his hands loosely linked between his knees. My phone rested beside his leg, and it was clear that he'd already healed from our encounter in the woods. Besides the fact he was no longer hunched over in agony, the skin beneath his torn shirt was clean and unbroken.

"You couldn't *pay* me to sit on that mattress," Laurie remarked, raising his brows at Collith. "In fact, you should probably burn those clothes when we're done here."

At the sound of his voice, I launched myself at him.

Laurie pushed off the wall and caught me effortlessly. I buried my face in his shoulder, his springtime scent assailing my senses. Laurie cupped the back of my head, and I heard him inhale, too, as though he was also reassuring himself I was real. "Hey, Firecracker," he murmured.

I pulled away reluctantly, but I couldn't bring myself to let go. My hands made involuntary fists in Laurie's shirt. He couldn't seem to move away, either, and one of his arms remained around my waist. Our faces were so close that I could see the delicate lines of his silvery irises. His breath touched my cheek like the tip of a feather.

"You shouldn't be here," I whispered.

"No," he agreed. "I really shouldn't. But I made you a promise."

I didn't ask him what he was talking about, or pretend to think about it—I knew exactly which promise Laurie meant. The memory lived under my skin like a whisper or a secret. *I will always come for you.*

By that time, Finn had returned. I stared up at Laurie, painfully aware that everyone was watching us. His hair was shorter, but other than that, he looked like himself. Maybe a little more serious than I was used to. We'd been reunited for an entire thirty seconds and he hadn't mentioned an orgy once.

Now I remembered something else he'd said. In the blink of an eye, I was back on that porch, and Laurie's voice floated past. Saying goodbye to me. Hurting me, even though I wouldn't admit it. *I allowed myself to get distracted.*

As if he'd heard the thought, Laurie finally stepped back. His expression wasn't neutral, exactly, but it felt like a door had closed between us. "I should go; I need to get ready for an event at Court. I'll check in later," he murmured.

With that, the Seelie King was gone. The only proof he'd been there at all was the smell of springtime in the air, lingering between me and Collith as if, even now, Laurie were taunting us. I finally moved toward the bed and grabbed my phone, avoiding his gaze. I didn't know what to say. No, I was *afraid* to say anything. Collith could probably sense that, too. I left feeling even more agitated than before, somehow.

Something moved in the corner of my eye, and a moment later, a tall form walked beside me. Light bounced off Gil's bleached hair, making it look a pale, sickly green. "I thought we were picking you up," I remarked.

"Couldn't wait," the vampire told me simply.

I understood; it was the bond. Gil had felt my fear just as strongly as I felt his thirst. In the beginning, I'd assumed that physical distance would make the magic between us easier to ignore. Instead, it was the opposite. We worried about each other, and the jittery feeling in my stomach never fully went away until both Finn and Gil were within my line of sight.

"Let's go" was all I said.

Gil nodded. "Would you like me to drive, love?"

I hesitated. Truthfully, the vampire's driving still frightened me. Though he'd been in the U.S. a few months now, Gil still tried to drive on the other side of the road when he was deep in thought.

I had a direct line to those thoughts, though. I knew what was distracting him—not just when he was behind the wheel, but all the time. Blood. Human blood. Always, eternally, forever. It was the blessing and the curse of being a vampire, especially a newborn one. It was the reason Finn didn't trust him. Well, the main one, at least.

If Gil sensed that I doubted his control, it might make him doubt, too. He needed to know he was strong enough to resist the call. He needed to believe I trusted him, even if there were nights I woke up with an inexplicable sense of unease and looked across the room to find Gil staring back, his stance unnaturally still. Like a predator about to launch from the shadows.

All of this went through my head in two seconds. On the third, I forced an easy grin to my lips and threw the keys at Gil. He moved in a blur, catching them one-handed.

Finn was already in the backseat. Gil opened the driver's door and said something I couldn't hear.

Better get out of here before they kill each other, I thought. I started across the lot without letting myself look back, noting the stillness as I went. The boys, the music, and the smoking woman were absent or silent now. Coincidence? Or had one of my companions scared them off to ensure our little conflict didn't have an audience?

"Where are you going?"

This time, I didn't react to the sound of Collith's voice. I kept walking, my attention fixed on the Taurus. "Somewhere even you can't find me."

"Guess some things never change," Collith remarked.

I stopped, my hands closing into fists. Gil raised his eyebrows at me through the window. Finn was watching, too. I knew they'd be out of that car in an instant if they sensed any danger. Rearranging my features into a calmer expression, I held up a finger and mouthed, *One minute*. Finn immediately turned away and Gil gave me a jaunty salute before he put his boots on the dashboard. I saw Finn say something to him, and the vampire responded with an obscene gesture that made Finn's nostrils flare.

Just as the werewolf's face began to lengthen, I spun to Collith and demanded, "What is *that* supposed to mean?"

"It means this is what you do," he said, shrugging. "It's your go-to whenever things get hard or uncertain. You run."

"If I throw a stick, will you leave?"

"Giving up your life for someone?" he continued, as if I hadn't spoken. "No problem. But tell that person you love them, or need them? You'd probably cut out your own tongue first."

I scoffed and made a dismissive gesture, turning back to the car. "I don't have time for this, Collith. Please, just trust me when I tell you that I left for everyone else's sake, not mine."

Collith materialized in front of me, and I stopped short, letting out an involuntary, startled sound. Finn snarled from inside the car.

"You're so close. Just bring it home," Collith said, ignoring the werewolf.

Bring it home? I frowned blankly. Then, all at once, I realized what Collith was doing, and my bewilderment vanished. I shook my head and let out a low, mirthless laugh. He was *antagonizing* me. Toying with my emotions, like a violinist plucking strings. Trying to get the truth out of me by a burst of terror or rage. Clever, clever faerie.

But Collith wasn't as clever as he thought. There was another reason I hadn't told him about the Dark Prince's visit, and it was partly why I'd fled from Granby. It was what kept me going, running, and hiding, even on the nights I missed my family so much I felt it, a physical ache in my chest.

Collith was a Nightmare now. What if Lucifer tried to use him, as he'd used Jacob Goldmann? As he wanted to use me? And if Collith knew the danger, he might do something moronic and noble, like offer his life for mine. I remembered the last time I'd been responsible for his death. All I had to do was close my eyes, and I saw his body on the kitchen table again.

Just like that, my ire faded. I shook my head again, slower this time. "It won't work, Collith. Just let me go. Please."

Hearing me say his name made those hazel eyes soften. "Laurie isn't the only one who made a promise, you know," he murmured.

Unlike that moment back in the motel room, I wasn't sure which promise he was referring to, exactly. I had to think about it. But the memory came within a few seconds, shining like a star in my mind. Burning bright. Painful and searing.

Don't give up on me, okay?
Never.

"Collith, you and I have broken every vow we ever made to each other," I reminded him, sounding as tired as I felt. Tired . . . and sad. I swallowed a sigh and forced myself to add, "But if you need me to say the words, then fine. I officially release you from your promise."

With that, I took another step toward the car, and once again, the sound of Collith's voice stopped me. "I will never stop looking for you. I will never relent. I am an immortal, and I've been to the depths of Hell, where light and time don't exist. Compared to those years, this is nothing, Fortuna. And until you're back home, where I know you actually want to be, I'll keep showing up. So do us both a favor and spare us from months of chasing and arguing. Just tell me the truth."

I turned to face Collith again. He stood with his hands shoved in his coat pockets, his eyes hard. Looking at him, I knew he meant it. I twisted my lips and mentally flipped through my options. "Well, I could just *kill* you. That would solve this little problem."

"Tell me," Collith said, his eyes steady. Batting my sarcasm away like it was nothing. Like he *knew* me. Like he didn't give a shit that I'd just stabbed him, or about any of the other terrible things we'd done to each other.

Something inside me cracked. And despite all my resolutions, in spite of all my reasons, I felt myself finally crumple. Giving in to Collith like I always gave in to him, because no matter how much I fought it, he still possessed some vital part of me I hadn't managed to take back.

My response was faint, almost a whisper. "Wings. He had metal wings."

CHAPTER TWO

THREE MONTHS EARLIER

*T*he devil himself stood in my doorway, and he knew my name.

For a moment, I forgot how to breathe. Not just *to* breathe, but literally how. Terror coursed through me, paralyzing my entire body as it went. Lucifer waited patiently for my response. His voice slipped through my head like a silk ribbon. *It's nice to finally meet in person, Fortuna Sworn.*

But I couldn't even pull the air back into my lungs, much less think of what to say or how to handle this. It felt like my runaway heart kept beating out his name. *Lucifer. Lucifer. Lucifer.*

I was still looking at the mirror beside us, and I watched the devil's eyes crinkle at the corners, as if he was pleased that I'd figured out who he was. I hadn't said a word, but my expression must've betrayed me, somehow. Shown a glimmer of recognition.

If he'd been beautiful before, seeing Lucifer smile was like watching the sun rise. My hold tightened on the doorknob. I couldn't stop myself from staring, and for the first time in my life, *I* felt like the plain one. This fallen angel's beauty lived up to the stories, the accounts, but it was more ethereal than the world's standards. His jaw was strong and graceful, and his cheekbones were high, like a faerie's. His lips were full and framed by the lines of a lean face. Like the fine, minute details of a carving. Golden hair fell across his forehead and against his neck, slightly longer than Oliver's. The color made me think of a lion.

At last, I pulled my gaze away from the mirror and back to the man standing in front of me. Jacob Goldmann was dying. The truth struck me like a blow to the chest, but I tried to hide my horror. I met his bleeding eyes and told myself to put on the mask of the Unseelie Queen. She felt nothing. She was cold, and cruel, and unafraid.

Even if the man in front of her looked like he was about to burst.

"This isn't real. You can't be here," I said finally. I resisted the urge to glance over my shoulder. Hello seemed to have completely disappeared, thank God. I didn't blame her.

"Is it so hard to believe that after millennia, I managed to climb my way out of the pit?" Lucifer questioned. Then he added, "You don't need to worry about your lover overhearing us—I've sent him away for a while. I didn't want any interruptions. None of your other companions will hear, either."

It felt like there was a hand around my throat. "Wh-what did you do to them?"

"Not a thing. They're safe, I assure you. A friend of mine has merely placed a sound ward around me, which affects anyone nearby."

By "friend," I assumed Lucifer meant a witch. I didn't answer. Jacob's skin looked chalky now, and his nose had started bleeding, in addition to the thin streams still coming out of his eyes. Worried I might vomit, my gaze shifted back to the mirror.

Until this encounter, I'd thought I was immune to the power of beauty. But Lucifer was shattering a lot of delusions I had let myself believe.

Realizing I'd fallen silent again, the devil let out a weary sigh and waved his hand. "Please point your gun at me if it helps you relax, Fortuna."

I hadn't even realized I was holding it, but that wasn't the only thing I found disturbing. The way Lucifer said my name was wrong, too. Easy, as if he had said it a thousand times and known me a thousand days. Once again, I squeezed the doorknob as though it were someone's hand, keeping me upright, lending me courage. I didn't know what this creature was capable of. I wasn't sure I could beat him.

The thought sent splinters of ice through my veins.

And yet, in spite of the fear that had frozen every part of me, something in my body responded to the devil's intent gaze. I didn't want to name it, but the truth whispered through my veins.

Attraction.

For an instant, I hated myself for feeling it, and I fought a wave of guilt and confusion. As I drowned, Lucifer's arm moved, slowly. I watched his fingers curl around the barrel of the gun and raise it toward his chest. He touched the weapon with disconcerting gentleness, as if it were really me he was touching. When I saw that, my guilt narrowed to a trickle, then evaporated.

Suddenly I was certain that divinity or knowledge wasn't what tempted Eve in the garden—it had been him. Just him. Like Laurie with his illusions and Collith with his heavenly fire, Lucifer was no ordinary fallen angel. His power had something to do with seduction, and I needed to ignore the heat in my lower stomach, because it wasn't coming from me. It was magic.

"What do you *want*?" I managed. My voice sounded strange, even to my own ears. Feeling foolish, I lowered the gun. Something told me it wouldn't work on him, holy bullet or not.

Lucifer didn't answer right away. He examined the loft with a polite expression, and there was a thoughtful twist to his mouth. "Do you know the meaning of my name?" he asked abruptly, refocusing on me.

It was difficult to speak, but he seemed to expect a response again. After several attempts, I managed to get out, "No. No, I don't know the meaning of your name."

He tilted his golden head. "Well, there's more than one

interpretation. Light bringer. Morning star. I am known for darkness, and yet, it wasn't always that way. I'm not evil, Fortuna. So please stop looking at me like I'm about to murder you in this stairwell." There was something about his weary tone, a sort of resignation that made the devil seem all too human. I caught myself actually wanting to believe him. Despite this, I didn't miss that he hadn't answered my question. An answer wasn't necessary, anyway, because I already knew why he'd come.

She's promised to him. That was what his witch had said to my parents, just before my father shot her in the face.

Lucifer wanted a host. One that wouldn't deteriorate in a matter of hours, like Jacob Goldmann. I held back a cringe at the sight of a hole opening in his cheek, and quickly turned back to the mirror again.

"How can I see you in the reflection?" I asked. "Honestly, I can't decide which one of you I find more revolting."

Part of me had been hoping to get under Lucifer's skin, to see his expression flare with temper. Instead, he looked down at me with a crooked smile, his eyes gleaming in a way that made the temperature rise between us. "There's that fire I admire," he murmured.

It was too similar to something Laurie would say, how he would act. Unnerved, I couldn't think of any of my usual comebacks or insults. As we stood there like two statues, the devil's hand reached up. For one breathless second I knew he wanted to touch my cheek. But then his fingers clenched, and his attention shifted.

I followed his gaze to a picture on the sofa table, which rested perfectly within his line of sight. It was of the five of us—me, Finn, Damon, Matthew, and Emma. We stood in the snow, wearing coats, hats, scarves, and gloves. Our cheeks were red from the cold. At first, Emma had been behind the camera. Then Cyrus had walked by and offered to take it. She'd run at us, her stick-thin arms outstretched. Both Damon and Finn had automatically moved to catch her, and I'd stood off to the side, laughing, my nephew in my arms.

It had been a good day. One of the last good days, though I didn't know it at the time. We never know it in the moment, when we're doing something for the last time. We always assume there will be one more night, one more conversation, one more laugh.

As if he could hear my thoughts, the devil's tone became speculative. "We can tell ourselves that we don't need them, but in the end, we'd be lying. Wouldn't you agree?"

He hadn't made a threat, not really, but it still felt like one. Remembering my helpless, slumbering family returned some of my senses, and the fear was pushed out by a surge of fury. I tipped my chin up to meet Lucifer's simmering gaze. My instincts immediately urged me to look back down, to concentrate on my feet or anything else except the creature filling the air with his power. I refused.

"Hurting someone I love will only make an enemy of me," I told him, keeping my voice low. "You really, really don't want that. You may be the devil, but I'm something worse."

Lucifer's eyes burned even brighter, as if my threat excited him. His voice was soft as he asked, "And what are you, Fortuna Sworn?"

The corner of my mouth tilted up into a wry smile. There was no irony in my voice, though, when I answered him. "If you harm anyone in this dimension, you'll find out. Trust me on that."

This was usually the part when my opponent started to get uneasy. *Danger*, their senses told them. Their brains finally urged them to look past the perfect face and see the monster beneath. They stepped back, or if they were too proud for that, they went silent.

But there was no hint of fear around Lucifer—not even the faintest flavor on my tongue. As if he had all the time in the world, the devil bent and whispered his next words in my ear. I kept my eyes on his in the glass as he said, "I think I would like to see the full extent of what you're capable of, Nightmare Queen. Something tells me it would be quite a sight to behold."

"Be careful what you wish for," I murmured back, ignoring how my core clenched at his proximity. Thankfully, the Fortuna in the mirror wore a cool expression, despite Lucifer's lips nearly touching my temple, the edge of one wing so close I could have run my fingers along the metal.

In an abrupt movement, I drew back and refocused on Jacob

Goldmann. The sight of him was a much-needed reminder of how this conversation could end if I wasn't careful. If I wasn't strong enough to resist the devil. I held up one finger and asked, "Will you stay there for a minute?"

My tone was courteous, and Lucifer's lips curved with bemusement, as if no one had ever made such a request of him before. "Very well."

Nodding, I turned and walked away, setting the gun down on the counter as I went. I could feel Lucifer's eyes on me all the way to my bedroom, where I stepped inside and reached behind the door. Calmly, I turned and crossed the wide space again. I held the item I'd fetched casually at my side, and the devil was so intent on my face that he didn't even bother glancing at what I now carried.

I looked him in the eye and said, "If you're still in there, I'm sorry, Jacob."

Lucifer realized what I meant to do a split second too late, and not even supernatural speed could save him. I hefted the sword with all my strength and swung it.

Beheading someone wasn't always like how it happened in movies—sometimes it didn't lop off with a single, effortless blow, especially when the target was moving. But Adam had made this sword, and it was still lethally sharp. I felt it cut through meat, cartilage, muscle, and bone, then hit Jacob's spinal cord. His body staggered, mouth gaping open as the two parts separated. I yanked my sword back and hacked at him again, this time finishing the job.

Jacob's head landed with a hard, dull sound, and then it rolled, leaving splatters of blood. My ears rang as I watched it come to a stop.

There was no time for remorse; there was no time to feel *anything*. I started to turn, my first instinct to summon Collith and ask for his help. I stopped short as a thought occurred to me. Oh, God. I kept forgetting that he was a Nightmare now. Even if Collith had only a fraction of my power, he might be strong enough to survive as Lucifer's host if the devil couldn't get his hands on me. But by some miracle, he didn't seem to know about Collith's new abilities.

Okay, so I definitely couldn't go to Collith for help or even tell him that Lucifer had been here. Knowing him, and how desperate he was for my forgiveness, my ex might make a deal of his own. A deal both of us would regret . . . just like the last one.

History was not going to repeat itself. I wouldn't let it.

"Lyari," I said quietly, letting the tip of the sword rest against the floor. Adrenaline was still gushing through me, so I hardly felt its weight, but there was a lot of blood. So much blood.

For once, my Right Hand actually showed up. She shimmered into view, standing near the kitchen island, and took in the scene without expression. Her eyes went to the sword in my hand first, then the mess on the floor, and finally the head lying a few feet away. "What happened?"

Her voice was emotionless. Her Guardian voice. Hearing it calmed me, somehow, and I recounted my brief encounter with the devil. Lyari waited until I was completely done to speak.

"You need to leave," she stated, calm as ever. But I could taste the faerie's fear on my tongue—lavender. Lyari's fear tasted like lavender. That was the moment it hit me, how much I had to lose. If someone as formidable as Lyari was scared, we were truly fucked.

Only the adrenaline, and the fact that my family's safety was at stake, kept me calm. I turned away and said over my shoulder, "Will you help me clean this up?"

Lyari's sharp voice seemed to come from a distance. "Fortuna, did you hear me? You and your family need to leave this place. Tonight."

"They don't want to run," I said faintly, taking a mop and bucket out of the pantry. I took them over to the sink and put the bucket beneath a stream of hot water.

"What they want doesn't matter anymore. You can't win this one. Not against the Dark Prince." Lyari picked up the head by its hair, grimacing, then vanished. She reappeared seconds later, her hands now empty, and did the same thing with Jacob's body. I found paper towels, took the bucket out of the sink, and got to work.

Unlike the fae, Nightmares bled red, and by the time I was done, the soapy water was the color of poppies. The only proof of Jacob

Goldmann's death were some bloodstains in the stairwell. Hauling the bucket up by its handle, I met Lyari at the sink. She was washing her hands with rough, impatient movements. Her braid fell over her shoulder and hid one of her pointed ears.

"Will you check on Collith?" I asked, staring at our reflections over the window. "My visitor said he 'sent him away.' If you find him, though . . . tell him not to come back. Not tonight."

Lyari nodded, a hard up and down, and sifted. Her terse silence lingered, along with the taste of lavender in my mouth. I'd never seen my Right Hand so rattled. It made me wonder what she knew about Lucifer that I didn't.

Don't think about that right now. Focus on getting them out. I exhaled, shakily, and tipped the bucket into the sink.

After I'd poured the red contents down the drain and everything was back in its place, I sent a group text. Finn, Gil, Emma, Damon, and Cyrus's names shone bright on the screen. Their phones would be on, since we'd made that a rule during our last safety briefing.

I double-checked my clothes for blood, then went down the hall to wake Nym. He still wouldn't touch the cell phone I'd given him, so it was pointless to send a text.

Somehow, I wasn't surprised to find him already awake.

The faerie was sitting upright in bed, his face turned toward the window. But there was nothing to see—beyond the glass, the sky was dark, and the trees were blackened hulks. Without looking at me he said, "Do you hear it? The ticking?"

"Yes, I do. I think it's coming from the clock I bought you. It's there on the nightstand, Nym. Will you join me in the living room?" When he finally turned in my direction, I kept my expression neutral. Part of me wondered if I was in shock. "We need to have a family meeting."

He bent his head. "Of course, Your Majesty."

"I told you, Nym. Call me Fortuna. Just Fortuna."

"As you wish, Your Majesty."

A small sigh escaped me. Leaving the door ajar, I went back to the living room and sat on the sofa to wait. Lyari moved to stand behind me, as if we were the Unseelie Queen and her Right Hand residing over our Court once again.

"Sylvyre is fine," she said, her gaze constantly moving between the windows and the door. Listening. "An alarm was tripped at one of his properties. He was speaking to the human police."

My eyes slid shut. "Thank you."

We waited together, neither of us speaking. I thought about what had just happened. I'd committed a murder, and Lyari had literally helped me get rid of the body. Somewhere along the way, this prickly warrior hadn't just become my friend . . . she'd become my best friend.

Best friends with a faerie. It was a strange world.

My family started arriving after that. One by one, they entered the room quietly. Finn emerged from the stairwell, his golden eyes instantly going to me. Dirt clung to half of his face, though it was obvious he'd tried to brush it off. He must've changed shape once he was done with his hunt, then fallen asleep in the woods somewhere. Distantly, I wondered how often he did that. It wasn't safe, no matter how strong he was. Not so long ago, I'd been taken by goblins during one of my own nights in the forest. We'd have to talk about it. Later, when we weren't about to flee for our lives.

Once everyone was seated, I didn't hesitate or mince words. I told them about Lucifer. About how he'd been wearing Jacob Goldmann like a flesh suit. About the reflection I'd seen in the mirror. Though I left out the grisly details of the beheading, I caught Finn's nostrils flaring and Gil's bright eyes darting toward the stairwell more than once.

"We have to go dark. Cut off all contact. Change our identities," I finished tonelessly. My hands were tight balls against my knees as I waited for their reactions.

Cyrus, unsurprisingly, decided to stay. Nym also expressed that he wouldn't be coming with us. When I pleaded with them, Cyrus agreed to hide in town for a while, and take Hello with him. I looked at Nym, and it felt like my mask had cracked. I begged him with my eyes. *Come with us.*

"I am difficult to catch, my lady" was all Nym said.

Dissatisfied, I opened my mouth to argue. Finn put a hand on my arm and stopped me. I glanced at him, and he gave a subtle shake of his head, gentleness moving down the bond. He was telling me to let it go. To let *them* go.

I clenched my jaw, half-tempted to disregard their wishes and bring them with us in handcuffs. But that would make me no better than the creatures who had imprisoned me and taken my choices away. I made a mental note to send a text to Ariel, asking her to keep an eye on Cyrus. Lyari could send me reports on Nym. They'd be okay, I told myself.

"Don't leave without saying goodbye," I said finally. "Please."

Cyrus nodded, and Nym put his arm across his waist and bowed. As the two of them left the couch, I turned to my brother, steeling myself for an argument.

He didn't protest about leaving, though. Neither did Emma. They just looked back at me with dark, worried eyes. "What's the plan?" Damon asked.

Some of the tension left my shoulders. I released a long, silent breath and reminded myself this battle wasn't over yet. "That's the other part you're not going to like," I admitted.

I told them what else I had decided while I'd been cleaning Jacob's blood off the floor. This time, there was some pushback, as I knew there would be. Eventually Damon and Emma did agree to split up, since I was the one Lucifer wanted. Staying here wasn't an option for them—the devil had already proven that he would use my family. While Cyrus and Nym might be able to defend themselves, Emma and Matthew were too vulnerable.

They weren't happy about it, but they agreed.

We separated after that, all of us going off to pack. No one spoke or made a sound, mostly because of Matthew, who was still sleeping. But I knew it was also because my family was scared. It was in the air and on my tongue, myriad flavors that didn't belong together and created a revolting taste. I couldn't offer any comfort, not without lying to them.

Suddenly I wished I'd made Lucifer's death slower, and more painful. I went to the closet and yanked two bags out, desperate for a distraction.

I'd just started filling the first one when Gil appeared in my doorway. His voice was low. "I'll be back in ten minutes, give or take. Don't have much to pack, but I should warn Adam. Let him know I'm leaving."

I straightened, a folded T-shirt in my hands. There was something in the vampire's expression that made me hesitate. "Gil, if you need to stay, I understand. I know Adam has been . . . helping you. If you're not ready—"

"I'll be back in ten minutes," Gil repeated.

I closed my mouth and gave him a small, worried smile. "Okay."

Once my bags were packed full and zipped shut, I texted Savannah to ask for witch-related help. Lucifer would be coming back, or one of his followers, or many. Some of them might be able to do tracking spells. Savannah spent most of her time in the Unseelie Court, though. What if she didn't see my message for hours, or days?

Nothing I could do about it now. Letting out a breath, I put my phone away and picked up the bags. I hadn't been able to find Hello, so I'd have to leave without saying goodbye to my fierce kitten. It was just one more reason to make sure Lucifer actually died a long, slow, painful death. *See you soon, wild girl*, I thought, looking toward every dark spot in the room. The small, fuzzy animal didn't appear, and I finally walked out.

Damon only woke Matthew up once the cars were loaded and running in the driveway. All the headlights beamed into the darkness. Little pieces of snow floated through the brightness, like dust motes in a sun-dappled attic. Damon emerged into the cold holding the boy in his arms. Emma and I had just said our goodbyes, and I could still feel her palm against my cheek, the press of her lips to my forehead. Now Emma sat in her vehicle, a light turned on overhead so she could see the map she held. She wore a thoughtful frown.

Cyrus, Nym, Lyari, and Damon faced me in the driveway. Matthew had already fallen asleep again. I swallowed and met their gazes, one at a time. "I will fix this," I said quietly. "I will find a way to kill him and bring us all back home. I promise."

They knew. All of them knew I didn't take promises lightly. I watched them react, each with varying degrees of emotion.

Surprisingly, Cyrus was the one to respond. "We know."

I paused, debating whether or not to hug him. My friend solved the dilemma for me by reaching over and giving my shoulders an awkward, brief squeeze.

"My cat—" I started as I hugged him back.

Cyrus's voice was firm. "I'll find her."

Before I could say anything else, he walked to his truck and whistled for Stanley. The dog leaped off the porch and bounded after his owner, his long ears swinging.

"Until next time, my lady," Nym said, giving me one of his sad, crooked smiles. A moment later, he sifted out of sight, probably back to the Unseelie Court or wherever else his bloodline lived.

You're stalling, Fortuna.

The thought belonged to me, but it sounded like Collith. Somehow he'd become the voice in my head, always urging me to be strong or good. I turned to Damon, and my stomach felt like a fist. I didn't want to do this, I thought suddenly. I didn't want to be standing here right now. We should've been upstairs, all of us in our beds, warm and dreaming. Nothing on the horizon but breakfast and routine. Lucifer had ruined that for us. I hated him. I *hated* him.

"I'll see you soon," I said firmly, ignoring the way Damon's face had gone blurry at the edges.

He shifted and put one of his arms around me, briefly pulling me to him. I felt his lips brush the side of my head. "I'll text you when we get to the first checkpoint, Tuna Fish. Be safe, okay? Don't try to be a hero."

I nodded jerkily and fixed my gaze on Matthew, fighting to keep tears at bay. My nephew's eyelashes were dark fringes, and he pressed a small fist against his cheek as he slept. He was a miniature version of my brother. I didn't want to risk waking him again, not when he looked content and good dreams were so rare. I leaned close, my eyes sliding shut as I imagined kissing his head. I forced myself to step back and meet Damon's gaze. "Call me if you need anything," I said thickly.

He nodded, his long face lined and solemn. "You, too."

A minute later, I watched Emma's SUV drive toward the road. The red taillights faded. The night crowded in close. I lingered, my breath clouding in the air. All I could think was, *I did this. I did this to us.* My newfound family was breaking apart and scattering to the wind, and it wouldn't be happening if I didn't exist.

"Fortuna?" Another figure materialized in the driveway. A tension inside me eased, and I knew, without looking, that it was Gil. He took one look at me and said, "What do you need?"

To say goodbye, I thought. Out loud I told him, "I just want to make sure Damon locked up. Be right back."

I ducked my head and returned to the barn, where I slipped into the shadowed garage and up the stairwell. Damon *had* locked up, so I used the spare key, avoiding the sight of the stained floor as I went in.

We hadn't even left yet, but already the loft had an abandoned feel to it. Every light was off, which was an anomaly in itself—there was always a light to guide the way, or greet us when we walked through the door. I hovered in the doorway and cast a final look around the room that had become so dear to me, every part of it filled with memories. The couch where Emma and I often watched Netflix. The island where our strange family ate breakfast together. The corner where Collith kissed me the day we ate pancakes and made love for hours on end. It was all I'd ever wanted for so long. A family. A home. My grip tightened on the edge of the frame, going white at the knuckles.

Then I turned away, pulling the door shut firmly behind me.

CHAPTER THREE

*C*ollith and I had been standing there for so long that my fingers were numb. The VACANCY sign flickered again, and the quiet sound it made jarred me. I blinked the memory away, and a fresh surge of urgency went through my body. If I'd had any doubts about running again, remembering the encounter with Lucifer had washed them away like a tide smoothing the sand.

With hardened resolve, I refocused on Collith. I knew he could sense the fear swelling in my throat, but I still tried to hide it behind a wall of anger.

"We're leaving," I said tightly. "Do *not* follow us. Do not look for us. Go home, or back to the Unseelie Court, or whatever you'd be doing if you weren't standing in this parking lot. I don't want you here and I don't need saving. If you came for answers, you have them now."

I paused, waiting for his response. I expected Collith to snarl or snap, continuing our heated back-and-forth as he so often did. But the furious stranger that had yanked me from the car was gone, and Collith's expression was calm, almost thoughtful. Maybe it was learning the truth about why I'd left, or seeing how terrified I truly was. Whatever the reason, my ex wasn't nearly scared enough at the revelation the devil himself was after us. After another moment, all he said was "Are you finished?"

I stared at him.

"That depends," I managed. "Did you hear any of it? This asshole won't stop, Collith. He's been hunting Nightmares for centuries. Until I figure out how to kill him, or find some other magical solution, anyone I . . . associate with is in danger. If you're smart, you'll disappear, too. Feel free to pass the message along to Laurie."

Anyone I love. That's what I had been about to say. Collith's eyes flashed, as if he'd heard the words, anyway.

"I'm aware of what 'this asshole' is capable of, Fortuna," he told me, still annoyingly composed. "I spent years being tortured in his realm. I may not remember him specifically, but I remember the pain. I remember how his demons broke me."

"Then why aren't you afraid?" I demanded.

This time, he didn't answer. The silence stretched, the noise of the running car behind us an ominous rumble. I studied Collith, frowning. I knew this faerie—well, as much as anyone could know a member of the fae—and there was a reason he'd shut down. Collith only withdrew when he was hiding something. Something I wouldn't like. I forced myself to look into his hazel eyes and tried to think like he did. At his core, Collith was analytical and calculating. He read Agatha Christie and studied history. He based most of his decisions off evidence and results.

And just like that, I understood. My voice was flat as I said, "You don't believe me."

Collith's face still didn't change, but somehow, that made his skepticism more obvious. Before I could say something we'd both regret, he finally broke his silence. "I do believe you. But no one I know has ever laid eyes on the Dark Prince, much less spoken to him directly. It's possible someone else came to the loft that night. Something else."

I made a humorless sound. I would never admit it, but his doubt felt like another betrayal. "Whatever. I have to go. Goodbye, Collith."

"Why didn't you tell us?" he called after me.

I faced him across the pavement. Knowing this would be the last night we saw each other for a long, long time, my gaze moved over his features again, starting at that stubborn lock of hair and ending at his full, solemn mouth. My attention lingered there, and I caught myself thinking about that kiss. Heat expanded in my lower stomach, making me clench.

Collith's eyes went dark.

He'd sensed my arousal, of course. Suddenly the distance between us felt like too much, and not enough. I was torn between the instinct to bolt and the urge to finish what we'd started an hour ago.

My resistance wasn't just because we had an audience. Months ago, before I found out about Collith's greatest secret and biggest deceit, I'd let him inside. Not only my body, but everything else. For the first time in years, I had allowed myself to *want* something. To dream of a bright future and warm somedays. Stepping back into the darkness had almost destroyed me.

I didn't think I would survive it again.

"Tell you what?" I said, after a pause that was just a beat too long.

I was stalling, and Collith probably knew that, too, the way he always seemed to know my secrets. But he played along. His low, soft voice drifted through the cold, and somehow it felt like a caress. "Why didn't you tell me and Laurelis about him? Why did you run without any explanation?" he asked quietly.

My heartbeat felt unsteady, and I was painfully aware Collith could hear it. Trying to regain control, I imagined myself as frozen as the ground beneath us. I decided to give half of the truth, because it made lies harder to detect. Collith had taught me that, too.

"I thought if you knew, you'd try to be a martyr. I don't need any more blood on my hands," I told him.

He raised his eyebrows. "It didn't occur to you that we might be able to help in other ways? Use our considerable resources, or add our strength to yours, if it comes down to a confrontation?"

"First I need to figure out how to *survive* another confrontation," I countered sharply. "I caught him by surprise at the loft, and something tells me he'll be prepared next time. We don't know how far his

32

reach is. What if you start asking questions and catch his attention? What if he uses you against me? What if he just rips your fucking head off to teach me a lesson?"

I stopped, breathing hard, as if I'd run a mile. But even now, Collith stood there without a trace of fear, his focus calm and steady. "You don't have to do this alone, Fortuna," he said.

"I'm not alone, and my people are waiting." As I mentioned them, I glanced back at Finn and Gil. It seemed like a small miracle they hadn't tried to kill each other yet. I started to take a step toward the car, but as an afterthought, I turned back to Collith and added, "If you even *think* about offering yourself to you-know-who, I'll make sure you regret it. The things he'll do to you will feel like nothing once I've had my turn."

My threat didn't have the effect I'd hoped for. A faint smile curved Collith's lips, and his voice was soft as he replied, "I don't doubt it."

There were a hundred memories tucked into his voice. For a moment, all I could do was stare, and it felt like I was reliving every moment between us since we'd first met at the black market. Locking eyes with him for the first time. Hating him. Loving him. Grieving together. Healing together. Hating him again. Now I wasn't entirely sure what I felt for this faerie king.

All I knew was that it hurt.

"Goodbye, Collith," I forced myself to say.

He gave no response. It didn't seem like there was anything left to say. Once again, I turned from him . . . and my stomach lurched at the sight of Laurie.

I gasped and pressed a hand against my chest. Distantly, I heard Finn snarling from inside the car again. He must've been taken by surprise, too. "How long have you been standing there?" I managed.

Just as Collith had, Laurie heard the words I didn't say. The question I was really asking. *How much did you hear?*

"Long enough," the Seelie King said. His tone didn't give anything away. I was used to his teasing, his smirks, the double meanings of everything that came out of his mouth. This strange reserve disarmed me, and I was barely aware of Collith coming up behind me.

Desperate for a distraction, I turned my attention to Laurie's appearance. Earlier, he'd said he needed to get ready. He wore a suit of red velvet, with lapels and sleeves made of intricate black lace. Rings gleamed on his fingers. The dark shirt beneath his jacket was unbuttoned halfway down, revealing a pale, sculpted chest that I'd once kissed and run my hands down—I didn't let myself remember the rest of that night.

As I finished my perusal of the silver-haired faerie, I could feel his eyes on me, too. I forced myself to look at him, and something about his expression made me resist the urge to raise my chin in defiance. "I'm surprised you'd deign to make another appearance. I thought you were going back to your precious Court," I said.

My tone came out more bitterly than I meant it to, and I caught a flash of surprise in Laurie's face before his mask settled back into place. As if he hadn't even known that I cared. As if he'd thought his choice to retake the throne didn't bother me. I swallowed, my gaze skittering away.

There was the briefest of pauses, like the hushed catch of a breath, and then Laurie murmured, "I make time for the things that are important to me."

My eyes flew back to his. I waited for a joke or a grin, but Laurie did neither. It was as if Collith weren't standing beside him, seeing everything, hearing every soft word. The Seelie King gazed at me with naked desire, and something close to tenderness, too.

My thoughts scattered. There he went again, catching me off guard, throwing me off when I most needed to be cold, and hard, and distant. I glanced from Laurie to Collith, struggling to remember why I had to drive them away. Why I'd run in the first place.

We can tell ourselves that we don't need them, but in the end, we'd be lying.

Lucifer's voice echoed through my memory, and suddenly Collith's nostrils flared. Feeling like I was back on solid ground, I stepped closer to the car and put physical space between us. I boarded up the walls of my heart and faced the faeries with fresh, cold resolve. They watched me with identical expressions that I couldn't define.

"Well, Collith can catch you up," I replied stiffly. "We really do need to go. The longer we stay, the higher the risk."

Laurie cocked his head. "Since when is Fortuna Sworn afraid of a little risk?"

But I didn't rise to the bait. Not this time. I walked over to the car and grasped the handle. A rush of heat greeted me as I pulled it open. I hated leaving like this, though. I hesitated, then twisted around, holding the edge of the door. Laurie and Collith hadn't moved. I gave them a crooked smile and said, "Try not to break too many hearts, Laurie. One of these days a witch is going to put a hex on you. Keep an eye on him, Collith, and don't forget that you're allowed to be happy, too."

I didn't give either of them a chance to respond. Quickly, as if I was worried they'd stop me, I lowered myself into the passenger seat and closed the door harder than necessary. Heat blasted through the vents, and it was the only sound. For a few seconds, I stared through the windshield and waited for Gil to say something, but he didn't ask if I was okay. He didn't ask where we were going. Neither did Finn. I knew it was because they understood. They knew me, probably better than anyone else in my life. Even Damon.

They could also feel everything through the bond. I'd gotten good at keeping them out, but right now I felt like a raw wound, ripped open and exposed.

Finn let out a whine, as if he could hear my thoughts, too. "Just go," I said hollowly.

Gil put the car into gear and drove toward the road. As the tires rolled over cracked pavement and lumps of ice, I noticed another figure standing at the edge of the parking lot. Short, square-jawed, muscular. A frown tugged at the corners of my mouth. I recognized him—it was the man from table six. Had he come here looking for me? Or was he just visiting someone else staying at the motel?

I gave a small, imperceptible shake of my head. Whatever. It didn't matter. He was irrelevant now, just like everything else in this town.

With that, I turned and fixed my eyes on the black horizon. I wasn't the one driving, but I'd learned to stop looking back. Looking back only brought pain and doubt.

And yet, despite this thought, my eyes darted to the side mirror of their own volition.

Laurie and Collith still stood there, dark silhouettes against the yellow light. As they got smaller, an ache started in my chest. It would probably be months until I saw them again, if not years. I didn't bother lying to myself, telling myself I didn't care—good riddance. They'd gotten under my skin. They were part of me, written into my story with permanent ink, and flipping the page wouldn't change that.

Seconds later, they were out of sight.

I let out a long, soundless breath, and rested my temple against the window. As the miles passed, each one taking me farther and farther from that parking lot, I thought about the way Collith and Laurie had been looking at me just before I walked away. My mind turned the image over and around, mulling, searching for an answer or a way to describe their expressions.

Then, in a rush of certainty, I finally put my finger on it. The abrupt change in their demeanors, the uncharacteristic solemnity.

They'd looked like they were preparing for war.

Wind whistled over the plains of the dreamscape.

For the first time in weeks, sunlight broke through the clouds. A flock of birds flitted past, their merry song filling my ears. With raised brows, I glanced behind me, then all around. Lately, Oliver had taken to meeting me beneath the tree. But tonight, there was no sign of the easel, or the painter himself. I was alone.

Trying not to let the paranoid whispers in my head become shrieks of panic—although the dreamscape had been quiet since we'd stopped hunting for memories, I hadn't fully been able to forget the monsters that lived beyond our peaceful hills—I left the tree's shade and walked toward the sea. It seemed more likely than the cottage. Oliver hadn't been spending much time inside since his shadow had attacked me there.

Just as I'd hoped, I found him at the edge of the cliff.

He sat on a small stool, his easel propped in front of him. His elbow shifted in and out of sight as his hand moved, undoubtedly holding a paintbrush. Most artists would face the horizon, but Oliver was positioned so his back was partly turned to it. I could see his face as I got closer. His expressive eyebrows were furrowed. The wind stirred his hair. His skin was still sun-darkened from our journey, and the golden tones made his freckles more subtle. The button-up shirt he wore was dark blue. It contrasted starkly with the white of the easel and the vibrant twilight hovering all around us.

Oliver would've felt my arrival, of course, and noticed my approach from the corner of his eye. But he said nothing as I walked up the beaten path and closed the distance between us. Once I reached him, I lowered myself to the ground and put my legs over the edge. Even now, my best friend didn't speak.

Since the night I'd decapitated Jacob Goldmann and fled Granby, Oliver had been quiet. Painfully, uncharacteristically quiet. At first, I'd thought he was angry at me. That the rift we'd repaired during our adventures was opening again. It had taken me several more nights to wrangle the truth from him.

Oliver was in pain. Relentless pain.

Lucifer had been trying to reach me through my dreams. Like the rest of my nightmares, Oliver was able to hold him at bay. Time and time again, I urged my best friend to let him through. *The devil can't hurt me here,* I insisted.

But Oliver was just as stubborn as I was.

Minutes ticked by, filled with the sound of distant tides and flocks of seagulls. Drawing my legs back from the cool spray, I crossed them at the ankles and hugged my knees, gazing at the colors seeping out on either side of the sun. Thin clouds allowed the dying light to break through, like dapples of morning shining through a stained-glass window. I knew the wild beauty was entirely the dreamscape's own, since Oliver no longer had control over the sky.

"What are you painting tonight?" I asked finally.

I'd expected more silence, or to wait a while for his reply, but Oliver answered readily enough. "I'm not sure yet."

He almost sounded like his old self again. Relief fluttered in my chest, making me realize how heavy I'd been feeling. How worried. "Are you ever going to let me see one?" I asked, smiling.

Oliver's eyes met mine, and he smiled back. "I *have* let you see them," he said.

I made a sound of disdain. "Liar. You've shown me two, maybe, and they don't even count. Who cares about landscapes?"

"Soon," he promised, his lips still faintly curved. He added more strokes to the canvas. I watched him for another minute, my thoughts wandering. The concentrated frown Oliver wore reminded me of someone else. Someone I had left behind and missed more than I'd expected.

"Nym likes to draw, have I told you that? I bet you two would hit it off," I remarked. But Oliver didn't respond this time. I watched his expression carefully, searching for a wince or the slightest tightening of his lips; I'd learned Oliver's tells when it came to his battle against Lucifer. I didn't see any now, and I wondered if he'd gotten better at lying. My voice was soft again as I asked, "How bad is it?"

Oliver kept painting. "He's eased up, actually."

"He has?" Unease trickled through me like the dark, freezing waters where we'd first encountered the ceti. I kept my body twisted in Oliver's direction, but I stopped seeing him. My mind raced through a list of potential reasons Lucifer would relent in his efforts for one night. "That can't be a good sign."

"Did something happen?" Oliver sounded distracted.

I hesitated. "You could say that. Laurie and Collith found me."

Oliver swore. He gave me his full attention, and his eyes were bright with urgency. He set aside his paintbrush and stood. "Way to bury the lead, Fortuna. Why are we sitting here talking about my paintings? You need to wake up. One of them might've led him right to you."

Staying where I was, I turned my head, squinting. The sunlight felt so good. I breathed deeply through my nostrils and leaned back. "I'll leave in the morning."

Oliver hovered over me. "You should leave *now*."

"Not yet. Can we just . . . sit here? For a little while?"

He must've heard something in my voice, because Oliver only stood there another second or two before he folded his body and settled on the ground next to me. "Fine," he said.

Guilt pricked at the sense of calm I'd found. All Oliver wanted was to be free, and I was terrified I'd lose him again if he kept feeling the sting of how little power he had.

"You have a choice, you know," I reminded him.

"I know I do. And I'm choosing to sit here, with you. Just for a little while," Oliver added, echoing my words. The wind mussed his hair some more, and it shifted into his eyes as they slid over and wrinkled at me in the beginnings of a teasing grin.

Gratitude swelled in my throat. I nudged Oliver's shoulder with mine like I'd done a thousand times before. "I love you."

He gave me a pitying look and tipped his hand back and forth like a seesaw. "Eh, I'm lukewarm about you. You snore in your sleep and you can be really annoying sometimes."

"Hey!" I shoved him, laughing. "Excuse you. I'm a *delight*."

He watched me with a soft, crooked smile. "It's been too long since I've heard that sound."

Slowly, my laughter faded. I gazed back at Oliver, and a familiar sensation spread through my lower stomach, a response to the heat in his eyes. Of its own volition, my mind flashed to the night we'd spent in the tent. Feeling his firm warmth against my back. His hardness between my legs.

Swallowing, I turned and refocused on the darkening sky. We both knew nothing had changed, and starting down this path would only lead to pain. There would probably always be a sense of attraction between us, so we needed to learn how to control it. Or ignore it.

But what if something did change? a voice whispered.

Another image blinded me—a memory of those strange, dog-like creatures I'd killed in the woods. Then I imagined the huge, twisted tree that had sprouted in the middle of my childhood bedroom.

A feeling popped in my chest, startling me, and the memories disintegrated. I was a Nightmare; I knew exactly what that sensation was.

Fear.

I switched gears abruptly, forcing myself to focus on the present threat in our lives. I still hadn't come up with a reason why the devil had retreated for tonight. Evil didn't rest, which meant I couldn't, either. I frowned at the open sea, barely noticing that the moon had come out, along with a dusting of smaller lights. The dusky sky had been covered in a drape of deep velvet, like the petals of a black rose.

What are you up to, Lucifer? I thought. *What are you up to?*

The stars didn't answer.

CHAPTER FOUR

*C*louds of hairspray filled the air around me, the scent and the taste of it going down my throat.

I held back a cough and reached for my makeup bag, eager to get out of the dressing room. Dancers talked around me, over me. We were in a town I kept forgetting the name of. I did know the name of the club, at least—Pink Paradise.

It was an accurate description, although the "paradise" part was debatable. Everything was pink, from the walls and the furniture to the lights and the costumes. I'd worked here for less than a week, and it was already getting old. This was not how I wanted to be spending my nights. I longed to be home, back in our warm loft, a fire crackling and the blue glow of the TV pouring over my family.

A sigh filled my throat, but I didn't let it out. Suddenly I felt heavy, and so, so tired.

"We're starting in five!" a voice rang out, sending a ripple of urgency through the girls. Our house mom, Shanice, appeared behind me in the mirror. She made an exasperated sound. "Violet, you're not even dressed yet?"

"I'll be ready in time," I told her, my hand steady as I drew a dark line across my eyelid.

"And don't forget, bags and coats go on the hooks along that back wall. I'm trying to keep a clutter-free dressing room." Shanice shifted her attention to the girl sitting beside me, a redhead who drove the clientele crazy with her ample curves and coy smiles. "Layla, check in with the couple in the first booth. He wants to buy his wife a dance."

Layla nodded, waving a makeup brush to emphasize that she'd heard, and Shanice bustled over to a dancer struggling with her G-string. The moment she was gone, I bent and took my gun out of my backpack. The hooks Shanice had mentioned weren't exactly convenient if I needed to access it quickly. I'd have to store it somewhere else tonight.

"So, what's your deal?" I heard Layla say.

I straightened, slipping the gun into my makeup bag. Thankfully, Layla was preoccupied with her reflection and didn't notice. "My deal?" I repeated.

"Yeah." She finished applying a layer of pink lipstick, then spun on her stool so she was facing me. She was so short that her feet barely touched the floor. "You intrigue me. First you walk in the door and Artie hands you a job without an audition. I've never seen him stammer like a high schooler before. Then there's the mirror thing."

"The mirror thing?" I knew I probably sounded like a moron, echoing everything she said, but it was the safest response.

Layla arched a perfectly-shaped brow. Her voice was matter-of-fact as she said, "You never look at yourself. Not really. You'll use the mirror to put on eyeliner, or to make sure your butt glue is doing its job, but nothing more. Most women glance at themselves as they walk by, and you don't even do that. So, what's your deal?"

People didn't usually notice details like that. Oh, they noticed me, of course, but few ever saw through the haze of lust to the person beneath. It meant that Layla was perceptive.

Perceptive people were dangerous.

"I've got bigger things to worry about, I guess," I said. Things like being hunted by the oldest, most powerful creature in the universe, and figuring out how to kill him. I reached for a tube of lip gloss. "As for Artie, you'll have to ask him. But with most men, their decisions just boil down to dick or dime. Usually they're thinking about both."

Layla laughed and got to her feet. "Oh my God. I'm totally stealing that."

I gave her a small, tentative smile. "Steal away."

She bent over to adjust one of her heels. After that, she straightened, took two steps, and paused. Layla's eyes met mine in the mirror. "There's a guy by the bar tonight, you can't miss him," she said. "He wears an orange and yellow windbreaker and only drinks vodka sodas. Don't waste your time. He never has cash."

I was so startled that all I could think to say was, "Thanks."

Layla nodded, smiling. "Anytime. Oh, and don't cover your beauty mark tonight. It gives you such a queenly look. Not that you need any help with that. Okay, see you out there."

Before I could respond, Layla followed another dancer through the doorway. I watched her go, shocked she could see my real face, and also thrown by her kindness. In every club I danced in, the other girls despised me. Despite what most people thought, this wasn't an easy job. We were competing for the same customers and the same wallets. And without fail, I always swooped in and took all the attention. Men fell over themselves to learn my name and get me into the VIP room. There wasn't a single night I found myself with free time or the need to go looking for work. Hell, I'd hate me, too. Yet there Layla was, talking to me without a trace of resentment in her eyes, offering tips. In another life, maybe we could've been friends.

But there was a reason I needed to keep my distance.

I raised my gaze, looking at the face in the glass. Slowly, I touched the beauty mark Layla had mentioned. It used to be a reminder of my mother. It still was, only now it also made me think of how afraid she'd been in one of my last memories of her, and why.

She's promised to him.

My hand fell away. I sighed and turned, reaching for my costume, which was made of pink leather. By the time the DJ started, I was ready, just as I'd promised Shanice. I followed a rush of dancers toward the door, the music and lights reaching for us.

Forcing a smile onto my lips, I stepped into the brightness, and my shift began.

The town might've been different, but nothing else was. The songs were the same, along with the men and the conversations. I went through the motions, swinging around poles, dancing in laps, accepting bills. I dodged personal questions and evaded wandering hands.

By the time two o'clock rolled around, my skin was dewy with sweat and all I wanted was a shower. I waved goodbye to Layla, who was still with a customer, and walked toward the dressing room. Halfway there, a man put his hand out and requested a dance in the VIP room. I was so tired that I didn't even look at him. I just mustered a weak smile and shook my head, murmuring, "Next time."

If he said anything else, I didn't hear it. I slipped into the dressing room, changed, and retrieved my backpack from the row of hooks. With a wad of cash in one hand and my car keys in the other, I walked through the club again. Two more men tried to get my attention. Ignoring them, I paid the house fee and tipped the bartenders, then the bouncers as I passed. I stepped into the night with a deep sigh of relief. Winter raced across my skin, and compared to the stuffy heat of the room behind me, it truly was paradise.

I did my usual scan of the parking lot, alert for any movement or power. Everything was still. It was so cold that not even the smokers were out. I exhaled, some of the tension easing from my shoulders. Soon I'd be with Finn and Gil. My boots crunched over a sheet of ice as I moved toward the car, eager to get back and do more research on Lucifer.

"Hey, Angel, wait up! No, sorry, it's Violet now, right?"

Hearing that name made my heart lurch into overdrive. It hammered in my ears as I whirled to face the owner of that vaguely familiar voice. When I saw who was coming toward me, his mouth stretched into a wide grin, I bit back a curse.

It was the customer from table six. At Sugarland. Back in Wyoming.

My instincts came alive. I didn't bother wondering what he was doing here, of all places—it was clear this human was in my thrall. Obsession shone from his eyes.

The power of a Nightmare affected everyone differently. Some people coveted it. Some people worshipped it. Beauty brought out whatever was in their hearts, and whoever this man was, it was clear that his wasn't full of good intentions.

I started to reach for the gun in the side pocket of my backpack, then remembered a beat later that I'd put it in my makeup bag for easier access during my shift. *Shit*. My makeup bag was still in the dressing room. I'd been so tired that I'd left without it.

"How did you find me?" I asked flatly, watching the stranger draw nearer. I was using a different name at Pink Paradise, but I must've made a mistake somewhere along the way. I wanted to know what it was so I didn't repeat it in the next town.

"I have some friends in the business. I made some calls and asked if they had any new dancers that were out-of-this-world gorgeous." He grinned at me again, as if he expected me to swoon at the compliment. He stopped and rocked back on his heels, plumes of air leaving his mouth as he added, "My name is Logan, by the way. Not that you asked."

"You're right. I didn't." Without another word, I turned and walked away. Putting my back to him made my skin crawl, and everything in me wanted to *run*, but I didn't know how unhinged this man was. A chase might just excite him.

"Aren't you curious why I went to all this effort?" he called, the night swallowing his voice.

I quickened my pace. "No."

His footsteps sounded behind me. "Hey, come on. Wait. I tried to get your attention earlier, but you blew me off. So just wait one second, all right? I promise I'll make it worth your while."

I kept walking. A moment later, the human's fingers closed

around my arm. I wrenched free so hard that pain shrieked through my shoulder. "Do *not* touch me," I snarled, spinning.

Logan held up his hands. "Whoa. I just want to talk. It's the least you could do. Look, let's go back inside, and we can—"

"I don't owe you a goddamn thing, and I'm not going anywhere with you."

The friendliness slid off his face, and his voice changed, too. "You think you're so much better than me?"

My mind raced. The car was still too far away. I was fast, but motivated humans tended to move fast as well. That left fighting or using my powers, and both options were last resorts. I glared at Logan, my free hand forming a fist. I was still holding my car keys, I noted distantly.

"You should know that the men who piss me off tend to end up dead," I told him. "If you just walk away, it's a win-win for both of us. You get to live, and I get to leave without another mark on my conscience."

His eyes narrowed. "Did you just threaten me? I could get you into a lot of trouble for that."

This was usually the point at which I said something that was the equivalent of waving a red flag in front of a bull. But I needed to lay low and avoid drawing attention, and that was more important than my itch to take this guy down a peg. So I gritted my teeth and forced myself to say, "I don't want any trouble. I want to go home, that's it. I'm asking you to leave me alone."

I started to turn. I hadn't taken a single step when Logan replied, his voice low with rage, "I didn't come all this way to be rejected by a fucking *stripper*."

He grabbed my arm again, yanking me backward. Even through my coat, his grip was biting. And despite all my plans and resolutions to stay cool, keep the peace, something in me just . . . snapped.

I regained my footing easily, using Logan's arm for balance to spin and pull free, leaving my coat in his hands. A chill raced over my skin, unheeded, as I took a giant step forward and aimed my keys at Logan's eye. But this human had done some training of his own,

46

probably a local Krav Maga class or some childhood karate, because he jerked out of the way as if he'd been expecting it. His other fist flew into my gut, winding me. Pain screamed through my body and I bent, wheezing. While I was incapacitated, Logan pinned both my arms to my sides, and I felt my spine slam into a truck behind us.

With a manic glow in his eyes, Logan bent to kiss me. I squeezed my eyes shut, screaming, and buried my nails in his flesh—somehow, I'd gotten one of my hands free. Logan shouted as I shoved his face away from mine. When he straightened, he looked like Ian O'Connell.

"I'm going to enjoy this," he hissed, holding his bleeding cheek.

It was Ian O'Connell's voice, too. Then I blinked, and Pink Paradise was gone. Bare, spindly branches reached over my head, blocking out the moon, and I was pressed against the hard ridges of a tree. Ian leered at me, enjoying the sight of my terror, and reached for the button on my pants.

That was as far as he got.

My power roared out of me, releasing in a violent explosion. I could see it, as if my desperation had made it stronger, given it physical form. Or maybe it had been there all along. It looked like black smoke, and the tendrils burst in a dozen directions, including where Logan stood. They went down his throat and into his eyes. He made a muffled sound, probably trying to scream. His entire body jerked like he was being ripped apart on the inside. I didn't care.

His fears were mine now.

His name was Logan Boon, and his greatest fear was mediocrity. Being mocked. Overlooked. Insignificant.

I didn't hesitate to make him exactly that.

I tortured him with a hundred different scenarios, the sorts of moments he'd only experienced in bad dreams. The girl he'd liked in high school laughed when he asked her to the prom. His father looked at him with disappointed eyes and said, *Why can't you be more like your brother?* His boss gave the promotion he'd so desperately wanted to his much taller, much more charming co-worker.

Over and over. Again and again. I hit him with image after image, and they felt as real to him as Ian O'Connell had felt to me. I kept going until I could feel Logan Boon's bleakness, his utter belief that he was worthless and better off dead. No one would notice his absence, anyway.

Only then did I stop.

I yanked my power back, blinking rapidly. After a few seconds, the crossroads and the tree were replaced by the parking lot of Pink Paradise. Logan stood in front of me, swaying, his eyes wide and glassy. His skin was gray and his lips were blue. I couldn't tell if he was even alive, and in that split second, it occurred to me how inconvenient it would be if he died. I swore and started toward him. I'd barely taken two steps when Logan fell to his knees so hard it sounded like his kneecaps shattered.

Then something slammed into him from the side.

It took my mind an extra second to comprehend what had happened. Yards away, a familiar figure with a head of bleached hair was hunched over Logan. The human jiggled like a rag doll from the force of Gil's movements, and I heard the undeniable sound of flesh tearing.

"*Fuck.*" I bolted toward them and grabbed Gil's arm without thinking, yanking it with all my strength—supernatural and otherwise. I almost lost my grip and slipped, but Gil didn't even budge. He just buried his face even deeper in the hole that was Logan's neck, and a squelching noise was the only response.

Normally, interrupting a feeding vampire was a death sentence, but this wasn't just any vampire. Gil was my family. We may not have shared blood or DNA, but we were connected by pain, love, and all the other things that forged two souls together.

We were also connected by magic.

Seeing no other options, I closed my eyes and imagined the bond between us. Usually, I saw it as ribbons of light or bright, glowing strands. Tonight, I pictured chains. Thick, unbreakable chains. I wrapped both of my hands around them and *pulled*.

Gil's neck snapped back, and his body bent as if there was actually a physical being controlling him. Logan hit the ground without any resistance. His head was detached from his body, I noted dimly. There was blood everywhere.

Worried that Gil would lose control again, I looked around, planning to get between him and the remains. He was nowhere in sight. I could still sense him, though, and I knew he was nearby. The sensations vibrating down our bond were dark and volatile.

This was bad, I thought. Someone could come out of the club any second. Luckily, an SUV hid us from view. My mind worked quickly, still in survival mode. I could fix this. I just needed to summon Lyari and get Gil—

A door slammed in the distance, and before I could react, there was the click of heels. A moment later, someone walked into view and spotted me. "Violet! You forgot your . . ."

It was Layla. In her small hands she held my makeup bag, which contained the gun that would've come in handy a few minutes ago. I witnessed the exact moment she saw Logan, or what was left of him. She trailed off and stared at the grisly scene we'd made, brows knitted together, eyes dark with disbelief. As though she was trying to decide if this was a sick, elaborate prank.

Apparently she reached the conclusion that it wasn't, because Layla's chest began to rise and fall in panicked gulps. She stumbled back, her heels kicking up dirt, and then she whirled. I opened my mouth to shout her name, but she was already gone. I wasn't sure what I would've said, anyway. I listened to the door slam behind her, thinking that Layla had managed to surprise me again—most humans probably would've screamed.

Silence crowded in close, and the stifled sounds of the club reminded me of how many more people could come out.

Okay. I let out a breath. Now it was *really* bad.

"Lyari," I said, bending over Logan. I wrapped my hands around his ankles and pulled, intending to drag him out of the parking lot. But I'd forgotten how muscular he was, and the asshole barely budged. How could one human be so *heavy?* I gritted my teeth and growled again, *"Lyari."*

While I waited for my Right Hand, I refocused on Logan and

49

braced myself. Gil wasn't going to be any help, and Layla was probably telling someone what she'd seen at that very moment. I had to get this body moved and buy us more time. I grabbed Logan's ankles again and leaned back to use my full weight, grunting with effort. Why couldn't a scrawny man have stalked and attacked me?

Every few seconds, I glanced toward the club. I got Logan to the edge of the lot, then behind a tree. There wasn't anywhere else to hide him, not even some bushes. For now, this would have to do.

Breathing raggedly, I straightened and looked at the trail of blood I'd created. *Shit*, I thought. The head. I'd forgotten Logan's goddamn head. Grimacing, I hurried over and picked it up by the hair. His eyes were still wide open, his mouth gaping. As I placed it beside the rest of the dead asshole that had assaulted me, one thing was abundantly clear.

Lyari wasn't coming.

"*Fuck.*" I closed my eyes and bent my head, hands forming into fists. If I couldn't depend on Lyari's help, there was only one other solution. One other way to clean up this mess before more humans came out and saw everything. I didn't have a choice.

Stupid, I thought, resisting the urge to hit something. I'd been so stupid tonight. If I'd done even one thing differently, like remember the gun or ask one of the boys to pick me up after my shift, I could've avoided what was about to come next.

I'd already wasted too much time, so I lifted my chin and forced myself to say their names. It sounded like someone was pulling my teeth. "Collith. Laurie."

It took exactly twenty-six seconds. They arrived at the same time, and I wondered if they'd been together. Both of them wore long coats, Collith in the wool one he'd been wearing when we first met, and Laurie, of course, in something much more elaborate. His clothes were blindingly white, and were those *feathers* on the sleeves?

Normally I wouldn't have been able to resist making a comment, but tonight, I was silent. With his hands shoved in his pockets, Laurie walked over to Logan's remains and examined them for a moment.

"What did he do?" was all he said.

The question made a flash of memory go off. *I'm going to enjoy this.*

I averted my gaze, pain bursting inside me like a flare. "It doesn't exactly matter anymore."

"He touched her. He put his hands on her." This was from Gil, but I still didn't know where he was, and his voice was nearly unrecognizable. It was as if a hand was grasping his throat, or he had a mouthful of rocks.

He sounded . . . *hungry.*

Laurie looked down at Logan's body again, this time with a mild, pleasant expression. "What a pity his death was so quick. At least being fed on by a newborn is fairly agonizing. Or so I've heard— strangely enough, it's not one of my kinks."

"Gil didn't kill him. I did. A human saw us and ran back inside. She's probably calling the police right now. I think . . ." I hesitated. "I think she saw my real face."

Laurie's expression didn't change. He just inclined his head in a thoughtless, graceful movement. "Go. We'll take care of this."

I bristled at the command, then realized how ridiculous my reaction was. I'd summoned them here. They were helping us. Swallowing, I nodded and turned away, searching for Gil in the shadows. There he was, squatting against the wall, his glowing eyes the only part of him I could see.

"Gil," I said softly, hoping the sound of my voice would penetrate his bloodlust. "I want to go back to the motel. Will you come with me?"

I chose my phrasing carefully. Gil was still in a primal state, but if I made it seem as though I needed something, I knew it would reach him in whatever dark place he was.

For a moment, nothing happened. But then Gil nodded and pushed himself up. I took hold of his fingers, slowly, carefully, wary of making any abrupt movements when his senses were so heightened. Holding the vampire's hand as if he were a child, I started in the direction of the car. Then I raised my gaze . . . and froze.

In the exact spot I'd been standing with Logan, there was a circle of soil. Streaks ran through it where Layla had recoiled. It clearly didn't belong, especially since the rest of the parking lot was pavement and ice, and I thought of the memory I'd been trapped in during the confrontation with Logan. There had been dirt at the base of the tree Ian had held me against.

More proof of the power that my parents had fought so hard to contain. The power Lucifer had been searching for. Killing for.

I caught Laurie giving me a speculative look, but now wasn't exactly the time to explain. Just as I moved to leave again, something else occurred to me.

"Laurie?" I turned back and met his gaze. "Don't kill her. Please."

"She saw your face, Fortuna."

"Please," I said again. I knew the risks, but this time, I didn't care. I couldn't bear to have more blood on my hands. Especially not Layla. She was kind, and smart, and she was the rare sort of human who didn't value perfection. That was how she'd been able to see past the power of a Nightmare.

I wouldn't lose any sleep over Logan's death, but if Layla was killed because of me, I doubted even Oliver would be able to keep those dreams at bay.

Laurie didn't say anything. I looked at him, waiting, and he just looked back.

"She won't be harmed," Collith interjected, his voice firm. My gaze swung to him, startled. He nodded at me, and there was a promise in his eyes. Even though he'd broken vows to me before—we both had—I felt the storm inside me subside, a little. My shoulders slumped, and I exhaled slowly, nodding back at him.

"Thank you."

After another moment, I broke our stare. Collith moved toward the body while Laurie seemed to be directing his attention to the club. He had a cell phone pressed to his ear, and he spoke in a clipped, urgent murmur. I led Gil to the car, and he finally seemed to regain some semblance of his former self. He folded himself into the passenger seat without any prompting from me. Hiding my relief, I circled the hood, and as I opened the door on the driver's side, I finally noticed my hands. They were stained with Logan's blood. I shuddered and got in, suddenly realizing how cold I was.

Our latest motel was about ten miles from the club. We were in Nebraska now, and this town looked like all the others. There were small houses, quaint churches, and several bars. Our motel was cleaner than the last one, at least, but the owner asked more questions than I liked. Finn had taken to staying in his wolf form so there was less risk of him being spotted, or someone coming across the bits of flesh, fur, and bone that were left behind after his transitions. Once or twice, I'd even found an entire pelt. Finn had also taken to hunting constantly, which explained why he hadn't arrived with Gil during the attack. The more distance there was between us, the more muted our emotions were to each other.

Thinking of Logan made me feel cold again. My grip tightened on the steering wheel, and I reached over to adjust the heat. It had started snowing, and small flakes scattered across the glass. I watched them gleam and glitter, trying to distract myself from an image of Logan and Ian's faces blending together.

"I'm sorry."

Gil's voice was so low that I almost didn't hear him. I glanced at him, but he kept his face turned away. I pursed my lips and refocused on the road. There was an ache in my chest that didn't fully belong to me—touching our bond had blurred things, connected us more intensely. I wished for the dozenth time that I'd remembered to get the damn gun tonight. Maybe then Gil wouldn't have felt my panic and flown to my rescue.

"It's the price we pay for power," I said quietly, switching on the windshield wipers. *Thump-thump. Thump-thump.* "The war inside you never ends. Sometimes you win. Sometimes you lose."

Gil made a soft sound. "And what about the price they pay? The ones who can't defend themselves?"

I hesitated, pressing my foot on the brake pedal. The sound of the blinker filled the cold stillness. Gil still wouldn't tear his gaze from the window, so I couldn't see his face, but I knew, somehow, that whatever I said next was important. God, why couldn't I be a more eloquent person? I didn't allow myself to take the deep breath I wanted, since Gil's sharp ears would hear it.

"For every life you take, you can save another. Use all your power in a different way. Be the better monster. That's how you bear it," I said, thinking of my own victims. *Morsels*, Gil called them. Or used to.

At last, he finally looked at me. He leaned against the headrest and gave me a crooked, sad smile. The green glow of the clock cast one side of his face in shadow. "Life isn't a ledger book, darling. I'm a vampire. My very existence goes against every law of nature or balance. No matter how many good deeds I do, I'm bound for Hell."

"Hey." I waited until his eyes flicked over at me, then gave him a faint smile of my own. "At least we'll be there together."

Gil didn't respond, but he reached over the center console and took my hand again. I laced our fingers together and tightened my grip. Maybe I didn't need the right words after all.

The snow had thickened outside, and wind howled beyond the glass. But Gil's mind had gone quiet. Neither of us touched the radio or filled the silence. We just peered out at the storm, speaking in a language only people like us understood. I knew the quiet wouldn't last. Now that I'd revealed where I was, Collith and Laurie would be back. I needed to figure out how to drive them away again.

But tonight, I would sleep.

Sleep and dream.

CHAPTER FIVE

The parking lot of the Super 8 was nearly full when we pulled in.

An entire day had passed since the incident with Logan Boon, and I was fighting to keep my eyes open. I knew I needed to stop, despite the restless feeling in my veins that urged me onward. We'd driven for twelve hours. There'd been no sign of Collith or Laurie, but that didn't prove I'd truly managed to evade them. Somehow, they kept managing to find me. Gil and Finn did regular checks for trackers, though, so I had no idea how they were doing it.

Letting out a frustrated breath, I pulled into one of the last spots left, and the brakes whined through the dusk. Gil immediately got out, the white box of his cigarettes flashing in the dim light. In the space of a blink, he disappeared. I stayed where I was, staring up at the brightly-lit sign. Just the thought of standing made me want to groan. After a moment, I sank against the seat and rubbed my eyes with the heels of my hands. As heat blasted from the vents, I mentally prepared for the conversation with the front desk employee. God, humans were so exhausting.

A hand touched my shoulder from behind, then gave it a careful squeeze. My eyes met Finn's in the rearview mirror. A soft smile curved my mouth. "It's good to see you," I said quietly.

I could tell from the gentling in his eyes that he knew what I meant. I didn't mind Finn's animal form—it had become a comforting habit to bury my fingers in his fur—but there was part of me that always worried when he was a wolf. What if those wild instincts consumed him? What if he went on a hunt and never came back?

At least I knew that wouldn't happen tonight. Not while Finn was confined to this shape and all the reason that came with it. The relief I felt was tinged with guilt. I knew Finn had changed back for me, because of me, even though he preferred the wolf. He'd probably felt my side of the bond unraveling.

It was wearing on my sanity, the relentless pace and the sleepless nights. Working, searching, running. Seeing Collith and Laurie again had been a catalyst of some sort. These past few months, I'd been putting all my fear, fatigue, and pain behind a brick wall. Then they'd come along and struck their fists against it, leaving cracks and crumbling blocks. I needed to slap some mortar down, keep going, keep fighting.

Staying in the car wasn't going to make any of that happen.

I suppressed a sigh and forced myself to kill the engine, then leave the warmth in favor of winter's bitter chill. Finn followed suit and beat me to the trunk, lifting our bags out. He left Gil's where it was, of course, and closed the trunk with pointed force. I rolled my eyes at him and moved to get the bag myself. After that, we crossed the lot to enter the motel, our exhales making plumes in the air.

Gil was huddled in the shadows near the front door. The orange tip of his cigarette glowed. I stopped and handed over his bag. "Are you coming?"

"Not yet. I can't . . ." He made a vague gesture toward the door.

"I understand," I said. I felt his struggle through the bond. Gil's fangs weren't out, his eyes weren't glowing, but I could sense the vampire beneath his skin. Clawing at it.

Standing there, it occurred to me that putting Gil in an enclosed space, surrounded by dozens of helpless, sleeping humans, wasn't the best idea I'd ever had. *Maybe we should just drive through the night . . .*

Finn must've seen the indecision in my eyes. "He'll be fine. We just need to rest," the werewolf murmured.

He was right. Getting back on the road would only gnaw at us more. Eat at Gil's control, Finn's restraint, my endurance. I nodded at the werewolf, relenting, and he went inside. I touched Gil's arm in brief, silent reassurance, then turned to follow. The only sound he made was the soft scrape of his shoe against concrete, crushing the butt of his cigarette. The first of many tonight, I suspected.

The lobby smelled like laundry detergent and pool chlorine. I checked in with the heavy-lidded woman at the front desk, who was even more tired than I was, if that was possible. She was so tired that she barely looked up, much less notice me enough to be influenced by my power. I was liking this hotel already. Never mind that I could see a spot of mold on the ceiling.

A minute later, the woman handed over two key cards and mumbled something I translated to "Enjoy your stay."

I gave her a bleary nod and stepped away from the desk. Finn took my bag wordlessly, refusing to give it back every time I tried to tug at the handle. We walked down the hall, and he pressed the button for the elevator. I opened my mouth to ask why we weren't taking the stairs, like we always did, since neither of my companions liked small spaces. A beat later, I figured it out. Of course—we weren't taking the stairs because Finn saw I was on the verge of collapse, and he was thinking of my needs instead of his own. Quietly watching over me because I refused to ask for help. I closed my mouth and watched the number change above the elevator doors, afraid I might do something stupid and cry. Luckily, the doors opened a moment later, and the two of us went inside.

We found our room in silence. As the door opened, I saw this one was a carbon copy of all the others. Thin carpet, two queen beds, an outdated TV on a stand. The door closed with a soft *knick*, and my thoughts turned to something else that had been bothering me today.

"I still think it's strange Lyari never answered my summons, or checked in with us afterward. Maybe she found something. Some new research, or someone who knows where we can find answers." I set my bag on the bed, every movement sluggish. If Lyari did come, I'd need to be ready. I glanced over at the dinky coffee machine on the desk and mumbled, "I should shower. She'll probably be here any minute with a fresh stack of books to read."

Finn stood near the doorway, watching me stride across the room and reach for the coffee packets. "You need to sleep, Fortuna."

"I will, I promise. Soon." I filled the small pot with water and dumped it into the machine. After double-checking the amount of grounds I'd used, I jabbed the BREW button with my thumb and turned to open my bag. Good thing this motel provided shampoo, because I kept forgetting to buy a new bottle. I gathered an armful of toiletries, gave Finn a distracted, fleeting smile, and hurried into the bathroom. His concern followed me the entire way.

I could've stood beneath that hot water for hours. But even now, I couldn't shake the sense of urgency. Just a few minutes later, I stepped out of the steam-filled bathroom, hoping Lyari had arrived.

I did a double take at the mirror hanging on the wall.

My heart was in my throat as I spun to face Collith. "Are you serious? You invited yourself into my motel room while I was showering? Okay, now this is getting—"

I cut short when something moved in the corner of my eye. Collith sighed and said, "I thought we agreed you'd sit this one out."

Laurie pouted from where he sat on one of the beds, his stomach muscles taut from how he was propped up. The buttons of his dress shirt were partially undone, lending him a more casual air. "I got bored. This seemed way more fun than the state dinner I just came from. Mermaids can be so dull."

I held onto the top edge of my towel with an unnecessarily tight grip. My gaze swept the room, confirming that my other companions were nowhere to be seen.

"How did you convince Finn to leave?" I asked tightly, refocusing on the faeries. Collith was the closest, so my eyes landed on him.

Laurie was the one who answered, though. He walked past Collith, who sat at the end of the other bed, his hands loosely linked between his knees. Laurie began to examine the room as he said, "The wolf may be unreasonably protective, but he's not an idiot. He knows you're safer with us than you would be with him. Where's the vampire?"

"In the woods, probably." I tried to hide my worry. Tried and failed, apparently.

"How cute. Is someone struggling with a little newborn guilt? Tell your fanged friend that human's death was just natural selection at work," Laurie said with a dismissive flick of his wrist. He finished his perusal of the space and faced me. I waited for him to comment on the atrocious wallpaper or the low thread count of the sheets. Instead, he lowered himself onto the bed in a single, graceful movement and patted the empty spot beside him.

I frowned. "Finn and Gil are coming back soon."

Laurie cocked his head, his eyes going distant as he listened to something I couldn't hear. "I got a room down the hall. The werewolf is making himself comfortable there. He just turned on the TV."

"This is insane." I shook my head and snatched up my pajamas. "Every second you spend with me, you're putting yourselves in danger. Please, just *go*."

"And miss a chance to see that towel fall off? Not a chance."

Collith muttered something in Enochian as I turned back to Laurie. His expression remained serious, his voice so matter-of-fact, but it felt like he was allowing part of our old friendship to slip past the kingly shield he'd put between us. Seeing that was the only reason I gave in. Or so I told myself. I shook my head at him, as if I found him exasperating, and unfolded the T-shirt still in my hand.

I pulled my clothes on, keeping the towel strategically draped. Sighing, I crawled down the length of the bed. Laurie watched me very, very intently, his eyes gleaming, and I gave him a look that said I knew exactly what he was thinking. I dropped onto my side, allowing my spine to rest against the Seelie King's rib cage, and stopped resisting the bone-deep exhaustion.

A second later, I felt the mattress dip in front of me. I didn't open my eyes, but I picked up on that subtle scent of someone who had grown up amongst secrets and shadows. Felt the shock of his skin as he adjusted himself around me like a wing or a protective shell. *Collith*. I resisted the urge to press closer. There were reasons why I shouldn't, even if I couldn't remember any of them right now . . .

With Collith's coolness on one side and Laurie's warmth on the other, I felt safe. Safer than I had in a long time.

"I'm so tired," I heard myself say. That voice didn't sound like mine, though. That voice belonged to someone creaky and gray.

"We know. Go to sleep, Fortuna."

I wasn't sure which one of them was the speaker. It didn't matter, anyway. I was already halfway over the threshold of consciousness, one foot on each side of the line.

Time became hazy. It overlapped with the past, and maybe a little of the dreamscape, too, images fading in and out of the dark. I was so far away from them that I couldn't tell what was real. I knew Collith and Laurie had come, that was real, and I was lying between them. What I wasn't clear on was whether I actually heard the conversation that happened next.

"Did it work?" Laurie murmured. The question clearly wasn't meant for me—my slowed heartbeat must've convinced them I was fully asleep.

Collith's voice was a rumble against my fingertips. When had I put my hand on his chest? "Yes. She lowered her guard long enough for me to sift through her fear. It's all true," he said.

If I hadn't been floating between realities, I would've protested the invasion of privacy. So *that* was why they hadn't tried to bring up Lucifer again—they'd devised a new plan and bided their time. If I wouldn't willingly give the answers, Collith would just take them. Loath as I was to admit it, his skills as a Nightmare were improving at an impressive rate. I hadn't even felt him inside my head. I probably should've been madder about it, but my reactions felt muted.

Laurie made a thoughtful sound. "We still haven't learned anything. Not really."

"Haven't learned anything? We know the Dark Prince is trying to rise again, Laurelis."

"Perhaps. Perhaps not. There are a lot of powerful players in this world, many of whom can disguise themselves or manipulate the senses," Laurie pointed out. "And Fortuna has caused quite a stir since her arrival at the Unseelie Court. It's possible she's caught the attention of the old things in this world. Things that have been sleeping for a long time."

"Well, whether it's truly him or not, Fortuna's fear was real. I know that." Collith's voice was tight.

I felt Laurie pick up a strand of my hair. There was a barely-perceptible tug, as though he was twining it around his finger. After a moment he said, his words low and solemn, "If it *is* the truth, then we're royally fucked, my friend."

"I'm not your friend."

Laurie heaved a dramatic sigh. "Must we keep pretending? This game has started to bore me. We're both cuddling the same girl in a very small, very lumpy bed. That seems like a friendly pastime."

Collith didn't acknowledge that he'd spoken. "Dark Prince or not, we'll deal with this new enemy like we've dealt with everything else . . . and pray that Fortuna doesn't kill anyone else along the way."

He was referring to Logan Boon. In an instant, I was back in that freezing parking lot, staring into Logan's bleeding eyes. If I'd been awake, I would've winced.

Laurie made another soft sound, but this one was almost sad. "You know," he said, "that's the difference between you and me. I would never ask her to change who she is."

"What do you care? You made your choice when you retook the throne," Collith reminded him coldly.

To my faint surprise, Laurie didn't rise to the bait. He just replied, his tone crisp with polite challenge, "So you have no intention of reclaiming your own, then? Is that what you're telling me?"

Now it was Collith's turn to heave a sigh. It had been a long time since I'd heard him make the familiar sound, and suddenly I felt the urge to smile, despite the direness of our situation. It was just so . . . Collith.

"I'm not telling you anything," he said to Laurie. He seemed more weary than angry, though. I found myself wondering how Collith had been filling these long months, now that he'd been relieved of his former responsibilities. Maybe he'd driven himself to the edge of sanity, too.

The two of them fell silent. If they'd been human, they would've felt the need to fill it. But we were Fallen. Creatures that had learned to exist in the quiet, because we'd discovered that it was the only way to survive. Minutes ticked by. Out in the hallway, a door slammed. I was about to float away when Laurie broke the silence again.

"You know she'll try to run again, right?" he said abruptly.

Collith paused. Then he admitted, "I'm surprised she's still here, quite frankly."

"Too stubborn for her own good. Want to place a bet on how long it'll take?"

Collith didn't answer, but some of the tension in the bed had eased. The energy between them felt lighter. I waited for Laurie to say something else, because he was Laurie, and he was always the one who extended a hand when it came to the people he loved. Like watching over Collith at the Unseelie Court, even after everything had gone terribly wrong between them. Or giving up his throne for me, knowing while he did it that I loved someone else. But when Laurelis Dondarte loved, he did it relentlessly.

Which was why I was unprepared to hear Collith speak first.

"Did you hear how they introduced her? At that first club?" he asked. His voice was thick, as if he was holding something back.

"Angel Jones. Jesus. That's got to be one of the worst stripper names I've ever heard."

Both of them shook with silent laughter. I was still lodged between them, and I felt their bodies moving. Laurie's ribs whispering along the back of my shoulder. Collith's chin against my temple. *Laurie and Collith? Laughing together?* I thought, nonplussed.

I braced myself for jealousy. But hearing their joy, feeling the power of their shared history, I only felt a tiny pierce of something. Something I couldn't name.

If Laurie responded, I didn't hear it; I couldn't hold onto reality anymore. I drifted deeper into the darkness, and my ears caught the faint sound of a roaring sea.

Then the dreamscape claimed me.

Once again, Oliver wasn't under our tree when I arrived at the dreamscape.

I searched the horizon, confirming that he wasn't near the cliff-side, either. The air was cooler than I was used to here. I'd get a sweater from the cottage and see if Oliver was there. I started walking in that direction, holding my hands out on either side of me so the tips of the long grass could tickle my palms. Despite the chill, the dreamscape seemed to have solidified in its current state of being. I wasn't sure if that was a good thing or a bad thing.

Something to worry about on another night. For now, I needed to find my friend.

"Hello?" I called, pushing the door open. "Ollie?"

At first glance, the cottage seemed to be empty. None of the lamps were on and silence clung to the air like mist. But there was a fire in the hearth, and it cast an orange glow over everything. Maybe Oliver was upstairs. I started to turn, frowning.

A sound reached my ears, and if it hadn't been so still, I probably would've missed it. A slight scraping, like something dragging along the wooden floor. I paused and scanned the room again, keeping my gaze low. This time, I caught sight of a shoe poking out slightly from behind the kitchen island.

"Ollie?" I rushed over to him and dropped to my knees. He was curled on his side, shivering. I helped him sit upright, noting as I did how much weight he'd lost. How had I missed that? "What's wrong? What can I do?"

Moving him seemed to make things worse. Oliver cried out, clutching his head in both hands. Desperate to help, I grabbed his arms without thinking. Alarm jolted through me when I discovered that my best friend's skin was slick with sweat, and beneath it, he was as cold as the wintry lands where we had once fought ceti and minotaurs. "Ollie, what can I do?" I repeated.

He didn't lift his head. "I don't think I can keep him out much longer."

"Then let him in," I said immediately. My voice was firm. "Just let him in. I can take him, I promise."

"Never," Oliver said through his teeth. "He's not coming near you."

"Ollie—"

"Water. I need some water."

I recognized the set to his jaw. The request for water was nothing more than a way to end the conversation, redirect my focus. I let Oliver win this round, simply because he was expending energy arguing with me. I bit back my protests and stood. I filled a glass and kneeled down again, picking up Oliver's hand to curl his fingers around the water.

Knowing it would only make him feel worse, I didn't let any guilt show on my face. It raged inside me, though, like a hurricane tearing a city apart. On the other side of reality, my body was resting and comfortable, tucked between two faeries. And here was Oliver, suffering, because of me.

"What can I do?" I asked a third time.

The words had barely passed my lips when the ground began to rumble. It was like thunder, but not. Dishes rattled in the cupboards. Oliver still didn't look at me, and his voice was hoarse as he said, "You can *run*. He's been whispering things to me. Or maybe . . . maybe I just overheard them. I can't . . . I can't tell anymore. But he knows where you are, Fortuna. You need to wake up and run as fast as you fucking can."

Goosebumps raced over my skin. I gripped his arm and shook my head. "I'm not leaving you like this."

Oliver's eyes snapped open, seeing something I couldn't. A vein stood out along the side of his neck. "Fortuna, he's almost there.

He's so close that he can see the sign of the town you're in. *Go*," he bellowed.

I scrambled back, my heart pounding in my ears. Lightning flashed outside the windows, or at least, I thought it was lightning. "Wake up. Wake up," I chanted, picturing the motel room.

Just as the entire cottage began to shake, my vision went dark.

CHAPTER SIX

*M*y eyes flew open.

I half-expected the bed to be empty, or for Laurie to be gone, at the very least. But both of the faeries I'd fallen asleep next to were still very present. They were everywhere, all at once, six feet of hard male on either side of me.

My mind absorbed the situation I'd found myself in. I was on my back, staring up at the shadowed ceiling. Laurie's arm was across my stomach, resting against it, and his hand ever-so-slightly touched Collith's. Collith was facing me as well, but his head was higher up on the pillow. He'd removed his shirt at some point, and his bare skin gleamed in the weak light slipping in from beneath the door. One of his legs was tangled with mine and his long fingers curled against the curve of my neck. As if he had been playing with my hair when he'd fallen asleep.

I got my leg free first. Laurie's arm was trickier, and I spent far too long lifting it off me. I kept darting glances at his sleeping face, convinced he was faking it. It seemed impossible that someone like Laurelis Dondarte actually slept. But once the weight of his arm was gone and I was free, he didn't stir. Moving as if the mattress were a field of landmines, I gingerly made my way to the end of the bed. My bare toes touched the floor and I almost let out a breath of triumph. When I settled my full weight on it, however, the wood emitted a low moan.

I froze for an instant, then dared to look over my shoulder. Neither of them had moved. Collith's chest still rose and fell in deep sleep, and Laurie's eyes twitched beneath the lids. I pushed myself up and retrieved my bag. There was no time to get dressed, but my coat was easy enough to shrug on silently.

Taut as a bowstring, I reached for the doorknob. Something stopped me. It was the same feeling I'd gotten the night I left Collith standing in the road, back at the last motel—the same weakness. An instinct to look behind or go back. I gave in to it again, twisting to see the warm bed I'd abandoned and the two figures lying in it. I didn't allow myself to think about the fact I'd woken up entangled with both of them. I traced each male with my eyes, committing the image to memory. They wouldn't find me this time, not if I could help it. I'd be more careful. After another moment, I opened the door and crept through.

The second I found myself alone in the hallway, I realized I had a problem.

Laurie mentioned that he'd gotten the boys a room of their own. But there was no way of narrowing that down, and I couldn't knock on doors without alerting Collith and Laurie. Swallowing a curse, I dug my cell phone out. I kept the message short and vague. *Time to go. I'll wait for you at the rendezvous point we agreed on. Hurry.*

This time, the rendezvous point was a gas station down the street. I pocketed the phone and pulled up my hood, then hurried down the stairwell. The elevator was slow, and the faeries could wake up any second. On the first floor, I slipped out a side door, fishing for my car keys at the same time. Cold air slapped me in the face. God, what state were we in, and why had we stopped here?

Daydreams about hot cups of coffee started to go through my mind. As I crossed the lot, I finally checked the time. It would be another day of driving, and today we'd go even farther. I had no idea if distance would improve my chances of evading Collith and Laurie, but it certainly couldn't hurt.

Just as I reached the car, I pressed my hand against the door and closed my eyes. More running. Would it ever end, or was this my life now? Even my time as the Unseelie Queen had been better.

I took a breath, let it out, and straightened.

"Where are you off to this time?"

I jumped and spun, my spine hitting the car. Laurie stood a short distance away, wearing that courtly, polite expression I was starting to hate. Damn faeries and their silent feet. "I'm going to punch you in the throat," I breathed, relaxing.

"Hard?" He sounded hopeful. I shook my head at him, but the corners of my mouth deepened. Laurie watched me with a faint, crooked smile. His voice softened as he said, "Admit it. You've missed me."

In an instant, it felt like the temperature changed or the air had shifted. I shoved my hands in my coat pockets and forced myself to meet Laurie's gaze. In the harsh lighting, with bits of snow drifting across his face, he looked like one of those pretty princes in a fairy tale. "I do," I admitted.

His full lips turned downward. It wasn't quite a frown. *Hurt*, I thought. But his voice was detached as he asked, "Then why leave without a single word? Do we truly mean so little to you?"

"Of *course* not." I started to move toward him, then thought better of it. My hands were fists in my pockets. I longed to confess everything. Confide anything. I lowered my eyes, thinking of the last time I'd been vulnerable around Laurie. The conversation that had haunted me for months. "Do you remember what you said to me on that hilltop? The day you took me to see the horses?"

Please. Don't do this.

Do what?

Make me fall in love with you.

"I haven't forgotten a thing," Laurie answered. The way he said it made my core tighten. I knew if I looked at him, I would be a fucking goner. But I'd already done this math, and we were an equation that didn't work. Laurie had also done it—it was why he'd left. He had made a choice, too.

Suddenly a spark of anger brightened inside me. Laurie wasn't the only one with questions. I felt my brows lower and I met his gaze again. There was a challenge in my voice as I said, "Then why come back? Why not just leave this to Collith? Like he said, you made your choice. Seeing you now, it's . . ."

Laurie's gaze was intent. I could feel him observing every movement, every thought that raced through my head. "It's what?" he said when I didn't continue.

I considered turning back to the car, but there was a hardness in Laurie's eyes that told me he wouldn't let this rest. "Confusing," I sighed. "Seeing you is confusing."

"There's nothing confusing about this, Fortuna."

He was wrong, I thought. Laurie had just made everything worse. I didn't have time to argue with him, though, so I decided not to even try. My gaze flicked toward the building looming over us. "I have to go. Keep an eye on him, okay? Don't let him do anything stupid." I hesitated. "And . . . tell him goodbye for me."

"Tell him yourself." Laurie's focus shifted, and I heard footsteps a second later. Collith's scent teased my senses.

"How do you two always find me?" I asked, looking between them. Suddenly I remembered that night outside Viessa's club. We'd been in fucking *Ibiza* and Collith had just appeared. He'd never revealed how he'd known where I was, and I'd gotten distracted after that.

I fixed my attention on Collith now, my eyes narrowed with resolve. He saw it, and I swore he almost smiled.

There she is, he thought. I heard the words in my own head, clear as a bell. But how?

When I discovered the truth, my heart softened.

Collith was terrified.

Ever since he'd found me at Sugarland, this faerie king of mine had been worried that something had finally succeeded in breaking me. Learning about Lucifer had only worsened it. He watched my face and listened to the words coming out of my mouth, secretly reliving his own time in Hell. That fear was what allowed me to slip past his defenses now, just for a moment.

"You think of us sometimes," Collith answered finally, his voice soft. He seemed unaware that I'd slipped into his head. "If you feel something strong enough, it can be just as effective as saying a name. It doesn't always work, though."

My eyebrows rose. "Uh, that would've been useful information to know before now."

"We thought you did." Laurie sounded amused. "Our young learn such things in the nursery."

I glared at him. "Well, I—"

Collith made a strange sound, cutting me off, and I frowned. Laurie and I both turned in his direction. Collith stood slightly hunched over, his expression twisted in pain and concentration. I started to say his name, but a guttural cry burst out of him, and he fell to his knees. Or he would've, if Laurie hadn't moved in a blur and put his arm around Collith's waist. He lowered him the rest of the way to the pavement, propping Collith up against my car.

Collith held his head, dark hair spilling between his fingers. "No," he moaned. "*No.*"

It was the same way Oliver had moved last night. Like something was tearing him apart from the inside. I knelt beside Collith while Laurie raised his phone, calling a witch, no doubt. Only magic could help Collith right now. I stayed within touching distance, my hands clenched into helpless fists. I was so consumed by what was happening to Collith that I didn't hear Finn's arrival.

"Fortuna," he said, drawing my focus to him. His golden eyes were overly bright, and his nostrils flared. "I know that scent."

Finn had been possessed by a demon recently. My stomach dropped as I grasped what this meant. Lucifer was here all right, and he was using Collith as a host for his grand entrance. Oliver had tried to warn me, and I'd wasted too much goddamn time. Once again, I'd put people I loved at risk.

70

"I want all of you to leave, *now*," I said sharply. I sought Finn with my gaze. "Get Gil and run."

The werewolf tensed, about to turn and do exactly that, but then Collith went still. His hands fell away from his skull, and he pushed himself off the frozen pavement. We all watched in wary, startled silence as he straightened his coat and tugged at the ends of his sleeves.

"That won't be necessary," he said in a voice that didn't sound like his. "I've come to offer a deal, Fortuna Sworn."

Then Collith smiled. In that instant, I knew my fear had come to pass. It was obvious whose words were coming out of his mouth. *Guess the cat's out of the bag*, I thought dimly.

Lucifer knew Collith was a Nightmare.

"How?" I said. My voice was flat. Finn had been branded, which allowed the demon in, somehow. It was the same for Jacob Goldmann. Collith bore no such scars on his body. At least, he hadn't the last time I'd seen him unclothed. But months had passed since then and I'd run without telling Collith about the potential danger.

"The mark is on his soul, Lady Sworn," Lucifer said, raising his eyebrows. He must've seen my guilt, and I didn't like that he could read me so easily. "Did you really think the Unseelie King could spend ninety years in my domain, undetected? The son of one of my most infamous residents? It isn't surprising that he doesn't remember—resurrection is a tricky business."

Doesn't remember? I echoed silently, disbelieving. Collith might not have retained the memory of getting branded, but he remembered plenty. My mind flashed back to those long months after I'd brought Collith back from Hell. I recalled his pain, his nightmares. He had been so destroyed by his years in captivity that he'd worried just *one* encounter with Lucifer might have broken me. Icy rage wrapped its fingers around my heart. I looked the devil in the eye and asked, "Are you the one that tortured him?"

He gazed back at me without a glimmer of remorse. "Not personally, no."

"It was the human, wasn't it." I still spoke tonelessly. "The night I killed Logan Boon. That's how you found me."

I supposed it didn't really matter anymore, but Lucifer still answered. "Actually, no. I learned of your whereabouts as soon as Collith did. I knew it would only be a matter of time until he found you again, so I've been making preparations since. Don't worry, I'll return your lover. I'm merely borrowing him for a few minutes."

Hearing this, my lungs loosened, and I could breathe again. So Lucifer didn't intend to use Collith as a host, then. Or at least not a permanent one. I traced his noble features with my eyes, trying to reconcile that it wasn't Collith anymore. The sooner we ended this conversation, the sooner we could get him back. "If you're hoping to use my body like you used Jacob's, there's no deal you could offer I'd ever accept," I told Lucifer.

The devil frowned. "I never wanted to possess you, my lady."

The sincerity in his voice caught me by surprise. I quickly remembered the list of reasons why Lucifer was my enemy. There were many. "The brand on my back would say otherwise," I said with cold loathing.

Laurie shifted, as if physically restraining himself. Until now, he'd been quiet during this encounter. I kept my focus on Lucifer, and I saw his mouth tighten after I'd spoken. Something about what I said had bothered him. "The brand is a mark created by Olorel. It simply makes passage between dimensions easier. That is why it is often used for possession," the devil said.

"You're lying. Want to know how I know?" I leaned closer and dropped my voice to a whisper. "Your lips are moving."

Lucifer just looked at me. I stepped back, answering the intensity in his gaze with a dull-eyed look of my own as I continued, "Otherwise why come to the house wearing Jacob? Why go through so much trouble to find me, make me a Nightmare again?"

"I wanted to meet you, and I couldn't reach you in your dreams, as there was someone preventing me from fully making contact," Lucifer countered. *Ollie*, I thought. As if the devil sensed something amiss, or my expression had given something away, he paused. His eyes flicked between mine. Then he murmured, "In hindsight, I see how the intentions behind my visit could've been misinterpreted."

If the devil had been in his true form, I might have been influenced by his beauty, his power. But it was Collith's body he wore, and I wanted this fucker *out*. "I don't think I misinterpreted anything," I said.

"As for the torment you endured at Belanor's hands," he went on, "please understand that he acted on his own. Belanor has always been overzealous in his devotion to me."

"Overzealous?" I repeated in disbelief. Echoes of my own screams drifted through my memory.

"Aren't you at all curious about my deal?" Lucifer questioned. I recognized the smooth attempt to change the subject. He still wanted something, and reminding me of what his number one fan had done wouldn't exactly help his case.

I didn't need to think about it. "No."

"Come to my dimension," Lucifer said, ignoring my response. "Do this, and I will give you the spell that will wake your brother. I had hoped to extend a less . . . complicated invitation, but then you beheaded my host."

I was so preoccupied by the first part of what he'd said, by the invitation to *Hell*, that it took me an extra moment to comprehend the rest of it.

"Wait, what do you mean, wake my—" My phone started vibrating. I pulled it out and glanced at the number calling me. My breathing went shallow again. I touched the screen and raised it to my ear. "Emma?"

"It's Damon, sweetheart." Her voice was hushed, and I knew Matthew must be nearby. "He just collapsed."

"It was Lucifer," I said dully, holding the phone with fingers that didn't feel like mine. "Don't bother calling for an ambulance. No hospital will be able to help him."

"What's happened?" Emma asked. There was a remarkable amount of composure in her tone, but I could still picture the deep lines that appeared on her forehead whenever she was worried.

I hesitated and glanced toward Lucifer. He'd turned away, offering the illusion of privacy, but I knew he could hear every word. "I'll explain everything when I can."

"You're not alone," Emma stated, hearing something in my voice. She made a determined sound and the line crackled with her exhale. "Okay. I'll keep Damon and Matthew safe. Be careful, sweetheart."

"Call you soon," I promised numbly, and hung up. I lowered my arm to my side, and Lucifer waited for my answer.

I said nothing; I was putting the pieces together. Going back. So *this* was why Lucifer had stopped pounding at Oliver's defenses for one night—he'd been focused on getting Damon. My brother was part of the "preparations" Lucifer had started making once he knew where I was. I should've known something was wrong. I should've called Damon the second I woke up.

Swallowing, I raised my head and looked at the creature wearing Collith like a flesh suit. "You just sealed your own fate. The second you put my brother under that spell, your life was forfeit."

My threat floated past Lucifer like a feather. He moved, but it was barely perceptible, as if he'd started to bow and caught himself. Instead, he straightened and stepped back. His silken voice became brisk. "Take some time. Think about it. I'll return after three days for your answer."

"What is it with bad guys and the three-day deadline? And if I don't accept your insane deal?" I demanded, taking a half step forward. "What then?"

Lucifer paused. His gaze met mine, and I tried to read him like he'd read me. Seconds passed, thick with tension and words unsaid. I was painfully aware of Laurie standing nearby, observing every moment, assessing every part of this interaction. The fact that he hadn't made a single remark spoke volumes. *He doesn't want to get on Lucifer's radar*, I thought. Even Laurelis Dondarte was scared of the devil.

Then Collith's body jerked, abruptly breaking our stare.

When he lifted his head again, breathing raggedly, it was clear Lucifer had kept his word. The person standing in front of me now had Collith's serious tilt to his mouth. Collith's scent and quiet presence. Relief expanded in my chest, but it was short-lived. I glanced at Laurie, who was looking at Collith with a grim expression, and I knew we were thinking the same thing.

We couldn't trust him anymore.

It was hitting me, finally—the reality of everything. Damon was under some kind of sleeping spell. Collith was Lucifer's puppet. Lucifer knew exactly where I was, along with the locations of everyone I loved. Not only was I losing this war, I was losing *badly*.

Needing a moment to myself, I took several steps away and put my back to everyone. There was a slight whooshing sound, and I heard Finn mutter something under his breath. Gil had arrived, no doubt. I felt him along the bond, and my only comfort was he seemed more stable. More grounded. For an instant, I worried if that meant he'd fed from someone's vein, rather than the blood bags Lyari had been obtaining for him. But I would've sensed it, right?

I pinched the bridge of my nose and took a deep breath. *One problem at a time, Fortuna.*

After a few seconds, I came back. Laurie was on his phone, his voice low and discreet. The other three stood perfectly still, exactly where I'd left them. I raised my head and looked at Collith. "He's going to kill my brother, isn't he?"

"We have three days," he started, then stopped. His jaw worked and his hazel eyes burned. He must've come to the same conclusion as me and Laurie, because after a moment he said, "You have three days, and you have our resources now. Everything has a balance. A weakness. Figure out his and use it against him. He may be immortal, but he's not all-powerful."

I was silent. I mulled over Collith's words, then Lucifer's, too. *Think about it*, the devil had said. Oh, I would think. Think and figure out how to save Damon *and* Collith.

Laurie had finished his call and rejoined our small band of misfits. One by one, I looked at the males forming a half-circle around me. Collith. Laurie. Finn. Gil. They were waiting for our next move. At least one good thing had come out of this—they believed me about Lucifer now.

"Change of plans. We're going home." I gave them a bleak smile. For months, I had dreamed of saying those words. Just one more thing Lucifer had taken from me . . . and one more thing he'd pay for.

Laurie's lip curled into something resembling a snarl, and I caught a glimpse of ferocity in his eyes. The part of his nature he kept so well-hidden that I kept forgetting it existed. "You're *not* handing yourself over—" he started.

"I don't intend to," I interjected. "But there's no point staying in more motels, or getting back on the road. He has Damon, Laurie. I might as well sleep in my own bed while I figure out how to beat the devil in seventy-two hours. Any chance there's a Door nearby?"

Laurie grimaced. "In this hovel? Unlikely."

I'd hoped to buy us more time at the loft, and the car was such a piece of shit that I wouldn't have minded ditching it. As it was, we probably had another day of driving ahead. Ignoring the wave of exhaustion that washed over me, I reached for my bag. Gil beat me to it, of course, and Finn opened the trunk. They loaded the bags and we all got in.

Just before I pulled the door shut, I glanced up at Laurie and Collith. "I'll text you from the road," I murmured.

Laurie nodded. Collith watched me with an unfathomable expression, a shadow in his eyes, and I fought a sense of déjà vu. Strange how much could change over the course of a few minutes, I thought as Gil started the engine. I'd started the day running away. Now it felt like I was running toward something. But what, exactly? Hell? Death?

I'd have my answer in three days.

The loft welcomed me back with a warm draft and soft lights.

We'd made good time on the road, but Emma and Damon had been hiding out in a town far closer to Granby, so they still beat us back. We had two days left until Lucifer's deadline now. Two and a half if you counted tonight, which I did. I didn't intend to sleep until my brother was safe again.

As I moved over the threshold, I noted that Emma must've made coffee recently, because its aroma clung to the air. There was something infinitely comforting about that smell. I lowered my bag to the floor, closed my eyes, and inhaled deeply, savoring this moment of stillness. Soon, Gil would come back from Adam's, Finn would finish his hunt, and the real work would begin.

In spite of the terrible circumstances that had brought us here, it was good to be home.

Soft sounds came from Damon and Matthew's room, pulling me from my thoughts. I opened my eyes and looked at the dark, open doorway that would take me to my brother. Emma had told me what to expect, probably hoping to make the moment easier. But there was nothing easy about this. No mental image to prepare me for seeing my little brother empty and still. There and not there. Everything that made him Damon—his sweet smile, that endearing cowlick popping back up every time he ran his hand over it—taken and locked away.

Halfway across the living room, I instinctively sidestepped the edge of the couch, where a certain kitten liked to hide and bat me with her paws every time I passed. When that didn't happen, a wistful pang went through me. Thankfully, I'd gotten a hold of Cyrus during the drive, and he'd be bringing Hello over tomorrow.

I'd also texted Savannah and Mercy, telling them what had happened to Damon.

While my family continued the search for Lucifer's Achilles heel, I needed help figuring out how to get Damon back. I wasn't going to Hell, and he wasn't staying under a sleeping spell. But now there was a clock on our search. Until today, I'd tried to avoid enlisting Savannah's help, save for a cloaking spell and asking how to avoid magical detection when we'd first fled from Lucifer. She was already trying to gain a foothold in our lives, and any help I received from her felt like allowing Savannah to get another step closer. I knew I should want her to be involved, for Matthew's sake, because no child should grow up without a mother.

No matter how hard I tried, though, I looked at Savannah and saw Fred getting ripped to pieces.

My thoughts moved to another person that I had spoken to during the long drive. While we'd been making our way through Iowa, I'd finally heard from Lyari. She hadn't made an actual appearance, as I'd hoped she would. Instead, I had to update her through text. There was no point in keeping our communications limited anymore—not now that Lucifer was holding my brother hostage.

When I asked Lyari why she'd been AWOL for two days, my Right Hand stopped responding altogether.

We still hadn't seen each other. She and Collith had been helping Emma move my brother, first from the bed and breakfast where they'd been staying when Damon collapsed, then from the car and into the loft. The second Damon was settled, Lyari disappeared again to discreetly resume hunting for new materials and witnesses. For anyone who had encountered Lucifer or knew how to neutralize him, if it could even be done.

Collith was stationed at Cyrus's for the time being. He couldn't be within earshot of our conversations, for obvious reasons, but there was no point in banishing him, either. Lucifer was well-aware of where we were, and having Collith's heavenly fire on our side could come in handy if any of my other enemies decided to pay a visit. He planned to contact the faeries who were still loyal to him and send them my way if they had any information.

Laurie was back at Court, of course, but this time it was at my request. He was making careful inquiries about Lucifer, as well.

Everyone had a role, a purpose. The odds were better than ever for finding a solution to our Lucifer problem. Why, then, did I have a sinking feeling it wouldn't be enough?

I finally reached Damon's bedroom, and I faltered on the threshold. The first thing I saw was Matthew's crib, which had been dragged closer to the bed. Through the bars, the swell of my nephew's body was outlined in a beam of moonlight.

The next thing I saw was Damon.

"Wow," I said softly. It was all I could think to say.

He rested in the center of the bed, covers drawn to his chest. Machines glowed off to the side, and tubes connected them to my brother. I followed those tubes to his face. There wasn't much to see—most of it was covered by a mask. Above this, his eyes were closed.

Standing there, I was struck by a memory. A flashing image of a face, much smaller than the one in that bed, but still similar in so many ways. Stretched into a wide grin, big ears standing out on either side of his head. *Come on, Fortuna. Get up. Let's play a game!*

My hand curled into a fist against the doorframe. I thought of the promise I'd made to that little boy.

"He's as comfortable as we could make him," Emma murmured, crossing the room. She'd been fussing with Damon's covers. She leaned against the wall near me and rubbed her arm. "I called up an old friend, a doctor who retired years ago. I explained what we needed as best I could without giving too many details. Nancy won't say a word to anyone, don't worry. She put in a Foley catheter and a nasogastric feeding tube. The monitor is so we can watch his blood pressure, heart rate, and oxygen saturation. Oh, and his temperature."

There was a concentrated expression on Emma's face as she recited the words from memory. Watching her speak made emotion fill my chest, and it sent an ache through my heart.

"Thank you, Emma," I said quietly, trying not to wake Matthew. My gaze moved from the crib, to the bed, and back to the woman at my side. All of them were paying the price for loving me, just as Mercy had once foretold. For a moment, guilt made it difficult to speak. I cleared my throat and added, "Not just for this. For . . . everything. I know it wasn't easy, leaving your entire life behind like that."

Emma gave me a shrewd look. Hearing, somehow, the words I didn't say. "None of this is your fault, sweetheart. You didn't threaten us or do this to your brother."

"No, but I could've done more to prevent it. I shouldn't have even let anyone move in here. Anyone close to me gets hurt. That's how it's always been." Pain sharpened the edges of my tone. Unbidden, an image flashed through my head. Mom and Dad, standing on a dark beach, white-faced and afraid.

"Which is exactly what he wants, you know. The devil likes his victims isolated and scared. Being surrounded by people you love isn't a weakness, Fortuna—it's a strength." Emma gave me a tender smile. Then she refocused on Damon and her eyebrows knit together. "Don't think I'll ever forget that sight, though. I didn't even know the witches had him. I woke up before the rest of the house and made some coffee . . . . then I looked out the window and saw our boy. They left him on the front lawn. There were rope burns on his wrists and ankles. The gouges in his palms were so deep they needed stitches. It wasn't painless, what they did to him."

There was a thickness to how she spoke. She was trying not to cry.

"As if he needed any more pain." A tear slid into the corner of my mouth, and its bitter taste burst on my tongue. I looked toward Damon's wrists, but they were tucked beneath the blanket. My brother would have more scars because of me. When he did wake up, would things between us be bad again? Had Lucifer shattered our fragile peace to pieces?

Emma squeezed my arm and pulled away immediately, knowing my aversion to being touched. "He'll heal. Damon's strength is different from yours, but he isn't weak."

She was right. My brother was certainly softer than I was, and yet he was every bit as fierce. He was just quieter about it . . . and maybe a tad less homicidal. I studied Damon's still, pale face, my lips twisted in thought. "Yeah, well, first we need to wake him up," I murmured.

"You'll figure out a way. You always do." Emma mustered another smile. "I'm going to get started on breakfast. Any requests?"

I gave a slight shake of my head, keeping my eyes on Damon. "No, thank you. I think I'm just going to sit with him for a while."

"Okay. I'll bring you some sugar with a side of coffee." She winked and turned, walking toward the kitchen.

Once Emma was gone, I moved deeper into the room. My gaze went to the recliner on the other side of the bed—Damon had sat in that chair a hundred times during the first few months of Matthew living with us. My nephew hadn't slept well, so Damon would rock him for hours and hours. I sank into it now, wishing I could time-travel back to those days. I'd have done things so differently.

In that better version of my life, Damon wouldn't end up in this bed.

Matthew shifted in his crib, sending a rustling sound through the stillness. I watched him for a moment, making sure he was asleep, then turned back to the bed. Looking at Damon's face felt like holding my palm down on a hot burner, so I reached beneath the blankets and searched for his wounded hand, bringing it into the open so I could hold it. Above the bandage, his skin was unnaturally cold, like a corpse.

The thought made feel sick. I gripped onto Damon so tightly that my fingers turned white.

Thankfully, a figure filled the doorway and distracted me. I looked over to thank Emma, assuming she'd come back with the coffee. The words faded in my throat.

Danny looked different from the last time we'd seen each other. Before, he'd been clean-shaven, and there was always a soft smile curving his lips. Now his jaw was covered in patchy stubble and his features looked haggard. There was also no hint of a smile around his mouth.

"What happened?" he asked quietly. He must've just gotten off a shift, because he wore his deputy uniform. The buttons gleamed from the lights behind him.

"That's a very long story." I hesitated, wondering how much I should tell him. In my world, knowledge was a double-edged sword. Sometimes it improved your odds of survival; sometimes it brought death.

"I'd like to know," Danny said simply. He stood there with such quiet dignity, and I thought, not for the first time, how much I liked this human.

Damon had decided to tell his boyfriend the truth, so I would follow his lead.

"Some witches found where he and Emma were staying. They put Damon under a spell to use him as a bargaining chip," I said. "If

I give them what they want, they'll wake him up. I have two more days to make a decision."

I waited for Danny to ask what the witches wanted. Instead, he just moved deeper into the room, circling the bed to stand on the other side. He gazed down at Damon. His stricken expression felt like a bullet in my heart.

"I'll get him back," I swore with hushed ferocity. "I promise, and our family doesn't make promises lightly. Nightmares may be lies, but we—"

"—don't have to be liars," Danny finished, his eyes still on Damon. He forced his gaze to mine and mustered a small, sad smile. "I haven't spoken to him in months, but I still remember every word he said. It's kind of impossible to forget, really. It's not every day you find out your boyfriend isn't human."

I tried to smile back. "No, I guess not. For what it's worth, I'm glad you didn't go running for the hills like most people would. You made my brother really happy."

"He made me happy, too." Danny's mouth tightened. He blinked quickly and cleared his throat. "Do you mind if I join you?"

I shook my head. "Of course not."

Danny crossed the room and folded his long body into the smaller chair opposite mine. We sat like that for a while, neither of us broaching the quiet. It wasn't an uncomfortable silence, though. I didn't get the sense that Danny blamed me for Damon's current state. I snuck a glance at him, wondering where he and my brother had left things. Danny had just mentioned they hadn't spoken in months.

I'd never asked Damon if he'd officially ended it. At the time, I told myself it was none of my business. But really, I just didn't want to know. I didn't want to hear that Damon had lost another person he loved. The very good, very kind man who saw Damon for exactly who he was.

Another item I could add to the "Fortuna's Fault" list.

Voices drifted through the loft, pulling my focus outward again. I recognized the rumble of one and the mocking lilt of the person who responded. Finn and Gil were back.

"Stay as long as you want," I told Danny, rising from the recliner. It rocked against the back of my legs. "And let me know if you need anything. Please."

I felt his eyes on me as I walked out.

Finn and Gil had already dug into the food Emma had made for them. They sat at opposite ends of the island. If they'd been cats, their backs would've been arched, their fur standing on end. I thought about asking them what the issue was *this* time. Then, deciding they were grown-ups who could handle their own conflicts, I walked past them and joined Emma at the counter.

She turned and pressed a warm mug of coffee into my hand. "Here you are, sweetheart."

"Thanks." I cupped it and shot her a grateful look. "I'm going to try calling Savannah again. Maybe a miracle will happen and she'll be somewhere with a signal."

"I've got the baby monitor," Emma said, waving it in the air.

"Thanks." I started toward my room. I'd need to use my real cell phone, since the burner was nearly out of minutes. I'd hidden it the night we'd left Granby, since I didn't trust that one of Lucifer's followers wouldn't break in and search for clues of my whereabouts.

The door was still closed. Wanting to get this over with, I opened it quickly and stepped inside. Part of me expected a stale smell, since no one had aired it out in months. But it just smelled like . . . home. I avoided looking at the bed where Collith and I had slept together the last night I was here. I also didn't look up at the faint outline of repairs done on the roof, a constant reminder of the day I'd blasted Collith through it with a spell.

Fixated on my task with an overzealous focus, I knelt next to one of the vents, pulled the metal piece out, and patted around for my phone. I fished it out of the darkness and straightened, plugging the charger in immediately. I waited a few seconds. Then, steeling myself, I held down the power button and the screen lit up.

It started vibrating the moment it was on. Forty-nine unread texts. I skimmed some of them, holding back a sigh. Though I'd sent vague messages to everyone I was close to, it apparently hadn't stopped some friends from telling me exactly what they thought about my latest disappearing act. Viessa. Bea. The only people I'd given a little more detail were Aerilaya and Adam, so everyone else was pretty pissed. *Yay.* For a moment, I toyed with the idea of not telling anyone I was back. But even I wasn't that cruel.

I drank my coffee and sent a few texts, then set my phone aside. My vision had started to get blurry. I went back to the kitchen for a caffeine refill, trying not to think about the sleepless hours ahead.

Emma, clad in her pink robe, paused on the way to the bathroom. The baby monitor glowed in her hand. "Oh, Danny left," she said. "He wanted me to tell you he'd be back in the morning, if that was all right. He was just going home for some sleep and a shower."

"Okay. Thanks." I gave her a bleary wave and shuffled over to the coffee maker. The bathroom door clicked shut.

When I saw the pot was empty, I got to work on a fresh batch. Amongst the slew of messages, there had been a new one from Lyari, informing me she was coming back within the hour—she'd probably texted both my phones to make sure I got it.

A few minutes later, my Right Hand knocked in her signature militant style. I picked up the mug I'd just filled and approached the door, fighting back memories about the last time we'd been in this loft together. Particularly the one where I decapitated Jacob Goldmann and his head bounced off like a grisly ball. Even now, I could still hear the wet, dull sound it had made on the wood.

I was wincing as I opened the door.

"Your stairwell still reeks of sulfur," Lyari said by way of greeting.

"Hello to you, too," I muttered.

"Hello. I got word to Nym, as requested, but my contact couldn't confirm that he'd understood the message. He just mumbled something about clocks and threw a shoe at her. Also, I secured the door downstairs, since it was completely unlocked when I arrived. Do you have any sense of self-preservation? At all?" She walked past me with an oversized box in her arms. It was so big that she couldn't see where she was going, and Lyari, usually so graceful and poised,

84

let out a pained grunt when her knee bumped into the edge of a side table. It might've been funny, if there was anything funny about why we were here. She set the box down and straightened, raising her eyebrows at me.

"Should we get started, then?" was all she said.

I'd been hoping to get some answers about her mysterious absences, but I didn't want to bring it up in front of the others. Finn and Gil were already sitting down, and once again, the places they'd chosen were notably far apart. I stayed where I was for a moment, hesitating. Then, relenting, I nodded and walked over to box.

As usual, the materials Lyari had brought focused on two things—the devil and magic. I rifled through the impressive pile of books and papers, giving each item a cursory glance. Only a few stood out to me. This time, Lyari had procured the journal of an American woman who claimed that she had journeyed to Hell to meet good ol' Luci. Beneath the journal, there was a stack of letters written in Enochian. Next to these, I discovered a large, cracked tome filled with spells. There was also a small wooden box. Inside it, I found newspaper clippings and a cassette tape.

"Okay," I said, closing the box. "Who wants what?"

Each of them claimed something from the pile, and we got started.

Time crawled by. For a while, the only sounds were the sporadic scratching of a pen on paper, or the fire making a log pop, or the hum of the refrigerator. Emma never came out of her room, and I knew she'd probably fallen asleep. Matthew hadn't stirred, either. Finn was listening carefully for any sounds from my nephew's crib, and the werewolf hadn't budged from the couch. His eyes were dark with concentration as they scanned one of the newspaper clippings. Firelight flickered over his serious face.

Two or three hours in, Gil set his book amongst the dozen others we'd already gotten through, then sank back down with a sigh. "Found another one," he said. "Confirmation that he's an invulnerable bastard. If any of it's true, that is."

I finished writing a note and looked up at him. "If any of what is true?"

"These letters were written by a faerie named Virion. Apparently he was a renowned swordsman amongst the fae. He wrote to his wife from a mental asylum—his words, not mine. I assume that's why a lot of it doesn't make sense. Basically, I've worked out that Lucifer killed their daughter, so Virion found the evil bloke, challenged him to a duel, and actually managed to win. But then Virion got word that Lucifer was alive and well in his world. After that, he did what any sane person would do and went to Hell." I opened my mouth. Gil already knew what I was going to ask, because he added, "Doesn't say how he got there, though. Or how he came back. Just that he kicked the devil's ass again. What a badass, eh? Story doesn't have a happy ending, of course. 'The Serpent King cannot be killed, in this world or the next.' He returned to Earth, but he was so fucked up that he ended up in the asylum."

"So that rules out going to Hell assassin-style," I sighed. I shifted against the throw pillow behind me, trying to get more comfortable. "And further proof there's no point in letting the 'Serpent King' possess me, then getting one of you to kill me. We already knew that from Jacob, though."

I caught my friends giving each other startled looks. Realizing I'd lost track of the sentence I'd been reading, I made a frustrated sound and read the whole thing again.

"I'll ask," Gil said to the others. He cleared his throat and ventured, "Fortuna, dear, was that second option actually being considered?"

I frowned, only half-listening. "I'm considering everything. Nothing is off limits when it comes to saving Damon."

Something made them look at each other again. I caught the tail end of that look, alerted by their silence. I didn't see anyone make a signal, but it felt like they all moved at once—Finn got to his feet and ambled toward the kitchen while Gil sprang up, his hand moving into his pocket for the ever-present box of cigarettes there. I frowned at them, my tired mind noting their behavior. Whatever their deal was, it wasn't the priority right now.

My focus went back to the journal in my lap. The ink was old, the paper even more so, and everything was so faded that it took extra time to decipher, despite it being in English. The journal must've been exposed to water at some point. I blinked hard and fast, trying to make myself more alert. Then I gripped the corner of the page and started again.

Lyari's arm appeared in my peripheral vision. At first, I assumed she was reaching for something new to read. But she didn't settle back into her spot, and after a moment I heard her murmur, "There is one person who might know something. She might've even met the Dark Prince."

I didn't look up from the passage I was reading. "We're not there yet."

"If not now, then when, Your Majesty?" she asked. Her voice lowered. "I know the truth. You're afraid to use the bond between you. You're afraid you'll hate yourself for it."

Slowly, I lifted my head.

So *this* was why Finn and Gil had moved away—to give Lyari a chance to talk about Gwyn. All of them had been trying to convince me to contact the huntress for weeks. She was ancient, and if anyone knew the devil's weaknesses, it would be her. And if she didn't willingly provide the information, it would be easy enough to force it out of her. After all, Gwyn was still under my control.

A control I'd been waiting for Gwyn to challenge. So far, her side of the bond was quiet. I felt her testing our connection sometimes. Toying with it. Once in a while, it almost felt like she . . . caressed it.

Without fail, I thought of the promise she'd made. Her voice sounded in my mind as though I'd spoken to her only yesterday. *Someday you will know what it is to choose between love and power. Someday you will be just like me.*

"You're wrong." I met Lyari's gaze, unflinching. "I'm afraid I'll enjoy it."

This time, she was the one who didn't answer. With an abrupt movement, I set the book aside and pushed myself up. I followed Finn into the kitchen, where he was leaning against the counter and eating a bowl of yogurt. I shot him a half-hearted glare for participating in the Gwyn intervention. The werewolf's bright eyes dropped, and he became wholly focused on stirring his precious little parfait. Coward.

"Would you like any coffee?" I called over my shoulder, glancing at Lyari.

"No. I don't understand the humans' obsession with it," she said as I poured, her tone disdainful. "I've never had cat pee, but I suspect it would taste like coffee."

I made a noncommittal sound, then took an obnoxiously loud sip, making Lyari cringe. I waited for her to glare at me, or make a barbed comment. That was our dynamic, and the foundation our friendship had been built upon. But Lyari just lowered her head and turned the page. I felt my eyes narrow.

Something is wrong, instinct whispered.

I suspected something had been wrong for a long time, not just since the night I'd killed Logan Boon and Lyari hadn't come. The fact we still hadn't talked about it wasn't lost on me. She was avoiding it, which was just further proof that my instincts were right.

Before I could bring it up, Gil came back. He reeked of cigarette smoke and his fingers were still twitching. Ignoring the gentle nudge of concern I sent over our bond, he took another book from the stack and swung onto the loveseat, his long legs dangling off the armrest. Every time he shifted, the smoke clinging to his clothes gave off a faint scent. By that time, Finn had finished eating and returned to his spot, too. He kept making pointed huffing sounds, his nostrils flattening. I ignored them and kept reading.

The writer's name was Goody Baldwin, and she was a witch.

In 1902, Goody was twenty years old. Amongst glittering New York society, it was expected that she marry soon, or be doomed to suffer every woman's worst nightmare—singledom. To her father's consternation, Goody had no interest in finding a husband, mostly because she was bad at talking to people. She was shy, and her interest in botany set her apart from others. Even the witches who ran in her social circles didn't share her enthusiasm. They found Goody as strange as the humans did.

Chastity Baldwin was Goody's only friend. She was Goody's mother, and a powerful witch in her own right. She was the one to teach Goody about horticulture and give her a journal. If it had been up to the daughter, they would've spent every waking hour in their family's greenhouse, performing magic and writing spells together, for the rest of time.

But there was a downside to their abilities, like with most creatures of power. While vampires battled bloodlust, and werewolves suffered agonizing pain with every shift, the Baldwin line was plagued by visions.

Mother is sick, diary, Goody wrote one day with a trembling hand. *The visions have taken their toll. They come too often.*

She was frantic to help, to ease her mother's suffering, so she turned to magic once again. When she wasn't at Chastity's bedside, Goody was in their greenhouse. Tinkering, searching, reading. The Baldwin women were meticulous record-keepers and Chastity had collected generations' worth of spellbooks.

But not even their knowledge could save her.

Chastity Baldwin died on August 6th, 1902. She was thirty-seven years old.

Goody's loneliness consumed her. She began to dream of speaking to her mother again. Such bright, vivid dreams that Goody developed an obsession. Even her handwriting became more frantic. *What if these dreams are a message from the beyond? What if there's a way to see Mother again?*

She had been taught, by her stern father, that every Fallen creature went to Hell after they died. *Our ancestors committed the ultimate treason*, he told her again and again. *We can never go back to God's world.* Goody had heard it so often the lectures began to roll off her.

She decided that in order to speak to Chastity again, she needed to visit Hell.

Goody got to work in the greenhouse. She had a talent for creating spells, and often utilized her knowledge of growing things to enhance her magic. This particular conjuration evaded her, though. Goody had underestimated the complexity of such magic. After

89

several months and countless failed attempts, she began to despair that she would ever be successful.

Then Goody discovered an old spellbook on her doorstep.

She assumed it was one of the other witches who'd left it there, someone who had guessed what she was trying to do. *Perhaps I do have another friend, diary*, she mused. There were components inside the grimoire that did assist Goody with her efforts. In a matter of days, she'd written a new spell.

And on the night she attempted it for the first time, it worked.

She opened a window, of sorts, between our worlds. The water was the most important part. Goody gazed into a porcelain bowl and prayed to see Chastity.

But it wasn't her mother who appeared in the water's reflection.

A face appeared in the depths. A stranger with masculine features and bright, golden hair.

At first, Goody was terrified. She tipped the bowl, effectively ending the spell, and ran out of the greenhouse. She didn't go back for an entire week. But the dreams of her mother worsened. They changed from wistful fantasies of seeing each other to Chastity being lost and alone. In the dreams, she called out Goody's name. She stumbled around in the dark. She wept.

Desperate to make contact, Goody returned to the greenhouse. She performed the spell again. The golden-haired stranger appeared a second time. He introduced himself, and Lucifer made no effort to hide his identity. When Goody found out she was speaking directly to the devil, she was afraid, yes—but she was also intrigued. This time, she didn't run. She asked about Chastity.

She felt the sting of disappointment at learning that Lucifer didn't know her mother or whether she was in his realm. It should've ended there.

And yet . . .

Goody went on to have more conversations with the person in the water. He was unlike anything her father, or the coven, or the church claimed him to be. Lucifer was kind, and intelligent, and funny. She laughed more with him than she'd ever laughed in her life. Even her terrible dreams stopped. They began to meet every night, and they quickly became friends.

Soon enough, Goody had fallen in love. It took her a month to work up the courage to tell him. To the witch's utter disbelief, Lucifer returned her feelings.

Goody's giddiness practically leaped off the page. *When I confessed the truth to him, Lucifer laughed. For an awful moment, I thought he was laughing at me. I was about to flee in humiliation when he reassured me he'd only laughed out of joy. Joy, diary!*

After that, it didn't take long for one of them to broach the subject of meeting. Since it was impossible for Lucifer to come to her world, Goody created a spell that would send her to his. Apparently some of her father's lectures still lived inside her head, though, because she didn't consider staying in Hell—the spell was designed so she could return.

The only problem was that Goody couldn't perform it alone.

Knowing her coven would never agree to help, she found a persuasion spell in the grimoire. My stomach tightened reading those words. I'd been rooting for Goody, somehow, despite her being long dead. But a persuasion spell took people's free will. I kept going, hoping that Goody had changed her mind.

She didn't hesitate.

Once the spell had taken hold of her coven, one by one, Goody arranged to gather on the next full moon. *Two days,* she wrote with nervous anticipation. *In two days, I can begin the search for my mother in earnest, and I will finally be in Lucifer's arms.*

There were no more entries after that.

I turned the final three pages, confirming they were blank. My lips twisted in thought, and I mentally reviewed everything I'd just read. After a few seconds, I flipped back to a drawing Goody had done beside the final spell she planned to do.

"Did you find something?" Lyari asked. It felt like her voice came from a distance.

"No. Nothing of use." Frowning, I skimmed the drawing with my fingertips. A woman—presumably Goody—was stretched out on a table, surrounded by her coven. Visible threads connected them, both to each other and to her.

Eventually, I became aware of how warm I'd gotten. Finn had been keeping the fire going, which was odd, considering he preferred cool spaces. *Taking care of me again*, I thought wearily. Reading for so long had made me sluggish. I lifted my head for the first time in hours, and squinted. Dust-speckled sunbeams floated through the window.

"Is it morning already?" I mumbled, sitting back against the couch. My spine cracked.

"Yes. We've been here all night." Wearing a pinched expression, her eyes narrowed with focus, Lyari briskly added a note to the legal pad in her lap.

Sweat clung to my lower back. I tugged at my shirt, then got to my feet. "Jesus, it's hot in here. I need to get some air."

Finn watched me go silently. Yawning, I stepped over the nest of pillows Gil had made. The constant adjustments and movements seemed to help him combat the bloodlust. It was empty now because the vampire was taking a shower.

When I got downstairs, the cold felt good on my skin. I stepped outside to let winter take some of the hot anxiety that had been coursing through my veins all night.

Light spilled over the treetops and frost glittered on our cars. I'd forgone a coat before going down the stairwell, and the chill sent goosebumps along my exposed arms.

As I closed the door behind me, movement drew my gaze toward the porch. I paused, then started walking in that direction. My shoes crunched on the gravel.

Collith was asleep in one of the rocking chairs. What was he doing out here? I stopped on the stairs, frowning. I turned to see what he might've been looking at, and within seconds, I felt my face clear in understanding. I knew what he'd been doing. From this vantage point, Collith had a perfect view of the driveway, the garage, the loft, and most of the trees that surrounded them.

He was watching over us. Over me.

He'd also been conducting some research of his own, apparently—papers covered his lap and lay scattered at his feet. The writing was Enochian. On one of the pages, I recognized Olorel's bloodline crest. Why would Collith be focused on this?

In that moment, I had a flash of intuition. A day ago, Lucifer had mentioned that shape was a mark of possession.

Collith was looking for a way to free himself from Lucifer.

I felt my mouth soften. After another second, I squatted next to the rocking chair and reached for Collith's hand. Unlatching his fingers one by one, trying to be gentle, I set the stack of paper aside and bent to pick up the mess. I put it in a pile on the side table. As I straightened, I noticed the purplish lines beneath Collith's eyes. I paused, worry churning in my stomach.

Faeries didn't get tired or weak . . . but goblins did.

There was nothing I could do to help him. I still hadn't figured out how to help Lyari, either. Both of them had been severed from their Court because of me, and both were showing signs of deterioration.

One problem at a time, Fortuna, I told myself, feeling the stirrings of panic. There were too many people to save. Too many mistakes to correct. Too many miracles to find. I felt like I was holding onto a dozen kites, desperate not to let them go, but all the strings were slipping slowly from my grasp.

I turned, intending to leave, and a splash of color caught my eye. There was a blanket hanging on the other chair. It was made of a wool that Emma claimed held mystical powers of restoration. I picked it up and unfolded the thick material. For once, as I settled it over Collith's shoulders, I allowed myself to believe in the impossible.

Just this once.

CHAPTER SEVEN

I didn't mean to fall asleep, but I must have.

One moment, I was sitting on the living room floor, surrounded by my pack and stacks of books. The next, I stood in a world of gray skies and writhing grass. Wind beat at me, raking its long nails through the sweater I wore. I squinted against it, doing a swift scan for Oliver. His golden head was usually like a beacon, shining off in the distance. Tonight there was only a darkening horizon, which looked like a newly-formed bruise.

I'd try the cottage first, as always. Hunching my shoulders against the cold, I bent my head and started running down the path. I tried to contain the jittery feeling inside of me, but it threatened to burst from my skin like fragments of a bomb. All I could think about was Damon, and Matthew, and the last time I'd seen them. Remembering how my nephew had put his small head on Damon's shoulder. So much love. So much trust. He'd lose all of that if I didn't save my brother.

I still didn't know how I would get Damon back. My pack had spent several more hours skimming old fae texts, and literature on the devil from every religion, every region. By the time darkness claimed me, neither Savannah nor Mercy had responded to my increasingly desperate texts.

I'd been waiting for them in hopes they'd have some kind of Hail Mary pass. Depending on their magic and knowledge so I could avoid what I'd been avoiding for months. But it was time. Today, I promised myself. Today I would contact all the other resources at my disposal. Viessa. Dracula. Even Gwyn, if it came to that. I'd ask for help. The thought didn't even make me cringe. Not when Damon's life was at stake.

The cottage was still off in the distance when I drew up short at the sight of Oliver.

He was halfway down the path between the cottage and the tree, his body rigid against the ground. Like last time, I knelt beside him and shoved down my self-loathing. I gripped his shoulder and bent over so I could see his face. His eyes were squeezed shut and his hair was damp with sweat.

"Lucifer?" I asked, but I already knew the answer. I just hoped for a different one.

Oliver managed a nod, his cheek scraping over the dirt. He sounded like he was being strangled as he said, "He wants to speak to you again."

I took a deep, soundless breath, grateful he couldn't see my face. My pulse felt uneven and thready. "Let him in," I forced myself to say.

Oliver shook his head instantly, his eyes opening to find me. "Fortuna—"

He cried out in pain again, cutting off whatever he'd been about to say. The second I heard that sound, I felt an inexplicable sense of control. The panic and the desperation couldn't touch me, because I commanded them not to. There were people depending on me to stay strong, to handle whatever came next in a way that would guarantee the survival of all of us. Including Oliver.

I kissed his temple, smoothing his hair back with my hand. "It's all right. Stop fighting him. You've done enough. It's time to rest, okay? Get some of your strength back."

"There are more weapons in the attic. I've been . . . I've been working on them while . . ." Another quake went through him, and he couldn't finish.

My mind worked quickly. Lucifer already knew Oliver was here, of course, but my best friend was weakened and vulnerable. I wouldn't put it past the Dark Prince to torment him, just as he was tormenting Collith, Damon, and all the others that had come before them. Maybe if I hid Oliver from sight, and kept Lucifer's focus on me, I could prevent that.

"Can you buy us any more time?" I asked calmly. "Just long enough to get you into the cottage?"

As an answer, Oliver forced himself upright, his arms shaking. He didn't try to evade me when I put my arm around his waist. He was heavier than I thought he'd be. After a couple minutes of struggling, we got him into the cottage and on the couch. It was a relief to be out of the wind. Oliver propped himself against a throw pillow, grimacing. His skin gleamed and the hand he put on the armrest was clenched into a tight fist. We didn't have much longer.

Breathing hard, I snatched a thick coat off one of the hooks. Once I'd shrugged it on, I glanced back at Oliver long enough to say, "Whatever happens, don't come out, okay?"

He didn't answer, and there was no time to wrangle a promise out of him. I closed the door firmly behind me, sending a silent prayer into the universe. I'd stopped believing God actually gave a shit a long time ago, but for Oliver, I would do anything. Pray, bargain, or grovel, it didn't matter. I refused to lose anyone else that I loved.

The wind came at me with renewed vigor. During the brief time Oliver and I were inside, the sky had succumbed to night and clouds. I started in the direction of the tree, wanting to put space between Lucifer and Oliver. Something drew my gaze to the cliffs, though, and I slowed. My heart launched like a frightened rabbit.

A broad-shouldered figure stood against the horizon.

Lucifer looked like a character from a gothic novel. He wore a long, dark coat with the collar turned up. The wings I'd seen in the mirror were bigger than I'd thought. Their beauty was strange, and jarring. Nym had once described wings as things of light. But there was nothing light about these. The feathers looked like they'd been forged out of metal, the edges sharp and gleaming. They spilled out of Lucifer's back and nearly touched the ground. Lucifer's bright hair—which was eerily similar to Oliver's, now that I thought about it—whipped around his perfect, oval face.

As I approached, he turned back toward the open sky and raised an arm in the air. Within seconds, the clouds shifted and a crescent moon shone through the wisps, allowing a faint light to spill over everything. The relentless wind slowed, then stopped altogether.

The devil had control over my dreams.

I filed the realization away as yet another reason I was outmatched by this terrifying being. From Lucifer's posture and the way he moved, the display of power seemed casual, more thoughtless than anything. But the devil didn't do anything without a reason. He wanted me to know he had power here, probably so I wouldn't try to remove his head again. I didn't have my sword, anyway.

I drew up alongside him and stopped, working to keep the fear out of my expression.

"Good evening, Lady Sworn," Lucifer said.

His voice. I'd never heard the full power of it before; he'd always been hiding behind a host. There was a husky quality to it that felt like a fingertip trailing down my spine, yet there was iron in it, too. This was a voice that had seduced thousands and commanded legions. I wanted to stand there and listen to it all night, and I also wanted to *run*. Run until my lungs were burning and I was on the verge of collapse, and there was so much distance between me and this immortal monster that I'd never hear him again.

My own voice was hard as I replied, "I still have two more days."

Lucifer inclined his head in acknowledgment. "You do. But I've come because you're in the midst of making a decision, and when one is making a decision, they should have all the facts."

As he spoke, the defined curve of his jaw moved. Every detail, every feature was like a living painting. I fixed my gaze firmly on the sea. "I have plenty of facts. Fact: I'd be an idiot to make any kind of deal with you."

In my peripheral vision, I saw Lucifer face me.

"Fact," he said. "There is beauty in my world. Hell is not what your stories make it out to be. Let me show it to you."

He made another gesture toward the horizon. The dreamscape seemed to ripple, and a dark mass formed in front of us. I almost stepped back, unnerved, but Lucifer moved his hand again in silent command. The sky obeyed. That dark mass parted, like rolling mist or clearing smoke.

I waited tensely, but nothing came out. No shapes formed. I frowned, unsure what I was supposed to be seeing . . . and then the lights appeared. A breath caught in my throat.

Hundreds, thousands of lights spread across the horizon. Faint lines solidified into buildings. No, towers. There were dark, spindly things in between them, like weeds reaching up from a dark sea. I couldn't quite make out what they were. The bright spots came from windows, the tops of the towers, and far below these, where I imagined there were roads and the noises of living things, like the cities from my world.

But it wasn't one of the cities of my world, that much was obvious. Enormous, winged things soared over the towers, and there was nothing earthly about them. Lightning flashed, or at least I thought it was lightning, and the bursts of light made the red sky look like an inferno.

It *was* beautiful, in a frightening, wild way, although I would rather die than admit that to Lucifer.

Was this really Hell? Or was it just another lie? Maybe the devil was making his world less horrifying so I would agree to his deal.

I knew he was waiting for my reaction, so I didn't give him one. "Funny, I thought there were supposed to be flames," I remarked.

"Some parts are still like that," Lucifer said. His voice sounded closer. "But there are other parts that don't make it into the stories. Some parts that deserve a chance to be seen."

I turned, unthinking, and a shock went through me when I saw the devil was right there. I was also standing closer to the edge than I realized, and my heel sent a rock skittering into the abyss. I stumbled. Lucifer's hands flew out to catch me, but I regained my balance.

He lowered his arms, standing so close now that I could see the blue in his eyes. His palms hovered over the backs of my hands, as if he was still thinking about taking hold. I was frozen, my entire being at war with itself. Torn between the instinct to run and the terrifying urge to stay.

As if he knew I was a flight risk, Lucifer didn't touch me—his fingers stayed just above my skin. He moved a hand up the length of my arm and over my shoulder, like he was memorizing every curve and plane. My hairs stood on end, goosebumps appearing, like my body was rising up to meet him. Then, when Lucifer's palm went downward, his thumb brushed my hardened nipple.

The warmth between my legs throbbed. I jumped and pulled away.

"Fact," I rasped. "You're a Nightmare-killer. You've murdered God knows how many of my kind."

Lucifer drew close again. "I didn't enjoy those deaths. And they did serve a purpose."

I barely heard him. I couldn't think. It felt like every nerve ending in my body was singing. I looked at Lucifer, my neck arched back, fighting the urges inside me. I reminded myself it was a lie, this reaction to him. Our mouths were a breath apart and I could feel the barest touch of his lips as he spoke.

"I want to know what you feel like," he said.

There was the distant sound of someone's zipper coming down. Mine, I realized faintly. Then Lucifer's fingers slid over my skin, down into my secret places. Why wasn't I stopping him? His fingers sifted through the thatch of hair between my thighs and gently eased them apart. A long finger slid inside me. I was so wet that he was met with no resistance, and I made a small sound, something partway between a gasp and a sigh. My hands were on his broad chest, but I didn't remember putting them there.

Lucifer put his mouth next to my ear. "Fact. You want me, Fortuna Sworn," he whispered.

I shoved him away, breathing hard from the wild cadence of my heart and the desire roaring through my veins. None of it showed in my voice as I spat, "I would rather light myself on fire. That would be less painful."

He just looked at me for a long moment, his eyes gleaming. "I can see why lovers flock around you. It's refreshing, your spirit. Incredible that it hasn't broken after everything you've endured."

"Stay out of my dreams," I snarled, zipping my jeans. My face was burning.

Once again, Lucifer seemed completely unaffected by rejection. He gave me a swift, fluid bow and said, "Two days, Lady Sworn. I will come for your final answer then."

Here's your answer. Go fuck yourself. I kept the volatile response inside, painfully aware that Lucifer held my brother's life in his hands.

With the faintest of smirks, as if he'd heard anyway, Lucifer stepped off the edge of the cliff and dropped out of sight.

A startled sound escaped me. I rushed over and peered down, half-hoping to see his body dashed against the rocks. But there was no sign of him, of course. The black water churned, reaching up the cliffside like frothy fingertips.

I moved back, letting out a pent-up breath. Had that really just happened? Had I really allowed the devil to touch me like that?

Remembering what he'd done to the sky, I tipped my chin up and sought that faint, thin moon. Even though Lucifer was gone, the crescent remained. It was confirmation that none of this was a dream, no matter how much I wished it were. Ironic—once, I would've given anything for this place to be tied to reality.

Thinking of Oliver, I glanced back at the cottage. The windows were softly lit, and I wondered how much he'd seen. At least Lucifer hadn't mentioned him, or used yet another person I loved against me in his efforts at persuasion. I knew Oliver would be waiting impatiently, anxiously. *I should go,* I thought. *I should tell him I'm all right.*

Just . . . not yet. I could still feel the imprint of Lucifer's hand on my body, and part of me worried Oliver would sense the fire. Sense the way the devil's touch haunted my thoughts.

I lingered there for another minute, gazing out at the star-speckled water. But I didn't see the sea anymore. Instead, I saw a city.

An eerie, beautiful city with a red sky and dark spires.

I didn't go back to sleep.

Instead, I got into my shitty car—the van was long gone, abandoned several states over—and drove to town. I'd left a note on the counter for anyone who might notice my absence and worry. There was no sign of Finn, and I hoped that meant he was just out on a hunt. *Going into town for a few hours. Love you.*

Fifteen minutes later, after brief reunions with Cyrus, Ariel, and Gretchen, I settled in a booth at Bea's. I'd brought a heavy, bulging backpack of research with me. Three of the books were journals that belonged to an ancient faerie named Lustina, mate to Shadi. I'd never met her, but the bloodline felt indebted to me because of what I'd done for Daratrine. There was no mention of Lucifer, specifically, but they were fascinating accounts of events that had occurred just after the Fall. Apparently an entire bloodline had gone missing, and the rest of the fae still didn't know what had happened to them. Why Lyari thought this was relevant to my search, I didn't know. Maybe because I had no idea what I was looking for, either.

As I reached for the next volume, I took a sip of coffee and grimaced. Not sweet enough. I added more sugar and stirred. The sky beyond the window slowly brightened. Now and then, dishes clinked in the dining room behind me.

Despite the noise, it was a slow morning. None of my old regulars had made an appearance yet. Good thing, since I didn't know what I'd say to them when the inevitable questions arose. *Where have you been? Why hasn't anyone heard from you? Are you coming back to work?*

The truth was, I wasn't sure whether I was still employed here. Bea hadn't come in yet, and though Gretchen had been happy to see me, I'd gotten the distinct impression I shouldn't expect the same reaction from her partner.

A figure stopped next to the booth. Without looking up from my coffee I said, "There can't be a crisis today, my schedule is already full."

"The only crisis here is that you came out of hiding and I haven't received so much as a text."

At the sound of the Unseelie Queen's voice, my head jerked up. When I confirmed that she was really standing there, I slid out of the booth to hug her.

"You're underground, V. Texts don't exactly reach you," I said as we pulled apart. Thankfully, she was wearing long sleeves and a thick coat, so our skin didn't make any contact.

Noticing the mess I'd made, I turned to clear all the clutter away. I could feel Viessa's eyes on me, shrewd as ever, but my demeanor stayed casual. Even as I made sure to cover anything that could hint at what I was researching.

"Are you hungry?" I asked over my shoulder. "Our cook's breakfast sandwich is legendary."

"God, no, that sounds awful. Humans eat like vermin." Viessa sat in the seat opposite mine, and I couldn't help but stare. I'd seen the faerie glamoured before, but that was in a dim club. Viessa had never looked so . . . normal. Her frostburn was gone, replaced with pink, healthy skin. Her lashes were coppery instead of frozen, her eyes a darker blue. Her rosebud lips shone with lip gloss.

"But I will take a Bloody Mary," Viessa added, setting her purse and coat neatly beside her.

I nodded and looked toward the bar, but Gretchen was occupied with a group of deputies that had just come in.

"Aerilaya, darling, it's wonderful to see you. I thought you'd died." Viessa lifted her head and flashed a brilliant smile. "What on earth are you doing in this revolting place?"

Ariel didn't look uneasy, exactly, but she stood too still. It was a dead giveaway for someone who practically skipped her way through life. "King Collith originally assigned me here," she said, her tone polite. "When he relieved me of my post, I found myself . . . unhappy at the prospect of leaving. And then I heard you'd given the Guardians a chance to honorably hang up our swords."

My ears perked. This was the first I'd heard of Viessa making such an offer to Collith's old guards. If she was feeling so generous and forgiving, why shouldn't that extend to Lyari? While the two faeries continued their conversation and Viessa ordered her Bloody Mary, I unlocked my phone to send a text to my Right Hand about it.

By the time I looked up again, Ariel was gone. I'd missed the end of their exchange, but I didn't miss the way she lingered at the order window. The discomfort she'd shown Viessa had been replaced with a soft expression. When I saw the blatant adoration in her eyes, I felt my jaw go slack. There was only one person in Bea's kitchen. One person she could possibly be looking at like that.

Why, Cyrus Lavender, you sneaky bastard. No wonder Ariel was so reluctant to leave. I had to give her credit, as well—she'd finally seen him. Too often, we overlooked other kinds of beauty because we were so distracted by what was in front of us.

"Damn," I said softly. "I'd forgotten that life can still have good surprises."

"I'll drink to that," Viessa said, bringing my attention back to her.

I smiled. "You'll drink to anything."

"I'll drink to that, too." She winked and then, as if they'd timed it, Ariel returned and set a glass down in front of her.

I wasn't in the mood, so I just clinked my water against Viessa's cocktail. While she drank, the new queen told me about the latest events at the Unseelie Court, and I spun half-truths about where I'd been these past few months. Faeries were good at picking up lies, so the best way around that was to use the truth. Everything I said was technically accurate. *I've made a lot of enemies. I didn't feel like my family was safe. I came back because my brother got sick.*

There were three empty, juice-stained glasses on the table when Viessa's demeanor changed.

"Something is happening in our world," she said abruptly, staring down into her drink. "I can feel it. A sort of . . . rumbling."

So *that* was why she'd come. I leaned back in the booth, considering Viessa's remark. I could sense her fear coiling between us. It had such a lovely flavor, like roses covered in a layer of fresh frost.

Focus, Fortuna.

She had to be talking about Lucifer. He was shifting players on the board. Making moves I couldn't see. For a moment, I thought about telling Viessa the truth. Warning her about Lucifer's presence here. But then I looked into her cold, pale eyes and remembered who she was. The Unseelie Queen. Fae.

Like Dracula, if she thought killing me would stop the devil from getting a foothold in this world, she'd do it. She wouldn't even hesitate. She might not enjoy it, because our strange friendship meant something to her, too, but she wouldn't hesitate. Of that I was certain. I turned my water slowly, watching sunlight bounce off the glass.

"Will you get a message to Nym for me?" I asked, raising my gaze to Viessa's.

She understood what I was really asking—I saw the glint in her eye, the knowing. Nothing in our world came free. The two of us might be friendly, maybe even friends, but she was still their queen and I would always put my family first.

"What do I get in return?" the faerie countered, playing the game effortlessly. There was a reason she'd been able to scheme her way to a throne.

"Information."

Viessa didn't pretend to consider it. "Very well. What is your message?"

I didn't need to think about it, either. My voice softened, and I imagined his sad eyes as I said, "Tell Nym his room is still here, if he ever wants it."

"I shall tell him. And what is this information you have to share?" Viessa asked, eyebrows raised.

I paused, thinking about the best way to word it. I had no idea if Viessa would accept it as my half of the trade, but it was the best I could do. My answer was halting. Hesitant. "When you leave this bar, pull your people in. All of them. And if there's a way to lock the Doors, do it. Because tomorrow night, something is going down. It could play out in a lot of different ways, but if the worst-case scenario happens . . . if the worst-case scenario happens, you don't want to be anywhere near here, Viessa."

She was quiet for a while, and in the silence, I could hear her unspoken question. *How do I know you haven't made this up just so I'll pass your little message along?*

I let my steady gaze be my answer. *You don't.*

Viessa searched my face, and for the length of a heartbeat, she let her glamour drop. The Ice Queen looked back at me, eyes empty as a frozen tundra, death on her lips and clinging to her fingertips. It was a warning. A promise, should she ever find out that I had deceived her.

At last she said, "My people won't make this easy. What am I to tell them if morning arrives and the sky hasn't fallen?"

"I'll get a message to you. If you don't hear anything, then you'll know . . . I failed."

Her finger tapped against the table. With each tap, the nail changed color. Pink, glamour. Black, frostbite. Pink. Black.

"Well, I suppose I should be going, then," Viessa murmured, getting to her feet. "This day just went from delightfully bloody to incredibly stressful. Thank you for that."

"Tomorrow," I said, giving her a small, tense nod. "I'll talk to you then."

"I'd say it's been fun, but you always manage to ruin my buzz, Fortuna Sworn," Viessa said as the door behind her opened. She pulled her coat on and stepped around Bea, who was only just arriving for the day. It wasn't like my boss to be so late, and a dart of worry pierced me. Was everything all right? Viessa walked out of sight, and Bea turned in my direction. I waved and gave her a small, uncertain smile.

She looked right at me.

Then she looked away.

It felt like someone had closed their fist around my heart. I'd been here too long, I thought suddenly. Everyone at home was probably wondering where I was. I'd also spotted Bella O'Connell, Ian's widow, and she was glaring at me as if she knew the part I'd played in her husband's death. Clearing my throat, I turned away and briskly finished putting the journals back into my bag.

Just as I started to get out of the booth, a champagne flute appeared in front of me. Orange juice gleamed inside the glass.

"Oh. Thanks, Gretchen." I looked up and gave my friend a polite smile. I didn't have the heart to tell her that a drink was the last thing I wanted right now.

She smiled back. "Everything is going to be all right. You looked like you needed the reminder."

"You're too good for this world, Gretch."

She dismissed this with a wave of her hand and went back to the other side of the bar. I sat there for a moment, trying to think of a way to get rid of the mimosa without drinking it. There wasn't anywhere to dump it, and I knew she'd see the glass at some point. Swallowing a sigh, I raised the flute to my mouth.

Someone rushed into the seat Viessa had just vacated and hissed, "Don't drink that."

"*You* again," I said, lowering my glass. It was Seth of the bloodline Arthion. His horns were gone, because he was wearing a weak glamour, but everything else was the same. The curly hair, a slightly over-pronounced jaw, and kind blue eyes. "What the hell are you doing here? And why can't I drink this?"

"I saw the bartender put something in it," he said, his tone insistent.

There was only one person behind the counter, but he couldn't mean Gretchen. I craned my neck, trying to see if there was someone walking away. But Angela and Ariel were on the other side of the room, and Cyrus never left the kitchen during his shift. "Who?"

A commotion made us both jerk toward the bar. Gretchen had dropped an entire tray of glasses, and I watched one of them roll over the tiles. I realized she must've been on her knees picking them up, because there was no sign of her. I waited a beat, expecting to see Gretchen stand up on the other side of the bar. When she didn't reappear, I frowned and got up, inexplicably uneasy. Someone else had noticed she was down, too. I could hear a voice call out for a doctor.

The morning rush had slowed, and I was the first one to get behind the counter. To my horror, Gretchen was on the floor, her frail body shaking. Black smoke emerged from her mouth. The instant I saw that, I knew—magic. Dark magic. Horror burned through my veins.

No one could witness her like this, and human medicine wouldn't help her.

Reacting quickly, I rolled Gretchen over, so her face was turned away from the bar. I could sense Seth hovering nearby. "Help me get her into Bea's office," I said with quiet urgency.

He nodded. People noticed us, of course, as we hurried past. A man raised his cell phone to his ear.

"No need for an ambulance," I said with forced calm. "She's just got low blood sugar. We're going to take her back to the office for a minute. Ariel, can you hold down the fort?"

The faerie had appeared where the end of the bar connected with the hallway, partially blocking us from view. I tried to communicate the need for discretion with my eyes. Ariel gave me a subtle nod and spun toward the gathering crowd. I was so grateful I could've kissed her.

"Nothing to see here," she announced. "Who needs more coffee? Regina, I know *you* want some."

Seth and I got Gretchen into the office. We set her carefully on the floor, and as I straightened, I took my own cell phone out.

"What the *fuck* is going on here?" Bea's voice said from the doorway. "Why did you tell someone not to call 9-1-1?"

I heard the hum of Seth's voice respond. I had no clue how he was going to explain this, but that wasn't my problem right now. I found the contact I needed and pressed down on the number with my thumb. A name filled the screen. SAVANNAH SIMONSON. As I lifted the phone, I noticed the open door and hurried over to close it. Seth and Bea were kneeling on either side of Gretchen, still going back and forth. Gretchen looked unchanged, her chest rising and falling weakly, but I didn't know how long that would last. I turned away and fixed my eyes on the wall of lockers, fighting the urge to bounce my leg.

I could count on one hand the number of times I'd prayed in my life. Today made one more. As I stood there and held my phone to my ear, I prayed to the God that had banished us and asked Him to provide a miracle. *Answer the phone, Savannah. Answer the damn phone.*

The line crackled. "Fortuna? Is everything okay?"

My relief was so overwhelming that I almost sobbed. Tamping the urge down, I held the phone tighter and explained what was happening, my words clipped and urgent.

"Repeat after me," Savannah said the moment I stopped speaking. I told her I would, and she fed me an Enochian chant. I faced Gretchen again and echoed the words the necromancer had said perfectly, syllable for syllable. After a couple minutes of this, Savannah switched back to English to ask, "Did anything happen?"

I could feel Seth and Bea's eyes on me, but I kept mine glued on Gretchen. Her white, still face didn't move or change. I waited another second or two before I said, "No. Is she possessed, Savannah?"

"Not if the incantation didn't affect her. If you saw her put something in your drink, a control spell would be my guess. Good news is, they're pretty easy to break. Bad news is, the spell can be fatal for humans near the end. As the magic starts to wear off, they break down. It's a reaction to the trauma."

The questions shot out of me like bullets. "What can we do? How long does she have? And can you get here in time?"

Her voice was soft, yet firm. "I can't do anything, but you can. You command magic, Fortuna. I've seen it."

A hundred arguments rose to my lips . . . but then I swallowed them. Forced them back down. If I didn't act, my friend would die. It was either try this crazy, desperate idea, or watch Gretchen slip away.

Bea would never forgive me.

"Okay," I said, breathing hard. I nodded even though Savannah couldn't see me, holding the phone so tight I worried it would break. "Okay. Tell me what to do."

"She would've had to ingest something for a spell this powerful. We're going to make one of the ingredients harmless, which will unbalance the entire thing and hopefully free Gretchen." Savannah rattled off a list of ingredients.

"Stay on the line," I said once she was finished. "I don't want to risk losing the signal."

"I'm not going anywhere."

To have full use of my hands, I put my phone on speaker mode while I found a piece of scrap paper on the desk, plucked a pen out of a sawed-off beer can, and wrote down the ingredients. "I need you to trust me," I told Bea. "I know how insane this looks, believe me. But if you want Gretchen to live, you'll do exactly as I say."

Most of the things on the list could be found right down the street, at the florist. The owner was a practicing Wiccan, and she had a small corner of the shop dedicated to white magic. Bea took the paper, her eyes going to what I'd written down then back to my face. As if she was debating whether or not I was insane.

She left without a word.

The next ten minutes were hell. As I waited for Bea and Seth to come back, I prepared Gretchen for the spell. I maneuvered her to the center of the floor and cleared everything away. The plastic chairs, the faded rug, the small garbage bin. All the while, Savannah was speaking in my ear, running me through the spell we were about to do.

I was wiping some worrying black fluid off Gretchen's chin when Bea returned, a plastic bag dangling from her hand.

I didn't waste any time getting started. We put some of the ingredients in a chipped bowl—the items Bea and Seth didn't find at the florist, they'd apparently found elsewhere—and I began the invocation. I didn't stop, not once, because faltering meant giving the doubt a chance to creep in. I placed the remaining herbs in the right places. I set the wicks alight. I did the spell *perfectly*.

And it worked.

More smoke seeped out of Gretchen's mouth. It reminded me of the night we'd extracted a demon from Finn, only not as violent. I glanced over at Bea, worried about how she was handling all this. My boss's eyes were huge, her mouth partly open. Savannah had gone silent. I checked my phone screen to make sure the call hadn't dropped. Reassured, I put it back to my ear and stared impatiently at Gretchen.

"She isn't waking up," I said. Bea shifted, and her knee cracked.

The necromancer stayed calm, just as she had throughout this entire thing. "That's normal. Her body just went through a shock. You can take her to the hospital, if you want, but she'll probably be conscious by the time you get there."

"My battery is about to die," I said, hearing the warning trill. "Savannah, I—"

"You're welcome, Fortuna." Savannah's voice had gone soft again. I knew things had changed between us today. I wasn't sure how that would affect Damon and Matthew, or if it even would.

But the prospect didn't frighten me like it used to.

We finally disconnected the call. Knowing that Bea was anxiously waiting for an update, I took my sweater off and tucked the thick wool beneath Gretchen's head. I'd been too frazzled to think of doing it earlier. The sight of her lying so still filled me with hot, heavy guilt.

"My . . . contact said to wait. She should come back to us soon," I told her worried partner.

Seth, who I'd pretty much forgotten about, got to his feet. He'd been kneeling behind us, probably ready to offer assistance the second we needed it. "I can hear people wondering if they should come in. They're worried about Gretchen. I'll go let them know she's all right," he said.

The goblin slipped out as quietly as he always seemed to arrive. Once he was gone, I leaned back and rested my spine against the desk. Bea stayed at Gretchen's side. I could see her fighting an inner battle again, debating if she should trust me. Her fingers curled around Gretchen's shoulders, and the short distance between us quivered with tension. *Don't ask me. Please don't ask me*, I thought.

"What the fuck just happened here, Fortuna?" Bea asked.

Her fear floated in the air, and when I sensed how powerful it was, it gave me the push I needed to overcome my own. No more avoiding. No more stalling. Bea deserved the truth, and it was time. I tipped my head back, resting that against the desk, too.

"The first thing you should know is that I'm not human," I started.

"Bea? What happened?"

We both jumped at the sound of Gretchen's voice. Bea made a strangled noise and bent over, hugging her partner fiercely. Nearly a full minute ticked by. When Bea straightened and met my gaze, her own was filled with wonder.

"I believe you," she said. She waited for me to keep going. Bea must've seen hesitation in my expression, because she gave me an encouraging nod. "It's okay, Fortuna. You can tell me."

I swallowed. *No going back now.* I glanced at Gretchen, who was still conscious, thank God. She was listening as closely as Bea when I continued. "The second thing you should know is that it's real. All of it. Those fucked-up fairy tales you grew up hearing? Most of them are based in truth. All the things that go bump in the night."

Bea absorbed this with raised brows. The expression made me wonder if she was in shock, a little. My boss leaned back on her haunches, and her grip on Gretchen loosened.

"*Fuck,*" she said, exhaling.

I nodded in weary agreement. "Yeah."

Bea looked down at her beloved. "Are you all right? Can you sit up on your own?"

Gretchen patted her hand in silent reassurance. Releasing another breath, Bea got up. She sat down behind her desk and opened a drawer. She reached inside, and a bottle appeared. Once she'd set it down, Bea twisted the cap off. She flipped her long, gray braid over her shoulder and angled her body toward me, making the chair squeak. She took a long swig of the whiskey, her throat moving with each swallow, and then the bottle landed on the desk with another hollow thud.

"Okay," she said. "Tell us everything."

CHAPTER EIGHT

An hour later, I pushed the door with the palm of my hand and stepped outside.

Sunlight beat down on my head. I felt drained. Empty. As I crossed the street, I checked my phone, and I was faintly surprised to see it wasn't yet noon. It felt like I'd spent so much more time in that small room with Gretchen and Bea.

During that time, I'd answered every single one of their questions—even the ones about Lucifer. But I wasn't sure where we stood now they knew the truth. Bea had wanted to take Gretchen to the clinic, despite Savannah's remarks, and they'd turned down my offer to go with them. They didn't say much to me while I was leaving. I was trying not to read too much into that, considering Gretchen had just been hexed and the foundation of their entire world was crumbling. Humans tended not to take it very well, finding out monsters were real and they were at the bottom of the food chain.

No wonder Bea and Gretchen couldn't get rid of me fast enough. I sighed and wondered if the relationship between us would ever be the same. *It won't matter, if you don't come up with a miracle by tomorrow,* logic pointed out. Panic fluttered at the edges of my heart.

I needed to get back to the loft and continue our search for that miracle.

My car was parked down the street, so I started toward it, pointing the key fob. The headlights flashed. I spotted a reflection in the window and paused, one hand on the handle. I'd know those horns anywhere.

"You're following me again," I said, turning.

Seth Arthion stood there. He was a young goblin, I thought to myself. There was just something distinctly youthful about his curly hair, lean face, and eyes the color of a wide, clear sky.

"I never stopped, really," Seth told me, shrugging in a way that seemed sheepish and defiant at the same time. The last time we'd spoken—not today, but months ago, before my family fled town—he'd asked to swear the Blood Vow to me and I'd turned him down.

"Why?" I asked bluntly. "What exactly are you hoping for?"

"What I said before. I want to be part of your Court." Seth lifted his chin.

An automatic refusal rose to my lips, but something stopped me. Maybe I was just tired of leaving things on a bad note. As I thought about what to say, realization hit me—Vulen. The telepath had mentioned Seth just before he died. In all the chaos of Lucifer's arrival and leaving Granby, I'd completely forgotten about it until now.

I fought to control my expression as the memory came back. It had been the night of the opera. I had arrived arm in arm with Laurie and Collith, thinking our evening would conclude with Belanor's death. We'd stood in that night-shrouded office and tortured his pet telepath. There had been so much blood, I remembered faintly. Rivers of it had been pouring out of the faerie's eyes when he spoke his last words. *Help him.*

I hadn't helped anyone lately, much less Seth. Guilt stabbed at me. I gritted my teeth and reminded myself I hadn't made Vulen any promises. I'd already broken one deathbed oath, and that was enough. I still heard Naevys's voice in my head sometimes, asking me to have faith in her son.

That was right before I'd found out he was a traitorous asshole and staged a coup in front of his entire Court.

Definitely broke that one, I thought with a wince.

Seth had been quiet while I contemplated. Desperate to forget about Vulen and Naevys, I refocused on him and saw the hope he couldn't quite hide in his eyes. Seth must be thinking my silence meant that I was considering his request, I realized. A heavy feeling settled in my chest.

Over the goblin's slender shoulder, I noticed a bench nearby. I pocketed my keys and said, "Do you want to sit?"

He nodded. We walked over to it, and I brushed some of the snow off. Seth sat on one end, and I settled in the middle, folding my arms against myself for warmth. The bench faced the antique shop. There was an old man on the other side of the display window, carefully arranging some books on a shelf.

I watched his progress as I said, "Vulen mentioned you before he died."

Seth's head turned in my peripheral vision. "You were there? I'd heard that he . . . passed on, but the goblin who told me didn't know anything else. What did Vulen say?"

After a moment, I tore my gaze from the old man in the window and searched Seth's expression. I wasn't sure what I was looking for. I just knew that Vulen had been loyal to Belanor, and part of me distrusted anyone even vaguely connected to either of them. "He just asked me to help you," I said eventually.

"That doesn't surprise me. Vulen was always kind. We stayed in touch for a while, after I left Court, but once my banishment started to take its toll . . ." Seth faltered again, then gestured to the horns. "I was angry. Maybe a little ashamed, too. I stopped talking to him."

The Seelie Court likes pretty things, Laurie had said to me once. It was unsurprising that those ancient, elitist assholes had pushed out one of their own and made Seth feel like there was something wrong with him. For a moment, I regretted that I hadn't burned that entire palace to the ground.

Out loud I said, my voice devoid of emotion, "How were you and Vulen connected?"

Seth squinted out at the street, and answered without looking at me. "He was my betrothed, in another lifetime. We grew up together, and our bloodlines have a long history of mutually beneficial unions. Vulen knew my secret, of course. The truth about how I felt in my body, and the changes I wanted to make. It would've been impossible to keep it from him, what with his mind-reading, but Vulen was happy to marry me and let me live how I wanted. In the end, I just couldn't do it. How did . . . how did he die?"

"I killed him."

I waited for Seth to ask why, or press for more details. After a few seconds, I realized he wasn't going to. There were a lot of potential reasons he had no interest in knowing, but if I had to choose one, I'd guess he wanted my acceptance so badly that the details of how I'd murdered his ex-fiancé were irrelevant. They wouldn't change anything for him.

The thought reminded me why we were sitting there. So I forced myself to say it, because I couldn't stay on this bench much longer and because he needed to hear it. "There is no Court here, Seth. You need to move on," I told him gently.

His lips twisted, and a stubborn light shone in his eyes. "Are you sure about that?" Seth said.

"It's nothing personal. I just have nothing to offer you. I'm barely keeping my head above water. Speaking of, I should go."

"Okay. Oh, wait. I wrote this down earlier." Seth reached into his pocket. He pulled out a piece of paper, neatly folded, and offered it to me. "It's my number. Just in case. I may be a goblin, but I can be useful. I'm good with computers, really good, which I know is strange for our kind. Guess I've always been strange. I can be useful," Seth repeated. "That's all I'm trying to say."

"I don't doubt it." His earnestness made my heart twinge. I raised my eyebrows. "And I happen to like the strange ones. Normality is overrated, if it even exists."

"But you still don't want me." Seth didn't say it like a question.

I sighed and made a helpless gesture. "It's not that I don't want you. Even if I were part of a Court—which I'm not—now is *really* not the time to be associated with me."

"Why?" he insisted.

Definitely a young goblin, I thought with a touch of exasperation. For a moment, I considered telling him about Lucifer. But even if I had time to fill Seth in on everything, he might do something stupid to prove himself worthy of my "Court."

"You wouldn't believe it if I told you," I said, sounding as tired as I felt. I tensed to get up.

"Try me."

"I would, but I need to get back. Clock is ticking."

I was about to stand again when my gaze went up to Seth's horns. I paused and allowed myself to really look at them. I felt the goblin's eyes on me, his fear filling the silence. It tasted like dandelions.

The horns were almost . . . delicate. The base of each one, nestled in his curls, was textured and strong. But as they rose and curved, the points became thin and deadly. Smooth, like polished bone. I'd never seen a goblin with horns, and I probably never would again. Not all of them developed what my mother used to call "touches," but for those that did, it manifested in different ways. The touch could be an extra finger, or pointed teeth, or black eyes.

The taste of dandelions was stronger now. I lowered my gaze back to Seth's, and I smiled. "I think your horns are beautiful," I said.

Seth stared at me. I lingered, hoping he'd see how much I meant it. After a few seconds, I gave him a small wave and finally left the bench, digging my keys back out. The car door opened with a whine. I put my bag in the passenger seat and started to get in.

"The mark on your back," Seth called. "I saw it once, and I forgot to ask about it when we finally met."

I paused and looked over my shoulder. "Ask what?"

He stood next to the bench, hands shoved in his pockets. "I just wondered why you'd choose the Leviathan Cross."

"I didn't. What do you know about it?" I asked, frowning now. Seth took a few steps closer and stopped on the curb.

"Not much," he admitted. "Just that it's the alchemical symbol for brimstone. But I can do more research on it. Like I said, I'm good with computers. I can access databases normal people can't."

I opened my mouth to ask what kind of databases. Then I decided that I didn't want to know too many details. Desperate times, and all that. "I'd love to know more, yes," I said. "Thank you. I'll send a text, so you have my number, too. If you find out anything interesting, will you let me know right away?"

As Seth nodded eagerly, I hid my worry that I'd gotten his hopes up. I'd been telling the truth earlier, and my answer wasn't going to change. There was no Court for him to be part of. I wasn't a queen. That part of my story was over and I had no desire to turn back the page.

I got in the car and drove home.

I must've gotten lost in thought, because when I killed the engine and stepped out, I was startled to see it had started to snow at some point. There were no footprints leading up to the door, which meant either everyone was here, or no one was. Anxious to start reading again, I shouldered my bag and hurried inside. The barn door slammed shut on the bitter wind, closing me in with dimness and silence. Light poured from the stairwell like a beckoning hand, and I ran up the steps.

Emma was baking.

"Welcome back," she said as soon as I walked in.

"Hey, Ems." I set my bag down and did a swift assessment of the kitchen. Mixing bowls, cookie sheets, and dough-crusted utensils covered the counters. Emma hadn't turned on any music—probably so she could hear the baby monitor on the counter, or any sounds from beyond the open door of Damon's room—but that didn't seem to lessen her determined cheer. There was a streak of flour on her cheek and she was humming something at the stove, stirring a pot of what smelled like melted butter.

I knew it was a show for Matthew, who sat in his high chair and pounded his little palm against a colorful lump of playdough. His life was in constant upheaval thanks to me. I swallowed down a rush of guilt and went over to him, pressing my lips against the top of his head. That innocent, warm smell greeted me, and I didn't want to pull away.

"Any change in Damon?" I asked, straightening.

Before Emma could answer, someone else entered the kitchen. I frowned at Collith as he joined her at the counter. "What are you doing here?"

"Emma didn't give me much choice," he said, taking a baking pan from her. With a gentle grip, Collith steered her to one of the kitchen chairs. Emma rolled her eyes at him but sat down without protest, her cheeks slightly pink. Traitor.

As I moved closer to the counter, I finally noticed the books on the island. "What are those?"

"Laurie brought some things, and I did, as well," Collith said.

Laurie had been here? I did a swift scan of the room, but it was empty, save for us four. With effort, I made myself refocus. I picked up one of the books and opened it to the middle. It made a cracking sound. "What are they?"

Collith reached for his coat, which was hanging on one of the wall hooks. "I know a kitsune in Kyoto. His species has vast knowledge of weaponry, particularly which ones can hurt Fallenkind. They even designed some of them, and created magic to make each design powerful in its own way. My friend has kept a record of everything. I thought it might be useful."

My eyebrows rose. "Actually, yeah, it could be. Thank you for this. Really."

Hearing the sincerity in my voice, Collith smiled. It was the first genuine one I'd seen since he'd found me in Wyoming, and for an instant, I felt warm. "You're welcome," he said.

We faced each other, and chemistry crackled between us. I cleared my throat and waved the leather-bound volume awkwardly. "Guess I should get started."

"Guess you should." Collith's smile was bigger now. I thought about hitting him with the book.

Remembering that we weren't alone, I glanced over my shoulder, hopeful Emma wasn't paying attention. I caught her watching us with a gleam in her eye. So *that's* why she'd dragged Collith over here, I thought, giving her a look. Emma pretended to be baffled, responding with a puzzled frown before she became oh-so-busy with the cookies. I turned back to Collith, hoping he hadn't picked up on our exchange.

"Thanks again for the books. I'll—" I stopped, hesitating. I'd been about to say, *I'll let you know if I find anything*. But that wasn't true, was it? Collith couldn't be part of our planning. He was only allowed at Cyrus's because we weren't bothering to hide our search for a way to beat Lucifer. He'd be expecting it anyway, and Lucifer was always two steps ahead. My mood darkened at the thought. Ancient, evil asshole. It made my life so much easier when my enemies were idiots.

Collith shifted in front of me. Realizing I still hadn't finished my sentence, I cleared my throat and said, "I'll bring them back over when I'm done."

He nodded. His gaze moved to Emma, and he gave her a warm smile, thanking her for the cookies. I closed the door behind him and immediately looked at her, ready to admonish her for interfering.

She faced me, a spatula in hand, and spoke before I could. "I don't know where the two of you stand, and I'm aware that it's none of my business. If you tell me to drop it, I will. But that young man loves you, Fortuna. It's clear as day. If the issue is something you can talk about, or work on, it's worth the discomfort."

She was so earnest that my annoyance faded. I picked up the book Collith had brought and held it against my chest, then used my other hand to steal a cookie off the cooling rack. "He's not a young man, Ems," I sighed. "And he may love me, but it's so much more complicated than that."

Emma was quiet for a moment. I couldn't see her face, but I knew she was trying to decide whether or not to continue. Her voice was gentle as she said, "There's nothing complicated about forgiveness, sweetheart."

"Forgiveness isn't . . ." Mid-sentence, something else occurred to me, and I went still. My gaze dropped to the baked good I was holding. Slowly I said, "Emma, these aren't your *special* cookies, are they?"

She shot me an indignant look, adding more to the cooling rack. "Of course not. Do you really think I'd drug you without your knowledge?"

"Yes," I said without hesitation. "Yes, I do."

Emma thought about it. "You're right, I would," she acknowledged. "But not right now. So eat the damn cookies and get to work."

She winked, giving me a tired smile, and I tried to smile back. As an apology, I shoved two cookies in my mouth. Then I tucked Collith's book under my chin and picked up two more in each hand.

Armed with snacks and research, I started toward the living room, intending to sit down for the next several hours. It was our last chance to scheme, because by the end of tomorrow, Lucifer would have come for his answer. I was trying not to think about it, or the panic that had been breathing down my neck might turn into a smothering embrace, and I needed to stay clear-headed and focused.

The squeal of brakes outside made me pause. I went to the window, curious, and peered through the frost-tinted glass. When I saw who stood below, a pet carrier in his hand, I made an urgent sound. I spun away and dropped all my cookies on the coffee table, rushing to the door without giving any thought to a coat.

"Where are you going?" Emma called after me. I was too far down the stairwell to answer.

Cyrus was home.

Sunlight filtered through the curtains of Damon's room.

Voices moved through the stillness like ripples across water. My friends were discussing the possibility of using dragonfire to break the spell on Damon. Cyrus, in his quiet way, rejected this idea. A second, less-familiar voice piped up and supported him.

Cyrus had joined us right after he got home, and he'd brought Ariel. The dragon and the faerie were now up to date on everything. Collith's predicament. The spell on Damon. Lucifer's twisted bargain. They'd wanted to help, immediately, and so our strange little army had added two more to our ranks.

But all afternoon, my mind had been on something else.

For the first time in hours, I was alone. Well, almost alone. Hello was curled in my lap, her purring vibrating against my palm as I stroked her. As Gil's voice floated through the stillness, followed by the low, annoyed rumble of Finn's, I sat in the chair next to Damon's bed and stared down at my phone. A name stared back at me. Another minute passed, then I quickly tapped the screen and raised the phone to my ear.

It went straight to voicemail. I couldn't tell if I was relieved or disappointed. Once the automated greeting had finished, I cleared my throat and held my phone tighter. "Hey, Bea. It's Fortuna. I just thought I'd call to see how Gretchen is doing . . . and how you're doing, too. With everything we talked about. I know it was a lot. If you have more questions, maybe we can meet somewhere and talk."

I hung up and released a long, tense breath. After a moment, my gaze went back to Damon.

In the harsh light of day, I noticed the subtle dips in his cheeks beneath the respirator mask. The slight darkness around his eye sockets. I stared at his pale face and silently willed him to open his eyes and look at me. When that didn't feel like enough, I leaned close and put my hands on his arm. The motion jostled Hello, and she leaped off me, complaining loudly as she wandered away. I just kept watching the quiet figure in the bed.

"Are you there? Can you hear me?" I whispered. "If you are, keep fighting, please. *Please.*"

My brother slept on.

Seconds later, Emma appeared in the doorway. She leaned her hip against the wall and brushed a strand of gray hair out of her eyes, drawing my attention to it for a split second. I couldn't remember the last time I'd seen her real hair color. Then my focus went back to Damon, and stayed there.

"Lunch is ready," Emma said. "You need to eat something. Coffee and cookies don't count."

I didn't move. She fell silent as she watched me. I told myself to say something, but I couldn't. My mind was too busy, too consumed with slow realization. Out of the corner of my eye, I saw Emma push off the doorframe and go to the other chair. It made a creaking sound as she sat.

"Damon is dying," I said quietly, my eyes still glued to him. "And my deadline is almost up. We're out of options. *I'm* out of options."

Emma leaned forward. "There's still time, Fortuna. Don't give up yet."

There was a note of urgency in her voice; she must've seen the shift in me. I'd felt like this before, and it usually resulted in disaster. Today would probably be no exception. It was time to use my own connections, which meant contacting Gwyn and Dracula. One was a psychopathic hitwoman and the other a deadly vampire with an overzealous mission to keep the shadow world hidden. It would be a miracle if involving them *didn't* end in disaster.

"I'm going for a walk," I said, standing abruptly. I knew if I put this off any longer, I wouldn't do it, and seeing Damon had revived the urgency in my veins.

Emma didn't offer to come with me. Maybe it was obvious that I wanted to be alone. After murmuring a swift, distracted goodbye to her, I walked back into the warm brightness where everyone else still sat.

The scene they made seemed like something from a really good dream. Danny had come back—out of uniform, this time—so there were several figures sprawled throughout the room, ancient books splayed in their laps or open beside them. Ariel rested with her head on Cyrus's stomach. The coffee maker bubbled in the kitchen and cast its familiar scent through the air. A freshly-stoked fire popped cheerfully, consuming the logs Finn must've recently added. Stanley, Cyrus's droopy-faced dog, was asleep on the wooden floor. Gil sat beside him, absently stroking the hound's head while he turned a page. His bleached hair glinted in the firelight. Nearby, Hello was now perched on her hind legs and batting at a piece of paper on the coffee table. The pile of notes in the center had gotten taller, just in the handful of minutes I'd been with Damon.

Saving the pile from Hello's mischievous claws, Lyari plucked her up and deposited the kitten on the cushion beside her, all without looking up from the book she was reading. Her lips were puckered in concentration.

My spot on the couch was still open, waiting for my return.

But I went past it, and moved past the kitchen, too. I felt eyes follow me to the door. Thankfully, none of them tried to offer company. I pulled on my coat and hurried down the stairs.

Crows chattered to each other as I stepped into the daylight. Their caws tore through the still, frost-laden air as I waved at Collith—he was on the porch, his eyes on me while he spoke quietly to someone on the phone—and the sound followed me down the driveway. Most of the people I kept company with these days had excellent hearing, and I wanted to make sure I was beyond earshot. I passed the mailbox, crossed the road, and stepped into the trees. Ice and dead sticks cracked under my boots.

Once the barn was out of sight, I took my phone out again and scrolled to a different name on the contact list. This time, I didn't let myself think before touching it. The line rang twice, and then a deep, rich voice filled my ear.

"A call from Fortuna Sworn. Fate has smiled upon me today."

"What can you tell me about the Dark Prince?" I asked without preamble.

Silence came from the other end. The sense of amiability between us faded, becoming something more intense. A faint, almost-imperceptible sound whispered against my ear, and I would've bet money that Dracula was communicating with one of his associates. He came back a moment later, and all he said was, "Whatever you think you know about him, you don't."

"His witches bespelled my brother, and he's offered me a deal to get Damon back." Dracula fell silent again, and I smiled, turning toward the horizon. I could picture the way he'd gone still, the polite expression that came over his face whenever he was evaluating, calculating. "Sorry, friend. Wherever you are, you wouldn't get here in time to stop me. One of your warriors might, but I'm pretty powerful these days. I could probably take 'em."

I waited for his response. Now that I'd told Dracula the truth about Lucifer, or part of it, at least, I found myself hoping he actually had something helpful to share. More seconds ticked by, sounding in my head like a tapping finger.

When the vampire spoke again, his voice was less friendly. "If you do make a deal, be on your guard, Lady Sworn. Give yourself a backup plan. A failsafe."

"You're afraid of him," I observed.

"My predecessors gave me a thorough education. I've seen classified information on cases the public knows nothing about." The vampire paused. "My training also included learning how to conduct exorcisms."

I'd been to an exorcism, once. I flinched at a memory of Finn snapping his teeth, his entire body twisting and jerking. "Did you speak with him?" I asked.

"Only briefly." Dracula paused. "He was perfectly pleasant. Yet somehow, I walked away from our encounter with the distinct impression I must never let that creature step foot in this world, or it would all be burned to ash."

He spoke of fire, but my heart felt like a lump of ice. I needed to think. "I should go. Thank you, Dracula," I managed. "If you think of any information that might be useful, like . . . oh, I don't know, the devil has a deadly allergy to cashews or can be killed with a unicorn horn, I'd appreciate a call."

"Until next time, Lady Sworn." Dracula hung up.

That hadn't gone nearly as bad as I'd thought it would. I put my phone away, surprised that I hadn't been forced into any bargains or received a single threat.

Hopefully my good luck would continue, because there was one more person I'd come out here to contact.

No time like the present. I sucked in a breath, held it, and released it into the cold. The faint cloud dissipated.

"Gwyn," I said.

A small breeze whistled in my ears. After a minute, the only one to appear was a solitary, nosy crow. It landed on a branch high above and watched me with gleaming black eyes.

I waited another minute before I called her again. "Gwyn of the bloodline Nudd, I summon you."

Once again, Gwyn didn't show. Either I was really bad at this whole summoning thing, or I was just being ignored. Somehow, I suspected the latter. Irritated now, I pulled my phone out and typed a brief message. *Call me when you get this.*

After I heard the subtle sound that meant it had been sent, I put my hands in my pockets and turned to leave. The crow called after me, its harsh voice echoing off the stark sky and hard snow.

Cyrus, Ariel, Gil, and Danny were all gone when I got back to the loft. Only Lyari and Finn were left, and they stood in front of the fire, clearly waiting for me. "Where did everyone go?" I asked, frowning.

"You have a visitor." Lyari inclined her head toward Damon's room. "We thought we'd give you some privacy. Emma took Matthew over to Cyrus's for something called 'ice cream.'"

I darted a glance at Finn, but his expression didn't change. His side of the bond was calm. It couldn't be Gwyn in that bedroom, then. Curious, I nodded and moved around them, heading for that open doorway. The last time I'd been in here, I'd left Emma sitting in one of the chairs. But it wasn't Emma beside the bed now, I discovered a moment later.

It was Savannah Simonson.

The feeling in my gut was a combination of resignation and apprehension. When I'd sent her that first text message, I knew it was likely only a matter of time until she showed up. The phone call from Bea's had only made it inevitable. I wasn't exactly making it seem like her son was in good, stable hands. Really, it was strange she hadn't come sooner.

Savannah's time at the Unseelie Court had treated her well. I wasn't sure what that said about the necromancer, but I liked seeing that she'd gained some weight, and her ribs were no longer poking out from her skin. Her autumn-colored hair had grown out to her shoulders, lending a softer look to her narrow features. Even her posture was straighter.

She looked like a faerie.

I sank down in the other chair and fixed my attention on Damon's monitors, scanning the numbers and images for any abnormalities. "You should've called first," I said.

"Why? So you could come up with an excuse to keep me away?"

Savannah's tone was bitter. Tearing my gaze from the screens above him, I stared at my brother and wished for the hundredth time that he was here. I didn't know how to have this conversation, and I also didn't want to speak for Damon. I had no idea how he'd handled things with Savannah when we left town. It was another question I hadn't asked, because the answer would only have added to my guilt.

"We're just trying to protect him," I said after a weighted pause.

Savannah didn't ask who I meant. She didn't need to. Her voice sharpened as she replied, "It's not like I'm trying to take him back to Court with me. I'm asking for a second chance. Haven't you ever needed a second chance, Fortuna?"

I opened my mouth, but whatever I'd been about to say stopped in my throat. My family and I condemned Savannah for her part in Fred's death, and yet I'd taken lives, too. She'd also betrayed us, yes, and yet . . . why was Collith worthy of forgiveness and not her?

As always, thinking of Collith made me hear his voice. It traveled through my body like an echo. *Holding onto anger is like drinking poison and expecting the other person to die. Choose mercy, Fortuna.*

I almost swore out loud. *Fuck.*

I was going to forgive the unstable necromancer who'd murdered my friend.

"I've worked around the clock to get better," Savannah said, probably mistaking my silence for refusal. "Why do you think I accepted the Tongue's offer to be his apprentice? He comes from a long line of fae who magically served the Unseelie King. He has centuries of knowledge that Mercy and other witches don't. He's been teaching me how to control my power. Last week, I raised a zombie and put it back to rest in less than a minute. I can even show you, if you want."

There was a tinge of pride in how she said this. I forced myself to meet Savannah's gaze. She really had changed—the Savannah I'd known was afraid and ashamed. Not this clear-eyed, quietly determined creature. I hadn't met a lot of people who faced the fears inside them. Most were content to stay frightened.

"I'm glad you're learning," I said. "That you're getting better."

It wasn't an answer, and we both knew it. Savannah's eyes filled with pleading, but there was defiance in them, too. "He's my son, Fortuna."

"I know." I looked at her steadily. I didn't say anything else, because I still wasn't sure what to say. Something had shifted, though—for the first time since Fred's death, the tiny flame of hatred in my heart was snuffed out.

Unaware of my thoughts, Savannah turned back to Damon, and I watched her lips press together.

"It was a soul removing spell, by the way," she said softly, touching his hand through the covers. "What the Dark Prince's witches did. Damon is still connected to his body, but barely. The threads are weakening. They can't hold him here forever."

Emma had warned me Damon's state was temporary, but hearing confirmation from Savannah only increased the agitation constantly simmering in my stomach. Then I replayed her words, and my mind latched onto them. *Still connected.* "Wait, if his soul is still here, does that mean he can hear us?"

Savannah shook her head. "I don't know."

As quickly as it had come, the hope dimmed. I couldn't help noticing them again, all those cruel changes in my brother's appearance. It hadn't even been two days. Maybe there had been more to Lucifer's three-day deadline than he'd let on.

"Why Damon?" I asked. My voice was hollow now. "Why did he choose Damon to take, of all the people who mean something to me?"

Savannah smoothed his hair back. The tenderness in the gesture startled me. I kept forgetting, somehow, that she loved my brother, too. "No matter how much you care about the rest of us, he's the last of your family. Blood will always call to blood," Savannah said.

"And there's power in blood," I murmured, thinking of all the rituals and spells I'd witnessed.

She made an absent sound of agreement. "That's how the Tongue does most of his spells."

All at once, it felt like a flare went off inside me. My gaze slowly rose back to Savannah's. "I have an idea, and I want to know if it's possible," I said.

Urgent, nearly breathless, I outlined what I'd read in Goody Baldwin's journal.

Savannah was already shaking her head by the time I finished. "You can't go to Hell, Fortuna," she said. "You wouldn't survive it. Damon is being kept alive by the life forces of at least a dozen witches. I can feel their power in this room. All you'd have is me, and maybe Mercy, if I can convince her to come. It would take us weeks—probably months—to find more."

Witches. The word made a mental image flash. A memory of the drawing Goody had done. All those threads. All that energy.

"Where does it say that anchors need to be witches? Why can't it be any powerful life force?" I asked Savannah. My heart pounded in my ears. But it wasn't excitement roaring through me . . . it was fear.

Her response was slow with unease. "What are you thinking, Fortuna?"

"When I was bonded to the Unseelie Court, I was the most powerful I'd ever been," I said, more to myself than Savannah. I'd half-forgotten she was there. I was looking at Damon again and accepting my fate. Coming to the same conclusion I'd come to earlier, when Emma had sat in that other chair.

My brother was dying, and there was no price I wouldn't pay to stop it from happening.

As I made my choice, I remembered the conversation I'd had on the bench with Seth.

There is no Court here.

Are you sure about that?

I swallowed, and then refocused on the necromancer who loved my brother. I stared at her for a moment, and she stared back with the same worried expression I'd seen on Emma's face. Then I lifted my phone and began to type.

"What are you doing?" Savannah asked. Her phone went off a moment later, and she glanced at the screen. I already knew what the new text said, since I'd been the one to send it.

"I'm calling a family meeting," I said.

CHAPTER NINE

On the morning of the third day, I was awake before the sun.

The light meant the others would arrive soon. I sat at the kitchen counter, tapping the side of a coffee mug while my lips twisted in thought. I strained to hear any voices or footsteps outside.

Last night we had decided—well, Emma had decided—that everyone needed to rest before we regathered. Her efforts were wasted on me, since I'd passed the night either pacing my room or tossing and turning in bed. But for the others' well-being, I had bitten my tongue and waited.

It was one of the longest nights of my life.

Savannah arrived first. She already knew the plan, since we'd discussed it at length before she'd left yesterday. I gave her a quiet, slightly tense greeting and offered a cup of coffee, which she accepted with a grateful look. Together, we went to stand in front of the fireplace and wait.

Lyari and Finn came up the stairwell next. The faerie claimed her usual post by my side, and Finn sank onto the couch. As we waited, I caught him giving the rug a fleeting glance. His expression gave nothing away, but the rug was where Finn usually sat when he was in wolf form. He wished he was in that form now, I knew. Now and always. Worry pricked at my heart, and I forced myself to look away.

Gil arrived shortly after that. He was alone, just as I'd asked him to be. I examined his expression carefully as he tossed himself onto the couch, wondering if I should've included Adam for Gil's sake. Contrary to how my request might've made it seem, Adam was a good friend and I trusted him. I just didn't fully trust Dracula, and I wasn't sure how much Adam passed on to his sire. I'd already taken a risk by calling him. The older vampire was merciless when it came to his life's mission, which was to keep Fallenkind a secret. To keep the peace.

If Dracula found out how much the devil valued my power, he might decide to help me . . . or he might decide killing me would effectively put an end to Lucifer's plans. I wasn't willing to roll the dice. These days, I had a lot more to lose.

The thought only solidified my decision, and I felt my expression harden. This was the right call, what I was about to do. The only call.

Minutes later, Emma walked in with my nephew, and Savannah instantly moved toward them. Matthew went into her arms without protest, his eyes still heavy-lidded. Cyrus and Ariel followed a few minutes after that. And finally, almost a half hour later than everyone else, Laurie came.

Emma called a warm greeting to the Seelie King from where she sat at the table, Matthew now secured in his booster seat beside her, and Laurie winked. He was dressed more casually than usual, if gray slacks and a dark blazer could be considered casual. His sleek, shining hair was straight, the left side tucked behind a pointed ear.

Every arrival noticed Savannah, who had returned to my side, and all had varying reactions. Confusion. Curiosity. Surprise. Speculation. I sat on one of the stools, facing the living room. It was nearing sunset now. Colors that looked like fire and paint moved over everything. Gil said something to Lyari out of the corner of his mouth, and to my shock, she snickered. Finn stiffened, his mouth tightening with annoyance. Normally, I would've sighed or thought about intervening. Tonight there were bigger things to worry about.

Feeling Laurie's eyes on me, I glanced over at him. He didn't look away or try to hide the fact he was staring.

"What?" I said quietly, not wanting to be overheard. Savannah had moved away to steal another moment with her son. Matthew touched her cheek with his food-laden hand, and when she playfully gasped, a noise of utter delight burst out of him. Savannah laughed.

"You've got that look on your face," Laurie told me, bringing my attention back to him.

"What look?"

He bent his head closer to mine, forcing me to notice how good he smelled, and his voice dropped to a conspiratorial murmur. "The one that comes right before the chaos. Normally I enjoy a good bloodbath, but seeing as I only recently lost and regained my throne, I'm trying to be on my best behavior."

I kept my eyes on the stairwell, trying not to react to his proximity. "I want to wait until everyone is here."

"Who else is coming?"

I did a swift, distracted scan of the room. "It looks like we're just waiting on—"

There was movement out of the corner of my eye, and everyone looked in the same direction. I turned quickly. When I saw who stood on the threshold, my mouth parted in surprise. "Nym?"

He stood there, holding an armful of clocks. All of them, I noted, were ticking. "Time" was all Nym said.

"Can I help you with those?" I asked, moving forward. I took the clocks from him, one by one, and put them on the counter. When we were done, I gave the faerie a warm smile. "It's good to see you. Did you come for the family meeting? I also left a message with Queen Viessa. Did she ever pass that along?"

Nym frowned at me, as if he was trying to understand the question. He looked even thinner than the last time I'd seen him. He wore a linen shirt and brown trousers a few sizes too big. There were no shoes on his feet, and I remembered what Lyari had said about Nym throwing them at her emissary.

"Just a little longer now," he said, bringing his gaze back to me. Then he nodded emphatically. "Yes. The family meeting. Yes."

Laurie had returned to my side, and he watched Nym intently. Finn, Gil, and Lyari also stared in our direction. They were gauging Nym, I thought. Trying to determine whether he was a potential threat. I deliberately took Nym's hands in mine and gave them a gentle squeeze.

"We're still expecting one more person. In the meantime, make yourself at home," I said. "There should be plenty of cookies left, unless Finn ate them all. They're on the coffee table."

Nym's eyes lit up with interest, almost childlike in its softness. He pulled away from me and walked over to the table, going right past the formidable figures still following his every move. He bent and picked up a cookie with the tips of his fingers. As always, Nym was fluid and graceful, despite his scattered thoughts.

He'd just taken his first bite when Danny finally came up the stairwell.

With the deputy's arrival, everyone was present. Everyone except, of course, Collith. I faced them, keeping my hands at my sides to keep them from fidgeting. My family waited patiently to hear the solution. To find out what magical, last-minute miracle I'd found after all our hours of searching.

"I'm going to accept Lucifer's offer," I said.

No one looked surprised, and no one spoke. They were giving me a chance to explain before they reacted. Hiding a rush of apprehension, I reached behind me for the journal and held it up.

"This belonged to a witch named Goody Baldwin. She created two spells. One that connected her to her coven, so she could draw on their energy, and one to send her soul to Lucifer's world. It's all here—the incantations, the herbs she used, everything we need. I'll make the deal to save Damon. Once I'm in Hell and I've gotten confirmation my brother is awake, I'll come right back. Lucifer won't be able to stop me, or trick me, because I'm not depending on his magic to travel there. I'll be relying on my own."

A failsafe, exactly as Dracula had advised.

Their doubt was so thick in the air that I half-expected a flavor to burst on my tongue. I looked from face to face, unsurprised by the reactions I saw. I'd expected this. I'd prepared for it.

"Give me another way. I'm all ears. We've been searching for months now, and all we keep finding are dead ends. Lucifer can't be killed. He can't be trapped. And from what we know about the spell on Damon, only the witches who cast it can bring him back. We don't have the time or the manpower to hunt them down, one by one, and force them to do it. Damon's body is weakening. If he doesn't wake up soon, those machines won't be able to keep him alive. This is the *only* way, and I'm doing it." I stopped, then cleared my throat. "That is, if some of you agree to the spell."

There was a pause. Gil turned his head, seeking out Finn, of all people. Neither of them spoke, and yet it was obvious they were communicating. For the first time, they looked like they agreed on something. Then Gil met my gaze and said, "Where do we sign?"

"If you need to think about it, we have a little time. It would be another form of binding yourself to me, and each other. You might even feel weaker, since I'll be using our connection to stay alive. To stay tethered to my body," I clarified. They needed to know what they were getting into.

Finn's dark eyes landed on the witch at my side, as if my warning was irrelevant. "Are you the one who will be doing the spell?" he asked.

Savannah visibly startled. It was the first time someone besides me had spoken to her. She hesitated, her expression betraying her surprise. Then she straightened and nodded. "Yes, I am."

There was a pause. I glanced at each person in the room, giving them a chance to speak. "Okay, then. You're all aware of the plan now. He'll come for my answer tonight, but—"

"I need a full moon for the spell," Savannah reminded me.

"That's tomorrow night, right?" I asked. She nodded, her lips thin with nerves. I nodded back, hiding any doubts I had behind a self-assured mask. "Then I'll buy us twenty-four hours, like I said."

"And if he doesn't agree?" This was from Lyari, who had been strangely quiet.

I'd been hoping to avoid that question. I looked down, pretending to be distracted by Hello, who was attacking my feet. "He wants my cooperation. Badly. I don't think I'll have any problems sweet-talking him into giving me one more day," I said dismissively.

Another pause filled the room. I stooped to pick up Hello, and I scratched her beneath the chin. The kitten's eyes closed in bliss and she started to purr like a small engine.

"Do you know how he'll arrive?" Laurie asked, his eyes flashing. I assumed his thoughts had turned to Collith, and the fact that Lucifer could control him like a puppet. It sent my own mind back to that terrible night in the parking lot, when Collith had looked at me but it wasn't really Collith. All the gentle parts of him erased, like they'd never even existed.

Shying away from the memory, I shook my head and said to Laurie, "He didn't specify, no."

"So you expect us to let you face the Dark Prince without any backup and without any way to defend yourself?" Gil questioned.

"That's exactly what I expect," I replied matter-of-factly, raising my eyebrows at him. My attention flicked to the window. "Actually, all of you should go now. I'll send an update to the group chat when . . . when I can. Nym, I'll try to get a message to you through Lyari or Savannah."

Everyone began to disperse. Their reluctance was obvious, but as I'd pointed out, no one had come up with any alternatives. I went over to Gil, then Finn, speaking to them in a low murmur. Once I'd gotten both to agree to stay elsewhere tonight, I stood back and watched my family leave. I mentally catalogued where everyone would be. Cyrus and Ariel at the house. Lyari at whatever mysterious place she'd been staying since her banishment. Danny at his apartment in town. Savannah and Nym back at the Unseelie Court.

That only left two people still in harm's way, and I had a plan for them, too.

"Emma," I said softly. She turned, raising her gray eyebrows. Beside Emma, Savannah was saying goodbye to her son. "Would you be willing to stay at Cyrus's place tonight, and take Matt with you? I don't want anyone nearby when you-know-who shows up."

Her forehead wrinkled. The door closed behind Savannah, and Matthew started to fuss. Emma rubbed his back in an absent gesture, her full attention on me as she asked, "You wouldn't be staying here alone, would you?"

"That's the plan. There isn't a single being on this planet who would be able to protect me, Ems. I doubt even an army could."

My words didn't exactly reassure her. "But no one should step into battle alone, if they don't need to," Emma murmured.

I reached out to tap Matthew's nose, making my tone bright in hopes of reassuring him. "I wouldn't be able to think straight if I knew you guys were here. This is the best way, I promise."

Surprisingly, Emma looked like she wanted to argue. But she must've decided against it, because she nodded and mustered a smile that didn't fully reach her eyes. In the same breath, Emma shifted Matthew, holding him with one arm so she could give my hand a fleeting squeeze. "Fine, we'll go. As long as you stop by to say . . . to say good night."

To say goodbye, she'd been about to say. I could smell Emma's fear, and it clouded her thoughts. I wish I had better words to comfort her. Everything that came to mind was a lie. As the silence between us got even longer, I thought about hugging them, but that would only worry Emma more. She knew physical touch wasn't something I did lightly.

"Of course I will," I said. "Look, Ems, I . . . there isn't anything . . ."

"Emma, dear, you simply *must* give me this recipe," Laurie declared. He came forward, holding a half-eaten cookie in one hand. He looped his free arm through Emma's and steered her away. She said something back, and though I couldn't see her face, I knew she was blushing.

Thank you, Laurie, I thought.

While the two of them spoke, Gil approached me, his hands shoved in his coat pockets. "You free for a chat?" he asked.

I nodded and reached for my own coat. "Sure. I'll walk you down."

Feeling Laurie's eyes on me, I turned and followed Gil out.

When we stepped into the cold, the vampire didn't speak right away. The clouds had thickened since I'd seen them through the window, and there were faint flurries now, too. I stopped beneath the lip of the barn, seeking protection from the wind. Gil was still silent as he faced me. He rubbed his jaw, and the ends of a tattoo peeked out from beneath his sleeve. Then he raised his gaze to mine, and the joke I'd been about to make vanished from my head.

"I've never had a normal family," he said abruptly. "To be honest, I never had much interest in it. Nicky was the closest I ever came. But then I ended up in that small, white room with you, and I finally got it. The point of all this. Meeting you has made it easier, losing Nicky. Going through all this newborn shit. You're like the kid sister I never had, Sworn."

"Meeting you made all of this easier for me, too," I said, disarmed by his sincerity. But I couldn't bring myself to smile. There was something in Gil's voice that made my heart fill with pain. I searched his expression and fought the urge to look away. "Why are you telling me this?"

Gil shrugged. "I just thought you should know."

With that, the vampire turned and walked into the gathering storm. I'd expected more, and I half-expected Gil to stop. But he was gone. Safe. I let out a breath and felt my shoulders sink.

I turned to go back inside, and I halted at the sight of Laurie. It felt like there was a hummingbird loose in my chest. "I'm surprised you're still here," I said, recovering.

My voice sounded normal enough. But Laurie didn't pick up on my cue, or respond the way he should've. The way I'd hoped he would.

"I'm always here, Fortuna. Even when I shouldn't be," he murmured.

He drew closer, and I stood utterly still, my eyes rapt on his face. Laurie studied me back. A look flitted across his expression that I'd never seen before, and for a moment, my friend seemed like a stranger. Before I could ask him about it, Laurie raised his hands and took hold of me. I felt his fingers on the sides of my neck, his thumbs resting lightly against the line of my jaw. When I didn't protest, Laurie began to lower his head.

Adam's training kicked in effortlessly, and I moved in a blur. I twisted Laurie's arm and wrenched it back, flattening him against the side of the barn. He made an amused sound and turned his head. His austere features started to bubble and shift.

Within seconds, I was holding Sorcha Cralynn.

"What gave me away?" she crooned.

"Besides the change of clothes?" I said icily. "There were a few things. Your smell. Your expressions. And then you touched me. That was your big mistake, really. Ever since he became king again, Laurie has been very, very careful to keep his distance. He hugged me once, I think."

I held her there for another second to make my point, then I let go. Sorcha stepped away and straightened her coat. My nostrils flared with resentment as I watched. Her composure hadn't slipped, not once, and I hated that I had such a small effect on her.

"Good. He's being smart," Sorcha said.

"What is that supposed to mean?" My voice was practically a growl. I knew I was falling right into her trap, but I couldn't help it. I never could when it came to Sorcha.

Her lip curled. "It means you're dangerous. To anyone who loves you or wants you."

"Oh, is that why you broke my heart? To protect yourself?" I demanded, and Sorcha rolled her eyes.

"Your delusions got tiresome a long time ago, but now they're bordering on tragic. You didn't love me, you stupid creature. I just bruised your ego. There's a difference, although I doubt you'll ever experience rejection again, so no point in learning, right? *Everyone* falls in love with the great Fortuna Sworn," she mocked. Voices sounded through the wall behind us, and we both went quiet, listening. After a moment, Sorcha stepped close again, and her tone became harder than I'd ever heard it. "Remember this, Nightmare.

Even if he gives in and goes back to you, he will never completely belong to you. There are some things too wild for cages, and Laurelis Dondarte is one of them."

"You care about him," I observed, looking at her with raised brows. "Wow, Sorcha Cralynn is actually capable of loyalty. Who knew?"

Sorcha's haughty expression changed for just an instant, revealing something akin to guilt—or regret—before she tossed her hair and turned her back on me. I followed her gaze and realized Laurie stood in the doorway of the barn. Sorcha had obviously sensed him before I did. How much had he heard?

The Seelie King gazed at the two of us with a remote expression. "Time to go, Sorcha," he said.

She didn't argue. Without another word, Sorcha sashayed over to Laurie, then slowed. As she passed him, she skimmed her finger down his arm. There was something sensual about it, and there was familiarity in the touch, too. Like she'd done it countless times. Just before Sorcha pulled away, she glanced over her shoulder. Her gaze met mine.

Then she said, "Ta-ta."

She waggled her fingers and slipped away, moving soundlessly over the snow. Her hips swayed back and forth. Laurie and I stayed where we were, watching Sorcha head for the trees.

"Wicked little thing," Laurie said, his face still impossible to read.

I felt my lips purse, and I couldn't stop myself from saying, "Exactly how you like them."

Dear God. Was I . . . jealous?

Thankfully, Laurie didn't seize the opportunity to tease or taunt me. His silver eyes shifted to the horizon. "The witch you mentioned," he said abruptly. "The one who went to Hell. How did it end for her?"

I hesitated. For an instant, I thought about lying. But there was no point, because Laurie would see right through me. I took a slow, soundless breath, but the air betrayed me, and swirls of heat appeared in the shadowed space between us.

"I don't know," I admitted. "There weren't any more entries after that."

"Lovely." He laughed, a brief and mirthless sound. "So the entire foundation of your plan, which is the capability to return from Hell with this spell, is based on the success of a witch who was never heard from again after she performed it."

It was then I realized Laurie was pissed. Deeply, visibly pissed. It was so unlike him that I fell silent, disconcerted. "We don't know that," I said finally. "There are a hundred reasons why Goody Baldwin stopped writing. She could've just started a new journal, for starters."

"Don't insult my intelligence, please. You *knew*, the entire time you stood there and fed us this story." Laurie gestured toward the loft, and the movement was so fast that his arm slightly blurred.

"Knew what?" I asked with careful detachment.

"That you wouldn't be coming back."

The coldness in his voice startled me. I felt my defenses rise, but I fought to hold onto calm. My hands formed fists in my pockets. After a moment, I moved away and reached for the door. As I grasped the handle, I faced Laurie again. At last I said, my own voice hard with conviction, "You can't say you wouldn't do the same if you were in my position."

"I wouldn't, actually. Because what you're doing is giving up. You're being a martyr, Fortuna. And despite what the legends say, there's nothing romantic about a martyr. It's just tragic."

The way he looked at me was a blend of scorn and pity. Laurie had never, ever looked at me that way before. But instead of getting pissed, I just felt a flash of hurt. It made it difficult to think, and I spent too much time trying to come up with the right response. Laurie misinterpreted my struggle as a stubborn silence. This time, he was the one to turn away.

"You said you'd never try to change me. That night." My voice was soft, but he still heard it.

Laurie stopped, and I knew him well enough by now to recognize that I'd surprised him. He moved closer to me again, searching my expression with a look in his eyes I couldn't decipher. "You heard us," he said.

It wasn't a question, so I didn't answer. I just gazed up at the silver-haired faerie who had, somehow, become very important to me. I didn't want to fight with him; I wanted to leave things on a good note.

I was about to try again when Laurie said, "Fine. You're right. I can't make this decision for you, however much I'd like to, because you're making the wrong one. For what it's worth, though, I'm hoping you'll change your mind. If Collith knew what you were planning, he'd say the same thing. On this, we'd be in complete agreement."

"See?" I said softly. "Miracles do happen."

I had hoped to make him smile, or shoot me a glare, at least. Instead, Laurie's jaw worked, and I'd only seemed to make things worse. I could see the two parts of him struggling. The reasonable side, the light, knowing he had to allow me to make my own choice. But the faerie—the hungry, roiling darkness that lived inside both of us— urged him to take the choice from me. Which one would he listen to?

I stared up at Laurie calmly. Waiting. The darkness looked out from his eyes.

Then he vanished.

Snow floated past the place he'd been standing. I stayed there, listening to the wind howl, and I hoped I got to see him again. We felt unfinished.

It wasn't the only thing in my life that felt that way.

Of their own volition, my eyes went to Cyrus's porch. Collith had been a constant presence there since we got home. But his rocking chair was empty, and I knew he'd probably left when he'd realized everyone was convening. We didn't know how much Lucifer was using his access to Collith.

Speaking of Lucifer . . .

My insides quaked. I quickly pictured my family's faces, and the sensation faded. I opened the door to the barn again and cast a final look around, memorizing every detail. The house, the glowing windows, the fat snowflakes still drifting down. The garage where Laurie had embraced me as I cried, the campfire where Collith and I had held hands in our silent grief, the trees where I played with Damon and Matthew. A soft smile touched my lips. After another moment, I went inside.

My three days were nearly up.

Oliver didn't like it.

He listened to my plan with an unreadable expression, but his mouth was pursed and there was a shadow in his eyes. He didn't interrupt or voice any opinions, even once I had finished.

We sat beneath our tree, me with my back against the trunk while Oliver sat in the canopy's shadow, one arm propped on his bent knee. I wore a long, white dress with a green sweater pulled over it, and the sleeves were just a bit too long. Every time I reached up to brush my hair away, I caught the faint, familiar scent clinging to the wool. *Ollie.*

When I'd first arrived, the sun had been hovering over the horizon, bathing the hills and fields in golden light. Now it was halfway down, and the devil still hadn't come. I'd fallen asleep waiting for him in the loft.

Succumbing to the need to fidget, I pulled some grass from the ground and began to tear the blades apart. I thought about that family meeting for the dozenth time. A frown tugged at the corners of my mouth. After a minute, I threw the handful of grass with more force than necessary, and it fell like confetti.

"There's something I didn't tell them," I said.

Oliver turned his head. "Tell who? Your family?"

I nodded without looking at him. "I think I know whose spell-book was left on Goody Baldwin's doorstep. In Kindreth's journals, she wrote of a witch who lived at the Unseelie Court. The witch supported Viessa's bloodline in their claim to the throne. She used her magic to bind faeries to her, so she could control them and ultimately get Folduin on the throne. Which means that the spell we're about to do tomorrow will give me the power to do the same."

"But you won't," Oliver said simply, realizing where I was going with this. What I was afraid of.

Nothing was ever that simple, though.

Like a terrible song on repeat, I thought of what Gwyn had said to me. *Someday you will know what it is to choose between love and power. Someday you will be just like me.*

I remembered Mercy Wardwell's warning, too. *Anyone who loves you will pay a price. It will cost you, as well.*

Then Sorcha's voice slithered through my memory. *You're dangerous. To anyone who loves you or wants you.*

My best friend must've seen my doubt. When he spoke again, something in his voice made me look at him, and he held my gaze steadily. "You forget, I know who you are, Fortuna," Oliver said. "I know you in a way no one else does. Not just because I grew up alongside you, and watched you become the amazing person you are now. It's because I'm part of the world you created. I can feel you with every breath, every heartbeat. Your essence. Your spirit. There's darkness in it, yes, but there's also a hell of a lot of light. So when I tell you that I know you won't abuse whatever power you claim, believe me."

He said all this so easily, and that's what affected me the most— Oliver talked as if he was telling me something absolute. These were facts.

My eyes flicked between his. Not for the first time, I thought about how much Oliver had changed. Somewhere along the way, the boy I'd known had been replaced with this strong, certain man. A man I had been keeping at arm's length, and who I tried not to think about during my waking hours. There was too much going on in my life—survival being a chief focus—and Oliver made everything more complicated.

Realizing I hadn't given a response, I broke our stare and looked down at our hands. I ran my fingers over his in an instinctive, thoughtless movement, and I heard the sound Oliver made. It was so faint that I knew he hadn't meant me to hear. Guilt filled my throat. I pulled back and looked away, wrapping my arms around myself.

"You haven't felt the rush of magic," I finally replied, resting my chin on my knees. "It turns me into a different person. Someone I don't even recognize. And that person . . . terrifies me."

This time, Oliver didn't respond right away. Like me, he returned his attention to the setting sun, frowning. I studied him from the corner of my eye. The light made his freckles more prominent. A five o'clock shadow dusted his jaw, and it made him look older. Harder.

"You could be wrong about the grimoire," Oliver said, oblivious to how intently I was looking at him. "It might not be the same spell."

I shook my head. "No. I'm not sure how it ended up in Goody's hands, then in Lyari's possession, but the spells are too similar. It can't be a coincidence."

Oliver started to answer, then something stopped him. His eyes darkened and his eyebrows drew together. He turned his face toward the horizon, and I had a feeling he did it to hide a flash of pain. My stomach sank.

"Ollie?" I said. Even as his name left my mouth, I was aware of exactly why his entire countenance had shifted. That didn't stop me from hoping I was wrong. But then Oliver looked at me, and I knew I wasn't.

"He's here."

I followed Oliver's gaze, and I stopped breathing.

A dark figure stood against the horizon.

I'd told Oliver, earlier, not to fight it if the devil came knocking on our door. It was better that he arrived this way. It meant no one else was hurt so Lucifer could have a body.

I turned back to my best friend, shoving down a surge of fear. *Don't let him see. Be brave for Ollie.* "You should go," I said.

I saw the rebellion in his eyes—he wanted to argue, and the old Oliver would have. But after a few seconds, he swallowed whatever he'd been about to say and stood up. Oliver reached into his pocket and pulled something out. A pocketknife, I saw as he flipped it and offered me the handle. The design was achingly familiar, and as I took it from him, I confirmed that it was my father's.

"I went off your descriptions of it," Oliver said. "The blade has been soaked in holy water."

I love you. I swallowed my words, too. We both knew this knife would do nothing against Lucifer's incredible power, but that wasn't what it was for. Oliver wasn't giving me a weapon; he was giving me a reminder. Something to hold and carry during the moments I was afraid or alone.

"Thank you" was all I said. All I could say. I rubbed the handle with my thumb, and then I stood, tucking the knife out of sight.

We didn't hug, even though I wanted to. Lucifer was waiting. He had to know what Oliver meant to me, but I wasn't willing to put on a display of it. Oliver knew this, too. We'd discussed it while I'd been filling him in on everything else. He hunched his shoulders—earlier, he'd given me his sweater and refused to take it back—and began the walk back to the cottage. I stayed where I was, watching Oliver go. Wishing I could run after him. His white shirt flapped against his long torso, and he looked back only once, his beautiful mouth a thin line of worry.

I turned toward that dark figure.

My heartbeat was loud in my ears. I watched the devil close the distance between us, the wind stirring the flaps of his long coat. Beneath it, he wore a gray suit with a black waistcoat. Everything about him was sharp and perfectly tailored. Laurie would've approved.

Don't think about Laurie, I told myself, swallowing a rush of fear. In spite of all my research, I didn't know what the devil was capable of. He already knew about my connection to the Seelie King, no doubt, just as he knew about every person I cared about. But I refused to allow him more glimpses into my life. Anything to protect them.

A few seconds after that, Lucifer reached me. He stood there for a moment, appraising my expression. I looked back without emotion, channeling the Unseelie Queen with everything I had inside me. *You are cold. You are powerful. You are unafraid.*

"Walk with me," the devil said.

I just nodded, and by some unspoken agreement, we started moving toward the horizon. My skirt brushed against the tall, whispering grass. I lifted it, baring my legs to the cool evening, and kept the cotton from getting caught. Lucifer didn't speak again. I knew he'd come for an answer, and this was it. I kept my focus on the fading sky.

"I'll do it. I'll . . . visit you in Hell," I said haltingly. Fear made my voice tight.

Lucifer kept walking, and a breeze stirred the ends of his hair. He squinted at the distant sea, and the dying sun painted his skin a striking gold. "I look forward to showing you my home," he remarked.

I stopped. It felt like someone had lit a spark inside me. I faced the formidable figure and raised my eyebrows. "Not so fast. Only a moron would take a deal without sweetening the pot."

Lucifer stopped, too. He looked at me, and the corner of his mouth tilted up. "I would expect nothing less from you."

I wanted to take a breath, for courage, but I knew Lucifer would see that. I met his gaze, willing myself to look back at him without a trace of fear. "I want the spell to wake Damon before I travel anywhere," I said.

Now Lucifer's eyebrows rose. "Are you suggesting I rely on your honor?"

My heart had started to quicken again. Was this actually going to work? To hide it, I gave a casual shrug. "I guess you'll have to."

"No deal, Lady Sworn," the devil said, shaking his head.

I hid my disappointment. I hadn't really expected him to go for it, anyway, but the last-ditch effort to avoid Hell had still been worth a shot. Lucifer's instincts weren't wrong about me—if he'd woken Damon before my departure, I probably wouldn't have held up my end of the bargain. I wasn't exactly dying to visit the underworld.

I was about to concede when Lucifer added, "I would be willing to negotiate the amount of time you are away, however."

"Great," I chirped, recovering from my surprise . . . and my annoyance. When I'd decided to accept Lucifer's offer, I hadn't even thought about how long I'd actually *be* in Hell. The devil had me so frazzled that I was missing things. Big, obvious things. Thankfully, none of this showed on my face as I looked at Lucifer and said, "Three days."

"Three *days*? You insult me. Two months."

"Do you have any idea how long that is in my world?" I countered. Whatever amount of time we landed on didn't matter, since I'd be using Goody Baldwin's spell as soon as I got to Hell, but I needed to put up the appearance of giving a shit.

"Two months is the blink of an eye," Lucifer said dismissively.

I scoffed. "Yeah, well, your concept of time is warped. Two weeks."

"Six weeks."

"Three."

"Done."

I went still, my heart picking up speed as I remembered how my other deals had concluded. I shied away from thinking about the one I'd made at the crossroads—the night I summoned a demon that came wearing Ian O'Connell's face—but then I saw Collith. I remembered that fall day we'd faced each other in the woods. The first deal I'd ever made. *Is that it, then? Now what?*

We kiss, of course. Shouldn't you know this part?

My gaze snapped to Lucifer's, and he saw a flash of panic before I could hide it. The devil stepped forward, raising his hands. I stiffened, expecting him to cup my face. Instead, his thumbs skimmed the edges of my jaw. The touch was so light that it felt like he hovered just a breath above my skin.

"When we kiss, Fortuna Sworn, it will be because you want to," Lucifer said.

Surprise whispered through me. Fighting against a tide of desire, I tipped my head back. My gaze lazily roamed his face, and I thought about all the Nightmares he'd killed. The terrible things he'd done. "You didn't care about my consent when you had me branded," I reminded him, just as soft.

Lucifer didn't answer. It was debatable whether he'd even heard me—I was giving him a look I'd given a thousand others. I was the spider, and Lucifer was the tiny fly caught in my web. Suddenly it didn't matter that he was the devil, or that power practically rolled off him. In that moment, he was just another morsel. Just prey. Our faces moved closer. Closer. Attraction heated between us. Desire stirred in my belly.

Just when I thought I had him, I hooked my foot behind Lucifer's ankle and yanked with all my strength, pulling the pocketknife out in the same breath.

It was a move I'd done hundreds of times before, mostly in practice, sometimes in self-defense when my admirers became crazed, like Logan Boon.

Lucifer didn't budge.

Instead, he caught hold of my wrists and used my weight against me. I tipped forward . . . right into his arms.

I regained my balance, but Lucifer didn't let go. His hands were like vices, and he wrapped them around my forearms, trapping me there. My chest heaved against his. I raised my chin and looked back at the devil, rigid with fear and defiance. "I'm not sorry," I said. "Had to give it a try."

But he didn't look pissed. Our bodies were still locked together, and I watched Lucifer's gaze drop to my mouth, our faces so close together I could see the golden rings around his pupils.

"You were worth the wait, Fortuna Sworn," he murmured.

I was so disarmed that I didn't wrench free as I'd been planning to, and Lucifer was the one to move away. He released his grip on me, holding the knife I'd tried to stab him with. I hadn't even noticed him take it, I thought with dismay. Lucifer tossed my weapon away, and it hit the grass with a dull sound. His voice became courteous again as he said, "I'll arrange for a coven to—"

"No need," I interjected smoothly. "The full moon. I'll come then. In my world, that's tomorrow night."

There was a pause. The corner of Lucifer's mouth tilted up again. "It won't work, you know."

"What?"

"Whatever you're planning, whatever scheme you've cooked up, it won't work. But I admire the effort." He leaned close. "May the best player win."

I started to respond at the same moment a woman's scream ripped through the dream.

I jumped, and something moved overhead. Lucifer's eyes flicked upward. I looked, too, and discovered the entire sky had turned red. Thick, vein-like things crept through the wide expanse above us. They were an even deeper scarlet than the horizon, and the longer I stared at them, the more those delicate strands seemed to . . . pulse.

What was this? What was happening?

"Fortuna," someone said urgently, their voice booming. "Fortuna, can you hear me?"

"You should wake up. That could be important," Lucifer remarked. I started to move away, but then the devil's arm blurred, and his fingers grasped mine. He bent, keeping his eyes on mine. "Until the full moon, Lady Sworn."

Before I could respond, Lucifer brushed his lips over my skin. It felt like an electric current traveling through me. I pulled my hand back, resisting the urge to rub it, and hoped he couldn't hear my wild heart. The devil's beautiful face was expressionless, but there was a gleam in his eye that told me everything I needed to know. *Fuck.*

A moment later, Lucifer's wings snapped open. He shot into the air, sending a gust of wind downward, and my hair blew back. "May the best player win," I said softly.

And then the sky started raining blood.

CHAPTER TEN

*B*loodlust waited for me on the other side of consciousness. It was a feeling I'd never experienced before, not even in the grips of deepest rage or harrowing pain. This was more consuming than feasting on someone's fear. A red haze half-blinded me. I was dimly aware that I had my face against someone's neck. A woman who smelled like expensive perfume and sweat. I was drinking from her, my hands tight on her waist, and I knew I needed to pull back. I could hear her heartbeat. It was slowing, dangerously. Soon, we'd be past the point of no return.

But the thirst . . . the thirst was stronger. I gripped the woman's waist tighter and tore even deeper into her flesh. A wonderful, horrible squelching sound filled the stillness. Blood flowed over my tongue, bringing euphoria along with it. My eyes fluttered and the mindless rage began to retreat.

"Hey! Hey man, stop that!"

The voice was familiar, I thought distantly. I kept drinking and forgot about it.

Then something slammed into me.

The blow was so hard that I went flying. I recovered mid-air, twisting to land on my hands and feet. I raised my head, teeth drawn back. The hiss that came from my throat was like no sound I'd ever made before. My eyes focused, and they zeroed in on the face of the one who'd interrupted my feeding.

It was Seth Arthion. Again.

He squatted and put his arms behind him, baring his own teeth in a threatening snarl. I rushed at him, and Seth braced himself. Just as we were about to clash, my name boomed from the sky, exactly like it had in the dreamscape.

"Fortuna!"

The goblin, the alley, and Gil's psyche rushed away. And then I was on my back, in my own bed, waking up with a gasp.

I already knew it would be Finn leaning over me, so as my eyes cleared and focused on his face, I didn't fight his hold on my shoulders. Instead, I used him to remain upright, my nails biting into the solid warmth of his forearms.

"We have to go," I said.

Finn nodded, his eyes preternaturally bright. I got out of bed and went to the closet, dressing quickly. When I emerged from my room, the werewolf was waiting by the door, keys in his hand. His other held out my coat. I pulled it on, my thoughts consumed by Gil. We went down the stairwell and outside.

Finn got into the driver's side of the car—he was probably worried my connection to Gil might overtake me again. If I was behind the wheel when that happened, I could drive us right off the road. I settled into the passenger seat, secured the seatbelt, and closed my eyes. As Finn drove, I put all my concentration into our bond. *Where are you, Gil?*

We reached town a few minutes later. It was the middle of the night, the bars closed and shuttered, so the streets were completely empty.

"Turn here," I said, following an instinct. I pointed at the closest street sign, which glowed bright green from our headlights. Finn put on the blinker, and as the silence resettled, I studied him. Soon, after Savannah performed Goody's spell, he would be able to tell for himself where our packmate was. I wondered if I'd really made him understand that. *Something I'll have to worry about later*, I thought faintly, looking away.

Because we'd found Gil.

The scene looked like an eerie, grisly painting. He was kneeling in the center of an alley, a streetlight shining down on him.

The light made it easy to see all the blood.

There was so much of it, I doubted the person it belonged to could still be alive. Wherever she was. I did a swift scan of the area, confirming we were the only ones there. Had Gil disposed of her, then come back here to clean up the rest?

Finn pulled up next to the curb, and I got out of the car calmly, resisting the urge to rush up to Gil. He'd never hurt me, I knew that, but part of me feared he'd attack Finn or bolt if he was startled. I knelt as close to him as I could get without putting my knee in the mess. The vampire didn't look up.

"Did you know," he said, "that when we drink from them, we get some of their memories? Not the insignificant ones, or the boring ones. We see the moments that impacted their soul. The moments that stay with them for eternity. Which is how I know that I just killed a woman with three children. I saw them in her blood. Cute little fuckers."

This last part was faint. Broken.

"Oh, Gil," I whispered. I raised my gaze to Finn, who had gotten out of the car and was standing closer than he normally would. Ready to intercept at the slightest provocation from the vampire. "Will you call Adam?"

Finn nodded and pulled his phone out. I stayed with Gil while the werewolf moved away, speaking to Adam quietly. Finn came back in less than twenty seconds. When I saw his grim expression, my stomach sank.

"The vampire is out of town."

Damn it, I thought. My phone call must've spooked Dracula. I would bet the contents of my entire checking account that he was putting precautions in place, shifting players around on the board in case Lucifer gained a foothold in our world.

It meant that we were on our own.

"Gil," I said evenly, "we can't stay here. Glamour won't hide all this."

He still didn't lift his head. His pale hands rested palm-up on his legs, and they were covered in rust-colored stains. If he hadn't been wearing all black, those stains would have been visible on his clothing, too, no doubt.

I wanted to take his guilt, his struggle. But some battles could only be fought alone. That didn't mean I couldn't send a little encouragement, though. I closed my eyes and imagined the threads between us. Gently, I sent my love into our bond.

But it had the opposite effect that I'd intended.

Moving with the speed of a newborn vampire, Gil gripped my shoulders in a sudden frenzy. Finn snarled.

"Don't make me stop," Gil pleaded, ignoring the werewolf. "Please don't make me. The blood isn't . . . I can't . . ."

Pain curled in my chest. I stared at my crumbling friend, thinking that if he hadn't left Adam to go into hiding with me, this wouldn't be happening. He would've learned control. The monster inside wouldn't be eating him alive, and we wouldn't be in this cold alley with gore gleaming on the dark concrete.

As Gil waited, I pasted on a calm expression, knowing he needed my strength right now. There was no time to fall apart. I cupped his face, and his hands moved to my wrists. It felt like part of me was dying.

"We can't take that risk. Not when someone else's life is at stake," I told him gently. Gil stared at me, wide-eyed with shock and guilt.

I swallowed, wishing I could give in to the voice crying out inside me. The one saying we should just go home, pretend this hadn't happened, and continue on as we had been. It was fine, everything was fine.

But everything was not fine.

Somewhere in Granby, there were three children waiting for their mother to come home, and she never would.

This was the right call, I told myself silently. If Gil hated me for it, so be it.

Even though I'd never done this before, I knew what to do, somehow. It was instinctive, like blinking or breathing. I reached for that bond between us, imagining it like a bright, glowing thing. My hold on Gil's face tightened, and I made myself say it, imbuing my will into our connection. "You will not drink from another living creature unless I give you permission. From now on, you can only feed from the blood bags. This is not a request."

My voice was firm. No one but me would ever know the thousand small deaths I experienced as I took Gilbert Payne's freedom from him.

Afterward, he didn't speak. He knelt there, swaying. His hold loosened on my wrists, and then his grip fell away completely. His eyes had gone dull. Looking at him, I wasn't sure which version was worse—the one who was being torn apart from the inside, or this hopeless shell. For once, I didn't blame myself.

I blamed Belanor.

If he hadn't been dead, I'd have killed him all over again, and it would have been much slower than the easy death he'd gotten.

"Can you walk?" I asked numbly. "We should get you into the car."

Still silent, Gil brought one leg up, then the other. He stood as if he was too heavy. His arms hung at his sides.

"I'll take him to Adam's," Finn said.

I imagined Gil staying in the empty garage all night, alone in his pain. I shook my head. "No. We're taking him home."

"Matthew is at Cyrus's," Finn reminded me softly.

I froze. *Shit.* That was too close for comfort, and Finn obviously thought the same. But it would kill Gil to know we didn't trust him anywhere near my nephew.

"He can come with me," someone said.

My head jerked at the same moment Finn's did. We both looked toward the mouth of the alley, tense. Finn's eyes glowed bright and my hand went under my coat, where the Glock was tucked against me. But then I saw the horns, and the familiar, round face. The second I laid eyes on Seth, I remembered that he had been here earlier. He'd seen Gil feeding and tried to stop it.

Now the missing body made sense.

"Did you bury her?" I asked flatly.

"No. I took her to the emergency room, actually. I couldn't stay, since the humans would've asked too many questions, but she was alive when I left." His eyes flicked to Gil. I paid close attention, but I sensed no fear around Seth when he looked at the vampire. Whatever had happened between them, it hadn't made Seth hostile or wary. "We shouldn't be here, though. Would you like me to take him?"

I opened my mouth to turn down his offer . . . just as I realized there *were* no other options. Emma and Matthew could've stayed with Danny, no doubt, but I'd already put them through so much. Asking Emma to pack up again and impose on Damon's boyfriend because I was afraid my friend would eat them? That was one conversation I'd do anything to avoid. Including accepting a near-stranger's help.

I pushed myself up and walked over to Seth.

"The bloodlust usually takes him a few hours to shake off," I said hesitantly. Could he really handle this? There was a reason Gil had been staying with Adam.

Seth shrugged. "I'm staying in a rental on the edge of town. There aren't any close neighbors, so he can come down without any . . . distractions."

"And what about your safety?" I asked.

His eyes flashed indignantly. *Ah*, I thought. *There's that Seelie streak.*

"I may be a goblin, but I'm still fae," Seth reminded me.

I couldn't argue with that. By all appearances, he wasn't injured, which meant that Seth must've held his own during that confrontation with Gil. Either that, or he knew how to get through to him.

"This is very kind of you. Thank you," I added. My voice was tinged with relief and sincerity.

Seth nodded, and my gaze went to Gil. I didn't know how much he'd heard, since it didn't exactly seem like he was in a listening mood. I returned to him, my footsteps the only sound in the alley. I lowered my voice instinctively as I said, "I'm not sure if you've officially met Seth, but I think we can trust him. He's offered to look out for you until . . . until things are calmer. Adam should be back soon. I wish you could come home, but—"

"It's fine." Gil didn't look at me. From this angle, I could see a layer of dried blood on the side of his neck. My mind flashed back to that moment he'd buried his face deeper into the woman's throat. I'd felt a warm trickle move down his skin, seeping from the gaping wound Gil had created with his fangs.

Right call, a small voice in my head whispered.

Seth had parked along the curb, too, and the headlights of his car flashed when he unlocked the doors. Finn got in ours, claiming the driver's side again. As Gil and I stopped next to it, I heard the faint whine of a window going down, probably so Finn could hear every sound Gil made. Normally, Gil would've heard it and done something to antagonize him.

Instead, the vampire just walked over to Seth's vehicle and lowered himself inside.

I followed him, then bent over so he could see me. My fingers curled around the edge of the door. "Gil . . ." I hesitated. "Do you want me to call Nicky?"

He stared straight ahead. The streetlight shone on his dyed hair and made the strands glisten. "I'm dead to Nicky."

I paused. "But you're *not* dead, Gil. I think it's important you remember that."

He turned his head, finally meeting my gaze again. "I'll be at the loft shortly after sunset," he said.

It took a few seconds to understand what he was telling me. My face cleared. "Oh, that. I don't care about the spell, okay? If you can't do it right now, or you don't want to, please—"

"I'll be at the loft shortly after sunset, Fortuna," Gil repeated. He reached for the door handle, and I moved out of the way. He closed it without another word.

"Okay," I said, knowing he could hear me through the glass. "If you need anything, call me, please."

It felt like I should say more. Gil had to get cleaned up, though, and all of us needed to drive far, far from this place. I touched the window with my fingertips, then walked away.

Seth had been standing on the curb to give us a chance to speak alone. I joined him there.

"I assume you know Laurelis Dondarte?" I asked, crossing my arms against the cold.

"I know of him, my lady, and I've seen him at Court, of course. I've never spoken to him directly."

"He told me once that the Seelie Court likes pretty things. But I don't consider lies, exclusion, and cruelty to be pretty. In fact, I think they're damn ugly." I looked at him. "You know what I do find beautiful? Courage. Authenticity. Kindness. Which makes you one of the most lovely people I've ever met, and I would be glad to have you in my . . . group, if you still want to be."

The goblin's eyes flicked away, but not quickly enough. I still saw the overly bright sheen in them. Seth blinked rapidly, and after a moment he answered, his voice thick, "I would be honored, my lady."

I couldn't smile, not with Gil sitting in that car covered in a human's blood. "I'll see you tomorrow night, then. Or tonight, I guess. I'll text you the address," I said.

"Don't need it." Seth's eyes darted away a second time, his shoulders tensing beneath his coat. "I know where you live."

He'd been out to the house? I hadn't noticed him, not once. Apparently even Finn and Collith had missed our friendly stalker. If the Seelie Court hadn't banished him, Seth Arthion would've made an excellent Whisperer.

Well, their loss was our gain.

I started to turn, shoving my hands into my pockets. But another thought occurred to me. I faced Seth again. "You might be making the biggest mistake of your life," I informed him. "I just thought you should know that."

The young goblin grinned. "Big mistakes make the best stories, anyway."

Now I did smile back; it was impossible not to. Seth Arthion had one of the sweetest smiles I'd ever seen. "Welcome to the family," I said.

"I won't let you down, my lady. This is for the best. Staying with me will make his withdrawals easier. Goblin blood tastes bad to them, but yours . . ." Seth hesitated.

I couldn't hide my surprise. Gil had never told me that. Neither had Adam. It said something about both of them, that they'd spent so much time around me and resisted the constant thirst scratching at the back of their throats. I'd felt it for myself now. I knew how strong it was.

With one more nod at Seth, I got into the car. I tried to look back at Gil as we left, but the interior was too dark. Only the bottom half of his face was faintly visible, and every inch of it was still crusted with blood. I twisted forward again and tried to let out a breath. Instead, the sound that came out of me was a small sob. I looked out the window, my chin wobbling.

Finn's big hand curled around mine.

Once town was behind us and my pain had quieted, Finn pulled his arm away, and I took my phone out. I brought Lyari's name up on the screen. But then I thought of her mysterious absences and distant behavior, and remembered my gut feeling that she was keeping something major from me. I scrolled to the name above hers and called it. The clock on the dashboard read 3:00 a.m.

After four rings, someone answered.

"Let me guess," his silken voice said in my ear. "There's another crime scene that needs cleaning up."

If a woman hadn't been hospitalized tonight, I probably would've responded with a mirthless laugh. Instead, I stared out the window, feeling hollow and bleak. It showed in my voice as I replied, "Have I ever mentioned that you have great hair? Like, seriously great. Beautiful, really."

"Yes, I am vain enough that flattery would usually work. Not this time, however. No matter how sad you sound, my lady. I'm not a free cleaning service you can summon whenever you have need of one."

A sigh filled my throat. I knew Laurie. I knew when he wanted something.

"What's your price?" I asked, ignoring the huffing sound Finn made beside me.

"A date."

I blinked. "Excuse me?"

Laurie's tone made me imagine a dismissive gesture. "Nothing fancy, don't worry. I know you have a lot on your mind. Dinner. Tonight. Your place."

"Fine," I said.

Laurie paused. And once again, even though I couldn't see him, I could picture him with perfect clarity. In my mind, the Seelie King was in his elegant bedroom at the palace, morning light gleaming over his bare skin as he held his phone to his ear. Maybe there was a naked figure asleep next to him—I ignored the pique of jealousy *that* detail provoked. During the silence that fell between us, the Laurie in my head raised his eyebrows.

He only cemented this image when he finally said, "No threats? No hustling, bargaining, or promises to skin me alive and disembowel me?"

I rested my temple against the glass. "If I disemboweled you, there would be no one to clean it up."

"I've taught you so well. Is this what pride feels like?"

I didn't even have the energy to roll my eyes. Instead, I just told Laurie where to find the alley and finished with, "I'll see you tonight, then. We won't have long. Savannah is coming to perform the spell at midnight."

"I'll bring everything we need for dinner," Laurie replied. "You just bring the wine and the sex swing. Actually, on second thought, I have those things, too, so never mind."

My lips twitched, but I didn't respond. I hung up, wondering how Laurie always managed to do that—make me smile when everything was terrible. I lowered the phone to my lap and peered up at the waxing moon. I was still leaning against the window, and as the tires rattled over some cracks in the road, the vibrations moved through my bones. Silence resettled in the car like dust, and that was when it hit me.

Holy shit. I was going on a date with Laurelis Dondarte.

I could feel Finn looking in my direction. When the seconds ticked past and I could still sense his eyes sliding toward me, I lifted my head and glared at him.

"What?" I demanded, exasperated.

He refocused on the road, and his voice was carefully neutral as he said, "I'll go on another hunt tonight."

Finn was too much of a gentleman to state his meaning outright, but I still got it. "No, you really don't need to," I told him firmly.

Finn shot me a dubious glance. "There's a scent," he began, hesitant.

"A *scent?*" I echoed. Then I held up my hand. "Okay, you know, I should warn you. You're coming between me and some pretty intense denial about what you can and can't smell, and we're room-mates. Don't take my denial, Finn. I've lost enough."

The werewolf stared out at the night, a faint smile curving his mouth. I turned my face back to the window, but I was smiling, too. *Amazing,* I thought. It was amazing that, in the darkest moments, when the sky was raining blood and there was death around every corner, these people I'd stumbled across brought me so much light. It didn't seem possible that only coincidence had led them into my life.

Then I remembered what Gil had said, once, about the God who had abandoned us. *Maybe He does take an interest.* I'd disagreed with him at the time, but now I wondered. My gaze went up to the moon.

I wondered, and I hoped.

Because in less than twenty-four hours, I'd be in Hell, and I needed all the help I could get.

My last day on Earth was quiet.

After everything that had happened, sleep held no appeal for me, so I passed the rest of the night making preparations. First, I wrote a letter to Gretchen and Bea, because I still hadn't heard from them and I couldn't bear to leave this world knowing they were afraid of me. Then I wrote letters for everyone else. I gave them the words that were so difficult for me to say out loud. I told them what they meant to me, and how much they'd changed my life for the better.

I just wished they could say the same for me.

I left the envelopes in the drawer of my nightstand, along with everything else Damon would need. The deed to the land Collith had put in my name, my birth certificate, and Bud's business card— when my life had started becoming more treacherous, I'd taken a page from my brother's book and updated my will. I'd even had Bud—Granby's only lawyer—draw up an advance directive, which Damon would find out about in his letter.

Once that was done, I considered packing up some of my things, but that felt too much like tempting fate. Contrary to what Laurie thought, I *did* plan to come back. Or hoped to, anyway. I was trying to be realistic about the odds of that happening, and I wanted to ease the burden on my family if the spell failed or something else went wrong. I wavered a little longer, and then I imagined Emma putting my clothes in boxes. I gave in to the urge and went downstairs to get some of the storage totes we'd tucked away.

I spent the morning putting what few belongings I had into those totes, and then I hid them in the closet. If my family knew how much I doubted the success of our plan, they might refuse to go through with it. But as long as my brother was under Lucifer's spell, there was no other option. Tonight was happening regardless of my own outcome.

After that, I changed into a sports bra and a pair of old track pants. Without the distraction of the letters or packing, my mind began to refocus on last night. I tugged on my running shoes and tied them distractedly, reliving the scene with Gil over and over again. The haze. The euphoria. The horror.

Shuddering, I tied my hair back and went into the kitchen, where I packed a small bag of provisions. I drew the zipper shut a minute later, and the sound it made was stark in the hushed stillness of the loft. I put my arms in the straps and tightened them. The solid weight of a water bottle rested against my spine as I hurried back down the stairwell, eager, for once, to be in the cold. The discomfort of winter's teeth scraping over my skin would divert me from everything else. It would be difficult to think, much less obsess about the bleak shadow in Gil's eyes or the broken pleading in his voice. *Don't make me stop.*

With a deep breath, I left the driveway and entered a world of naked trees and untouched snow.

I'd stopped jogging during our time in hiding. It had seemed like too much of a risk. Unknown terrain, strangers everywhere, and we were always trying to avoid attracting attention.

All those reasons were gone now.

Today I ran like I'd been wanting to for months. Like the world was on fire, because it was, and all my efforts to put it out only seemed to fan the flames. I didn't think, or obsess, or worry. There was just the burning in my lungs and the jolts of my feet against the ground. I ran for miles, until the sky lit up and sunlight sparkled over the snow. I finally slowed down when I comprehended how far I'd gone and that my mouth was dry with thirst. I pulled the bag off and sat on a flat rock, then rummaged for the water bottle. I drank deeply, enjoying the feel of the cool water sliding down my throat and warm sunlight on my skin. I ate one of the granola bars, too, chewing leisurely while I looked around. At last, the noise in my head had gone silent. The woods had become a peaceful place for me again.

I lingered there long after I'd finished eating. But eventually I stood and started walking in the direction of the house, my legs slow with reluctance. Part of me wished I could just keep going and see what awaited on the horizon.

The thought made me pause. I pictured the quiet loft I'd be returning to, and I remembered that ringing, awful stillness. Why was I in such a rush to get back, anyway? Wherever I was, all I could do was wait.

Decision made, I readjusted my grip on the backpack straps and turned around, facing that beckoning horizon.

I spent the entire day out there. Exploring parts of the woods I'd never ventured through before. Following the length of a dried-out creek, just to see if I could find the place where it ended. Trailing my fingers along every tree that I passed.

The sky began to deepen, the bright blue sinking into a brooding indigo. By the time I decided to go home, I almost felt ready to face the creature that was coming for me. Almost.

It took another hour or two to retrace my steps. When the barn came into sight again, I was cold, tired, and sore, but my roiling emotions had settled. I walked up the stairs with a heavy tread and quiet veins. The loft was dim, sunlight slanting over the floor in burnt ribbons. I'd been gone longer than I thought. I stopped in the kitchen, tapping my finger thoughtfully against the counter. I wasn't sure when Laurie was coming, but there was still some time before sunset. I might as well take my last hot bubble bath.

Ten minutes later, I was doing exactly that. I sank into the tub and the bubbles closed in over me. Tension hovered in my shoulders and between my eyes as I waited for images to accost my thoughts. But my mind remained quiet, empty. Maybe it was the fact that midnight was only a few hours away now. I was feeling that strange numbness again, the sensation that seemed to keep happening whenever my life was in danger.

I was just starting to relax when the bathroom door opened.

Laurie came in and leaned against the counter. In a flash, I was standing, water streaming down my body. I was too startled and too aware of how naked I was to be furious. "I thought you'd be coming later," I blurted.

Laurie's eyes were dark. They scanned me quickly, and his fingers tightened around the edge of the counter. "I couldn't wait any longer" was all he said.

There was something in his voice, some kind of tension or shadow that made my mind clear. I reached for the towel on the hook and wrapped it around myself. My voice was stiff as I said, "If you're here to collect on my debt, this isn't—"

"I didn't know," Laurie cut in.

I frowned, stepping out of the tub. My feet sank into the plush rug. "What?"

"When I made my choice," he answered. The line of his shoulders was taut, and his body practically thrummed with energy. "When I retook the throne. I didn't know."

"Didn't know what?" I asked. I tried to sound exasperated, but my heart was hammering. I knew exactly where this was leading. *Don't go there, Laurie.* I tightened the towel and raised my gaze, knowing he'd see my apprehension, because he saw everything.

Just like I feared he would, Laurie pushed off the counter, his movements a little too fast. It was a blatant reminder of what he was. *Faerie.* His hair caught the light, strands of it glimmering like stars as he drew closer. One of his hands slid around my waist while the other cupped my cheek. In spite of the agitation coming off him— he'd really worked himself up before coming here—his touch was gentle. He skimmed his thumb along the edge of my jaw, and even that simple touch started a fire inside me. I closed my eyes. I knew this was a bad idea. At the moment, though, I was having trouble remembering why.

"This," Laurie whispered, then he bent his head.

I turned my face away, but of its own volition, my hand reached up and took hold of Laurie's wrist. I felt his nose skim my cheek, and a quake went through me when I heard his soft inhale, as if he was enjoying my scent. I looked at the mirror beside us, and the picture we made felt surreal. His moonlight hair gleamed, splaying starkly against the stiff, royal blue collar he was wearing. Never in a hundred years would I have believed I'd end up in this position with the Seelie King. When had I allowed myself to fall for this danger- ous, beautiful creature? It was different than what I felt for Collith or Oliver, I thought as Laurie's lips brushed my skin. With Ollie, what we had felt like water. Soothing, beautiful, familiar. Collith was wind and earth. Inevitable, powerful. Laurie was fire. Crackling, hot, hungry fire that affected everything in its path, no matter how fast you ran from it.

But I was good at running.

"You made the right choice," I forced myself to say. "It would've destroyed us, the sacrifice you made. Both of us knowing what you gave up."

"I didn't realize you were a seer," Laurie remarked. His hand was still on my jaw, but he didn't try to turn my face. His breath teased the tender skin of my ear, and that's when I found the strength to pull back. My towel had loosened, somehow, and I grabbed the edge of it with both hands, going toward the door. Why did Laurie always show up when I was naked? Near the threshold, I stopped and faced him again. I gathered a barely-perceptible breath, but his eyes still darted down, lightning-swift, noting the movement.

"I can see the writing on the wall, okay? I'm not an optimist like Collith. I'm not brave like you. Not when it comes to . . ." I swallowed. But of course Laurie knew what I'd been about to say.

Not when it comes to love.

Laurie's expression shifted. I saw the intention in his eyes a beat before he reached for me, and I had a beat to deny him. Push him away.

Instead, I met him halfway.

Laurie's kiss was hot and thorough. His mouth moved against mine as if no time had passed since our last night together, and he tasted so good. His body pressed me into the wall, displacing my towel again. It fell open, baring my entire body to the chilly air. But I wasn't cold. Laurie's hand was a fist in my hair and the other ran up my bare side, stopping just short of my breast.

Only then did he pull away.

"You should get dressed," he said. "I'll start on dinner."

I stared at him. My lips felt swollen from his hard kiss. "Wait. What?"

Laurie looked at me like I was an idiot. "Dinner. The consumption of food. There must be at least one participant, but when you make it two, everything gets so much more interesting."

I resisted the urge to kick him and settled for a glare, but Laurie was already strolling out, hands shoved in his pockets. Cocky, arrogant bastard. Scowling, I picked up the towel, wrapped it roughly around myself, and went into the bedroom to get dressed. But *not* because Laurie had told me to.

A few minutes later, I emerged into the great room. The ends of my hair dripped against the back of my denim dress, and I rolled the sleeves up as I walked up to the kitchen island. There were two cloth bags resting on the middle of it. Laurie was taking items out, one by one, subtle muscles rippling beneath his shirt. The jacket he'd been wearing now hung off one of the barstools.

I stopped on the other side of the counter from where he was working. After a moment, I slid onto one of the chairs. "What are you making?"

"Portobello steaks with avocado chimichurri," Laurie answered promptly, bending to open one of the drawers. "I checked with Emma to make sure you didn't have allergies to anything. But if you don't like it, we can always make a reservation somewhere else. I have a friend who will set aside a table for us."

"I'm sure you do," I replied with a small, private smile. He was just so . . . Laurie. I watched him for another minute. He removed dishes from the cupboards as if he'd been in this kitchen a thousand times. "Do you need help with anything?"

In response, Laurie retrieved a bottle of wine from the bag. He made short work of getting the cork out, then fetched two long-stemmed glasses from the liquor cabinet. He circled the island, dragged one of the barstools out, and poured. "I say this with love, darling, but you'd only slow me down."

I decided not to argue. I reached for one of the glasses and took a slow, cautious sip. The wine was exactly how I liked it—red and just a tad sweet. I didn't think it was a coincidence. I took another drink, turning the stem between my fingers while I continued to observe Laurie. The watch on his wrist glinted as he started to chop the parsley he'd just rinsed in the sink. "Who taught you how to cook?" I asked.

Laurie smiled. A strand of his hair came loose, and he tucked it behind his pointed ear as he replied, "My governess, of course. Her name was Florence, and she didn't give a shit that I was fae or royalty. She didn't spoil me like the rest of the staff, and she taught me skills the other courtiers looked down upon. Cooking, cleaning, laundry. She wanted me to have a good head on my shoulders when I took the throne. To be different from the rulers that came before me."

I thought of Laurie's kindness. He wasn't perfect—I still hadn't forgotten that he'd murdered Ian O'Connell—but he was also the one who'd left a chair for me in the tunnels of the Unseelie Court, just to make my visits with Naevys more comfortable. And he hadn't even taken credit for it.

"Well," I said, my voice soft, "I think she succeeded."

Laurie set a cast iron skillet on the stovetop and glanced at me over his shoulder. As always, he heard the words I didn't say. "But?" he prodded.

I hesitated. In the silence, Laurie turned one of the burner dials, and the ignition clicked. A small, blue flame materialized. "But I've been to your Court," I said quietly, raising my gaze to his. "I've seen how humans are treated there . . . and the faeries who don't conform to the archaic standards the old ones enforce."

My mind filled with an image of Seth's open, honest face. I blinked it away, nervous for Laurie's response. He'd come back to the counter, and he slid a spoon through an avocado, his fingers deftly guiding the curved edge around the pit. At last he answered, his face expressionless, "Then come change it."

Laurie didn't look at me, but there was a challenge in the way he spoke. His meaning was clear. He knew I didn't want to be queen, and here he was, offering me a crown.

But Laurie's answer didn't have the effect he'd probably intended. I pursed my lips and focused on the glass of wine I was still holding, working to control a surge of anger going through me.

"Or you could," I countered. My voice was hard. I looked up at him. "You got your throne back, Laurie, and you did it with hardly any bloodshed. You used your intelligence, and your charm, and your connections, and you defied an ancient spell to reclaim your power. You don't need me to make the Seelie Court a better place. You've proven that you're more than capable of accomplishing the impossible."

A muscle twitched in Laurie's jaw. He turned away and tipped a bowl of mushrooms into the skillet. As the sound of frying intensified, he reached for a wooden spoon resting on the counter. "Tell me about your parents," he said abruptly.

The randomness of the topic made me frown. It was also not an easy topic. But there was still a strange tension between us, like Laurie and I were locked in a battle of wills, and I wasn't about to be the first one to back down. "It happened in the middle of the night," I bit out. "I was having a bad dream, and then—"

"Not how they died," Laurie interjected, his bright eyes darting my way. He'd started cooking our steaks. "I want to know how they lived."

For the second time tonight, I stared at him blankly. It felt like it had been a long, long time since I'd thought about my parents without also thinking about that night. That dark, bloody night. It was easy to forget that the dead were so much more than how they'd died. Mom and Dad had led rich and passionate lives before a killer invaded their house.

"They were the best," I said finally, raising my brows at him. "Seriously, Laurie. I had the most *amazing* parents. I won the fucking parents lottery."

The Seelie King looked at me. The hard lines around his mouth softened. "Tell me about them," he said.

So I did. I told him all the small details that only family knew about each other. The small details no one else really cared about, yet somehow, it felt like Laurie did. How my dad was the one who'd given me my sweet tooth, and he used to keep caramel squares in his pockets. How Mom always read her books with a puckered, severe expression, even when she was reading something light and fun. Laurie listened to all of it, asking questions now and then, his expression attentive and open.

The feeling I had was reminiscent of a day I'd had with Collith once, before everything fell apart. Like the two of us were at the edge of change, and something beautiful was on the horizon, or something painful. With Collith, it had been the latter.

But this was different, I reminded myself as Laurie took plates out of the cupboard, steam rising from the pan on the stove. Whatever secrets he was keeping didn't matter. Whatever came of this dinner didn't matter.

In a few short hours, I'd be trading places with Damon.

Thinking about the spell dimmed my mood, and I couldn't ignore the storm clouds hovering over us anymore. I stood near the table now, my hand resting on the back of a chair. "What is this, Laurie?" I asked finally.

It was the question I'd been wanting to ask all night.

Our food was ready—the aroma in the air was making my mouth water—and two tall candles flickered on the table, which I'd just finished setting. Walking over with two plates, Laurie set them down and pulled out the chair I was touching. "This is a ceasefire. A pause," he answered.

"Wow, you *really* don't think I'll be coming back," I joked, sitting at the head of the table.

Laurie settled in the chair to my left and took a sip from his wine glass. He set it back down and began to slice into his steak. Once again, he kept his focus on the task in front of him instead of looking at me.

"It's true, I think your plan is sloppy and dangerous," he said. His voice had tightened again. "I think magic isn't as predictable as you're acting like it is. And I also think none of that matters, because even if you weren't doing this spell, you would've taken the Dark Prince's deal.

"But then I think about the conversation you overheard in that revolting little motel. I have my faults, but I'm not my brother. I won't put you in a cage . . . no matter how much I may want to."

Even now, Laurie didn't look at me. It wasn't because he was ashamed, though. As my gaze lingered on him, it felt like a light switched on in my head.

"You're still angry with me," I realized. *That* was what I'd been picking up on since he got here, but I hadn't recognized it because Laurie didn't get mad. Not toward me, at least. "Why? Because of the martyr thing?"

Laurie put his silverware down. His eyes met mine, and they flashed as he said, "Yes, because of the 'martyr thing.' You're giving up, Fortuna. Where's the stunning creature I used to know? Where's the firecracker?"

My defenses rose. I held my fork tighter; I hadn't even touched the food yet. "You're one to talk. You went into Creiddylad's tomb without knowing if you'd come out," I pointed out.

"That was different." Laurie shook his head and started eating again.

I scoffed. "Oh, yeah? How do you figure?"

Laurie's palm slammed down on the table with a thunderous *thwack*, and the entire thing shook. "Because it was *me* making the sacrifice!"

His voice echoed through the room. The candles quivered. I sat ramrod-straight, glaring at him. I could feel my nostrils flaring in response to the swell of power between us. The Nightmare in me, rising to the faerie in him. Logically, I knew Laurie would never hurt me. Didn't I?

"I think about it, you know," he murmured, probably seeing the question in my eyes. He unclenched his hand and plucked his wine glass off the table, swirling it calmly. He took a drink and went on, "I weigh the pros and cons of locking you away. You'd hate me for a while, of course, but you change your mind about people. I've seen it. Not to mention the fact that Nightmares have a long life expectancy, and most minds can't hold grudges for centuries. You'd probably forgive me eventually. And I'd have plenty of time to wear you down."

His thoughtful tone sent a breath of ice through my veins. "Why are you telling me this?" I asked.

Slowly, Laurie set the wine glass back down. His eyes burned into mine. "I believe that, sometimes, you mistake us for men, Fortuna. You forget what we truly are. You think like a human, and you live with their limitations."

Now it was my turn to shake my head. "I don't understand what you're saying."

"Don't you?" he said, watching me intently.

It felt like everything went still. I was having trouble breathing again, but this time, it wasn't because I was afraid.

"I came tonight because you love me," Laurie said, ignoring how I physically reacted to this. He said it so casually, as though he were speaking a fact. "I wasn't certain before, but these past few days confirmed it. Months ago, when I faced an eternity without you or my throne, I let fear dictate my choice. I'm here to clear the air, because the thought of you going to your death without knowing the truth is unbearable. And the truth is this.

"Things have changed. I've changed. If you survive this, I want to be with you in any capacity you're willing to give me. I don't need all of you, and I'm not asking for it—I just want a small piece."

I sat there, frozen, my eyes so wide that I knew I probably looked like a deer in headlights. Was he expecting an answer right *now*? "What made things change?" I managed, trying to buy myself some time.

Laurie opened his mouth to reply at the same moment someone knocked on the door.

"I got it," I said to Laurie, practically leaping up from the table. He just reached for the wine bottle.

I hurried over to the door. As soon as I opened it, Collith lifted his head. The sight of him made my heart shift inside me, just as it always did. He wore the wool coat he'd been wearing on the day we met, and his dark hair glistened with droplets from outside. I wondered if it was melted snow, or if it was raining.

"I came to say goodbye," he said. His hazel eyes flicked toward Laurie, but he didn't seem surprised to see him here.

I frowned. "You're leaving?"

Collith shook his head. "I'll be here until you don't want me to be. But I saw Finn before he went on a hunt, and he told me I should come see you."

Meddling werewolf, I thought darkly, knowing I wasn't really mad. I couldn't be angry with Finn even if I wanted to be. I swallowed a sigh and refocused on Collith, peering up at him with one hand on the doorknob. "Okay, yes. There's a small chance this may be the last time we see each other."

I didn't think I was risking anything by saying that—Lucifer already knew that I planned on arriving tonight. I watched Collith's face for his reaction, alert for any signs that he might not be alone in his head. Before Collith could say anything, a creaking sound disrupted the stillness.

"Have you eaten?" Laurie asked, his voice coming from directly behind me. I jumped, and he put his hand on my waist. His palm was warm.

"Don't have much of an appetite," Collith said. He noticed the wine bottle on the table. "But I'll take a drink."

Laurie didn't respond, and when Collith looked at me, I realized they were leaving the decision in my hands. I was calling the shots. Why did it feel like I was agreeing to more than a drink, though? I glanced back at Laurie, then at Collith. My hold on the doorknob loosened, little by little, until my hand fell away completely. "The wine won't be dry enough for you," I warned Collith.

It was as much of an invitation as he was going to get, and both of them knew it. Collith stepped inside, and Laurie went to the liquor cabinet to fetch another glass. I returned to the table and refilled mine and Laurie's. By the time I turned, the two fae males were already standing there. Collith's coat hung on one of the wall hooks next to the door.

Laurie accepted his glass from me and held it up. "To Fortuna."

Collith took his as well. He didn't hold it up, but his gaze met mine. A hundred memories passed between us, and they were in Collith's soft voice as he echoed, "To Fortuna."

The clink of our glasses rang in the silence. We drank. Tension quivered in my belly as I brought my glass back down, and I held the stem a little too tight, making the red liquid inside slosh dangerously near the rim.

"Why don't we sit?" Laurie suggested suddenly. He inclined his head toward the living area. "It would be a shame to let a perfectly good fire go to waste. We can bring the food over, since you still haven't touched yours, Fortuna."

"Okay," I said. Surprisingly, I didn't need to think about it.

Music played gently from the speaker in the kitchen while we settled in the other room. Sitting on the couches felt too formal, so I went right over to the fire, making myself a small nest of pillows before I lowered myself down. Collith rested against the base of the couch, facing me, and Laurie sat between us, arranging all the food between us. The Seelie King propped an elbow on his knee and brought a grape to his lips with his other hand, the picture of lazy nonchalance.

I steeled myself, waiting for him to say something along the lines of *Let's play a game.*

"Here's something you don't know about me," Laurie said casually, watching the flames move through his wine glass. He hesitated, his pale lashes brushing against his skin as they flicked down. "Sometimes I feel terribly lonely."

"Really?" I said, frowning. "You? But you have your inner circle, and your sister. I would've thought . . ."

Laurie shrugged, reaching for another grape. He popped it into his mouth. "Physically, I am rarely alone, you're correct. It can just be an isolating thing, responsibility."

Everyone in this room knew exactly what that felt like. We'd all been rulers. I wanted to ask Laurie if it was worth the cost, that throne he'd fought so hard to retake.

"All right. Here's something you don't know about me," Collith said, drawing our attention to him. He nodded at Laurie and raised his glass, acknowledging the rare glimpse of vulnerability our friend had given us. "I was a spy in the Vietnam War."

Laurie scoffed. "You were *not*. I would've known. Must we start the lies so early in the evening?"

"You were distracted. If I remember correctly, some important dignitary was coming to visit, and they were bringing a huge party with them. Since you couldn't keep tabs on me yourself, you sent someone. I just bribed him to give you false reports and leave me the fuck alone."

It felt like the temperature had dropped. Laurie's jaw worked, and his eyes blazed like light shining through ice. "You could've died, and I wouldn't have known," he said.

They stared at each other.

"Okay, just how old *are* you two?" I interjected.

"Don't try to change the subject. It's your turn." This was from Laurie. Slowly, he pulled his gaze away from Collith and refocused on me.

"I never agreed to this," I protested. The males just waited, and I shook my head. "Fine. Something neither of you know about me? Okay, uh, I despise cauliflower. Like, really hate it."

I pretended to shudder. Collith and Laurie both spoke at once, immediately dismissing this as an answer. I sighed and took another drink of wine.

It wasn't that I was afraid to be vulnerable. I just truly couldn't think of anything. Collith and Laurie had gotten so many pieces of me since we'd barreled into each other's lives. They knew about my parents, my powers, my pain. They knew my faults and my fears. They even knew about Oliver, to an extent.

But then I did think of something. There *was* one thing they didn't know. One thing no one knew, not even Finn, or Gil, or Damon. It wasn't a secret, exactly, but until now, it had only belonged to me.

I repositioned myself on the pillows and let out a breath. "Okay. It was while we were on the road. Me and the pack, I mean. We had all this downtime in motels, and since I was constantly researching you-know-who, I just needed a break sometimes. I have no clue what made me do it, since nothing about my life is stable, and I don't even know if I'll be alive tomorrow morning"—both of them reacted to this, Collith's eyes darkening, Laurie's mouth tightening, which I ignored—"but I started looking into schools. And then, I don't know, I started thinking about maybe going back."

I shrugged, my fingers tugging at a string attached to a throw pillow in my lap. I could feel both of them looking at me, and I wasn't sure what would be worse: seeing pity or apathy. So I focused on that small, delicate string, wondering if pulling it out would make the seam come undone.

"If you need a letter of recommendation for any applications, I'd be happy to provide one," Laurie said, making my eyes fly to his. He shrugged. "My name is known in some veterinarian programs because of donations I've made to rescues over the years."

"If you're looking at schools in Denver, I own a property in the area," Collith put in, giving me a soft smile of encouragement. "It's vacant right now. You're welcome to it on the nights you want to stay in the city."

I sat there quietly for a moment, trying to think of what to say or how to express the sensation inside me. It felt like something soft and bright was in my chest. In the end, of course, I didn't have the words. But I knew they could probably hear it in my voice when I simply said, "Thank you."

Laurie winked, and Collith's foot brushed against mine. A wordless, sweet touch. I took a sip from my glass to fill the silence, but I didn't pull my leg back.

After that, the three of us proceeded to do something we'd never done before.

We . . . hung out.

Later, I wouldn't remember how it happened, or at what point we forgot our tension. It was probably Laurie's doing. Over and over, our laughter rang through the night. Collith and Laurie told me more stories from their earlier years. They constantly interrupted each other, arguing about the true order of events or whether certain details were correct. I told them about being Angel Jones. The wine must've loosened my tongue, because I also shared how, my first night on the job, I'd fallen off the pole and rolled into the crowd. To this day, I still wasn't sure how, but in the fall I'd managed to break a customer's nose with my boob.

Collith and Laurie *roared*. My gaze went back and forth between them, and I knew I was grinning like a moron. For the first time in months, I felt warm, and safe, and happy.

Those weren't the only things I was feeling, though.

Throughout the night, there were touches. Small touches. A hand on the small of my back. A thigh graze. A finger curling briefly around mine. Every time one of us got up for those mundane, beautifully normal things that people do—to get a drink of water, use the bathroom—we found reasons to move closer or pass close by.

Once again, Laurie stood to get another bottle of wine. Did this make our fifth? Our sixth? I'd need to stop drinking soon, so I was sober for the spell. But that time hadn't come yet. I leaned back on my arms, relaxing, and Collith stayed where he was. His eyes were hazy with desire as they roamed my body.

Seeing that look, heat surged between my thighs. I instinctively clamped them together. Collith's gaze flickered, noting the movement. He did it so fast that I would've doubted whether I really saw it, but the way his nostrils flared told me all I needed to know.

Our eyes met. Held. I could see the past in those depths, our shared history. It had been so long since I'd touched anyone like that . . .

The throbbing between my legs intensified.

Collith pushed away from the couch, and then he leaned on one knee, bending over me. I felt his long, splayed fingers sliding up the backs of my calves, my knees, my thighs. When he reached my ass, his hands cupped me firmly, and he used that firm grip to lower me to the floor. Collith eased his body down, too. I watched, breathless, as he kissed me through my underwear.

I didn't make a sound, but my fingertips flattened against the floor, and I felt my toes curl.

"I've missed this," Collith murmured, keeping his eyes on mine as his hand moved.

I swallowed. I was having trouble remembering reasons why this was probably a bad idea. "So have I," I admitted in a whisper.

I sensed Laurie returning from the kitchen, but Collith didn't pull away. Still holding my gaze, he slid his fingers beneath my underwear and circled my clit slowly with his thumb. Pleasure exploded through me.

When I turned my head, biting my knuckle to keep from crying out, my eyes locked with Laurie's. He'd taken the spot Collith had just vacated, his wrist propped on his knee again. He watched my face intently.

Without thinking about it, I reached for him. Laurie reached back, his rings gleaming as our fingertips met halfway. His gaze moved to Collith, who paused in his administrations. A wordless communication passed between them.

Something about that look made me remember Laurie's remark at the dinner table. His silken voice moved through my mind. *You think like a human, and you live with their limitations.*

Without warning, Collith pulled away and got to his feet. He reached down before I could ask if something was wrong. I gripped his hands and stood, my dress falling back into place. He kissed me again, as if he couldn't help himself. I stood on tiptoe and buried my fingers in his hair. Collith began to move, and I moved with him. Laurie strode ahead. I heard the sound of a door opening.

We were making our way to the bedroom, I registered dimly. Probably a wise move, since someone could come back to the loft. I allowed Collith and Laurie to guide me over the threshold and into the shadows, overwhelmed by what they were doing with their mouths and hands. My bare feet moved onto the rug in the center of the space, and something about the sensation brought me back to my senses. I pulled away from Laurie reluctantly. Collith stood behind me now, his hands on my waist. I felt his lips skim the side of my neck.

"Wait." I could barely hear my own voice over the sound of my wild heart. "What if Lucifer is watching?"

Laurie gave me a slow, wicked grin. "Then let's give the prick a show."

I stared at him. At both of them. Silence trembled between all of us, and it felt like even the air was holding its breath.

And I made a choice.

Slowly, I stepped back. I stepped back again, right at the edge of the rug, and my hands rose. I unbuttoned my dress, taking my time, and it fell to the floor in a pool of cotton.

For the first time in my life, I laid myself completely bare, and I wasn't afraid. I looked back at Collith and Laurie without flinching, and I let them see me. Not just my body, although I was still wearing a bra and panties—I allowed them to see the depths of what I felt. I knew these males. They still had their secrets, no doubt, but everyone hid something.

I trusted them.

Laurie came toward me, and his fingers curved around the back of my neck, unexpectedly gentle for him. I raised my face. While I lost myself to his taste, his tongue, Collith approached from behind again. He brushed his lips over my shoulder, his fingers tracing the lines of the tattoos that only we could see.

As one, the two of them worked their way down slowly. Kissing, caressing, breathing, licking, and stroking on either side of my body, from my neck to my hip bones. I felt one of them unsnap my bra. Another pulled my underwear down. Then, as though they could read each other's thoughts, they worked their way back up, still at an agonizing pace. Like we had all the time in the world.

When Laurie's mouth closed around my nipple, and his tongue began to flick it, my sex ached and clenched. I was still the only one naked, but I was far too impatient to give both of them the same treatment they'd given me. "Take your clothes off," I commanded softly.

They obeyed.

We moved together in whispers of clothing and bare skin

brushing. Laurie and Collith undressed each other, too, kissing each other's throats, jaws, and shoulders. Within a minute, the last shirt fell onto the floor, and they stood in their full, fae glory. A thrill went through me as I considered the cocks in front of me. Two of them, both impressive in their own ways. Collith's was length and elegance. Laurie's had girth, and there was a move he did with that thick width that I still thought about sometimes.

And tonight, they were mine.

I touched Laurie first.

My fingers trailed down his erection. I stroked the shaft lightly, as if it were fragile. I knew it was anything but, and I also knew it would drive Laurie crazy. My head tipped back so I could meet his gaze. Laurie liked eye contact. But the fierce way he was looking at me made my own wild desire ignite. I wrapped my fingers around his cock now, squeezing it, and rotated my wrist in a rhythm he began to match with his hips. Laurie's eyes never wavered from mine.

Once he was so hard that his cock stood to attention, my motion slowed. I turned my head and reached out with my other hand. I grasped Collith's cock, then slid my fingers down to cup his balls. On the way back up, I carefully dragged my nails along the tender flesh. I watched as Collith's chest started to rise and fall, listened as his breathing became more labored.

Watching him get turned on, seeing how much he responded to me, sent a searing rush of arousal straight to my core.

Smelling it, Collith's eyes went unnaturally bright. He hauled me against him and claimed my mouth. I raked my nails down his stomach, enjoying the feel of his firm muscles as they rippled against my touch. While I was frantically kissing Collith, Laurie lowered himself to the floor. He grasped my hips and turned me. As my back settled against Collith, he shifted his mouth to the side of my neck, his hands cupping my breasts with just the right amount of roughness. Distantly, I was aware of Laurie's face pressing against my thighs. I opened them for him without thinking, angling my body to give him better access.

At the feel of Laurie's tongue, my knees buckled. Collith's arm instantly wrapped around my waist, catching me, and he held me up as though I weighed nothing. I was no longer capable of coherent thought. Only seeing, and touching, and wanting. The curve of Laurie's ass. The arch of Collith's neck. Brown curls. Long eyelashes.

Soon, I began to feel the familiar build-up of heat and pressure. I never wanted it to end. I didn't even care about reaching that wild crescendo.

My body came apart. I released the longest, toe-curling moan I'd ever made. After a few delicious, torturous seconds, my entire frame went slack, and I still couldn't think in anything but a hazy sort of way.

Then one of them hilted himself within me. Laurie, I realized through the rush of sensation. My core tightened again, squeezing around his considerable girth. Laurie was just as dominant, just as insistent as the last time we'd been together, but now his edge was counteracted by Collith's tenderness. While he pounded into me, again and again, Collith trailed his fingers around my nipples. Tipping my head to rest on his shoulder, I reached back blindly. Collith realized what I wanted and shifted to accommodate me. I found his hard shaft and wrapped my fingers around it, starting an insistent rhythm. Collith swore in my ear. His hips moved with my hand.

I hadn't known it was possible, to connect to two people like this. All of us, all at once, everywhere. Laurie was still thrusting. He kissed Collith, then me, and it felt like I didn't know where I ended and they began.

Laurie gave a deep, masculine groan as he came. Seconds later, Collith's warmth spilled over my fist. We sank to the floor and rested against one another, taking some time to recover. Sweat gleamed on my skin. My head was on Laurie's chest, my legs tangled with Collith's. Both of them had their arms above their heads, and their fingers touched, palm-up on the rug.

After another moment or two, I raised my gaze to Laurie's. "This is the part where you disappear, right?" I said.

There was another pause. Laurie looked at Collith. I sensed something pass between them again, which seemed to be happening more and more these days. Collith got up and went into the bathroom. He returned with a towel and gently cleaned off my hand. After that, he gathered me into his arms and handed me to Laurie. He followed us as my silver-haired faerie turned away and moved toward the bed.

"My darling," Laurie said, setting me down, "we're just getting started."

I shivered.

CHAPTER ELEVEN

A full moon glowed on the other side of the window. I sat next to my younger brother, bent forward so that I was propped on my elbows. For the thousandth time, I thought about the promises we'd made to each other. *I'll take care of you.*

So much had changed since then, but not this. Not my love for Damon.

And yet, since Laurie and Collith had left, the sense of calm I'd been feeling about my decision was nowhere to be found. I'd been hoping to rediscover it here, at my brother's side, staring at his pale, vacant face. So far, the agitation roiling inside of me hadn't eased.

"Are you ready?" Savannah Simonson asked from the doorway. She'd arrived an hour ago to start making preparations for the spell.

No, my heart whispered. I had so much to live for now. So many people I didn't want to leave behind. Once, I wouldn't have felt a single twinge of regret at the thought of death. Now everything inside me longed to stay.

I turned my head so Savannah could hear me say, "Is everyone here?"

She shook her head. "We're still waiting on Finn. He's the last one, though—everyone else came. They're in your room."

"Wow," I said faintly. It was all becoming real. "They all came? Even Nym?"

Savannah gave me a small, hesitant smile. "Even Nym."

My gaze lingered on Damon for a few more seconds, and then I stood. "I better check on them."

When I turned, I caught Savannah looking at Damon, too. Her expression was inscrutable, and a whisper of unease went through me. Did any part of her blame Damon for her dark transformation? Or resent him for claiming full guardianship of Matthew?

That little detail might be different after tonight, I realized as I followed her out of the room. If Damon didn't wake up, and something happened to me, Savannah was fully within her rights to take her son back. He was at Danny's right now, since I didn't want Matthew on the property when such a dangerous spell was being performed. What if it was Savannah, and not Damon, that picked him up in the morning? What if this didn't work, or it was all a trick? What would happen to my nephew?

I was a Nightmare. I knew fear better than any other creature, and I recognized the signs—I was letting mine take control. Forcing myself to take slower, deeper breaths, I paused in the living room. My hand landed on the back of the couch as I focused on the air going in and out of my lungs. I heard my own voice, an echo from the past that never fully faded. *I'll take care of you.*

Okay. I could do this.

I had just started toward my room when the door to the stairwell opened. Laurie entered first, looking unusually disheveled, followed closely by a scowling Collith. Each of them bore fresh injuries. Laurie was holding one of his wrists, which looked broken, and dark blood trailed down from Collith's nose.

"What is this?" I demanded, going up to them, examining both for any wounds that weren't healing. Thankfully, all the ones I found were either scabbing over or fading.

Laurie flashed me a cheerful grin when I moved his head, checking the deep cut beneath his right eye. "I caught this fool at a crossroads. We exchanged words."

As soon as I heard the word *crossroads*, I went still. My fingers lingered on Laurie's cheek as I turned to look at Collith. "You were going to offer yourself to Lucifer," I said flatly.

He kept his focus on the wall across from us. His jawline was rigid. "And I still plan to. It's the obvious solution. If he wants a Nightmare so badly, he can have me. Not you."

"Even if he wanted you, which he clearly doesn't, the bastard isn't getting any more Nightmares," Laurie snapped, his silver eyes flaring. "You're not thinking clearly, you noble idiot. What do you think Lucifer will do to our world once he has a body? He's never struck me as the peaceful sort."

"Keep your voices down," I cut in. "Collith, for multiple reasons, you need to leave. The most important one being I don't want Gil to smell your blood."

"I don't know what you're planning," he said, ignoring me, "but I do know that you haven't thought through the consequences. You have no idea what it really costs, making a deal with the Dark Prince."

I should've been furious—here Collith was, accusing me of not considering the consequences, when offering himself to Lucifer would've had monumental repercussions—but I could feel his fear. When I reached for it, I glimpsed an image I hadn't seen before. Collith's body, broken and crumpled on a floor of stone.

Sylvyre stood over him, smiling.

"What does it cost, then?" I asked quietly. Laurie was silent, and I suspected it was because he wanted to know the answer, too.

"Your fucking soul," Collith said, and there was a bleak shadow in his voice now. His urgency had given way to remembrance. Before I could pull him away from the past, Collith spoke again, and I knew it was too late.

"You think you don't need it," he said. His eyes were haunted. "You tell yourself it's worth the sacrifice. But there's no pain that matches it, existing without that part of yourself. And it is existing, Fortuna, because there's no living once he claims your soul. Not even you can come back from that."

Collith met my gaze, and in spite of all the lies he'd fed me since we met, I knew he was telling the truth. Doing this spell would probably be something I'd come to regret.

But it changed nothing.

Collith was still standing there, desperate to save me from the same fate he'd endured. Looking at him, sensing the swiftly unraveling thread of his control, I decided to tell a lie of my own.

"Hey." My voice was even softer now. "Everything is going to be all right. You're blowing this out of proportion."

"I saw the drawer, Fortuna," Collith said.

My stomach dropped. *Shit.* The lube. Earlier, while we were in bed, Collith had gone into the nightstand looking for the lube I kept there. No doubt that was when he saw the documents I'd left for Damon. I swallowed a sigh. Guess there would be no lying my way out of this one.

"I'm an adult, Collith, and I'm sound of mind. I get to make my own choices," I told him.

His expression was carefully blank—just as I had an Unseelie Queen face, Collith had one from his time as king—but there was a storm in those hazel eyes. "I can't let you do this," he said.

It wasn't a threat, though. There was a shift in his voice, almost pleading. He couldn't manipulate me this time, or take my free will. But I knew there was a part of him that wanted to, just as there was in Laurie.

I put my hand on Collith's chest and rose to kiss his cheek. I lingered there for a moment, my lips against his skin, and tried to memorize his scent. His hand pressed against the small of my back, hard, but he didn't touch me beyond that. Maybe he didn't trust himself to.

As I sank back down on my heels and met Collith's gaze, I sensed Laurie moving away. "I made a promise to your mother, did I ever tell you that?" I murmured.

185

Surprise flitted across Collith's austere features. "No. You didn't."

"I told her I'd have faith in you," I said. I swallowed down a rush of fear and reached up to cup his face. "And I do. I really do now. You and I aren't the same people we were in the beginning—if it comes down to it, I trust that you'll do the right thing. Because you're *good*, Collith. I know you think you're broken, but there's so much light in you. The cracks just let it shine through that much more."

I smiled at him, hoping he saw how much I meant it. Slowly, the pressure of Collith's hand lifted. I knew he was about to pull away. On impulse, I rose on my feet again and put my hand on the back of his neck. Our eyes met for an instant, and then I kissed him with the same hungry, unchecked frenzy I'd experienced during our mating ceremony. Collith gripped me back, his tongue tasting me deeply, fingers raking down my spine while the other hand pulled me even closer. My body came alive again, as if Collith's touch was my own personal sirensong.

Luckily, he had more self-control than I did. Collith ended the kiss, but he still lingered, pressing his forehead against mine. "I love you," he said roughly.

Before I could react, he sifted, and my arms fell to my sides. I didn't move.

"Am I banished, as well?" Laurie asked.

I turned my head, following the sound of his voice. The impish faerie leaned against the wall, arms crossed over his chest. Considering his question, I gave Laurie a long, hard stare. "You can stay, but if you interfere with this spell, Laurie, I promise you this. I *will* hold a grudge for the rest of my life, however long that may be, and I will *never* speak to you again."

Laurie stared back at me. His expression gave nothing away, but I knew him—he was searching for weaknesses, evaluating the seriousness of my claim. After a moment, he inclined his head and said, "Shall we?"

He made an elegant gesture, and I walked past him. We finally joined everyone else in the bedroom. Moonlight spilled over the windowsill, casting a glow over the tense stillness. Savannah stood near the bed with an open spellbook balanced on her palms. Everyone else was scattered. Cyrus and Ariel stood with their arms around each other. Nym was curled in the armchair, frowning at his palms. Gil and Seth were seated on the floor, their heads bent in conversation. Apparently some bonding had taken place during their time together. I was glad.

"Fortuna?" a sweet voice ventured. I turned to Ariel, unsurprised that she was the first one to speak. She flashed her dimples at me and said, "It is an honor to serve you again."

Collith asked you to do this, didn't he? I thought, searching the faerie's bright, open expression. Ariel was loyal to her king, first and foremost, and not even Collith's dethroning had changed that. I also knew why he'd asked her to do this. It wasn't to spy on me, or get access to me. Collith just wanted someone he could trust at my side.

I smiled at Ariel and told her, "The honor is mine. Thank you for making my friend so happy."

She grinned at the male at her side and bumped his hip with hers. This brought my attention to Cyrus. He looked back at me without flinching, eyes as clear as a summer sky. Looking at him, I realized that I wasn't the only one who had changed since all this started.

"You're a beautiful person, Cyrus Lavender," I said. "Thank you for giving me a home when I didn't have one."

The dragon stepped forward, bent, and hugged me. I recovered and hugged him back, closing my eyes tightly. After a few seconds, Cyrus let go and moved back, putting his arm around Ariel again. My gaze lingered on the two of them, happiness swelling in my chest.

Sensing another presence behind me, I turned to face Emma. This was a goodbye I'd been avoiding, too. Emma knew, of course—her eyes glistened with the sheen of unshed tears as she smiled, cupping my face in her rough hands. "Never forget how strong you are," she said. "Or that you are *loved*."

I blinked rapidly and nodded. I didn't trust myself to speak. Slowly, she let me go, too.

After Emma, I went over to Seth and Gil. The goblin's eyes were bright with excitement, and I swallowed the words I'd been about to say to give him another chance to back out. Somehow, I knew it would hurt him. "When I get back, we should actually hang out," I said.

Seth beamed. "Absolutely."

I forced myself to face Gil. Sparing me from an awkward speech, he sighed and hooked his arm around my neck, pulling me to him. To my relief, the coppery scent of blood was gone. "You're a pain in the ass, did you know that?" my friend said, the words muffled as he squeezed me.

I uttered a brief, watery laugh. "So are you."

His hold loosened and I pulled back, taking a shuddering breath. There was more I wanted to say, others I wanted to embrace one last time. But Savannah kept looking at the moon, and I knew we needed to begin. As I returned to the center of the room, I touched Nym's sleeve in passing, acknowledging him. He just dipped his head in a slow, reverent bow.

Feeling self-conscious about the number of eyes on me, I got into bed and lay down, just as the necromancer had instructed me to. I adjusted the covers, and the future members of my Court stood all around the bed, except one.

Finn arrived just as I was starting to get worried.

He must've been at Bea's, because I recognized the scent on his clothes from the countless times I'd thrown my uniform in the laundry and that smell wafted up. Grease and coffee. I searched the werewolf's expression, wondering if he'd been hoping to see the girl who reminded him of his daughter. I had hoped those days were behind him. That things were getting easier for him.

He didn't look at me as he moved to my side. I knew Finn wasn't okay, not entirely, but just the sight of him loosened some of the tightness in my chest. It was easier to breathe, too. I felt the back of his warm hand brush against mine, and I let out a small breath.

Hearing it, Finn reached for the bond between us. Gentle encouragement shone from his end like a star. A reminder that I wasn't going into this battle alone. With fresh resolve, I adjusted my head on the pillow and focused on the ceiling.

As everyone else drew closer, there were four figures who stood apart.

The first was Laurie, of course, being king of his own Court and all. Emma was the second. She was human, and Savannah didn't think she'd be strong enough to survive the spell. But the older woman had insisted on being here for moral support. Adam kept his distance, as well, and I wondered for the hundredth time if his allegiance rested with Dracula or himself. He'd come back from his mysterious trip in the afternoon, and only the knowledge that I wasn't completely abandoning Gil made it possible to leave.

Adam caught me looking at him, and I realized we'd never said goodbye. I'd been a little distracted since getting his text, considering it had been while Collith and Laurie were here. *Take care of Gil*, I mouthed, knowing I didn't need to say anything else. He was Adam; words weren't his thing, anyway.

The vampire nodded. He didn't even hesitate. Seeing that, even more of the pressure in my body eased.

"All right, then. I think we have everything we need to get started. Stand in a circle around Fortuna, and hold hands, please," Savannah said.

Everyone moved to obey, and their shadows slanted over the wooden floor. Cyrus. Ariel. Nym. Gil. Seth. Finn. I didn't know what Viessa would think about losing two of her people to me, but right now, I didn't care.

Despite Finn's presence, it still felt like we were missing someone. I didn't let myself look at the last person who'd stayed at the edge of the room.

It wasn't Collith. If I'd been able to ask him to be part of the spell, I knew what he would have chosen. He'd all but admitted to Laurie, when they thought I was asleep at the motel, that he hadn't let go of his throne. So he would've opted out, no matter how badly he might want to be part of my life.

But Lyari had surprised me—she was the fourth one who stood against that far wall. I could still hear her voice in my head, saying that she wouldn't be part of the spell tonight. Had it really only been two hours ago?

My mind went back. Two hours ago, I'd emerged from my room, drawn by the sound of footsteps. Collith and Laurie were still getting dressed. Lyari must've been waiting for the three of us to finish our . . . activities, because I found her pacing in front of the fire.

The instant she'd heard the door open, she'd spun and blurted, *I can't do this.*

I'd paused, the crackling fire the only sound in the loft. I knew, without turning, that the room behind me would be empty—Laurie and Collith had sifted to give us some privacy. Frowning, I faced my Right Hand across the high-ceilinged room, and she waited for my response with cold, distant eyes. It was the way she used to look at me when she was a Guardian and I hated the fae. Back before trust grew between us, and eventually, friendship.

That friendship was why I'd pushed her, of course. If Lyari was part of the spell, her transition into a goblin would stop. It was such an obvious solution.

Our argument still rang in my ears.

Tell me what's going on, Lyari. Maybe I can help, I'd said.

Her lips were thin with irritation. *There's nothing "going on."*

Then give me a reason. If you can do that, I promise I'll drop it. It's your life. But at least give me one reason to explain why.

In the end, she'd refused to answer.

Hiding my frustration, I finally allowed myself to look at Lyari. It felt like the distance between us had widened even more, and she stood in a dim corner, her expression half-hidden.

"Are you sure?" I asked her.

Lyari shook her head, and I got that sense again. I heard that faint, insistent thought. *Something is wrong.*

But the time had passed for a heart-to-heart. I could only hope that Lyari took care of herself while I was gone, and that we'd have another chance to repair the bridge between us.

"Okay," I said. "Let's do this."

Tension rose around me. Offering any sort of comfort seemed like it would just make things worse, so I ignored it. My gaze met Laurie's across the room. Warmth and longing filled my heart.

"If you go through with this, you'll probably die," he said matter-of-factly.

I glared at him. So much for a mature goodbye. "That should tell you exactly how sure I am," I countered.

I was lying through my teeth, and both of us knew it. But we also had an audience, and Laurie had learned my family was a hard limit, so he didn't call me out in front of them. Smart faerie.

Savannah cleared her throat. "Before we begin, I need a name."

I frowned up at her. "What?"

"For the spell," she clarified. "The wording is very specific, and in order to direct the magic, I need to give it a focus. Does your new Court have a name?"

"It's not a . . ." I started. Then I stopped myself. Why was I fighting this so hard? Because I was so afraid of being a queen again? That wasn't what was happening here, not in the same capacity. These were people I cared about. People I trusted. The fact they were standing in this room with me was proof of how different we were from the faerie Courts.

Savannah was still waiting for a name.

I thought about it, my gaze falling to the floor while I drew a complete blank. As the silence lingered, I noticed the shapes slanting over the wood. Shadows. They were neither darkness nor light. Something always in between. My eyes shot back up, and I studied the faces around me. It fit perfectly.

"The Shadow Court," I said.

It was a moniker the Unseelie Court was known by, and it was fitting, but I would claim it for us nonetheless. We were the gray ones, the strange ones. The wounded and the vulnerable. The strong and the dangerous. They made us powerful, our shadow selves. Our eternal struggles. We wouldn't be ashamed of them anymore.

Now, we would claim them.

"Okay, then. The Shadow Court it is." Savannah took a deep breath, her fingers curling around the edges of the book.

There were certain moments in life when you had the thought: *My life is never going to be the same after this.* I'd learned to take note of such moments. I looked at the people I loved, and I wasn't afraid.

Savannah called the magic forth using ingredients she'd gathered and the words pouring out of her mouth. There was a bowl on the nightstand, and at one point during her incantation, Savannah dropped a match in it. Smoke coiled through the room. As Savannah picked up a knife, I felt it. A slight temperature change in the room.

Magic.

The first half of the spell—the bonding part—was exactly how I remembered from the times I'd performed it with Gil and Finn. We all did our cuts and vows. There were a few alterations, because there was a group of us, instead of two people. The others had to exchange blood, as well, not just with me. Bonding them made all of us stronger.

Within seconds of the final blood exchange, new threads appeared in my mind. They were bright and golden.

Before I could marvel at them, Savannah's voice came from a distance. "Fortuna? Fortuna, it's done. We should be able to proceed with the second part of the spell."

Once again, my eyes flicked around the bed. This time, I could feel the connections to them. Connections that had always been there, but now they were marked with magic. Amplified. They felt . . . right.

The easy part was done. Now came the part that had sent me to my brother's side earlier tonight, needing a reminder of why I was doing this. Why any of us were. Knowing this could possibly be the last time I spoke to my family, I swallowed and thought about what I wanted to say. For once, the words came easily.

"I love you. You should know that, before all this goes to hell. Literally." My eyes moved beyond them, including Emma, Lyari, and Adam in what I was saying. I smiled at them and added, "Thank you for finding me. For being my family."

When it was clear I'd finished, Laurie pushed off the wall. He rounded the bed and stopped at my side. He didn't say anything, and the rest of the room faded away. We looked at each other silently.

It felt like we'd been here before. At the Unseelie Court, just before I battled Jassin. At the mouth of an ancient tomb, just before Laurie sacrificed what he valued most to spare me from doing the same. We'd survived every time. We always survived, and then we found each other on the other side.

"I can do this," I said. A slight waver in my voice betrayed me. I tipped my chin up and looked at Laurie. "Right?"

The corners of his beautiful mouth turned downward, and his brows drew together. I could see the struggle in his starry eyes—he still didn't approve of my choice. He was probably pondering the cage he'd mentioned earlier, and whether he should put me in it until the full moon had passed. I waited patiently, trusting him to make the right decision, just as I had with Collith.

Finally Laurie said, his voice soft, "You're the bravest creature I've ever met."

They were the same words he'd given me as I prepared for the fight with Jassin. I felt my heart shift, as if it were releasing a faint sigh. I hoped Laurie could see the truth in my eyes, because even now, I couldn't bring myself to say it out loud. *I love you, too,* I told him silently.

He saw it. Of course he did. I watched Laurie's expression change, as if my admission hurt him but also brought a rush of joy. His long fingers clenched as he fought, more than ever before, against the urge to pluck me up and whisk me away, like he was one of the fae from those old, twisted fairy tales.

"You can start, Savannah," I said, shifting my attention to the figure hovering behind Laurie.

Slowly, the Seelie King moved away, and a wide-eyed necromancer stepped up to take his place. To my relief, Savannah's voice was steadier than the hands holding that spellbook.

"One more thing," she told me. "Magic always seeks balance. For every spell that is done, it comes with at least one way it can be undone. Look for a sign when you first arrive in the Dark Prince's dimension. It might be subtle, like a stray thought or a doodle you feel compelled to do. It could be words, or an ingredient. There's no way of knowing for certain."

"Great," I responded weakly. I could sense the unease coming from the people around my bed. Quickly I said, "What do you need from me?"

"Nothing. Just try to stay still." Her focus moved away from me, and her next words were directed to my family. "Repeat after me. Concentrate on your intent as you speak."

They began to chant. It was a low, eerie sound, and tension built in my shoulders as I waited for something to happen. I wasn't sure what I expected. But the seconds ticked by, the chant went on, and nothing changed. Was the spell even working? I fought to hold back an anxious frown.

And then . . . something did happen.

The sensation was subtle at first. Almost indiscernible, like the smallest of slivers tucked beneath my fingernail. I stared up at the ceiling, focusing completely on my body. The voices of my Court faded into a background hum as the imaginary slivers went deeper. They became shards of glass. I felt my mouth open in the beginnings of a scream, but an explosion of agony silenced me.

It felt like I was dying.

Then I was falling through light, flipping and turning, with nothing but air and panic to grab onto. There was a rushing sound in my ears, and I couldn't hear my family's chants anymore. It felt as though I was being put together and pulled apart all at once. I couldn't sob or beg for help. At some point, I heard a single sound leave my throat, something akin to a whimper.

Heat surrounded me, so intense that I knew there would be no surviving it. While the pain ripped me apart, I was blinded by images. Disjointed, senseless scenes. Crowds. Battles. Creatures I'd never seen the likes of before. Clouds. Stars. I kept falling, relentlessly enduring that vivid pain, my mouth stretched in a soundless scream. A cruel, colorful parade of panic and images went on and on, and there was no end in sight.

The end did come eventually. There was another flash of light and agony, and after that, beautiful, merciful darkness. By the time it closed in around me, I was ready for it. I went into it willingly.

A small eternity passed. I was floating. Everything was quiet, peaceful. I was nothing and no one. There was only a vague sense of existence, and even that didn't matter.

Then I woke up in Hell.

CHAPTER TWELVE

When I opened my eyes again, I was so disoriented that I felt like a newborn.

I blinked, putting a word to the action, and struggled to form more coherent thoughts. It was a sensation similar to waking up, a sort of hazy confusion as dreams and reality collided. I didn't think I was awake, though. There was something against my back and everything was so dark. I blinked some more, trying to look around. But the dream was too unfocused, or maybe there was something wrong with my eyes. I still didn't panic. Every dream ended, after all. I just had to wait.

Then something moved.

I was in a room of sorts, I thought faintly. Something big had detached from the ceiling. Whatever it was drew closer, and it became a looming blur. I frowned up at the shape, still too bleary to feel anything like fear or alarm. It was too dark to make out any of its features, but I could see the outline of wings. The sounds coming from its throat seemed like the language of an insect, all chitters and clicks. Even now, I felt no fear. This was just a strange dream. Nothing could truly hurt you in a dream, could it?

I didn't know my own name, much less what was or wasn't possible.

Noise erupted into the silence. The creature launched into the air, flapping its wings. The darkness swallowed it, and a moment later, something else moved. This shape was on the ground, walking on two legs, and it was much smaller than the one I'd just faced. My vision was beginning to clear. I blinked some more and watched it come toward me. A bright light flickered near its head. Other shapes were behind it. They carried lights, too. *Torches*, I thought.

They crowded the room, and I cringed away from them. I huddled in the shadows, still devastatingly disoriented. They were talking, I had managed to put that much together. But the words were meaningless and guttural.

A few seconds after that, I finally realized that I was naked.

With limbs that didn't feel like mine, I brought my knees to my chest. A curtain of hair fell into my eyes. As I sat there, watching the blurs argue amongst each other, a new thought occurred to me.

What if this wasn't a dream?

I must've made a sound, because the shapes suddenly quieted. One of them dared to approach. It knelt next to me with slow, deliberate movements. It spoke again, and I stared into its black eyes, startled that I could actually see them now. I could see everything.

Long, dark hair draped over its massive shoulders. It had two slits in the middle of its face, and teeth that could only be described as fangs. They were so big they hugged the curve of its top and bottom lips. Its fingernails were black, and the ones on its long, arched feet looked more like black claws.

But this creature's most jarring feature was its skin—every inch was gray and mottled. The texture looked like scabs, or maybe scales.

My gaze shifted, taking in the details of the creatures filling the room behind it. They looked similar, with slight variations in height, build, and facial features.

The quiet didn't last long. Their voices were loud again, their eyes wide and wondering as they took me in, this strange thing that clearly did not belong. I tensed, on the verge of moving away from their torches and stares. Before I could, the creature in front of me turned and said something to them, its voice low and sharp. Once they'd fallen silent, it faced me again, and it repeated the words it had been saying.

Suddenly, in a burst of clarity, I understood. It was speaking in English, my own tongue.

"What's your name? Are you hurt?" the creature was asking.

I still didn't answer; I couldn't. The memories were coming back now, in all the brightness and the noise.

I remembered finding my mother's body in a shadowed hallway. Peering out a window at my brother's empty garden. Meeting a hazel-eyed faerie through the bars of a cage. Then the images starting coming even faster and closer together, and I couldn't process them quickly enough to fully grasp all the information. So much pain. So much death. But . . . there was joy, too.

The creature closest to me shifted, drawing my attention back to it. *Him*, I corrected silently. He was wearing a ragged loincloth, so I couldn't tell for certain, but I was pretty confident.

I realized I'd never responded to his questions. This one emanated kindness, while the rest eyed me with curiosity or distaste. But still I could not bring myself to utter a sound or syllable. I squeezed my knees with white fingers and grappled in vain for a coherent thought or sentence. There was a reason I was here, I knew that now. I'd come to this place seeking something.

My new friend said something else. The crowd dispersed quickly after that, though some moved slowly or grumbled under their breath. Even then, I couldn't speak. When the quiet stretched and thinned, my rescuer stood. I tried to protest by reaching out a feeble hand toward him. I needn't have worried; the creature came back within seconds. There was something tucked over his arm.

He squatted again, handing the blanket over in such a way that we didn't touch. The material was scratchy and gray. I draped it over my shoulders and managed a tiny, tentative smile. The creature closed one eye. A wink.

Now that my eyes were working, and my brain had finally rebooted, as well, I took stock of my surroundings again. It was an enormous room, but I absorbed the smaller details. Much like the Unseelie Court, the space was lit with torches on the walls. The ceiling was so high up that I couldn't make out anything at the top. Whatever I'd seen when I first woke up—that huge thing with wings—was tucked deep into the darkness. It could stay there, as far as I was concerned. Farther down, there were narrow openings in the walls that had the feel of an afterthought, like, oh, maybe the occupants of this place might like some light or fresh air. The make-shift windows were too far away to see anything through, however.

At ground level, there were two sets of doors. One small and square, the other vast and tall. The square set looked like it led into a lift of some kind, surrounded by a metal frame and made of wire mesh. Or this world's version of it, at least. The doors opposite were wide open, but at this angle, I couldn't see what waited beyond.

And all around me were . . . rocks. Piles and piles of rocks. Some were absolutely massive, reaching for the ceiling, and many more were smaller. One of those piles was what I had been leaning against this entire time.

"Is that your name? Rain?" the gray-skinned creature asked, making me jump.

As soon as he pointed it out, I realized that while I was looking around, I'd been muttering under my breath. A single word, over and over again, like a mindless chant. *Rain. Rain. Rain.*

It felt like a lightning bolt shot through my heart, and I heard a voice in my head. Another memory.

Magic always seeks balance. For every spell that is done, it comes with at least one way it can be undone. Look for a sign when you first arrive in the Dark Prince's dimension. It might be subtle, like a stray thought or a doodle you feel compelled to do. It could be words, or an ingredient.

Savannah's spell. The missing piece.

In order to trigger the spell again, and get back to my world, I needed to find rain.

The gray-skinned creature was still waiting for an answer. I raised my gaze, holding the blanket so tightly I could feel the bite of my nails. When I spoke, I expected my voice to be a thin rasp. Instead, it was steel.

"My name is Fortuna Sworn," I said. "And I'm here to see your king."

Hell wasn't a pit of flames.

Lucifer had told me it wasn't, but now I knew he'd been telling the truth. As one of his creatures carried me through the city, I looked around with bleary curiosity. It felt like we were on the outskirts. There were oddly-shaped shanties on either side—or at least, I thought they were shanties. The walls looked like they were made of packed dirt. We weren't alone in the street, but the figures I did see—they looked human—were either lying on the ground or walking listlessly. With the flickering horizon and dark sky, everything had an eerie feel to it.

Savannah's spell had worked. I was in Hell.

Traveling between dimensions had taken its toll, though. Not just mentally, but physically. Back in that vast room full of rocks, I'd quickly discovered I couldn't walk. After watching me attempt to stand half a dozen times, the gray-skinned creature had unceremoniously lifted me in his arms, which were as thick as the branches on my tree in the dreamscape. He'd carried me outside without comment and started in the direction of the skyscrapers I had seen in my dream.

"Where are you taking me?" I mumbled. I didn't even try to fight him. Talking took up too much of my energy.

The creature's answer made his chest rumble, and I felt the vibrations against my shoulder as he said, "The king's tower."

Hearing those words made the fog around my mind begin to dissipate. Though seeing Lucifer was inevitable, not to mention necessary, I felt a rush of panic. Now I did fight the urge to struggle. Seeking a distraction, I tipped my head back to appraise the creature's stoic face. It took me several seconds to say, "What is your name?"

He kept walking, his eyes fixed on the road ahead. "I don't have one, my lady."

No name? But why? Because he hadn't been given one, or because he'd forgotten it?

Before I could decide whether or not to pry, something darted past us—it looked like a cat, but the cats I'd seen didn't have fan-like webbing on their backs or fangs that nearly touched the ground. I still didn't have full use of my arms or legs, but I could move them. I pointed at the animal and asked, "What is that?"

"It's called a bajang," the creature carrying me said. Then he added, like an afterthought, "They survive off blood."

Oh. Lovely, I thought weakly.

Other things moved in the shadows, too. Some of them had eyes that glowed. They must've been intimidated by the creature carrying me, because nothing came into the open or tried to attack us. I wanted to ask my champion more questions, but I knew I needed to conserve what little strength I had for the encounter with Lucifer. The words I couldn't say crowded in my throat. How could I feel everything even though I didn't have a body? Were souls endlessly tortured here, as my world believed? And most importantly, what was that *smell*? It clung to the air like mold, so putrid that my nose was beginning to sting. The creature carrying me didn't seem to notice.

Those questions became quieter as I stared at the strange new world I found myself in. The deeper we went into the city, the more it changed. The packed-down street became a smooth road of stone. The shanties became buildings, no, businesses. There were neon signs—they had electricity here?—and the streets and sidewalks overflowed with so many different animals and creatures that I found myself questioning if this was a dream again. And the *noise*. Contraptions that looked like steampunk carriages rolled past, and the beasts pulling them had long trunks where a muzzle would be on a horse. They brayed and stomped their cracked hooves. Figures lounged against walls, many of them naked, not all of them human-looking. Were the ones that did look human souls from my world?

It was too loud to ask the creature above me, but at least we'd left the stench behind. The urge to gag subsided as I continued to take it all in.

By the time we arrived at the tower, it felt like I was in a glittering metropolis . . . if a metropolis usually had scaly creatures and bloodthirsty cats walking around. In this part of the city, I even saw a machine that resembled a car. As my gray friend drew to a stop, I didn't need to ask if this was the tower he had mentioned. I arched my head back, looking up at the intimidating structure.

It was like something out of a dark fairy tale.

There were no buildings on either side of the tower because it took up the entire block. Its sides were made of sharp-edged, gleaming black surfaces that looked like marble. The doors reminded me of the entrance of a church. They were shaped in a pointed arch, and the surface of each one was covered in markings and symbols I didn't recognize. As I stared at Lucifer's giant monstrosity, I finally put my finger on why his tower was so menacing.

There wasn't a single green or growing thing in sight.

The creature with no name carried me up the stairs, and soon we entered a gleaming lobby. Once again, I thought of a church. The floor was made of black tile and the ceiling was far, far above our heads. I raised my gaze, then did a double take. I registered what I was seeing, and it felt like the air froze in my lungs.

The lobby wasn't empty.

On the far side of the space, there was a single elevator. Standing in front of the doors were three enormous creatures. I might've compared them to dogs or wolves, but each of them had what looked like a serpent's tail, a mane of snakes, and feline paws. Thankfully, the beasts didn't seem to find us a threat. All three of them were lying down, watching us from between slitted eyes. One was even sleeping.

Cerberus, a voice in my head whispered. The mythology from my world must've gotten some of the details wrong.

It made me wonder what else we'd gotten wrong.

I was stiff, anticipating that these . . . things would still try to eat us. My mind was already assessing the distance between us and them, trying to figure out if we could reach the doors faster than the dogs.

"They will not harm you as long as you don't press the button," the creature holding me said, nodding toward the small, hand-sized square beside the elevator. It glowed like a normal elevator button from home.

Hearing this, I relaxed a little. But not much. "Will you put me down?" I asked. "I'd like to try walking again."

He heeded the request instantly, and I used one of his thick arms for balance as he set me upright. I released him to see if I could stand on my own. My legs were shaky, but at least they supported my weight now. I turned to thank my gray-skinned friend and found the space beside me empty. He was gone.

A few seconds after I noticed this, a low-toned *ding* echoed through the room. The elevator opened, and a woman came out. Or at least, she looked like a woman. She was tall and willowy, dressed in black clothing that clung to every curve, and her platinum blond hair gleamed in an elegant updo. She walked past the three beasts as if they were nothing more than chihuahuas, and one of them gave her a half-hearted growl. She ignored it, her focus trained solely on me. Her heels clipped against the tile. Then she got close enough for me to see her face, and I realized this was no woman.

Her eyes were white. Completely, creepily white. Where an iris and pupils should've been was an empty space, like someone had sucked all the color out.

"Welcome, Lady Sworn," the stranger said in accented English. She drew to a halt, keeping a healthy distance between us, and I wondered if some of the city's stench lingered on me. Her expression revealed nothing as she added, "Please, come this way."

The beautiful blond made a gesture that indicated the elevator, and I just nodded. My mouth tasted like ash and my stomach had started churning. Was it possible to vomit in this dimension, considering I'd left my real body back on Earth?

Oblivious to the danger, Lucifer's lackey turned and strode away without waiting to see if I could keep up. I hurried after her, relieved to find my legs were a little stronger now. It took us several seconds to cross the vast room. Compared to the noise of her heels, my bare feet were soundless on the gleaming floor. I was still wearing nothing except the scratchy blanket, and I held it tighter around me as we passed the three beasts. Their black eyes followed our progress, their heads turning slowly.

My new guide didn't offer any comfort or reassurance. She pressed the button with black-tipped fingernails, and the doors opened immediately. We got on without a word, and the blond passed her hand over a screen. It came awake, white symbols racing over the dark surface. I recognized Enochian, but my grasp of the angelic tongue was still rudimentary, at best. The words also moved too quickly. Blondie pressed something at the top of the screen and stepped back. Still silent, she folded her hands in front of her and raised her pale gaze. While she focused on the glowing number above the doors, my gaze flicked around, noting the floor-to-ceiling window behind us and a camera tucked in one of the corners overhead.

A moment later, the elevator shot into the sky like a bullet, and I almost lost my balance. As I stumbled, I glanced over at Blondie, expecting to see a smirk. She just stared at the symbols changing over the doors. I wanted to ask her if the person who'd taken her eyes had also taken her personality. Self-preservation stopped me—I didn't know what this creature was capable of, or whether she had a temper. My instincts said she was a demon, and I knew better than anyone what demons were capable of.

Remembering that night hardened something inside me. And my legs finally stopped shaking.

A second later, I heard that *ding* again, and the doors slid open. A long walkway loomed ahead. The left side was made of normal walls and doors. The right was made of arches, a low wall, and pillars. There was no glass in the openings, and in a way, the result reminded me of the Colosseum in Rome. But the Colosseum probably didn't have as many cameras as this place, I thought as I noted more of them, tucked into shadows and pockets. Were the cameras a security measure? Did that mean the King of Hell could actually be harmed?

We hadn't gone very far down the walkway when Blondie opened one of the doors. She stood to the side, waiting for me to go in first. My focus sharpened, and my heart kicked into overdrive.

This was it. This was the moment I would come face-to-face with the Dark Prince.

And all I was wearing was a smelly blanket.

There was no time to panic, because in the next moment, we entered a room that could only be Lucifer's office. It seemed strange that the devil even had one. For some reason, I'd always imagined him in an empty world of fire and eternal suffering. Not this normal-looking space that could be from my own world.

To my relief, its owner was nowhere to be seen. But the relief was immediately followed by a burst of impatience. I just wanted to get this meeting over with so Damon would be awoken and I could start the process of returning home.

"There's some clothing on the sofa. It should be your size. Would you like any refreshments while you wait?" Blondie's tone was bland, her eyes flat. She hadn't moved from the doorway.

"There's food in Hell?" I asked, darting a glance toward the sofa. Just as Blondie had said, there was a folded pile resting on one of the cushions. I turned back to her, but the demon just looked at me. Waiting. I knew it was probably safe, since Lucifer needed me alive for his nefarious purposes, but the thought of eating made my stomach roll. I shook my head. "No, thanks."

Without another word, Blondie retreated and closed the door.

I made a beeline for the clothing and put everything on hurriedly beneath the blanket. The soft, dark pants fit perfectly, and the sweater, also black, settled on my frame as if it had been made for me. Whoever had brought the outfit had even thought to include a pair of slip-on shoes with low heels.

Now that I was alone—and no longer naked—my gaze darted around curiously, and I paid closer attention to the details of Lucifer's inner sanctum. By the right wall there was a mammoth desk, complete with an intricate chair, stacks of paper, and an advanced-looking computer. What did this creature have to write, I wondered? The floor even had a rug laid out. It was a disorienting pattern, all swirls and never-ending lines. One of the walls was made of glass, and another was covered in a floor-to-ceiling bookcase. Overhead, a chandelier cast a glow over everything.

Definitely not what I would have expected.

"You certainly know how to make an entrance," someone said from the doorway.

I spun, making a startled sound. I knew that voice.

Lucifer leaned against the doorframe.

The sight of him sent my thoughts into a dim frenzy. It was the first time we'd truly laid eyes on each other. Stood in each other's presence. No more dreams, no more hosts.

It was just me and the devil.

He looked like he'd stepped out of the pages of *GQ* magazine. Lucifer's muscular body was clothed in black slacks, a white button-up, and a jacket. It was still jarring, seeing him in a style from my world. The sleeves were shoved casually to his elbows, revealing forearms that were hard and defined. His biceps strained at the material. He also wore expensive-looking leather shoes.

There was no sign of the metal wings.

"Welcome to my dimension, Fortuna Sworn. I apologize for your reception. Had I known how you'd be arriving, I would have made far more ideal arrangements," he said courteously.

"Where . . ." I touched my throat and cleared it, using the pause to scrape my composure back together.

"It may take another day or two for you to fully recover. Traveling between dimensions isn't as simple as walking through a Door. We're fortunate that you awoke in one of the seven cities. Imagine if you'd landed in the Waste." Lucifer straightened and stepped aside, gesturing to the open doorway. "Follow me, please."

I stayed where I was. "Where's my brother?"

Lucifer put his hands in his pockets. "I've already reached out to my contacts in your world. Witches should be performing the spell to put his soul back in his body."

"Prove it."

"I plan to," he said patiently. "But in order to do that, I need you to follow me."

He was still standing by the door, and he inclined his bright head, indicating the walkway beyond. I stood there for another second, feeling stubborn and paranoid. But I hadn't come all this way just to hide in Lucifer's office. I raised my chin and walked past him, unable to shake the feeling that I was putting my back to a deadly predator. The devil stepped out and closed the door behind us, moving with the same thoughtless grace that Collith and Laurie did. The comparison unsettled me.

I turned, intending to examine my surroundings and push any thoughts about Collith and Laurie from my mind. A small creature darted across our path, and I couldn't stop the startled sound that escaped me. Even in the brief glimpse I'd gotten, there was no missing its big, hairy legs and numerous eyes. I fought the instinct to go right back into that office and lock the door.

Lucifer paused, too, but he was watching me instead of the shadows, where more of those things were scuttling. "They're called mazzikin. Mostly harmless. Pests," he said dismissively.

Mostly harmless? I eyed one of them. Seeing the mazzikin made me think of the other strange species I'd glimpsed since coming to this dimension. "What were those creatures that found me? The ones with the gray skin?" I asked.

The devil started walking, forcing me to do the same, although I didn't love getting closer to the mazzikin. He tilted his head as he considered my question. "Ah, that would be a baloc demon. They are the only ones who can work the mines, because their bodies are able to withstand the heat."

Demon? I echoed silently, blinking. It made sense, of course. And yet I hadn't thought of that sad, nameless creature as one of the things I loathed with every fiber of my being. Could it be that demons were like faeries, and some of them had the capacity to be good? The possibility made me frown.

"The one who brought me here was . . . very kind," I said. "He spoke English."

"Some of them do. It's easy enough to pick up, hearing it from the souls that reside in the city."

"Reside?" I echoed with raised brows. "So they're not being tortured?"

Before Lucifer could answer, my gaze shifted. I registered the view, and I stopped in the middle of the walkway, staring. I sensed Lucifer coming to stand beside me, and a cool breeze carried his scent to me.

"Welcome to the First City, Fortuna," he murmured.

It was the place Lucifer had shown me in the dreamscape. From this vantage point, it was even more alien and unnerving. Interspersed amongst the modern-looking skyscrapers, there were the black, jagged bits of rock I'd noticed before, standing up from the ground far below like enormous claws scraping the sky. But it seemed like there *was* no sky—the space above the towers and streets was unending darkness, broken only by brief, strange flashes of red, like colored lightning or a flickering fire. Winged things circled the air like vultures, just like I remembered.

As I leaned over the ledge to see one more closely, I thought about the remark Lucifer had made. *We're fortunate that you awoke in one of the seven cities.* I pulled back and looked at him. "Earlier, you said something about cities. But I was taught there were seven circles in Hell. Are they the same thing?"

Lucifer smiled at me, and for an instant, it felt like my heart forgot to beat. "Well, I don't know about circles, but we certainly have seven cities, yes. This world is mostly wasteland and fire. I placed seven settlements throughout the planet, directly where its most valuable resources are. What else would you like to know?"

He waited, and there was a light in his eyes I hadn't seen before— he liked my questions. He liked sharing this place with me. I frowned, annoyed that I was actually having a civil conversation with the devil. I hadn't forgotten everything he'd done, and he didn't deserve civility.

In an abrupt movement, I stepped closer to the low wall and looked far below. I did it mostly to hide my frustration, but then I noticed all the activity. I'd been too disoriented to notice much during my time on those streets. It occurred to me that I could've walked right past someone I'd met before. Or some*thing*.

"Are they all demons?" I asked. My fingers dug into the stone ledge as a memory lashed at me. *Trees overhead. Ian McConnell's leering face. Headlights on a dark road.*

"Demons, souls, and an assortment of other creatures, just as it is in your world."

"So the dead really do come to Hell," I murmured, tortured by the thought. The people I loved, the family I'd surrounded myself with, tended to see the world in shades of gray. Some of the things they did might be considered evil, to a judge and jury. Did that mean they were damned?

Lucifer considered this. "Death is simply the degeneration of a body. The soul is untethered from the dimension the body formed in. Hell is one of the dimensions it can travel to. Heaven is another. And there are many, many others in between. Some choose to remain in the world they died in."

It took me an extra beat to understand his meaning. "Ghosts. You're saying ghosts are real?" I managed.

"Of course." He cocked his head. "You find that difficult to believe? In spite of what you are and everything you've seen?"

I didn't answer, because my mind had already moved on to another question I'd always wanted to know the answer to. I was about to ask Lucifer whether it was true, the belief that all Fallen creatures went to Hell. But before I could say a word, the devil lifted his hand and brushed a strand of hair out of my eye.

He'd never touched me before, not in his true form.

The feel of his skin brought heat, and lust, and fear.

Seeing my reaction, Lucifer's expression shifted, and he didn't move away. My gaze dropped to his mouth. For the first time, I understood what it must feel like to be one of my victims. To be terrified and wanting at the same time. I fought a rush of urges, all of them conflicting. *Run. Move closer. Flee. Find out what he tastes like.*

A delicate cough shattered the stillness.

Lucifer didn't react, but I jumped and moved backward, as if we'd been caught doing something we shouldn't. My eyes darted to the walkway behind Lucifer, where an old man stood, looking as though he had been plucked from the pages of a novel. He had two tufts of white hair, each one sticking over a large ear. His frame was bony and stooped. His clothes were loose and threadbare.

But then my gaze lowered, and I realized this was no old man. In the place where his feet should've been, shoes or bare toes poking out from the hem of his pants, there were hooves.

"Samael is causing trouble again, my liege," the stranger said, politely ignoring my stare.

Irritation flashed in Lucifer's eyes—Samael seemed to be a sore spot for him, I noted silently, wondering if this information might be useful later on. Was Samael a person? A place? Oblivious to the way my attention had intensified, Lucifer gestured between me and the newcomer. "Fortuna, this is Roger. I trust him above all others, so he's been charged with your care. If you need anything, he will bring it. I'm afraid the display of your brother's good health will have to wait."

Out of everything Lucifer had just said, my mind latched onto one detail more than the rest. *Roger?* The devil's most trusted demon was named *Roger?*

Then I realized Lucifer was leaving. And he'd conveniently avoided showing me proof that the spell over Damon had been lifted. I also hadn't asked about the weather in this dimension, and specifically, when I could expect a friendly rain shower.

"Wait. I have more questions," I said tersely, brushing past Roger to charge after his master. I followed Lucifer up a wide staircase, our feet making soft sounds against the stone. "Wait!"

He didn't, so I stayed on his heels. As we neared the top, though, the sky distracted me, and I tipped my head back to see more. It was the same dusky red it had been the last time, the roiling clouds flashing constantly, like there was an eerie strobe light hidden somewhere inside them.

Then we emerged into the open, and I found myself in a courtyard. But it was a courtyard from a nightmare or a gothic novel. Pillars lined the circular roof, all of them connected at the top, and they were a different stone than the rest of the tower—they looked older, somehow, and obsidian. The carvings on them were strange and jagged.

Lucifer strode to the center of that stone circle, and I looked up again, noting the frozen creatures perched above us. Gargoyles.

In many ways, they looked fae. Pointed ears, long bodies, high cheekbones. But that was where the similarities ended. These statues had snouts instead of noses, their spines were curved, and they had been given wings. Their wings were different than Lucifer's, though, as if they'd been plucked off enormous bats and sewn on. The carvings were so detailed that I could see thin, veiny lines in the stone. The toes that curled over the edge of the stone had claws. The way the creatures perched reminded me of birds that gathered on building ledges and laundry lines.

Lucifer's voice floated across the rooftop. "The gargoyles like you."

"Funny. What is this place?" I asked, refocusing on him.

The devil was pulling on the wings that I'd seen before. They looked heavy, but he handled them as if they weighed nothing. *How does he get them to flap?* I wondered. There had to be a spell on the wings so they responded to his thoughts or impulses.

Once the straps were secure, Lucifer faced me, and one of the gargoyle's shadows fell across his golden features. "This is where I sacrifice innocent souls to the blood moon," he said.

My mouth went dry. "How often—"

"I'm joking, Fortuna. This planet doesn't even have a moon."

"Hilarious," I muttered.

"The other cities are run by my brothers and sisters, but I'm often called away to settle disputes or handle other . . . difficulties. I simply use the roof to leave the tower." To drive his point home, Lucifer extended his wings to full height. They were absolutely massive, and again I wondered how he controlled them. I wouldn't let myself ask, though. Lucifer looked down at me and raised his eyebrows, as if he'd heard my thoughts. "You said you had more questions?"

This was it. Here was my chance. But then . . . I hesitated. I really thought about the ramifications of this conversation. There was no way to organically work in questions about rain, as he'd inevitably know that I wasn't feeling some whimsical need to dance in a thunderstorm. What if Lucifer found out that I needed rain to return home, and he kept me from it?

I couldn't trust the devil. Not only was he the greatest trickster of all time, but he'd almost killed my brother to get me here. There was no telling what he would do to keep me.

But I'd charged up here after him, and he was waiting, offering a chance to ask my question.

"Your wings," I said lamely, my cheeks burning. "What are they?"

"God saw fit to take the first pair, so I made some of my own." He inclined his head and added, "I shall settle the matter of your brother in the morning. Sleep well, Lady Fortuna."

. "You—" I started furiously, but a gust of wind cut me off. Lucifer was in the air now, his bright wings flapping. The sight of him hanging there in the flickering sky, his metal feathers catching the light while his golden hair stirred, made my mind go blank with awe. The devil peered down at me, his carved face half-hidden in darkness. Then he flapped his wings harder, and a moment later, the night swallowed him.

Silence descended upon the rooftop.

Once Lucifer was gone, I could think clearly again. But now there was only one thought left, as if the beat of Lucifer's wings had sent all the others tumbling away. One stunned, terrifying thought.

I am so fucked.

"May I show you to the guest suite, Lady Sworn?"

At the sound of that voice, I almost shrieked; I'd half-forgotten there was someone else here. I spun toward Roger, Lucifer's most trusted minion. His question sank in, and that was when another realization hit me.

I was spending the night in Hell.

If I was being realistic, it would probably be more than one night. A part of me really must've believed I'd be able to activate the spell immediately, because I felt tendrils of panic creeping into the edges of my thoughts again. What if my worst fear came true, and I was stuck here? Even if I did show my hand and ask Lucifer for help, there was no guarantee he could send me back.

To top it off, I still wasn't certain if Damon was okay or not. Even if I had the second half of the spell, I couldn't leave until I knew my brother was awake. I felt Roger's eyes on me as I stood there, my mind working frantically, trying to figure out my next move. The panic twined deeper, thickening, breaking apart all logic and reason in its path.

Then, just as I was about to completely succumb and start hyperventilating, a voice sounded in the stillness.

You're the bravest creature I've ever met.

A hush fell over my thoughts. I could hear my own heartbeat, and as the thuds resounded through the rest of me, I saw him. Them. Laurie's roguish grin. Collith's soft smile. They were quickly followed by images of the others I'd left behind. I couldn't feel any of the connections between us, but I knew they were there.

The panic slowly retreated. After a few seconds, I comprehended that I was staring up at the gargoyles. They stared back, their strange faces forever frozen in expressions of curiosity. I brought my gaze back down. Roger was still waiting for an answer, his thick eyebrows knitted with concern. Our eyes met, and I lifted my chin.

"Lead the way," I said.

CHAPTER THIRTEEN

*T*he guest suite was warm and welcoming.

It was decorated in shades of brown, gold, and cream, which created an instantly soothing effect. The devil did everything for a reason, and I doubted interior design was an exception. He wanted me to feel at home here. Why? I scowled at the enormous, plush-looking bed. I also cast scornful glances toward the vaulted ceiling, the mirrored armoire, and the elegant nightstands.

To my surprise, the room wasn't empty—to our right, standing on two legs, there was another demon. The creature was like an oversized lizard. Its yellow eyes widened at the sight of us, and it leaped onto the wall, skittering over to another door and vanishing into an adjoining room.

I didn't remember recoiling, but suddenly there was a wall against my back, and I stared at the other doorway.

Guess who wouldn't be going in *that* room tonight?

Roger noticed my reaction. "That was just Narfu, my lady. He is a drar'ereth demon. Relatively harmless, unless you touch his tail."

"His . . . tail?" I repeated.

"Yes." Roger didn't go into detail, and I wasn't sure I wanted to know, anyway. He bowed and said, "If you need anything else, please don't hesitate to ask. I am at your disposal."

He paused, waiting for my response. I hesitated. It was another chance to ask all the questions I still had, but caution stopped me. This was the creature Lucifer trusted most, and Lucifer was a monster. Which meant that I couldn't trust anything that came out of Roger's mouth. And whatever questions I asked him would go right back to his master. So I just looked at the demon and said, "Thank you."

He bowed a second time and closed the door, hardly making a sound. Thinking about the grime on my skin, and how good it would feel to shower, I turned toward the doorway Narfu had fled through. I could see the gleam of tile and light reflecting off a mirror. Of course there was a potentially violent lizard in the bathroom I needed to use. This was Hell, after all.

Tomorrow, I decided numbly. I'd shower tomorrow.

As I stood there, absorbing the room, the tower, all of it, it felt like a tsunami was crashing over me. A gigantic wave of sorrow and longing. I missed my family. I missed *home*, and it felt like I had never been farther away. The people I loved weren't just across state lines, they were in another fucking world entirely, and I was alone. Truly, utterly alone.

Twice now, I had managed to collect myself. Twice now, I'd controlled the fear. I knew there wouldn't be a third. Tears welled up in my eyes. Seeking any form of comfort, I lay down on the bed and curled myself into a tight ball. I didn't let myself cry, not fully, but the blanket beneath my cheek became damp and cold. At one point, I started to shiver. Something stopped me from getting beneath the covers, though. Maybe it was the fact I was still covered in sweat and dust.

Time passed.

Eventually, I decided to risk checking the bathroom. I was desperate for a shower, and in the hour or two that I'd been here, I hadn't heard a single sound come from that open doorway. Maybe ol' Narfu had slipped through a window. One could only hope.

I let out a small breath and scooted off the bed. I stood there for a moment, listening closely. The silence rang in my ears. A dozen possible scenarios went through my head, but somehow I mustered enough courage to cross the room, walking on the tips of my feet. I reached the threshold of the bathroom and leaned forward, peering up first, because I'd seen plenty of horror movies and getting mauled by a giant reptile was *not* the way I wanted to go. The ceiling was made of smooth stone, and it was empty. My gaze darted around the rest of the bathroom. Relief expanded in my chest.

No lizards in sight.

There was a window, which explained where he'd gone, although that seemed too generous a term for what I was looking at. It was more of a tall, narrow opening in the stone wall. I turned my back on it and fixed my attention on the huge, glass-walled shower.

That's good, I thought hopefully, moving toward it. *At least there's water here.*

I didn't waste any more time after that. Within a minute, I was naked and standing beneath a hot, gentle stream. I scrubbed my body until it was pink, using the bottle of soap on a shelf. It wasn't labeled, but it had a pleasant, subtle scent, and the substance was the same as body washes I'd used in my world. Bubbles slid down my body and surrounded my feet.

At least another hour had passed by the time I emerged from the bathroom. As I adjusted the towel wrapped around my hair, I felt more like myself. Actually, it was the most normal I'd felt since waking up in this world, all those hours ago. Steam rolled past me, and I went into the closet. Lights turned on automatically as I passed the rows of clothing. There was so *much*, and I only had to examine a few items to confirm what I already knew—everything was in my size. Lucifer had prepared for this.

She's promised to him.

The witch's voice echoed through my head, and I wondered how long these clothes had been here. Days? Months? Even longer? Disturbed, I pulled on the softest-looking things I could find and left the closet in a rush. Then I paused on the threshold, realizing that

I hadn't bothered to do any exploring earlier. Sloppy. I needed to do better, if I actually planned to survive Hell and all the monsters that lived here. Including their master.

What if there was another way in and out of this room? My eyes went to the other side of the space, where the walls were covered in long, intricate tapestries woven with gold thread. I moved toward them, tugging the towel off my hair as I went and tossing it onto the bed. Once I got to the opposite corner, I started walking the length of the wall, pressing down on the tapestries. I wasn't sure what I was looking for, exactly, but I knew I wouldn't be able to sleep tonight if I didn't examine every inch of this place. My palm pressed against something smooth and cold.

In an instant, I knew these weren't wall tapestries—they were curtains. I found the edge of one and pulled it aside, listening to the rasp of hooks sliding along the pole.

On the other side of the glass, there was an atrium, of sorts. An open space, surrounded by windows that peered into other rooms. There weren't any plants here, either, but like the rest of the devil's city, there was an eerie beauty to it. The space was filled with what looked like a rock garden, complete with places to sit and a waterfall that came out of the far wall, crashing into a pool far below. It sent a white mist through the air.

Then I looked up, and my mind went blank.

Across the enormous space, standing in another room with a glass wall, was Lucifer himself.

A startled jolt went through me. I must've been crying longer than I thought, if the devil was back from his mysterious business. Luckily, he hadn't noticed me yet, and I couldn't pass up the chance to stare at him unobserved.

Lucifer was in his bedroom. The lighting was dim, the masculine space lit by two lamps and a fire that blazed from a massive, stone hearth. But the details of that hearth would have to wait, because I only had eyes for the male standing in front of it, his elbow propped against the mantel. He peered down into the flames, holding a drink in his other hand. He turned the glass absently. The dress slacks he'd been wearing were gone, along with that crisp white shirt. Instead, the devil wore no shirt at all. Firelight moved over his body, revealing ridges and swells of hard, carved strength. He wore gray sweatpants, slung low around his hips.

Desire lit in my belly, deep and low, hard and hot.

Then, without warning, Lucifer turned.

I froze as our eyes met. The Dark Prince sipped at the amber liquid in his glass and brazenly looked me up and down. When I saw that, a whisper of intuition crept through me. *He knew I was here the entire time.*

Before I could react, Lucifer raised his drink to me in a wordless salute. His expression made me think of his remark from our last conversation in the dreamscape. *May the best player win.*

An hour ago, I probably would've blanched, or maybe even bolted. But that shower had done wonders, and I wasn't going to accept whatever fate Lucifer had in store for me. I'd fight tooth and nail to get back to my family. And if I failed, I'd try to take a pound of the devil's flesh with me as I went.

I gave him a cold smile, extended my arm, and put up my middle finger.

I was still flicking him off as I stepped back and yanked the curtains shut.

I thought it would be impossible to fall asleep, but I did.

One moment, I was curled up on a strange bed, trying to keep the terror at bay.

The next I was opening my eyes to stars.

I rose slowly, looking down at myself. I wore my favorite running clothes, and the dream had gotten every detail right, even my faded sneakers. I frowned when I realized I was resting on black stone. The air was painfully cold.

"Please, allow me," a familiar voice said.

Fingers gently took hold of my elbow, lending me balance as I got up. I lifted my head, already knowing it would be the devil standing there. He wore the same clothes I'd seen him in when I first got to Hell, but the jacket was gone now. The buttons undone at his collar showed glimpses of a hard, golden chest. I was about to wrench my arm from Lucifer's grasp when I got caught in the beauty of him again. His vivid eyes, his full lips, the alluring slope of his jaw.

Lucifer let go and moved back. My cheeks burned, realizing that he'd been the one to pull away first, and not me.

I glanced around us, only intending to take stock of my surroundings. But when I saw where we were, I found my gaze lingering. This wasn't the dreamscape, I knew that much. I wasn't sure why I was so certain, since there were parts of that world I'd never seen. I just couldn't shake the feeling of . . . fear. Curiosity. Awe.

We were on a rock. The part that was smooth enough to stand on was the size of an elevator. Then the edges dropped, plunging down into a rolling mist that stretched as far as the eye could see. It should've been creepy, or menacing, considering how many monsters that mist could be hiding. But the stars were big and bright. The mist was ever-moving, like the surreal, frothy waves of a monster-infested sea. There was no hint of the red sky, only empty darkness.

"What is this? Where is—" I stopped short of saying Oliver's name, worried it would make him vulnerable, somehow.

Lucifer kept his gaze on the horizon. The starlight lent his skin an ethereal glow and lit up strands of his thick, golden hair. "Don't worry, I haven't harmed your . . . friend. He's tucked away, or suppressed, for lack of a better word."

A chill went through me at hearing him talk about Oliver. "How?" I asked.

What I really wanted to know was if he was stronger than me. If he was keeping Oliver away so easily, what chance did I have of using my abilities against him? Since getting to Hell, I hadn't sensed a whisper of fear from Lucifer.

As though he could hear my thoughts, the corners of the devil's mouth tipped up in a faint, amused smile. "You are in my domain now, Lady Sworn. My power is unmatched, even against curious creatures made by an artist such as yourself."

Oliver had kept bad dreams away my entire life. Nothing ever overpowered him, no matter how terrible or strong. As I considered the implications of this, Jacob's voice whispered through my memory.

Sometimes, he can reach you in your dreams.

I frowned, and my arms tightened against my body. "What is this place?" I asked abruptly.

Lucifer noticed the movement—the flick of his eyes was barely perceptible, but I saw it. He stepped closer again and held out his arm. Then I blinked, and Lucifer's missing jacket was dangling there in a silent offering. I hesitated, knowing I should reject him. It was cold, though. Like, really cold.

I took the jacket from him and pulled it on, trying not to scowl. Why did I feel like I was losing a chess match?

The jacket smelled like him, of course. A scent that made me think of sandalwood. I wondered what Hell's equivalent would be to that, since I doubted they had any trees. I pulled the jacket tight around my body and ignored how that scent made something in me stir.

"This is one of the highest points of Hell," Lucifer said, turning back to the view. "It has no name. I discovered it several decades after the Fall. We're not actually here, of course. But if we were, and you were still in the physical shell you wear on Earth, you'd be dead."

"You flew all the way up here?" I asked, peering over the edge. I'd never considered myself afraid of heights, but seeing so much open air sent a nervous whisper through me.

"No. I climbed."

My gaze shot back to Lucifer's. "You *climbed*? Why?"

His blue eyes lingered on mine for an extra beat before he turned again. "After the Fall, all of us were scattered, and most of the planet was cast in darkness. Our wings were not designed to withstand another environment for extended periods of time. In a matter of days, they'd weakened and fallen off. We became wanderers. Alone, cold, in pain. I started losing my grip on sanity. One night, I decided to end it. I made a plan to throw myself off the highest edge I could find. I started climbing. I reached the point where I knew the fall would kill me. But then . . . I kept going. It became important to reach the top. To see light. I don't know how long it took me—days, maybe weeks—to reach this spot. When I did, I looked at the stars and remembered who we were.

"Everything changed after that. I climbed back down, and I learned to hunt. I found others in the wilderness. We became strong again."

I didn't know how to respond. I was also fighting a sense of déjà vu. Collith had done this once—come into my dreams, shown me a place that meant something to him. My grip tightened on Lucifer's jacket. History was not about to repeat itself. I wouldn't let it.

"I thought there weren't stars in Hell" was all I said.

He looked at me from the corner of his eye, eyebrows raised. "Hell may surprise you, my lady."

I didn't reply. I gazed out at that spill of light over the mist, mentally latching onto a lifeline of hope. If there were stars, then it seemed possible that rain existed, too. I had to get back. Not just for my Court. Faces flashed in my mind. *Collith. Laurie.*

"You've come to depend on them," Lucifer remarked, making me go still.

So he *did* have access to my thoughts.

I felt another prickle of unease at the revelation. I wanted to ask Lucifer how much he could see, hear, but what really mattered was keeping him out. I reverted back to my lessons with Collith, imagining an impenetrable wall. I needed to protect them. Keep Lucifer's focus on me.

"I don't depend on anyone," I said flatly.

He made a soft sound. I couldn't tell if it was a sigh or a laugh. "I didn't take you for a liar. How common . . . and disappointing."

"Let's be clear about one thing." I took the devil's jacket off and held it out. I forced myself to look at him, and I summoned all the revulsion I felt for the things he'd done. "I don't give a *shit* what you think about me."

He searched my gaze, taking the jacket without any protest.

Lucifer's voice was a soft, speculative murmur as he said, "Did you know that we are our innermost selves in dreams, Lady Sworn? I find something comforting about that."

"I find it comforting that I'm going to kill you someday," I told him coldly.

Lucifer just smiled. "I'm glad you're here. Please let me know if there's anything you need. As you're now aware, I'm just across the way."

Before I could respond, he waved his fingers, and my eyelids became heavy. Unbearably heavy. I fell backward, but a bed caught me. It was so warm, so soft, and I was so tired. I nestled deeper into the pillow and released a long, contented breath.

"Sandalwood. He smells like sandalwood, and it's *delicious*," someone with my voice said. I was too far away to care.

I fell asleep to the sound of a soft laugh.

CHAPTER FOURTEEN

*D*arkness greeted me when I came back to reality. My new, harsh, terrifying reality. The fire was almost dead, and the room was freezing. I sat up and looked around for a clock, hoping I'd missed one earlier, but there was nothing on the walls. And there was no cell phone resting on the nightstand, of course.

Not knowing the time made me feel disoriented. My latest encounter with Lucifer didn't help, either. Needing to feel more grounded, I got dressed and made a plan. It was simple. First, I'd summon Roger. Then I'd ask him to bring me to Lucifer. Once I got to the Dark Prince, I'd demand to see the evidence my brother had been resuscitated. After that, I would start a conversation about the weather patterns in Hell.

And once I figured out where to find a little precipitation, I'd go from there.

Calmer now, I walked over to the door and poked my head out. There was a guard standing farther down the walkway—it wore a helmet, so I couldn't see its face, but the demon had a male build and what looked like a lion's tail, and he turned his head in my direction. "Is Roger available?" I asked.

Holding the hilt of his sword, the guard bowed and walked toward the elevator. I retreated back into the bedroom to wait.

Less than a minute later, I heard the unmistakable sound of hooves against stone. There was a gentle knock on the door. I hurried to open it, and Roger bowed so deeply that I could see his frail spine, even through the burlap-like material of his shirt.

"Good evening, my lady," he said, straightening. The tufts of hair around his ears were a bit neater than the last time I'd seen him, as if he'd made an effort to smooth them down. "Would you like a dinner tray?"

This created even more questions. If we didn't have physical bodies, why did we seem to have all the same physical needs? How did Roger even know it was dinnertime? But I had a plan, and I didn't want to spend precious time chitchatting with a demon. I shook my head and replied, "No. I just need to see Lucifer."

"Of course, my lady. My lord is in his office, and he instructed me to bring you anytime you'd like."

Roger bowed again and shuffled back, allowing me to pass. In doing so, I caught his scent, and it was more pleasant than I'd expected. He smelled like books and harsh soap.

We started walking in the direction of the elevator. Since we were the only ones here, minus the horrid mazzikin I could see darting through pockets of shadow, the quiet between us felt painfully obvious. I didn't know what to say, and I didn't trust this creature, even if his name was Roger. So I bit my tongue and kept my eyes on the path ahead.

To my surprise, he was the one to break the silence. "You slept a long time, my lady. Fourteen hours."

"Fourteen *hours*?" I echoed, my eyebrows raised. How could that be? It had only felt like a few minutes.

"Yes, my lady. His Majesty grew concerned. He even dream-walked, so he could make sure you were all right."

I mulled over this information, trying to keep my expression neutral. If Roger was telling the truth, I must've been sleeping like the dead if I'd gone that long without seeing the dreamscape or having nightmares. Or had Lucifer continued to suppress them? Then I thought about the second part of what Roger had said.

"Is that what you call what he does? Dreamwalking?" I asked. A hint of scorn slipped into my voice.

Roger must've heard it, because he was silent for a moment. As if he was considering his next words carefully. His voice was slow as he said, "It costs him to do it. It weakens him. In all the years I've served my lord, I've only known him to dreamwalk a handful of times. The last occasion was many, many years ago, when he intervened in the Hunt. He couldn't bear to watch you die, my lady."

I frowned at the demon in confusion, mentally turning those words over. *The Hunt.*

Something in my mind clicked. I thought of the mysterious figure who'd led me to Creiddylad's tomb. I heard my father's frantic warning. *That wasn't me, in your dream, do you understand?*

But the hunt for Creiddylad wasn't years ago; it was only a few months. Then I remembered how time moved differently in Hell.

So it *had* been Lucifer in that dream.

Until this moment, I had never truly considered why he'd intervened. I didn't believe Roger's story about Lucifer having a heart, or giving a shit about what happened to me. He'd probably been desperate to save my body.

It also meant that Lucifer had been watching me for years. I thought of that creepy closet again, full of clothing perfectly tailored to my measurements, and held back a shudder.

"Are you cold, my lady?"

Now I swallowed an annoyed sigh. Demon or not, I couldn't take this *my lady* shit anymore. "Roger, you can just call me Fortuna. Please," I added.

"Oh, my lady, that's so kind. But I could never do you the dishonor."

I was about to argue just as Roger slowed, making me realize that we'd arrived. I recognized the door from when I'd come here with Blondie. This time, there was a single guard outside it. When I got a good look at him, I hid the startled leap in my throat. Like

Blondie, the guard was beautiful, almost fae in appearance . . . but with one major caveat.

He had scales instead of skin.

Tiny, sand-colored scales. He also had a strong jaw and dark eyes, and his inky hair curled boyishly against the back of his neck.

Politely ignoring my scrutiny, the guard nodded at Roger and opened the door for us, standing with one hand on the hilt of his sword, just as the other guard had.

As I moved over the threshold, Lucifer turned from his desk. I felt the devil's power again, a forceful swell that made my skin tingle. He was dressed more casually today, the black suit exchanged for a blue, crewneck pullover that clung to every swell of muscle. I ignored the way my body reacted at the sight of him, and Lucifer politely pretended not to notice. But he was an original angel—his senses were so powerful that he could probably detect the slightest shift in my temperature, let alone hear the way my pulse had quickened. My face burned as he gestured at the scaled guard and said, "Lady Sworn, this is Dagan, my head of security."

I looked over my shoulder and realized that Roger hadn't followed me inside. Only Dagan stood there, his expression open and friendly. Despite his armor, he bent in a deep, fluid bow, and his voice was a pleasant rasp as he told me, "It is an honor."

I frowned at the sincerity I sensed in him. Was it an act? And was I a complete fool for wanting to believe it? Yes, I decided. It wasn't just foolish, it was idiotic. This was Hell, and no one could be trusted. Not creatures that seemed like nice old men, and certainly not courteous guards with kind eyes.

I turned my back on Dagan without saying anything.

While I'd been distracted, Lucifer had closed the distance between us. I jumped when I registered his proximity, but moving away felt like an admission of something, or revealing a weakness. So I forced myself to stay where I was, my head tipped back. I held my breath to avoid his heady scent. Lucifer peered down at me, his vivid eyes flicking over every detail. "You look well-rested. I'm glad. There are some that don't survive the journey to my dimension," he remarked.

What a cheery conversation starter. Too bad I wasn't in the mood for small talk. "Is my brother awake, or not?" I asked curtly.

Lucifer didn't miss a beat. "He is, yes. I'm sure you would still like your proof. It's here in the tower, but we'll need to go down a couple floors. Shall we?"

Those words. They were the equivalent of a trigger or a flash bomb. For an instant, I saw Laurie standing there. Silver hair instead of gold. Silver eyes instead of blue. His lips curved faintly, always on the verge of a smile. His voice soft and slow, as if he knew a secret no one else did. *Shall we?*

When the image faded, and Lucifer was the one in front of me again, I expected to feel a pang of loss. But I just felt steadier. More grounded. I met the devil's gaze and said, "Let's go."

Two or three minutes later, we were in the atrium.

From this vantage point, the rock formations were even stranger. They stretched over our heads like naked, time-worn trees. My shoes made soft sounds against the path, but the deeper we moved into the room, the louder the water got, and it drowned out my footsteps.

When we reached the center and the space widened, I looked up, automatically seeking stars. Forgetting that this wasn't Earth, and there was a ceiling between me and anything remotely familiar. As I stared at the smooth stone, I heard Oliver's voice in my head, more familiar than any sky or song. *The first thing we always do on a dark night is look up. Always.*

I refocused and saw that Lucifer had gone to the edge of the water. His hair gleamed from the glow of a nearby light, which stood on a dark pole like a lamppost. The pool was round, and bigger than I'd thought. The ripples from the waterfall didn't quite reach the edge. Lucifer reached down and picked up a small knife I hadn't noticed. It had been resting on a stone, and the blade reminded me of the swords at the Unseelie Court. Clear, almost like glass. Without hesitation, Lucifer slid the edge through the fleshy part of his hand and held it over the water. He looked back at me, his lean, golden face shifting into the light. "There's a mirror at the bottom," he said.

My heart leaped. *A mirror?* Lucifer's blood must activate a spell, I thought, my eyes darting to the water. I didn't hesitate to get closer now, and I stared at the bottom of the pool. Just as Lucifer had said, I could see smooth, unbroken glass there, reflecting every ripple and fragment of light. I waited, practically holding my breath, as if I'd jinx the magic with a single intake of air.

Within seconds, Damon's face appeared in the mirror.

"Oh," I said faintly, exhaling in a rush. I didn't mean to—the sound slipped out involuntarily—but I didn't care. I put my hands on the rocks, using them for balance as I knelt down, wanting to get closer. The image was already changing. Damon must've been bending down, because he reappeared holding Matthew. I pressed a hand against my mouth and blinked rapidly. Oh, this was good. This was really good. My family was safe. They were okay, and together, and smiling. Nothing else mattered.

My blinding happiness dimmed as another thought occurred to me. What if this was a trick? What if the spell was only showing me what I wanted most, instead of reality?

I leaned back, frowning. The spell had ended, and the faces in the water were gone.

"It isn't enough," I said.

Lucifer looked unsurprised. "It has to be. If my word had no value, no one would bother making deals with me."

Right. The devil and his deals. My jaw clenched, and I pushed myself up. Roger wanted me to believe his master cared for my well-being, and yet it was one of Lucifer's deals that had caused more harm than anything I'd ever been through.

At the same moment I had the thought, I realized that I was looking at the knife in Lucifer's hand. The edge was still stained with his blood. Whatever it was made of, he was vulnerable to that blade. It could cut him. Suddenly I was imagining it. Getting close to him. Seducing him. Grabbing for that knife.

Time slowed.

Stick to the plan, Fortuna, a voice inside me urged.

I blinked, and my thoughts cleared. The plan. Yes. I'd confirmed that Damon was alive and well. Now I needed to complete

Savannah's spell and get my ass back home. Trying to stab the devil was definitely *not* on that list, and it was pure delusion to think that I'd succeed where hundreds, probably thousands, before me had failed. He was an original angel, for chrissakes.

I let out a breath and walked away from the pool, stopping once I could no longer see the water. Beyond the windows around us, I could see glimpses of sky. There were more clouds than last time I'd been conscious, and when I saw that, hope went off inside me.

"Looks like rain," I murmured, wondering how much it would take to trigger Savannah's spell. A single drop on my skin? Standing beneath the downpour?

I felt Lucifer looking at me. "There is no rain in Hell, my lady."

"There has to be," I blurted, my stomach sinking. "I mean, this is a big world, right? There must be rain *somewhere*."

Lucifer didn't respond. His eyes were intent on my face, and in an instant, I knew I'd made a mistake. He could see how upset I was. How much I cared. I turned away to regain my composure, and my mind raced. If Lucifer was telling the truth, it meant that I had no way of getting home. Not without his help, at least. Revealing my dilemma to him would probably result in another deal that would entrap me further, or bring around the end of the world. It was a toss-up, really.

Okay, so I couldn't tell Lucifer. That gave me three weeks to find some rain or figure out another way home. Magic existed in Hell, I'd seen it. And magic seemed to respond to me.

The only problem was Lucifer. I had to buy myself enough time to leave this tower alone, and search the city for a miracle. But he seemed determined to be a gracious host.

I needed to drive him away, I decided.

I'd barely finished the thought when Lucifer asked, "Would you like a tour of the tower?"

"No." My lip curled. "I don't know what your game is, and I don't care. I'm not playing. I don't want anything to do with you. You may put on a good show, but I see you—I see past the pretty face. You're still the same prince that rebelled against your daddy and lost. You're trapped in a cage, and you call it your kingdom. All because you can't bear the truth."

When I stopped, Lucifer was silent, and I noticed the slightest movement in his jaw. A shadow, like a muscle had flexed. *There*, I thought. I'd finally gotten to him. *Fortuna, one. Lucifer, zero.*

I waited for his response, my heartbeat slightly uneven. It didn't seem likely that many people got to mock the devil and survive it.

"I am not the only one who turns a blind eye," Lucifer said. I expected his voice to be hard, cold, but he spoke to me softly now. Almost as if he . . . pitied me. There was sadness in his eyes.

I bristled, and I opened my mouth to demand what *that* meant. Then I caught myself, realizing I'd nearly played right into his hands. This was how the devil wove his web. This was how he manipulated and warped people's minds.

Little did he know that *he* was the one getting outsmarted now. I would play Lucifer's game, and I'd do it better.

"Stay out of my dreams tonight," I said calmly, raising my gaze to his. "Or you'll learn what it really means to meet a Nightmare."

With that, I turned and left the atrium. I felt Lucifer watching me the entire time, but I didn't look back.

Fortuna, two. Lucifer, zero.

The next time I woke, there was a demon in my room.

I didn't shoot upright, which was my first instinct. Instead, I forced my body to remain still and follow the creature with my eyes. It was the same one that had been here before. What had Roger called him? Narfu, that was it. I watched his movements, warily at first, but as the seconds went by, my unease began to fade. The giant lizard appeared to be . . . cleaning. He was delicate about it, too. The towel I'd used last night had fallen onto the floor, and Narfu retrieved it with the tips of his claws. When he straightened, I noticed there was a collar around his neck. It was thick, and made of some sort of metal. There was dried blood around the edges.

Narfu began folding the towel with surprising dexterity. While he was distracted, I slid my legs to the side of the bed, moving slowly. Narfu's head jerked upright, and he froze, still holding the towel.

"I'm not going to hurt you," I said, daring to move closer. "I just want to look at the collar."

He didn't respond, and I wondered if he understood English, or whether he was even capable of speech. Somehow, I doubted it. Narfu watched me approach with round, bright eyes, his body posture similar to how a stray dog might act around a human. Wondering if the human was there to hurt him, or help him.

He wasn't the only one who was intimidated—the demon was at least seven feet tall, and his claws looked like they could slice through me like butter. I made a deliberate effort to avoid glancing at them again, and I stood on tiptoe, peering more closely at the piece of metal rubbing Narfu raw.

It reminded me of the collars that were linked to an invisible fence, except the two prongs were buried in his flesh, instead of just resting against it. Suddenly I didn't care what purpose it served, or whether those prongs were preventing Narfu from devouring me whole. The collar needed to come off. Was there a clasp, or a latch of some kind?

A knock sounded through the room. Narfu's eyes widened, and he let out a girly squeak. In a blink, he'd scuttled into the bathroom and, undoubtedly, through the window. *Damn it*. The collar would have to wait.

"Who is it?" I called, turning toward the door. Somehow, though, I knew exactly who stood on the other side, even as the question left my mouth.

His voice drifted through the air a moment later, confirming the certainty in my veins. "Would you accompany me to breakfast, Lady Sworn?" Lucifer asked.

I swallowed and started to move away, wanting more distance between me and the beautiful creature in the hallway. "I'm busy. Can I ignore you another time?"

"You agreed to spend time with me, my lady. I honored my side of the bargain."

I made a scoffing sound, knowing he would hear. In seconds, I'd crossed the room. I swung the door open and held the edge with one hand. At the sight of Lucifer, a strange combination of coldness and heat sweep through me, which I promptly ignored. I tilted my head as if I were unaffected by him.

"Did you?" I challenged. "I'd be a fool to trust your word and a bespelled mirror. You don't exactly have a glowing reputation."

"You're right. I don't. I wouldn't trust me either, if I were in your position. So I'll make this an opportunity." Lucifer turned and signaled to someone down the hallway. Probably Dagan.

His response caught me off guard, and I was instantly wary. "How?"

Lucifer smiled, and once again, it felt like I'd gotten the wind knocked out of me. He sounded almost . . . boyish as he said, "I've heard you have some skill with a sword."

I raised my eyebrows. "You've heard, or you saw it for yourself while you were squatting in Belanor like a toad?"

"Fight me, then," Lucifer responded, unruffled. "Let me catch a glimpse of the legendary Nightmare Queen. To level the field of experience between us, I will use my non-dominant hand. If I win, you must come to the dining room and have breakfast with me."

"And if I win?" I asked without hesitation. I'd gotten good at this. Too good.

Dagan returned, and he was holding two small, blunt-edged swords. Lucifer kept his focus on me as he took them. "If you win, I will subtract three days from our contract."

I paused. Lucifer probably thought he'd piqued my interest, but I was thinking quickly, trying to determine the smartest move here. I didn't want to subtract anything from the contract, because that meant less time to find a solution to my little problem. Lucifer would get suspicious, though, if I didn't jump at this chance. He just had to believe my hatred for him was stronger than my desire to get out of here.

It wouldn't be a tough act to sell.

"Or I could just stay right here and ride out the three days," I countered. I gave Lucifer a withering look. "That would be preferable to sharing a single meal with you."

To my disappointment, he didn't react to the insult.

"You hide your fear well. I suppose you've had far too much practice. But what are you afraid of, I wonder? This?" Lucifer indicated the swords. "Or . . . this?"

The devil's voice softened, and with his free hand, he reached up to tuck a strand of my hair behind my ear. His fingertips skimmed the side of my neck in a questioning, feather-light caress, and the simple touch sent my thoughts scattering. I reminded myself to stick to the plan. Drive him away. This was doing the opposite.

I'm not afraid of you. I willed myself to say it, and imbue my tone with venom. I told myself to look at Lucifer as if he repulsed me. But the words stuck in my throat. I needed to say *something*, because staying silent would practically be an admission that he was right.

In my desperation, I said something easier, and something far worse.

"Deal."

"May I come in?" Lucifer asked, giving me no chance to panic about what I'd just agreed to.

My only response was to step back. I was mentally scrambling, desperately trying to think of a plausible reason to change my mind and reject Lucifer's offer. But he was already in the room and presenting one of the training swords, the hilt extended toward me. I took it to buy myself more time. We moved into the center of the space and faced each other. I opened my mouth to blurt out an excuse, any excuse, for why I didn't want this fucking deal.

Then Lucifer said, "I dare you."

My gaze snapped to his. The air between us heated, and I reminded myself that it wasn't real, this thing he made me feel. This ache deep inside me. *Don't fall for it, Fortuna,* reason insisted.

Lucifer had figured out my weak spots, though. He knew exactly what to say to goad me. Taunt me. Tempt me. I'd changed in a lot of ways, over these past few months.

But there were some things that never changed.

"Three days," I said, moving into a fighting stance, "and I get to come and go from this tower as I please, without you. *And* you take the collar off Narfu."

I didn't expect to add this last part. It had popped out like my mouth had a mind of its own. I just hadn't been able to get the image of that giant lizard out of my head. But it wasn't the image of the collar, or the crusted blood around those prongs—it was seeing him handle that towel with such care. Before meeting Narfu, I hadn't known reptiles could have such expressive faces, and seeing his puckered with concentration had changed my fear of him. Of demons in general, although I wasn't ready to delve into that yet.

"Always trying to 'sweeten the pot,'" Lucifer remarked. There was admiration in the gleam of his eyes. "Very well. Three days off your contract and you may have your freedom, on the condition that you take a guard with you at all times. But the collar stays where it is, I'm afraid. That I cannot grant you. Narfu comes from a violent species, and the collar keeps his impulses in check."

There was a finality in Lucifer's response that made it clear any argument would be met with failure. "Fine. Let's get this over with, then," I said.

We both lifted our weapons. Lucifer ran his sword along the length of mine, and there was something . . . intimate about the movement. About the way his eyes held mine. I didn't let him provoke me, though. I kept my focus on his body language. The subtle shifts and flickers in his expression. Everyone had a tell, and I would find Lucifer's.

Then he launched into an offensive charge, and I forgot to even think about tells, much less look for one. God, he was fast. There was only time to parry and swing, sidestep and feint. Before long, I felt a drop of perspiration slide down my temple.

"You've managed to surprise me, Lady Sworn," the devil said, drawing back.

We circled each other. After a few seconds, I realized that wasn't all we were doing—Lucifer and I were mirroring each other. It was effortless. Instinctive. Almost as if we thought the same way.

Silently recoiling from the possibility, I looked at him and felt my lip curl. "Funny. Nothing about you has surprised me," I replied.

In truth, Lucifer was a magnificent fighter. Before this, I'd considered Laurie and Adam to be the best I knew. But the devil would give them a run for their money, just like he was giving me a run for mine.

And then I lost.

I got tired, and my technique became sloppy. Lucifer flicked his wrist, getting his blade beneath mine, and then he gave it a hard jerk. My sword hit the floor with a hollow sound. I followed it with my eyes, my chest heaving. When I looked up again, the tip of Lucifer's sword was already at my heart. We stared at each other. I struggled to control my breathing; I didn't want him to know how much effort I'd been putting in.

Then Lucifer's arm fell, and the spell between us ended. "You are a worthy opponent, Lady Sworn," he said.

I couldn't think of an insult. As I turned away and retrieved the other sword from the floor, it felt like there was a scream trapped in my gut, a building pressure made of frustration and rage. I gritted my teeth and shoved it down, then faced Lucifer and said curtly, "I need to shower."

"Of course." He stepped forward and wrapped his fingers around the hilt of my sword, startling me. I let go and moved away like a skittish horse. Lucifer's eyes flickered as he noticed this, and his mouth tightened. But his voice was courteous as ever when he added, "Take your time. I'll wait in the dining room."

I didn't bother responding. Still fuming, I turned from him again and crossed the room without looking back. A moment later, I closed the bathroom door with more force than necessary.

After my shower, I stood in the closet for so long that my hair began to dry. What did one wear to breakfast with the devil? I frowned as I surveyed the rows of clothing. A dress was way too formal, but I'd feel self-conscious in jeans. Minutes later, I finally settled on black leggings, a form-fitting slip, and a filmy, button-down shirt over both. I left it open, and rolled up the sleeves to my elbows. As I turned toward the door, I considered using some of the makeup I'd found in the bathroom. No, I decided. Lucifer would think I was trying to impress him. I did allow myself to use a hair clip from one of the drawers.

Calmer now, I slipped on the same shoes I'd worn yesterday and left the room.

Roger was waiting for me in the hall. "Good morning, my lady," he said with a bow.

I thought about ignoring him, but I couldn't bring myself to do it. No matter how many times I reminded myself what Roger was, and who he served, I looked at those white tufts of hair around his ears and couldn't hate him. "Good morning," I mumbled back, averting my gaze.

We didn't head in the direction of the elevators, and Roger walked beside me to lead the way. "The dining room is on this floor, my lady."

"What would it take to forget this 'my lady' business?" I asked.

The demon's hooves clicked gently against the flagstones. He considered my question with his hands clasped behind his back. "I doubt you'll find a single creature who would do so, my lady. The title is a sign of our gratitude and respect."

"Gratitude?" I repeated, baffled. "I haven't done anything. I just got here."

Roger's papery voice became earnest. "You've brought hope back into this tower. We love our master, Lady Sworn. He may not be perfect, but every demon here longs for his happiness. Ever since he found you, my lord has been different. We all see it. He is . . . better."

Better? The word seemed like an odd choice, and I frowned. I was out of time to ask more questions, though. Where the walkway ended, there was a pair of double doors. They stood open. There wasn't anything welcoming about the sight, because I could see the space beyond them, even before we reached the threshold a few moments later.

The dining room was menacingly beautiful. The walls seemed to be made of the same dark, gleaming stone as the rest of the tower, but one side was entirely glass, providing an incredible view of the city and the red horizon. A painting hung over the massive fireplace at the left side of the space, which crackled in the stillness. There were three imposing figures on the canvas. It was evident from the styles of clothing they wore that this painting was very, very old. Lucifer was easily recognizable in the middle, but I'd never seen the two people standing on either side of him. The only thing they all had in common was their beauty, although the others had darker coloring. Lucifer was like a shining beacon or a bright flame, and something told me it had always been that way for him. It was how he'd led a rebellion against the most powerful being in the universe.

The thought made my mood darken even further. Sometimes I managed to forget who I was really up against, and just how low my odds were of surviving this.

I tore my gaze away and focused on the lone figure near the end of the table. As soon as we'd entered, Lucifer had stood from his chair. He wore a suit again, this one gray, and of course it fit his muscular frame perfectly. Dagan stood nearby, along with another guard I hadn't met. She reminded me of Lyari, in a way, with her pursed lips and straight spine.

"Good morning," Lucifer said, as if we hadn't just dueled with swords in a bedroom. *Everyone here is so goddamn polite,* I thought irritably.

As Lucifer pulled out a chair for me, I realized Roger was gone. Once again, the old demon had quietly disappeared. I really needed to ask him how he did that. With those feet, it should sound like he was wearing heels.

Lucifer waited for me to approach, but I made no effort to hide my reluctance. I stayed where I was and toyed with the idea of sitting at the opposite end of the table. But there was a possibility it would make me look cowardly, rather than defiant. And Lucifer would probably just remind me of the deal we'd made.

Scowling, I walked toward him and settled onto the chair, making a point of yanking it closer to the table without his help. As Lucifer returned to the place he'd been sitting, I noticed a glass of water beside my plate. I snatched it up and drank the entire thing. I hadn't realized how *thirsty* I was.

From the corner of my eye, I saw Lucifer signal to someone. Within seconds, another demon came up behind me and set another glass down, then took the one I'd emptied. She was less human-looking than the others I'd seen—there was a sharp, black beak where a nose would usually be, she had feathers instead of hair, and she moved strangely—but I still didn't like her serving me. I didn't know if she was here by choice, or if she was a slave.

Lucifer, of course, must've noticed something in my expression. "Saida," he said, picking up his own glass with long, graceful fingers, "would you reassure our guest I'm not the beast she believes I am?"

The demon turned to me. Her brown eyes were wide, but I didn't sense any fear around her. "Safe, in the tower," she said, nodding emphatically. "Nestlings here. Warm here."

I glanced from her to Lucifer, wondering if he'd set this up. "So you work for room and board?" I asked.

Lucifer said something in a language I had never heard. Saida listened carefully, her expression attentive. When he was finished, she nodded again, even harder this time. Her feathers bobbed with the movement. She spoke in the same language Lucifer had used, her tone eager. Suddenly, in a burst of recognition, I realized they were speaking Enochian. A rudimentary, rough-edged version of it, maybe, but I knew certain words. *Death. Monster. Children.*

"She says her people were dying out," Lucifer told me, translating. "Their land had been overridden by the tol'gadak, predators that breed like cockroaches and are just as hard to kill. She'd lost several nestlings by the time she came to the First City."

Saida looked at me as he spoke, and there was pain in her eyes.

That was the moment I knew it wasn't just an act. Not all of it, at least. I met Saida's gaze and nodded at her, speaking in a language we'd both be able to understand. Grief could bring anyone together . . . even a Nightmare and a demon.

Sparing me from a response, Lucifer addressed Saida in her tongue again. Whatever he said was clearly a dismissal, because she bowed and moved away from the table. I still didn't like being waited on, but I'd probably hurt Saida by refusing. I reached for the fresh water she'd brought and tried to think about something else. My focus went to the glass in my hand.

"What is that?" I asked suddenly. "Why do we need to sleep, or drink, or shower?"

Before Lucifer could answer, Saida reappeared. She set a plate on top of the one resting in front of me, and quickly retreated again. I peered down at foods I'd never seen before. There were round, white balls that looked like uncooked dough. Next to them was bread, toasted and covered in something that seemed identical to butter. There was also a pile of pink stuff that jiggled when I touched it with my fork. *Nasty*, I thought. Apparently my stomach didn't have the same issues I did—it rumbled at the sight.

"The needs you mentioned are all in your head," Lucifer said, probably hearing the sound. "Technically, you don't need any of those things. But your mind still believes you do, and that belief is powerful enough to manifest the physical response."

I gave him a doubtful look. "You forget, I've walked through your city. I saw how those souls are living on the outskirts. They're starving."

"It's entirely of their own doing, I assure you. A soul's suffering ceases the moment they realize their limitations are self-imposed. A good thing, too, seeing as there simply aren't enough resources on this planet to sustain every soul."

I stared at the food. Besides the ethical problems I had with it, I'd grown up listening to stories about people who were dumb enough to eat or drink with a faerie. Lucifer wasn't technically fae, but he had their cruelty, and their craftiness, and their hunger for power.

Maybe he'd bespelled the food to make me more agreeable to his plans, or to fall in love with him.

Okay, so I won't be touching anything on this plate, I thought. Once again, I sought a distraction or a topic change. My gaze went back to the painting.

"Who are they?" I asked, nodding toward the three figures.

Lucifer took a sip from his glass before answering. He set it down and followed my gaze. "On the left side is my sister, Mammon. The other is my younger brother. Asmodeus."

"He's your favorite," I said, hiding my surprise. I could hear affection in the devil's voice, a genuine warmth I'd never expected from him.

Lucifer made a weary sound. "He's impulsive and reckless. There are more riots in the Second City than any of the others and I'm always cleaning up after him," he groused.

"That doesn't change the fact he's your favorite."

Lucifer's voice softened. "Yes. Yes, he's my favorite."

What do you know, I thought, watching him, *the devil is capable of love*. It could be another act, put on to make me trust him or like him. But either way, it changed nothing. Even monsters had souls. Finding out Lucifer had one didn't absolve him of all the terrible things he'd done.

Looking at the painting again, I started to ask about Mammon, then stopped myself just in time. His family didn't matter. The details of his personal life were completely irrelevant. I wasn't here to get to know the devil. I was here to learn his weaknesses or anything else that might help me escape.

I poked at my food, trying to think of questions that would provide useful information. My mind moved to magic. "How does it work?" I asked abruptly. "The deals, I mean? You can't travel between worlds, but garden-variety demons can?"

I half-expected Lucifer to dodge the question.

"It's a spell," he said without hesitation, meeting my gaze. "The crossroads, the Witching Hour—they're all ingredients. It was cast by a powerful witch who meant a great deal to me. Her intention was to give me access to your world, so that I might not be so isolated here, but magic is unpredictable at the best of times. The results weren't quite what the witch intended.

"That spell is also what grants my demons the ability to manifest and harness magic in your world. Unfortunately, the spell doesn't hold enough power to carry my own. Every time the magic chooses me, I feel a great rush of pain, and then the spell fails. The summoner goes on their way, thinking that their mother was wrong and making deals with demons is just an urban myth."

"If only," I muttered. Thinking once again of the deal I'd made, my hatred returned in a rush. The demon had been from this world, where they looked to Lucifer for command. He was their king, their god, and cruelty like that didn't flourish without encouragement. I needed to remember that, no matter how charming their king might be.

As I sat there stewing, something else occurred to me. "Wait. How did you plan to send me home, if getting there is so impossible for you?" I demanded.

"My witches were prepared to act as an anchor, and when the time came, they could've easily pulled you back. But since you arrived here without them, that option is no longer available. It's a good thing you have means of your own to return." Lucifer noticed I'd stopped touching my food. "Are you finished, my lady? Would you like a tour of the tower?"

By some miracle, my pulse wasn't racing, but my mind certainly was. Lucifer had been my backup plan, my failsafe in the event I didn't figure out a way to activate Savannah's spell. If he couldn't help me, and I wasn't able to find rain in this world, I was well and truly screwed.

After a moment, I realized I hadn't responded to Lucifer's invitation. I opened my mouth to turn him down . . . then I remembered my plan. Truth be told, a tour would be helpful. If I was going to sneak out of here, or have a private conversation with one of the demons living in this tower, I needed to know the layout. The blind spots.

"Fine," I clipped out.

Lucifer rose. I did the same, resisting an impulse to take the knife off the table. I knew shoving it into Lucifer's eye wouldn't kill him, but it was still fun to imagine. I kept the daydream close to me as we left the warm dining room and moved down the cold walkway together.

A door came up on our left, and Lucifer inclined his head toward it. "That one leads to my bedroom," he said.

I half-expected him to say it in a suggestive tone, or for our pace to slow, but Lucifer just kept going. Halfway down, we arrived at the elevator, and he stopped. As I halted next to him, I noticed another door at the very end of the hall. I looked at Lucifer, waiting for him to say something. His focus stayed on the elevator. *He doesn't want to draw my attention to it*, I thought.

Which of course made me more determined to see what was behind it.

"What does that one lead to?" I asked, walking away. There was a flutter of apprehension in my throat as I dared to reach for the knob.

Lucifer's arm flew out, and in a blink, his palm was flattened against the door. I'd discovered it was locked, but that didn't seem to matter to him. His breath tickled the shell of my ear as he replied, "Something you're not ready for."

I turned my head, even though putting our faces so close made my heart pound harder. "What does that mean?" I asked evenly.

The devil looked into my eyes. He wasn't searching for anything, or assessing. He just . . . looked. "Someday I'll tell you, and I'll show you what's behind that door. But there's still fear in your eyes when you look at me, Lady Sworn. When that's changed, you'll be ready."

His voice was soft, and my body reacted to that husky sound, as if Lucifer had cast another spell on me. In a frantic attempt to outrun the feeling, I ducked beneath his arm and hurried back down the walkway, clasping my hands tightly behind me. Lucifer returned to my side at a casual, unconcerned pace. Once the doors slid open, he led me into the elevator and made a selection on the screen.

"Most of the floors are just office suites," he told me. "But this one is an exception."

The elevator moved so quickly that it only took seconds to arrive. The doors opened, and the light hit me first, spilling into the space like dusk-tinted water. It took my vision a moment to adjust. Once it did, I blinked rapidly, half-convinced I was still asleep and this was all a dream.

It was a library. A vast, beautiful, surreal library.

The old Fortuna would've been mildly impressed. She hadn't been a huge reader, and she'd found books about as exciting as doing taxes. But since Collith had come into my life, I'd spent a lot of time combing through ancient texts and stories. Somewhere along the way, I had started to like those written words. To enjoy the feeling of skimming my fingers over a page.

"Are some of these in English?" I asked hopefully, arching my head back to confirm there were more bookcases a level above us, too.

Lucifer nodded, watching me with an unreadable expression. "Many."

I left his side to move closer to the books, and their wonderful scent teased my senses. Whatever these volumes were made out of, they still smelled like old paper, just like the ones from back home. Part of me wanted to start browsing the shelves then and there. Lucifer was here, though. What if he stayed and asked what I was reading?

There was a painting over the fireplace here, too. A portrait, I discovered as I gave it my full attention. She looked human, but that didn't mean she was. The female stood next to a rosebush, looking back at the artist as if they'd caught her unaware. She wasn't wearing any clothing, yet somehow, there was nothing scandalous or forbidden about it. It was as though the female was unaware of her body, or the fact that it wasn't covered. Her hair was long and pale. Her smile was shy, but there was something bold about her eyes. *I have a secret*, they said.

Unsettled, I turned and rejoined Lucifer near the elevator. Like the painting upstairs, I wanted to know more about it, but I couldn't bring myself to invite a conversation with its owner. I felt him appraising me again, probably sensing something amiss. But Lucifer didn't pry. After the doors opened and we went inside, he touched the screen and sent us downward. Really downward, I noted uneasily. The elevator kept going, and going, and going. When it slowed, the air was notably colder. I felt goosebumps spread all over me. *It's all in your head*, I reminded myself, resisting the urge to rub my arms.

"And here is the final stop of our tour," Lucifer said. It was the first time one of us had spoken in at least a minute.

Ding. The doors slid open. I expected another walkway, or a modern hallway. Instead, an earthen path loomed ahead of us. Looking at it made my pulse spike. The other end of the passage was hidden in darkness, and the rest was lit with torches. Thick, bolted doors lined the uneven walls on either side. There were barred openings in each of them. Echoes traveled through the freezing dim. Far, far away, probably miles beneath our feet, someone was screaming.

It reminded me of the dungeons at the Unseelie Court.

"What is this place? Why are you keeping people down here?" I asked. My voice was stiff; I was thinking of my own time in a cell. I remembered the cold and the pain. The fear and the helplessness.

Was this where Collith had been tortured?

Lucifer answered as we walked deeper into the earth. "They're all here for different reasons. Most have information I require. Many are broken souls that are too dangerous to be free. A select few tried to kill me. And some of them put themselves in."

Put themselves in? I frowned. "What do you mean by that?"

Lucifer kept his eyes on the path ahead of us, acting as if he didn't hear the moans and sobs floating from those cells. "Most of the souls who arrive at my domain choose to do so," he said. "Just as you thought of Hell during the spell that brought you to me, the newly dead think of it as they leave their bodies behind. It's why Collith Sylvyre came here. This is where, in his heart of hearts, he thinks he belongs."

The revelation almost made me falter.

Oh my God, I thought. If Lucifer was telling the truth, Collith hadn't come here because he was Fallen. He hadn't been tormented because it was what he deserved. Instead, it was his innate goodness—his maddening nobility, part of the reason I'd fallen in love with him—that had sent Collith to Hell.

Later, I told myself. I would think about that later.

Because right now, there was a body hanging in front of me.

We'd entered one of the cells. As I moved deeper into the room, my stomach flipping at the sight of that mutilated figure, I glanced around quickly. The ceiling was higher than I'd thought it would be, but everything else was pretty standard for an ancient dungeon. Stone walls, cold floor, dim light.

The body mounted on the far wall looked like raw meat. It must've been a demon of some sort, because I saw one of its blood-streaked ears, and the tip was pointed. It hung there by chains, and judging from the smoke coming off the creature's wrists and ankles, those chains had been recently doused in holy water.

I wasn't exactly torn up about a demon getting its just desserts, but I didn't want a front-row seat, either. I faced Lucifer, frowning. "Why would you show me this?"

"Because this is the one who made a deal with you, Lady Sworn," he answered, and a shock went through me.

There was a dull roar in my ears as I turned back to the demon, expecting to recognize it, somehow. But it had been wearing Ian O'Connell's face at the crossroads. Now it was a creature with claws for fingers and a misshapen head, its pained grimace revealing rows of small, sharp teeth. I didn't look away, though. I kept looking for the creature that had almost destroyed me.

Lucifer's voice lowered, and there was something frightening about how calm it was. As if he was keeping his emotions under tight, careful control. "I had no hand in what happened to you, and if I'd known, I would've stopped it," he said. "I'm not omniscient, and demons are a chaotic species by nature. They're extremely difficult to control."

It was a relief to turn away from the demon. I gave Lucifer a faint, bitter smile. "Sounds like excuses to me. I knew a king who talked that way once."

"What happened to him?" he asked.

I pictured Collith. I remembered the look on his face as I threw our sapphire down, and a shadow passed over my heart. "He lost everything. His cowardice caught up with him."

"He lost everything . . . or you took it?" Lucifer asked. I didn't answer, and he regarded me thoughtfully. "There is no shame in taking what you want, Lady Sworn."

His remark made me think of Gwyn, and the comparison cleared my mind. People like them only cared about power. Lucifer didn't care about my pain, or my revenge, or whatever secret guilt I had about the urges inside me. He was just playing the game.

"I held up my end of the bargain. I'm leaving now," I said, turning toward the door. Lucifer's next question stopped me.

"Shall I do it, then?"

I frowned, and gave a slight shake of my head. "Do what?"

Instead of answering, Lucifer stepped close to the demon. He pulled a knife out of its stomach. I hadn't even noticed the hilt, since it had been buried in guts and all. Lucifer returned to my side, holding the knife loosely. He kept his gaze on the demon as he said, "End this pathetic creature's life."

Was *that* why he'd brought me here? I didn't bother pretending to be offended at his assumption that I was the sort of person who went around killing. Because I was. Logan had proven that. Instead, I fell silent. I stared at the demon and wondered what it would feel like, killing it. Satisfying? Cathartic? Maybe even freeing.

Every child had a monster in their closet. Not every child opened the door and slaughtered it.

That's what I imagined it would feel like.

But something held me back. I kept staring at the demon, and there was an uneasy sensation in my stomach. Stillness filled the cell. I wavered, going back and forth between the urge to run and the longing to stay. A longing that grew stronger with every second.

Then I heard another voice in my head. This time, it wasn't Laurie or Oliver—it was Collith. Beautiful, infuriating Collith with his flaws and his ideals.

Choose mercy, Fortuna.

Taking a life, no matter how dark, decrepit, and poisonous it was, was still taking a life. It left a mark. I'd learned that the hard way. I could close my eyes and see the face of everyone I'd ever killed, even the deaths I had enjoyed.

Sometimes, mercy wasn't for someone else's sake. It was for your own. Collith knew that, too. Every time he'd intervened, and I'd thought he was judging that dark part of me, he was really just trying to protect me.

Damn it, I thought. Another sigh filled my throat. I was about to step back when the demon opened its eyes.

And that was when I finally recognized it.

It couldn't hide its eyes that night, I realized, watching the creature focus on my face. They may have looked like Ian O'Connell's, but it had been this thing behind them. This thing's soul, its essence. Evaluating me. Watching me. Leering at me.

How charming. You thought I would want your soul. That's not how it works, sweetheart. No, I take something that you value.

My hands curled into fists.

I wasn't going to kill it, I told myself silently. I wouldn't go that far. But . . . I didn't see anything wrong with punishing it a little. Making this monster feel even a *fraction* of the pain it had made me feel, and the countless other victims that it had destroyed with its deals.

I wouldn't use a knife to draw out its screams, I decided.

For the first time since arriving in Hell, I reached for the other part of myself. I closed my eyes and summoned the darkness.

Nothing answered.

I frowned and reached even deeper. Focused harder. It was just . . . empty. The place inside me, that vital, awful, wonderful, beautiful place where euphoria and energy lived, was like a barren desert or a forgotten attic.

My powers were gone.

CHAPTER FIFTEEN

*D*ays passed.

I spent most of my time in Lucifer's library, trying to make sense of the texts. Some of them were in Enochian, but most were written in languages I'd never seen before. There were also books filled with Spanish, Arabic, and Chinese, but I couldn't exactly read those, either. I was looking for any references to rain, or any images of water falling from the sky.

And if I happened to come across a super-helpful passage about how to kill the devil, well, bully for me.

Lucifer, it turned out, was a gracious host. He extended break-fast and dinner invitations. His staff cleaned and restocked my room daily. When he wasn't in a meeting or on a call, he offered to play games or go for a walk. I rebuffed most of his efforts. I acted like I was just running out the clock. I pretended to be bored, or annoyed, or outright hostile. But all the while, hour after hour, I couldn't escape the terror. It had started as a seed, and every time I thought about the reality of my situation, it grew.

I was in Hell without any way out, and I was powerless.

How would it affect my Court, being connected to me, lending strength to me, for an indefinite amount of time? Would my body eventually weaken and deteriorate, like Damon's? What if it killed my Court members instead?

I had no answers, no solutions, and no one to ask. And that was why I'd basically moved into the library.

One morning, I leaned over my usual table, brows furrowed in concentration. An atlas rested in front of me. Much like everything else here, it was vastly different from what I knew. I couldn't figure out what the lines were supposed to represent—borders? coastlines? rivers?—and the writing was in one of the languages I'd never seen before. From the reading I'd done these past few days, I had begun to suspect there were as many species of demon as there were Fallen, and they'd created their own dialects.

But I didn't care about demons or how they spent their eternity here. I'd been staring at this atlas in hopes of learning more about Hell's regions. Lucifer couldn't be trusted, and he might have lied about the rain. It was a big world with a lot of resources. There had to be different biomes, right?

I became rough in my desperation, and I turned the page so hard it made a snapping sound. Thankfully, the paper was thick and coarse, and it didn't tear. I let out a breath of relief before I refocused, a tide of hope rising inside me. It sank right back down when I saw the page.

This map was even more confusing than the last one.

A blaze of frustration roared through me. Suddenly I wanted to push the table over and stomp on the atlas until it ripped and broke apart. I wrapped my fingers around the table's edge, battling myself. Trying to breathe through the fear that my anger was really masking. I wanted to go home. I wanted to run through the woods and hear the crunch and crackle of snow and leaves. In another burst of desperation, I decided to do the next best thing.

I went up to the roof.

I was so distracted that I barely noticed the mazzikin. They nipped and batted at my ankles, but I just rushed into the center of the open space. I stood there for a few seconds, breathing. But the fresh air didn't help as I'd hoped. It felt like a nuclear war was brewing in my head. Unable to remain still anymore, I began to pace the length of the rooftop, or what I had mentally started calling Lucifer's landing pad.

It only took him a few minutes to show up.

I heard Lucifer murmur something to Dagan. One by one, all the guards went down the stairs. Even guards I hadn't been aware were there, I noted with annoyance. I'd have to work on that. Their shoes made soft sounds against the stone, and all the while, my relentless pattern continued. Back and forth. Back and forth.

Once Lucifer and I were completely alone, the words spilled out of me.

"I need to get out of this tower. You can't just keep me here the entire time. What kind of 'visit' is that?" I demanded, still moving. "I'll tell you. It's actually called kidnapping."

Lucifer stood with his hands behind his back. He watched me with a calm expression. "What's wrong?" he asked.

"Well, let's see. Maybe I'm a little tense because I'm in *Hell*," I snapped, tossing a glare at him. I kept pacing.

Lucifer didn't react to the hard edge of desperation in my voice. He stayed silent while I did a few more laps. "Would you finally like to see my world, Lady Sworn?"

I'd reached the other side of the roof, and it took a moment for his words to float over to me. My head jerked up, and when I realized he'd extended his wings, I slowed. Flying together would require him to touch me. The thought only made my agitation worse. We hadn't even kissed and I ached for him like we'd been doing this dance for years.

I was on the verge of saying no when another thought occurred to me—going with Lucifer would be a chance to ask more questions. To search for *rain*.

Swallowing the denial that had been rising to my lips, I managed to meet Lucifer's gaze without flinching. Looking at him sucked me in, as it always did. I fought the magnetic pull and said, "Okay. Sure."

He came toward me. He didn't move quickly, but I still wasn't ready when he bent and picked me up, one of his arms looping beneath my knees while the other supported my back. I wrapped my arms around his neck instinctively, bracing myself as he lifted into the frigid night. Air rushed past us, and I forced myself to let go of Lucifer once we were off the ground. I didn't like how my body reacted to his proximity, his *smell*. It was the sandalwood scent I remembered from my dream.

I deliberately shifted my focus, and Lucifer's wings were the obvious choice. The way the feathers moved was mesmerizing, like some strange, metal kaleidoscope. I followed the length of his wingspan, marveling at how huge it was, and that was when I noticed how small the tower had become. Lucifer took us up, and up, and up. Within a minute, we were so high that my nerves got the better of me, and I grabbed hold of his broad shoulders. I knew if I looked at him, he'd be watching me with a soft smile. I was determined not to give in to the urge. My eyes went up to those otherworldly flashes, which were higher than I'd thought. If we'd been in my world, only an airplane would have been able to reach them.

Lucifer took me into the heart of the storm.

At first, I flinched at every burst, convinced we were about to get fried and then plummet to the ground. I also found the silence disconcerting—there were no claps of thunder or echoing rumbles. It was just dim and quiet, almost like a room with the curtains drawn. Then the sky brightened again, and in those brief moments, I caught glimpses of the city below. The roiling clouds. The tip of Lucifer's strange, beautiful wing.

"They're completely harmless," he told me, his eyes glittering with amusement. "We call them light storms."

"Very creative." I'd meant my response to be biting, but the effect was somewhat ruined by a nervous waver that slipped in. I still hadn't let go of Lucifer's shoulders. He didn't point it out, and I pretended not to notice.

He was so much warmer than I'd thought he would be.

We soared through the flashes of red lightning that had seemed so eerie and ominous from a distance. Now I saw a strange sort of beauty in them. The wings Lucifer had forged for himself glinted and reflected the storm happening all around us, inside us. Or inside me, at least. I couldn't pretend to feel nothing as he carried me through his world, my shoulder resting against his hard, broad chest as if I knew him. Trusted him.

Why did it feel, more and more each day, like I did? Like there was a piece of my soul that recognized him, just as it had recognized Collith in Creiddylad's tomb?

I reminded myself that this was what the devil did—he was a master of manipulation. He'd had millennia to perfect the arts of deceit and seduction. The thought made a knot form in my stomach.

Lucifer glanced down at me. After a few seconds, the line along the right corner of his mouth deepened into a questioning smile. I didn't answer, or even react, but my gaze lingered on him for another moment before I looked away, refocusing on the landscape far below. Jagged, black mountains clawed at the sky, and billowing columns of orange smoke burst from the cracked ground.

It struck me anew that Hell wasn't what I'd always imagined it to be. The bible was hardly an accurate resource, but Collith's fragmented memories had depicted a dark place. When I'd found out I'd be coming here, I had prepared myself for fire everywhere, the air full of screams, pain and blood in each encounter. And yet . . . I'd encountered kindness in this place. There were cities and histories, just like in my world. There was even beauty.

That didn't mean Hell was all sunshine and rainbows, though.

Dark growths had appeared along the landscape below. My mind kept wanting to call them trees, but the name wasn't accurate. They looked more like bone than anything living. Black bones, sticking up out of the ground, with craters in the center of a few. There was something ominous about this place, more than anywhere else I'd been so far. I held my hair back to peer down more intently. "What are those? Volcanos?" I asked.

Lucifer didn't take his focus off the horizon. Without looking at me he said, "That is where Abaddon resides. He has been asleep for several centuries. It wouldn't be good for my world if he ever awoke, not as he is now."

"Why?"

Lucifer paused, and I felt my eyebrows go up in surprise. Since we'd met, he had made a point of answering all my questions. This was the first time he'd faltered in his efforts at transparency. I watched his expression closely, intrigued by his hesitation. His fingers flexed on my knee.

"As Fallen have evolved in your world, so they have evolved in mine," the devil said vaguely. He turned his face away.

I wanted to ask what Abaddon had become, but there was a distance in Lucifer's voice. I thought about pressing him. What did I care about his feelings, or his opinion of me? Something held my tongue, though. We tilted in the air, and Lucifer began the journey back to the First City. Neither of us spoke again.

Even after we landed, the Dark Prince didn't say much. Once he'd set me back on my feet, Lucifer bowed and left the roof, his long strides urgent and distracted. He went down the stairs, and his golden head vanished through the archway. I watched him go, frowning.

It was late. There was no way to know the time, not up here, but I could feel sleep tugging at me. The agitation that had sent me up here in the first place was gone, leaving a hollow feeling in its wake. Tomorrow. I'd continue my search tomorrow. I waved wearily at the guards—the ones I could see, anyway—and followed Lucifer down.

I didn't encounter anyone during the walk back. I thought I caught sight of Narfu's tail once, but as usual, he was too fast for me to track. Even security stayed out of sight. I reached my room without talking to another soul, and when I shut the door, an unexpected pang of loneliness hit me.

I tried to distract myself by changing. Washing my face. Brushing my teeth. When I left the bathroom and moved toward the bed, my gaze flicked to the windows. I found myself wondering if Lucifer was restless, too.

Giving in to curiosity, I pulled the curtains aside. Lucifer's were also open, revealing that his bedroom was dark and empty. There were no lights on in his office, either. I stared into the unmoving shadows, my mind going backward. I thought of what I'd learned about Lucifer and how he spent his time.

Suddenly, I knew where he was. I could feel the knowledge in my gut, with the hardness of certainty. I got dressed again. I slipped out of the room like a thief in the night, successfully avoiding the mazzikin's notice.

There was a guard standing in the hall. In a low murmur, I asked him to take me down to the cells.

As soon as the doors slid open, I was greeted by the shoulders of two more security guards. They stood on either side of the elevator. I emerged hesitantly, waiting for one of them to speak or move, but they may as well have been statues.

It seemed Lucifer hadn't instructed them to keep me out of here. He wasn't trying to hide anything. It almost felt like a dare.

There was no sign of him, though, or Dagan. The passageway was empty, and low sounds were swallowed by the darkness. Moans. Footsteps. Sobs.

Something drove me forward, away from the brightness of the elevator. Deeper into the ground.

As I passed, I started looking into some of the cells.

Most of the prisoners were souls. I'd expected all of them to be secured against the wall, like the demon I'd seen, but many were sitting or sleeping. Very few of the conscious ones noticed me. The handful that did gave me looks of pleading. One started to get up, shaking, and I remembered what Lucifer had said. *Many are broken souls that are too dangerous to be free.* I hurried on, feeling guilty and helpless.

Seconds later, I reached the end of the passageway and discovered that it continued in a T. I looked left and right, then back at the guards, who hadn't budged from the elevator. They were too far away to make out their expressions. I could retrace my steps and ask them, I supposed, but there was a good chance they wouldn't understand anything I said.

My powers, I thought. I reached for them automatically, thinking

I'd try to sense if someone in these cells was experiencing more fear than the rest. To see if anyone's thoughts happened to be filled with an image of a tall, golden-haired being. But my abilities were still gone, or dormant—I reached for them and felt the same sensation I had experienced after Cyrus had burned the Nightmare part of me away. Empty. Cold.

The reminder made my stomach tighten.

Just like that, I wanted to pace again. I clenched my hands and glanced down both passages, debating quickly now. I had a fifty-fifty shot of picking the right direction. I liked those odds. Following an impulse, I turned left and kept walking. There were no more guards in sight. Save for the eerie sounds echoing through the dark, it felt like I was completely alone.

I passed cell after cell. Prisoner after prisoner. I wasn't sure how far I'd go, or if I planned to walk the other way. I wasn't even sure what was driving me right now. Maybe I wanted to catch Lucifer unawares, here where the polished facade fell away and he was his true self. Maybe I wanted a reminder of what he was capable of after days of knowing him only as an attentive host. I glanced into the next cell, half-hoping, half-dreading that I'd find what I was looking for.

I did a double take . . . and stopped.

It can't be.

I stared, waiting for the scene to change, hoping this was some kind of fucked-up trick. But the prisoner's features didn't change. The details of the room stayed solid and static.

After a few seconds, I reached for the rusted, metal handle and pulled the door open. It was unlocked. That was because the cell's occupant was chained to the wall, exactly as the demon had been during Lucifer's "tour."

I didn't remember having walked inside, but suddenly I blinked and I was standing in front of him. My nightmare. My enemy. My torturer.

Belanor.

He was almost unrecognizable.

I didn't know how to feel, what to think. I stood there, frozen and staring. All I could do was breathe, even though I knew oxygen didn't exist here, and technically I didn't have a body. But it felt like I did, and right now, I'd half-forgotten how to pull air in and out of my imaginary lungs. I looked at the bloody, blackened lump of flesh hanging against the wall and said nothing, even when his eyes rose to mine. They were the only part of him still untouched, still reminiscent of the faerie who had tortured me.

It felt like the past was in the room with us. Suddenly I could hear the echoes of my own screams. Feel the sizzle of my flesh. I relived the sleep deprivation, the cold, the terror. Belanor's body began to shake, but then, in a dim burst of clarity, I realized I was the one shaking.

"He can't hurt you, Fortuna. Not anymore." Lucifer's voice was directly behind me, and I knew if I moved, I'd feel his chest against my back. I couldn't bring myself to put space between us. I was too busy breathing.

When I stayed silent, Lucifer moved, appearing in my peripheral vision. Even down here, in the murky dimness of so much pain and anguish, he shone brightly golden. A thing of beauty, surrounded by the ugliness he'd created.

"You burned him alive," I said eventually.

In response to this, Lucifer put out his hand. Between one blink and the next, a flame appeared there, hovering just over his palm. It was the same color as Collith's, but more controlled. It crackled in a cluster of blue heat. So Lucifer had the gift of heavenly fire. Somehow, I wasn't surprised.

"There's something so purifying about fire." The devil studied his hand, turning it this way and that, admiring the blaze. Or maybe considering whether to use it again.

"I thought he was your biggest fan." My voice was quiet. Hollow. I'd turned back to Belanor. He seemed to have lost consciousness now; his eyes were closed, and the pained movements of his chest had slowed.

Lucifer closed his fist and snuffed out the flames. I felt him looking at me. "No fan of mine would've endangered your life," he said.

His words brought the memories back again. *Spider legs on the wallpaper. A branding iron glowing red. Blood splattered across sand.* My hands curled, and I felt the bite of my fingernails. "I think he did a little more than 'endanger my life,'" I heard myself say.

"Exactly." Lucifer's arm shifted, and after a moment, he held something out. "I understand that he was killed by his brother. Would *you* like to do the honors this time?"

I glanced toward his offering and saw that it was a knife. The edge of it was crude but sharp—it would tear Belanor's throat open and ensure a slow, painful death. I didn't reach for the small blade, but I didn't look away from it, either. My insides turned to crashing waves and roaring winds. The tempest howled so loudly I couldn't hear anything else. I pictured Belanor choking on his own blood. I imagined the sounds he'd make. I felt the satisfaction it would bring me.

Away. I had to get away.

I turned and walked out of the room.

I didn't know where I was going, so I let my feet lead the way. They brought me back down the passageway, past the cells, and into the elevator. I didn't say a word to the guards. My ears rang as the doors closed and the elevator shot upward. When it stopped, I stepped out and kept walking. I felt detached from my own body, and I barely registered the sight of the sky.

Near my room, I finally slowed to a stop. I approached the low wall that separated me from a perilous fall to the streets below, resting my hand on one of the pillars. The stone was smooth and cool against my palm. I stared out at the winged beasts swooping slowly through the flashes of light. The image of Belanor's destroyed face was replaced by a daydream. I saw myself leaping onto the back of one of those creatures, seizing hold of its curved horns, and forcing it to fly up, up, up, through the layers between the universes, heading home. *Home.* A sharp, piercing sensation filled my chest, and I held the pillar tighter.

A moment later, there was a slight scraping sound behind me. I knew Lucifer had done it on purpose, to make me aware of his presence. I straightened my spine and blinked rapidly, clearing my eyes as best I could. I still didn't speak, so Lucifer did.

"I sense the ferocity in you. The hunger," he said. "You've just been conditioned to believe you should contain it."

I made a disdainful sound. "You know, that sort of thinking is how you got kicked out of your daddy's house."

I'd hoped the reminder would sting, and drive him away. Instead, Lucifer moved to stand beside me. Roused by a spark of defiance, I turned from the sky and met the devil's gaze. He already knew I was afraid of him, and that another part of me was drawn to him, but I wouldn't give Lucifer the gratification of seeing it. Not this time.

Then he ruined everything by leaning in and pressing his forehead against mine. I closed my eyes instinctively to avoid his gaze, his closeness. Lucifer inhaled as if the scent of me was intoxicating. My insides quaked, but I was even more terrified to open my eyes. They were still closed when I forced myself to step away.

He was like Gwyn, I thought, raising my face to Lucifer's. Time and power had stripped him of whatever compassion or goodness he'd once had. I couldn't let him get to me. No matter how long I was trapped down here, I needed to keep finding ways to resist the devil's allure. I looked directly at him and gave a small, mocking smile.

"Is this it?" I asked softly. "Is this your big plan? Coax me to the dark side, warp my mind, and finally use that to get what you want? I see you, Your Majesty. You're just a lonely, spoiled prince."

"You see nothing. But you will." Lucifer turned away. Then he paused. He came back, hands in his pockets, and leaned close to murmur, "By the way . . . I'm the fucking king."

His scent was all around me, masculine and intoxicating, and my gaze dropped to his mouth of its own volition. With one last, lingering look that sent a whisper of heat through me, Lucifer turned again. This time, he left me there, moving soundlessly down the walkway. Moments later, he was out of sight.

Once he was gone, I turned and frowned at the dark horizon.

I didn't go back to bed for a long, long time.

CHAPTER SIXTEEN

*R*oger informed me the next morning that Lucifer had gone away.

It was the opportunity I'd been waiting for. Since my search in the library had proved to be fruitless, it was time to go into the city and speak to some souls. One of them had to know a witch, or a spell that could send me back to my dimension. Lucifer had never explicitly stated that I wasn't allowed to leave the tower, but it was implied. I couldn't operate the elevator on my own, and every time I stepped out of my room, Roger or Saida was there. Once, it was the female guard that I'd seen with Lucifer.

I wasn't a prisoner, but I wasn't free, either.

The answer came to me while I was lying in bed. *Narfu*. Narfu was my ticket out of the tower. He could climb through windows and down vertical walls. With his help, I'd bypass the elevator and the risk of discovery altogether.

There was just the tiny matter of communicating this plan to him.

I also hadn't seen the demon in several days, which meant I needed to get more aggressive. Especially since I wasn't sure when Lucifer would leave again. He didn't hover, by any means, but he always seemed to be nearby. I probably wouldn't get another chance like this by the end of my three weeks here.

Roger was still standing in the hallway outside my room, waiting for an answer. He'd just asked if I would like to have my breakfast in the dining room.

"Actually, will you send Narfu to me?" I asked. "There's something I need him to . . . clean."

The old demon looked concerned. His forehead wrinkled. "Is everything . . . well, my lady?"

"Yes, everything is fine. Just send Narfu as soon as you can. Thank you," I added.

Roger bowed and walked backward, moving out of view. I closed the door and went over to the bed, where I perched on the edge and tried to look as unthreatening as possible. I wore a black button-down and another pair of leggings. My feet were bare because I'd just been about to put on some socks when Roger had knocked. Layers were a necessity in Hell—despite the stories of eternal fire and unbearable heat, this world was cold. So cold even my soul could feel it, apparently.

Narfu arrived without making a single sound. One moment, the doorway to the bathroom was empty. The next, I noticed something in the corner of my eye, and I turned to find the giant lizard standing there. He watched me with the same petrified expression he'd had last time.

"Hello," I said cautiously, getting to my feet. The demon cataloged every movement I made, his scaly body tensed and ready. I kept my hands where he could see them and didn't try to approach. "I don't think we got to officially meet. I'm Fortuna. And you're Narfu?"

There was no understanding in his gaze. He looked from me to the room, undoubtedly searching for whatever I'd told Roger needed cleaning. When he turned his head, my attention went back to the collar he wore.

"Do you know what that's for?" I asked, gesturing toward it.

Narfu just stared at me.

I reminded myself that I'd summoned him to get out of this tower, but even as I thought it, I couldn't ignore the damn thing around his neck. I moved as slowly as I had the last time, and walked around the bed. Narfu's big eyes darted up and down, noting my feet and my expression, looking like he couldn't decide which he found more terrifying. But he didn't move. I got close enough that I could make out the details of the collar again. Keeping my hands where Narfu could see them, I edged around to his other side, hoping a different vantage point would reveal more.

There *was* a way to take it off. It rested just to the left of the prongs, out of sight from the angle I'd been looking at it from before. There were three small holes, and at the very bottom of each, I saw the glint of a button or a lock mechanism. The design was unexpectedly simple after all the technology I'd seen here, but still effective—no way was Narfu getting his big, lizard fingers in those holes. Only a soul or a human-shaped demon could reach the release buttons.

Well, only a soul, a human-shaped demon, or . . . me.

I hesitated for the length of three heartbeats, hearing them in my ears as I paused and considered the potential consequences of doing this. Then I looked at those prongs again, and saw the hardened blood around them.

Since warning Narfu would probably make him panic or move, I stood on tiptoe and fit my fingers into the holes without a word. The collar popped open and the prongs retracted.

Narfu's eyes flared with pain, and his lips lifted in a hiss. Long, pointed teeth filled my vision and now I was the one to freeze. Then I blinked, and the demon was gone in a burst of scrabbling nails. The only sign he'd been there was the heavy, blood-crusted collar dangling from my hand.

Okay, so maybe Narfu isn't an option, I thought faintly, unable to shake the sense that I'd just come very, very close to death.

And now I needed to come up with a new plan to get out of the tower.

"Fuck. *Fuck.*" I let out a breath and swung away, mentally kicking myself. I went back into the closet, where I hid the vile collar beneath the skirt of a voluminous gown. As an afterthought, I finally pulled on a pair of socks. Maybe I'd feel more clear-headed if I wasn't freezing. Rubbing warmth into my arms, I left the closet and strode over to the fireplace. It had been tended to before I awoke, or sometime in the middle of the night, because the flames were bright and full. Within seconds, I started pacing in front of it. I glared down at the floor, my mouth twisted in thought.

I spent the rest of the morning trying, and failing, to come up with an escape strategy. Every plan I made had holes in it, or failed when I did a mental run-through of possible scenarios. I couldn't bribe or trust any of the demons in this tower, because they were undeniably loyal to their master. I couldn't sneak out without the cameras seeing me. This floor was too high up to dangle a rope from the window, Rapunzel-style, and scaling down the side myself would be impossible. Then there was the issue of the terrifying beasts in the lobby. They'd let Blondie pass, sure, but I wasn't interested in testing whether they'd do the same for me.

Eventually I grew tired of the guest suite, and I went back to the library. Roger accompanied me, of course, and he made more polite conversation during the short walk. He talked about a species of demon who lived in the north, a harmless race that communicated to each other with flashes of light from their antennae and floated through clouds of poisonous fumes like butterflies in a field. I listened to his friendly chatter without any rude comments or interruptions—against my better judgment, I'd started to like Roger.

Once the elevator doors opened, I said goodbye to him and stepped out alone. The library was as welcoming as ever, with a fire blazing in the hearth and warm lights scattered throughout, making the rugs and books glow, or flicker with soft shadows. But tonight, it didn't have its usual calming effect. I was frowning as I went to a new section and started at the top left, just as I'd done with the others I had gotten through. I wasn't even sure what I was looking for, at this point. I just couldn't stay in that bedroom and do nothing, or drive myself insane by going in circles. I carried a stack to the table I often used, the stone surface smooth and gleaming.

After another hour or two, I shoved a book back in a burst of frustration. This one was in English, which should've made it more helpful. Instead, I now possessed a vast amount of useless knowledge about a region called the Lowlands. I stared at the shelves without seeing them, considering all my options for the thousandth time. There had to be a way. There was always a way.

It felt like I was on the verge of screaming when I heard him. Heard his strong, gentle voice. *Sometimes it's not about being stronger. It's about being smarter.*

The memory soothed me more than the library ever had. Even when he couldn't reach me, Oliver was there. Guiding me. Loving me.

I sat there and tapped my finger against the table. Maybe I was going about this all wrong—I couldn't overpower Lucifer, or evade him. This was his domain and these were his people. His rules.

Instead of trying to get around the devil, I had to go *through* him.

What did I know about Lucifer, now that I'd been roommates with him for several days? Well, I knew that he valued the promises he made. He liked deals and games. He wanted me to trust him. How could I use that?

The thought was a spark. An idea began to form, and soon enough, it spread like wildfire.

I ran through the scenario, and this time, it worked. There would be variations, of course, and I couldn't predict Lucifer's mood or his exact reactions, but it worked. The hardest part would be the role I had to play. I needed to make the devil believe he stood something to gain, and that something was me. I swallowed at the thought.

No time for that. Adrenaline rushed through me now, the heady rush of realizing I might actually pull this off. I started to pace again, this time in front of the window. For the remainder of the day, I prepared. I imagined outcomes. I considered the exact words I would say.

That was how Lucifer found me.

The *ding* alerted me that someone was arriving, but I didn't stop. I was nervous, agitated, and I didn't feel ready for what was about to happen. There were so many ways I could fuck it up.

"Always pacing, Lady Sworn," that husky, familiar voice remarked. "If you'd like to go for a run, I can make arrangements."

I finally slowed, then turned. My lungs gathered the smallest, most subtle of breaths, and I thought of my family. I met Lucifer's gaze and raised my eyebrows at him. "How did you know that I'm a runner? Have you been spying on me?"

"I saw your running shoes when I came to the loft. Right before you cut off my head," he said wryly. There was a gleam in his eyes, as if the memory amused him.

I bet Jacob Goldmann didn't find it so amusing, I thought, wishing I could say it out loud. Remind Lucifer of the fact that I knew he was a cold-blooded murderer. But I was playing nice tonight. I kept my mouth shut and gave him a swift, expressionless once-over. He wore what looked like a designer sweater, and I was struck by the strange thought that Laurie would appreciate the devil's fashion sense.

"Will you join me in the dining room tonight?" Lucifer said, halting next to the table. His fingers rested on the cover of the book I'd shoved away.

It was the same question he asked me every night, and I'd been expecting it. Depending on it, actually. Almost every time he extended the invitation, I said no. But Lucifer would get suspicious if I changed my tune for no apparent reason, so I pretended to hesitate, turning my face toward the window. I stared at those distant flickers and tried to focus on why I was doing this.

Why, then, could I only think of flying? Flying through that dark sky, my shoulder against a warm chest, the wind in my hair and my eyes as I lost myself to that vast, foreign horizon.

I gritted my teeth and shoved the memory away. I'd hesitated long enough. I spun back to Lucifer and hurried past him, muttering as I went, "Fine. But only because I'm desperate for a change of scenery."

He didn't say anything, but his amusement permeated the air around us as he followed me toward the elevator. I jammed the button with my thumb, since it was the only part I could actually do. The doors slid open immediately, and we got on together, facing the doors at the same time.

"Have you found anything interesting during your time here?" Lucifer asked. He pressed one of the symbols on the screen, and I tried to watch without making it obvious. I was still trying to figure out what each of them meant.

"Not a thing," I said flatly. It wasn't even a dig or an attempt to piss him off—I really hadn't found a single goddamn thing in that library. Suddenly I wondered if that was by design, and I fought the urge to give Lucifer a suspicious look. His stance was relaxed, his expression calm as ever. A king in his castle, completely assured of his power and hold over everything.

Well, we would just see about that.

Ding. The doors opened again, and the two of us strode down the walkway. I couldn't tell if it was my own nervousness, but the air between us felt like it crackled with tension and unspoken words. We were both hiding something, and neither of us was about to give. Tonight's game had only just begun.

I took a subtle, fortifying breath and kept my gaze on the open doors at the end of the hall. Dagan and the female guard stood on either side of the towering entrance. I'd gotten so used to them that I no longer reacted to Dagan's scaled skin or the black claws the female had in place of fingernails.

The dining room had been prepared for our arrival. Along three walls, sconces glowed bright. The fire was high and vibrant, casting its heat all the way to the doors. With fluid, long-legged strides, Lucifer went over to the table. He wrapped his long fingers around one of the chairs and pulled it out for me, flashing a charming smile that revealed slight indents in his cheeks. Not quite dimples, but close, and they drew attention to his sharp jawline.

Heat spread through my lower belly again. Why did the evil ones always seem to be the hottest? I fought back a scowl and sat down, handling the chair more roughly than was necessary as I pulled it closer to the table. Lucifer sat with more grace, of course, and that infuriating smile still hovered around his lips.

Once again, I reminded myself I was playing nice. I couldn't ask the devil where he'd been all my life and if he could crawl back there, or tell him that he looked like a before picture. We'd both know that last one was a lie, anyway. I gritted my teeth and reached for my glass of water just as Saida appeared and set down two plates of steaming, elegantly arranged food. Lucifer thanked her and stood to retrieve the wine bottle.

"Would you like any, my lady?" he asked. I shook my head. It was probably a moot point, avoiding the wine when I'd been drinking the water, but I also wanted to stay clear-headed. Lucifer just turned and poured some into his own glass, then returned to his chair. "The chef prepared one of his favorite dishes in hopes you'd come tonight. It's called bazzollath."

I noticed that he didn't tell me what, exactly, the dish was. I would probably vomit all over it if I knew.

The origin of the meat didn't matter, though. Just like every other meal we'd shared together, I didn't eat it. I just pushed the food around my plate or flattened it with my fork. Lucifer didn't try to force a conversation, and I decided to use the silence to my advantage. I waited until he had nearly finished eating before I made my first move.

"I'm bored," I declared. "Let's play a game."

Lucifer didn't bat an eye. He sat back in his chair and regarded me for a moment, holding his glass of wine in a light grasp. I still couldn't guess at his thoughts, but I'd learned enough about him at this point to know his wheels were turning. Once more, it struck me how similar Lucifer could be to the males I'd left behind in my world. I wasn't sure what this said about my own mind, that I was continually drawn to people like him. Probably something I should bring up in my next therapy session.

First, though, I needed to get home.

"Very well. Lady's choice," Lucifer replied at last, just as I felt my resolve harden all over again.

I looked down at the table, my brows furrowed. I allowed a few seconds to pass. Then I lifted my head and said, "Truth or dare. The first one to yield loses the game, of course."

"I suppose the winner gets something out of it?" Lucifer asked, sounding amused again. As if he knew exactly what I was doing. He made a gesture to Roger, who dipped into a bow and slipped from the room.

As Lucifer refocused on me, I felt my heart quicken. This was it. This was the first pivotal moment for the new plan I'd come up with. I had rehearsed what to say during all those hours of preparation. My thoughts tended to muddle whenever I was around Lucifer, and I couldn't let that affect my chances of getting home.

"If you win, I will have dinner with you every day this week," I stated.

Lucifer cocked his head. He didn't argue with my suggestion, which meant I'd done well with that part of the plan, at least. "And if you win?" he asked.

I commanded my pulse to slow down. *Breathe, Fortuna. Just breathe.* When I answered, I sounded steady, and even the oldest courtiers of the Unseelie Court wouldn't have known that every nerve ending in my body was burning with anxiety. "If I win, I am free. I get to leave this tower whenever I want, and none of your people can come with me, or follow me."

I stopped, and I fought the instinct to hold my breath. Lucifer would hear my lungs go still and realize how important this was. Seconds ticked by, the silence disturbed only by the fire's crackle. Then, instead of giving me an answer, Lucifer turned in his chair and said something to Saida in Enochian. The demon nodded and hurried out.

She returned less than a minute later, holding another bottle of wine in one hand and two glasses in the other. Lucifer took the bottle from her, and once she'd put the glasses down, Saida removed the old ones. As she retreated, Lucifer poured. I gave the wine a puzzled glance and kept waiting for his response, expecting him to warn me of the untold dangers beyond the tower. But in the end, he just raised his glass and said, "There's a truth spell on the wine. Once you drink it, the game has begun."

My confusion cleared. *Damn,* I thought. They did things a little differently in Hell. I hesitated, peering down into the glass as if I could see magic shimmering on the surface. "Will the wine force me to perform dares, too?" I asked.

Lucifer held my gaze. "No. I will never take your choice from you—free will is much more entertaining. In that, at least, my father and I can agree."

My interest was piqued. Lucifer didn't talk about God, or his past, or the dimension he'd been cast out of. However adamant I was about not wanting to know him, I couldn't deny that I was curious.

But now wasn't the time to satisfy a little of that curiosity. Lucifer had fallen silent, and I realized he was waiting for me to make a choice. I'd already made it, though. I wanted to see my family again, and there was nothing I wouldn't do to achieve that.

Even a game of truth or dare with the devil.

Stillness hovered around us again. Just like that moment in the library, I didn't want to agree too quickly. Lucifer might know I was up to something, but I could still hide the depth of my planning from him. The fire popped and sent a flare of light across the room, bathing one side of Lucifer's face. Without looking away from him, I finally picked the glass up and raised it. "To the truth," I said.

Lucifer's eyes gleamed. "And to daring," he replied.

Our glasses clinked. It felt like the small vibration traveled through my entire hand, and the sound was like a bell in the big, quiet room. Apprehension filled my throat, so I washed it down with wine. I couldn't bring myself to meet Lucifer's gaze, so I looked up as I drank, absorbing the unexpectedly sweet flavor. We set our glasses back on the table at the same time.

I waited, expecting to feel the spell take hold. But everything seemed normal. That didn't mean the spell hadn't worked, though—sometimes magic was subtle, or virtually undetectable. The game had probably started the moment I swallowed. Trying to hide my reluctance, I settled against the back of the chair and brought one knee up to hug it. "I guess I should go first, since I was the one to suggest this."

Lucifer quirked a brow. "I'd be happy to break the ice, my lady."

"Okay, great," I chirped. The spell had made this game more

dangerous, and I wasn't about to turn down a chance at avoiding one turn. "Truth or dare?"

Lucifer appraised my expression. "You expect me to say 'dare.' Why?"

"Because you're temptation. You're supposed to be this wicked, wild creature. Of course you would want to do something on a dare," I said dismissively, taking another sip of the wine. I'd already had some, so the damage was done. Might as well enjoy it.

Lucifer looked sad. Sad, and maybe a little angry. "I am not temptation" was all he said.

Do not feel bad for the devil, Fortuna. He was just trying to make me sympathize with him, and get me on his side. I wasn't going to fall for it. I took another drink of wine and raised my eyebrows. "Well? You never chose. Truth or dare."

"Truth."

My first instinct was to ask him something about magic, or the prisoners below the tower. I opened my mouth to do exactly that, but then I heard myself say, "If you're not temptation, what are you?"

Lucifer sipped from his glass. I couldn't get a read on his expression, and he matched my matter-of-fact tone when he answered, "I am desire. I am a reflection of what you want most."

My eyebrows shot up. "So you're like a Nightmare?"

"Ah, but I already gave you one truth. It's your turn. Truth or dare?" Lucifer asked, giving me a look that said, *Uh, uh, uh.*

It had been worth a shot, at least. As Lucifer waited for my response, I was tempted to finish the glass of wine for some liquid courage. This was another part of the evening I'd carefully considered from all angles. The truth was too dangerous, I'd decided during all my plotting in the library. I didn't know what sort of questions Lucifer would ask, and now I'd just had wine that made lying impossible. Which only left one other option.

I ignored a flutter of fear in my chest and answered, "Dare."

Lucifer grinned. His entire face lit up when he did that, and it was like sunlight—beautiful and golden and too bright. I looked down quickly, trying to control my reaction. He plucked something off his plate and held it out to me. It looked like cheese. "I dare you to eat this," he said.

I frowned, automatically taking it from his fingers. I was careful not to make any skin-to-skin contact. "That's it?"

Lucifer gave me a single nod. "That's it."

I kept frowning at him, convinced there had to be a catch. But the devil just looked back calmly, his hands folded on top of the table. Firelight danced over his features. I popped the small square into my mouth, intending to swallow it immediately. But then the flavor registered. Holy shit, that was good. Like cheese, but . . . sweet and spicy at the same time. *Damn it.*

"There. Happy?" I said tonelessly. I looked at Lucifer with flat eyes.

"Very."

The warmth in his voice, and the intent way he was looking at me, made my entire body flush. "Your turn," I said quickly. "Truth or dare?"

"Truth."

"You said you're a reflection of what I want most. So you're like a Nightmare?" I repeated.

"No." Lucifer tilted his head, his mouth pursed in thought. A lock of that shining, golden hair fell over his brow. He refocused on me and leaned forward, resting his elbows on the table. "Say what you wanted most was acceptance. You would not look at me and see a vision of yourself surrounded by friends or adoring fans, but you would feel whatever that dream makes you feel. It's more subtle than that, of course."

Hearing this, I felt sick . . . and maybe a little impressed, too. No wonder the devil inspired such devotion and loyalty. No one stood a chance against power like that.

Oh, God. What did it mean, then, that I'd taken one look at him in the mirror and felt an immediate sexual rush?

I tipped my wine glass back again.

Lucifer was silent as I gulped it down, finishing what was left. He waited to speak until I lowered the glass. "Truth or dare," he said.

The wine did help. I felt less jittery, and there was no waver in my voice when I looked him in the eye and answered, "Dare."

"Touch me."

I blinked. "What?"

Lucifer didn't answer. Instead, he stood up and came around the corner of the table. His scent assailed my senses again, threatening to undo my clarity and resolve. He bent into a bow and held out his hand. He didn't say the words again, but I heard them. Our eyes caught and held as his dare whispered through my mind. *Touch me.*

I looked at his hand as if it were something dangerous. If I didn't take it, I would lose the game, and then I'd have to join him for dinner every fucking night. Seven nights of this tense silence, this push and pull, this relentless temptation. Regardless of what Lucifer said, that's exactly what he was to me. The wildness in him called to mine like a sirensong, and if I got too close, I might drown.

I just needed to stay afloat long enough to get back to my family.

Without letting myself think about it anymore, I reached for Lucifer, and my fingers curled around his. He pulled me up from the chair, picked up our drinks with his other hand, and led me away from the table. We walked across the room and stopped in front of the fireplace, where Lucifer turned to face me. The light moved over his thick, wavy hair, making certain strands glint and gleam as he let go of my hand and gently pressed my wine glass into it.

"See?" he said softly. "Nothing happened. You didn't catch fire, or get bewitched."

I wasn't so certain.

I tipped my head back and forced myself to meet Lucifer's gaze. His eyes glistened with so many secrets and depths that it was dizzying, like peering down into clear ocean. "It's your turn" was all I said.

Lucifer lifted his drink wordlessly. I only hesitated for a beat before raising my own. We clinked our glasses, drank, and the game went on.

Again and again, Lucifer opted for truth. Again and again, I forced myself to pick dare. I kept bracing myself for him to take advantage, force me to do something terrible, but his dares only involved food. He'd brought our plates over from the table, and every time my turn came back around, he selected something new to put in my hand. Despite how alien it all looked, the flavors were good. Some of them were comparable to things I'd eaten at home, and others were like nothing I had encountered before.

There was only one thing on the plate that I didn't like. *Hate* would be a more accurate word, actually. When I registered the taste, I wrinkled my nose in revulsion, and Lucifer laughed at my expression. The sound sent another flutter through me.

Saida came back to clear the plates, and she also brought a new bottle of wine. Lucifer gave her a warm thanks as he took it. The demon blushed and scurried away.

We kept drinking, and I stopped worrying about the truth spell. I couldn't feel it, and it wasn't relevant to my part in this game, anyway. After a while, it felt like the wine flowed through my veins instead of blood. Our back-and-forth became less restrained. I began to say whatever popped into my head.

"Have you influenced me with your power?" I asked bluntly. I pointed my wine glass at Lucifer, almost spilling it on the rug. "And don't you dare pretend you don't know what I'm talking about."

We were sitting in front of the fire now. One of Lucifer's long legs was stretched out beside me, his calf nearly touching my hip. Neither of us had acknowledged it. I felt loose and warm, like my body had started to thaw.

"No, I have not," Lucifer responded. As if he knew exactly why I was frowning, another smile hovered around the devil's lips. "What you feel is like calling to like. Soul reacting to soul."

Sure, I thought, resisting the urge to roll my eyes. I didn't believe it was our souls that kept colliding—it was our darkness.

The thought sobered me up a little. I drew away from Lucifer, realizing how close I'd been leaning. Guilt and unease settled in my chest. *It's the cozy fire. And the wine*, I thought. My gaze fell on the glasses next to us, both of them empty now, along with the two bottles we'd finished. I needed to get out of this room. What came next wasn't going to be any easier, though. Neither of us had yielded and my plan was still in action. I hid the way my insides trembled.

"I think I should probably go to bed," I said.

"I'll escort you up," Lucifer said, just as I knew he would. He got to his feet and once again extended his hand. It was still my first instinct to ignore it. But now, more than ever, it was important that Lucifer believed I was softening toward him. I steeled myself and allowed him to help me up, sparks going through my fingers. He released me right away, and we left the impromptu picnic area we'd made.

On the way to the elevator, we passed Dagan and the other guard. It didn't feel right to ignore them, so I gave both a small, awkward wave. Dagan returned the gesture with a kind smile. *Shit*, I thought, facing forward quickly. I was starting to like Lucifer's staff.

Less than a minute later, we arrived at the door to my room. It was time for the second part of tonight's plan. Or the third. I wasn't sure, I'd lost count somewhere along the way. I was actually glad I'd had so much wine, because it made this easier.

I was about to seduce the devil.

Fighting the urge to swallow, because I knew he would hear it, I faced Lucifer. "Truth or dare?" I breathed, my eyes on his mouth.

Lucifer paused. I didn't look up at his eyes, so I couldn't tell if it was surprise or caution that made him go still. But his stillness didn't last long—not after I brought up my hands and laid them on his chest. Slowly, the King of Hell bent his head. A lock of his soft hair brushed my forehead, and I felt his hand curve around my waist.

"Dare," he said, his voice huskier than usual.

Adrenaline shot through my veins and hit my heart like an electric jolt, sending it into a rapid beat. Lucifer had done *exactly* what I had hoped.

All night, I'd been holding onto a single dare. Waiting for this moment. Praying for my chance.

It was the wild card. The surprise move on the chessboard. The twist ending of the movie. I'd thought of it while I was pacing in the library, and I'd known, in my gut, this would work and win me the game. The only problem had been getting Lucifer to actually agree to a dare.

Thankfully, the devil was male—however ancient he might be, however intelligent and cunning, he still thought with his dick. That was a given no matter what species I was dealing with.

So I smiled up at Lucifer with all the satisfaction of a hunter finding an animal in the trap, or the cat who'd cornered a mouse. "I dare you to show me what's behind that mysterious door," I said.

There was another pause, and I could have sworn the temperature dropped. Lucifer looked down at me. He was probably working out that I'd planned this. So much depended on what he did next. *Everything* depended on it. My heart beat so hard that I could hear it in my ears. I used it to mark the seconds. *One. Two. Three.*

"I yield," the devil said at last. "You win our wager, fair queen."

Excitement sent my heart into a rising crescendo. "You'll honor it?"

"Of course I will." His voice was soft. "I'll notify my staff in the morning."

"Okay. Thanks. Well, good night, I guess." It felt like such a strange, stilted note to leave on, considering everything we'd said tonight, but I had no idea what else to say. I gave Lucifer an awkward nod and began to turn away, reaching for the doorknob.

"Lady Sworn," Lucifer said. I turned back. He kept his eyes on mine, and there was a soft vulnerability in the way his demeanor shifted. "My name is Heilel."

I went still. It was such a simple statement, just four words, but it was the first piece of himself that he'd ever given me. It changed things, somehow.

I felt a rush of fear, and I spun back around, desperate to hide my reaction from Lucifer. He would figure out what I was really afraid of. For some reason, the thought of him knowing that was more terrifying than anything else I'd seen in Hell. I reached for the doorknob again.

"Allow me," Lucifer said, his hand already on it. I hadn't even seen him move. I felt his breath on the back of my neck, and another ripple of desire went through me, stronger this time. It felt like there was a tiny voice in my head, pleading. Urging.

Give in. Give in. Give in.

God forgive me, I wanted to. I really wanted to. It felt like I was hanging off the edge of a cliff, holding on with just my fingertips. I needed something else to grab onto.

A new question formed in my head.

I spoke over my shoulder because I couldn't bring myself to fully face him. "Truth or dare?"

He searched my gaze, a faint line between his eyebrows. As if he'd stumbled upon something strange in his path, and he didn't know what it was. "Truth," Lucifer said.

No surprise there—the devil had been surprisingly forthcoming this evening. He was either determined to win my approval or, just as I was nervous about what truths I might reveal, worried about what my dares could expose.

But the truth was always worse. Strange the devil hadn't figured that out yet.

My voice was quiet. Like the whistle of air just before an ax fell. "When was the last time you did something good?"

Lucifer looked back at me, and his expression was impenetrable as ever. The silence stretched on. And on, and on.

When it became apparent that he wouldn't—couldn't—answer, I felt my lips curve into a small, humorless smile. "That's what I thought," I said. "Good night, Lucifer."

He flinched as the name cut between us. We both knew it was my way of throwing his gift back in his face. I'd never tell him how those soft words floated in my mind. *My name is Heilel.*

Without waiting for a response, I put my back to him and stepped inside the guest suite. I didn't look back, but I could feel Lucifer's eyes on me as I closed the door. I leaned against it and willed my heart to slow down.

I knew, without looking or feeling, that my underwear was wet.

It was physical proof of what I'd been trying so hard to deny. This was the part where I usually reminded myself that it was magic, whatever I felt for Lucifer. That I completely loathed him, and there was no part of me that actually wanted the monster who had destroyed so many lives, my own included.

But this time, that didn't matter. I didn't need to comfort myself with pretty lies, because I had one triumphant, beautiful truth. I'd won. I'd *won*. I had gone toe-to-toe with the devil, and I had walked away the victor. How many people could say that?

Tomorrow, I would leave the tower.

The moment I fell asleep, Lucifer was waiting.

But this was different than the other dreams. Tonight, there were no open skies or distant, crashing sea. My eyes darted around, widening.

I was in a room with mirrored walls. The only piece of furniture was a single, enormous bed with a black frame and red sheets. The lighting was low, gleaming on a smooth wooden floor. Dimness and shadow clung to every sharp angle and deep corner. But I wasn't on the bed or standing in one of those corners.

I was hanging from a chain.

Lucifer wasn't here, but I knew he had to be responsible for this. I was stretched taut, my wrists bound and tied to the ceiling to display my naked body. One of the lights beat down on me, putting a spotlight on whatever was about to happen. Just as I started to struggle, the door opened, and I froze.

Lucifer came through.

In the space of a breath, my heart was hammering. I worked to control my expression as he closed the door behind him, every movement graceful and measured. He looked like he'd just finished a long day in his office. His sleeves were rolled up to his forearms, and he wore no jacket or tie. His hands were in his pockets and his feet were bare. Every inch of him was casual, pensive. Almost absent.

Before I could say anything, Lucifer stopped in front of me and lifted his head. There was a dangerous glitter in his eyes that I didn't like . . . or maybe a part of me liked too much. Without a word, Lucifer took his hands out of his pockets and reached up. Slowly, he began to unbutton his shirt. He pulled it off his shoulders, one side at a time, and let the shirt fall to the floor.

I'd seen him like this before, my first night in Hell, but it was different up close. Muscles rippled beneath his smooth skin. Dominance and power rolled off him like a scent. His hands rose again, but this time, they went to his belt.

My eyes jerked back up to Lucifer's. It was a futile effort to hide how much I wanted him to undo that belt; I knew he could smell my reaction to him. Lucifer didn't acknowledge it, though. He didn't even pause. The belt was already off, and then he undid the button on his slacks. He was wearing boxer briefs underneath. The lights shone down on his muscled thighs, then his calves. Next, Lucifer hooked his thumbs in his briefs and pulled them down. This time, I didn't look away or pretend not to watch. Once he stood completely naked before me, the mirrored walls revealed every angle of Lucifer's body, too.

He was perfection.

Silence shivered around us. There were a hundred things I could've said. I could have insulted him, or spat at him. But I just . . . hung there. Staring at Lucifer like people usually stared at me. After a few seconds, I wrenched at the chains, more to shake myself out of my daze than to break free.

"Careful. You'll hurt yourself," Lucifer said. It was the first time either of us had spoken. He gripped my hips with big hands, anchoring me at the perfect distance. He held me firmly, slightly beyond his cock, withholding what I was secretly desperate to feel.

"Stop this," I snapped. But the waver in my voice made the command far less effective.

He just chuckled, and the sound sent shivers down my spine. "Would you like to know a secret, Lady Sworn?" the devil asked.

I didn't answer, because I worried my voice would betray me again. When it became clear I wouldn't speak, Lucifer took hold of my ankles and parted my legs. Desire burned through me.

"What secret?" I said through my teeth, jerking uselessly at the cuffs again. But I didn't know who I was fighting anymore. Without taking his eyes from mine, Lucifer poised himself between my parted thighs, and I stopped breathing. I felt the tip of his long, thick cock brush against my entrance.

With that single, fleeting touch, all my resistance melted away. I was practically trembling now. I knew if Lucifer pushed his way inside, I wouldn't fight him. I stared up at his golden face, breathing hard, hoping he'd do it and yet dreading that he would.

But he didn't take advantage of my weakness. Instead, Lucifer leaned close and whispered, "This is the secret . . . I'm not the one controlling this dream. You are."

"You're a fucking liar," I said automatically. Even as I denied it, though, I felt a jolt of shame. I had that immediate, sinking feeling you get when you know someone is right. My half-hearted attempt to close my legs only made me clamp down harder on Lucifer's hips, effectively bringing him closer to me. A whimper lodged in my throat.

Lucifer was losing control, too—gone was the remote expression he'd worn earlier. He hauled me against him. It would only take the single, slightest movement for his hardness to slide into my hot, wet entrance. I bit my lip to stop myself from begging him for it. Lucifer watched the battle raging in my eyes, and when it became evident I wouldn't yield, I swore he began to glow. As if his frustration had become sparks beneath his skin.

"Let me in," the devil growled. The dark desire in his voice sent another quake through me.

Never. My chest heaved against his. I wanted him like I'd never wanted anything before. My mind told me desperate, hungry lies. One time wouldn't hurt. Just one time. It wasn't even real. I stared into Lucifer's pretty blue eyes, then looked down at his lips. I imagined what they'd feel like on my clit.

"No," I whispered.

He stared at me for a beat, and once again, I couldn't define the look in his eyes. Then Lucifer's hands fell away and he stepped back.

I'd been wrapped around him like a pretzel, and as my legs swung toward the floor, the chains snapped.

At the same moment I heard that, and felt the jolt through my arms, I woke up.

Propping myself up on my elbows, I looked around wildly, convinced Lucifer would be here as well, because I couldn't ever escape him. But I was alone in my bed. Alone and . . . aching.

A fire still burned in the grate. It cast a soft-edged glow over everything. Moving more slowly now, I sat upright, my eyes going to those curtains on the other side of the room. They were shut. Nothing moved as I scanned every piece of furniture, every shadow.

Once I was sure the room was really empty, I eased back onto the bed. One second passed. Two. My hand stole downward, trailing along my inner thigh. Just I was about to touch the part of me yearning for Lucifer, that small voice returned. *Fight him, Fortuna.*

"*Fuck.*" I yanked my hand back out and let it flop onto the covers. A heavy sigh slipped out of me, and I stared up at the ceiling restlessly. As I waited to fall asleep again, I chanted those words like a spell. My heart beat like a dark rhythm.

Fight him. Fight him. Fight him.

CHAPTER SEVENTEEN

Sweat streamed down my collarbone and the base of my spine. Breathing hard, I glared at the dummy in front of me as if I had a personal vendetta against it.

The gray, lumpy thing gazed back pitifully. No one had thought to give it eyes or a mouth, and its whole body was lopsided. Its placement on the short stand looked precarious, but so far, I hadn't been able to knock it over. I prowled around the dummy in a restless circle, silently reminding myself that it was all in my head, the exhaustion. I should've been able to keep hitting for hours without stopping.

Holding this thought tightly in my mind, I launched forward again, swinging, striking, kicking, spinning. An ache began in my side and I ignored it determinedly, whacking the dummy so hard with the edge of my sword that a dent appeared in its side. Satisfaction ebbed through me; I was getting stronger.

I was back in the library. It was still too early to begin my excursion into the city, so I'd found Roger and asked if he could bring back one of the practice swords Lucifer and I had used for our little face-off the other day. As I passed the hours training, I kept going to the window and peering down. There was no such thing as night and day here, but there were certain stretches of time that were quieter than others. Safer. I'd learned that much, at least, during my time here. The busier the streets below, the more likely I was to run into trouble.

Lucifer wasn't entirely to blame for my bad mood. Some of it, strangely enough, was because of Narfu. I had spotted the demon on my way to the library. He'd scuttled out of sight, but I'd seen his neck—there was still no collar. No reason for the fact that he hadn't claimed his freedom or seized the opportunity to leave this tower.

I'd just started whaling on the dummy again when the elevator doors opened.

I didn't stop or look to see who it was, but judging from the way my entire body lit up, it could only be one person. From the corner of my eye, I saw Lucifer lean his hip against one of the pillars. He crossed his arms over his chest and watched me. I was suddenly conscious of the thin tank top I was wearing, and that I hadn't changed out of the tiny shorts I'd fallen asleep in.

The last time we'd seen each other had been just a few hours ago, when we were both very naked . . . thanks to me.

Tension shot through my jaw, and I forced myself to unclench it. I kept going, waiting for Lucifer to bring up the dream. Instead, he kept his focus on my movements with the sword and said, "I can teach you."

I already have a teacher, thanks. I forced back the sharp response and struck the dummy again. "I'd rather go flying" was all I said.

"Maybe later. Come downstairs for breakfast." Lucifer inclined his golden head, and it glinted in the firelight.

"Maybe later," I said, mocking him. Fuck it. I was done playing nice, anyway. I'd gotten what I wanted from him. I hit the dummy, grunting.

Seconds later, someone else arrived on the elevator. I heard the familiar *clip-clop* of Roger's feet, and the intensity of Lucifer's focus finally moved away from me. His head bent as he and Roger had one of their secret conversations. Whatever the demon said made Lucifer's eyes darken. I observed them as subtly as I could, making sure not to falter in my training.

Once they were done, Roger bowed and stepped back. Lucifer nodded at me in a silent goodbye, his expression distracted. He strode back onto the elevator, where Dagan was already waiting. I'd finally stopped fighting the dummy, and I stood in the center of the room, my gaze locked with Lucifer's as the doors closed between us.

I couldn't focus after that. Even after he had been gone for several minutes, my strikes were off. I wasn't punching with as much force. Roger stood in the shadows, keeping his face turned toward the windows. Eventually I swung away from the dummy, growling. A burst of temper almost made me throw my sword at the wall. I took some deep breaths and placed it calmly on the table.

Roger moved forward. "Are you finished, my lady?"

"Yes." I started toward the elevator, knowing the demon would follow. As he reached my side, I thought about the hours ahead. I could *not* spend them in that bedroom, where the sight of the rumpled covers would remind me of last night. Of why, exactly, I'd been tossing and turning so much. "Actually, will you take me up to the roof?"

"Of course, my lady."

A minute later, I rushed off the elevator, arching my neck back to breathe in the open air. It didn't matter that the need for oxygen was all in my head, I swore it helped. I passed below the stone circle that connected all the pillars, and walked through the shadows of the gargoyles that perched on top. For a split second, I could've sworn one of them moved. I halted in the middle of the circle they made, but I was still restless.

Roger must've sensed that I wanted to be alone, because he bowed and walked backward, away from me. The elevator doors opened and shut with his departure.

I tried to focus on today's plan. I'd need a weapon before I left the tower. But I had never seen a gun here, and the knives were undoubtedly kept in the kitchen. A room I'd never seen, even during Lucifer's tour. I could probably ask Roger to take me there, but he would undoubtedly tell Lucifer about it.

Wait. I frowned and came to an abrupt halt, realizing, belatedly, that I had started pacing at some point. Technically, I wasn't a prisoner. What if I just . . . *asked* for a weapon?

My thoughts were disturbed by the faint rustle of wingbeats above. I spun around, and I hated how the breath caught in my throat.

Lucifer was like some beautiful statue in a fairy-tale courtyard. He'd landed on the ledge, and he stayed crouched there, head bent, hands folded loosely between his knees. The horizon rumbled behind him. He must've just been somewhere cold, because his cheeks were dark and his hair rested over his forehead in half-frozen waves. The devil's wings loomed behind him like dozens of strange stars, catching every flash and flicker of red.

I took one look at Lucifer and knew something was wrong. It felt like his pain was a current that traveled from his heart to mine. Not one muscle in his face moved. I found myself wanting to ask what had happened. I bit my tongue, hard. *Don't say a word, Fortuna. You don't care about his problems.*

Lucifer still hadn't looked up. When he finally spoke, his tone matched his expression—detached. "They called me Light Bearer. The Shining One. Now I am the Destroyer. Lord of Filth," he said.

You don't care about his problems. I walked over to the ledge and peered down at the street. It was finally starting to get quiet down there. To fill the silence, and also to stop from asking Lucifer anything regarding his personal life, I heard myself say, "I like the painting in the library. It's beautiful."

Lucifer didn't seem caught off guard by my comment. As his thoughts shifted to the portrait several floors below our feet, a soft light entered his eyes. "Her smile was more dazzling than the sun on its youngest days."

"What was her name?" I asked. *That sounds like a personal question, Fortuna,* the little voice in my head remarked. I ignored it.

"Her name was Persephone." Lucifer paused, as if saying it out loud affected him. Lines had smoothed out in his face when he regained his composure. He raised his gaze to mine and added, "She was one of the first humans, and she came before Eve."

My curiosity stirred. I couldn't stop myself from saying, "Persephone was real? And there were humans before Eve?"

Lucifer finally got down from the wall. He reached beneath his shirt, exposing a chiseled abdomen as he undid the straps that secured his wings. A staff member scurried forward to take them, a demon species with thorns growing out of her face and arms. I hadn't even noticed her up here, and as she passed me, I realized why—beneath the thorns, the demon's skin was the same texture and color as the pillars. She could camouflage to match her environment.

"The world didn't begin with two humans," Lucifer said, bringing my attention back to him. "It began with several. Beings formed of different genetics and traits. Unfortunately, their names have been lost to time."

"Interesting." It actually was. I hesitated, then said, "The tattoo on your wrist. It's her name, isn't it?"

I half-expected Lucifer to deny it, or evade the question. "Yes," he said simply.

I wanted to ask more questions, but we were already in dangerous territory. This felt too much like a civil conversation, and unless I was tricking Lucifer into something, there was no reason for it. I couldn't forget who I was talking to, or everything he had done.

Before I could turn toward the elevator, Lucifer shifted closer to me. He kept his eyes on the horizon as he asked, "Have you ever wondered why they call it the Battle of Red Pearls? Angel blood is bright. Blinding. Not the red, sticky mess humans make."

I hesitated. *Walk away, Fortuna. Stick to the plan.* "I'm guessing it has something to do with Persephone."

"Yes." A muscle bunched in his jaw. "It was her blood that splattered over the gates first. Her blood that began the war."

"What happened?" My voice was soft. Lucifer's power was so strong, and now that I could smell him, it was getting more difficult to think.

But the devil didn't answer. He tore his gaze from those distant flickers of light and looked at me. "Weren't you planning an excursion this morning?"

"It can wait an hour or two," I said. It was the truth, I told myself. I could still leave the tower anytime I wanted. The city would be quiet for a while, now that most of the souls and demons had retreated into the darkness. I looked back at Lucifer as if I had all the time in the world. "What happened to the woman in the painting?"

He held his hand out to me. "See for yourself."

I frowned at first, confused by the gesture. Then I understood, and I felt my face clear. Lucifer was an original angel, which meant he probably had the ability to communicate mind to mind. If I touched him, and lowered the walls around my thoughts, he could show me his memories.

That was about as personal as it got.

I tipped my head back and met Lucifer's gaze. He waited patiently, and something about his expression reminded me of the game we'd played last night. I heard the question as if he'd asked it out loud, his husky voice in my ear. *Truth or dare?*

I took his hand.

He went to the Garden because he was curious.

It had been years since their creation, and his siblings hadn't stopped talking about them. The humans. One of the Maker's favorite designs. All His designs were wondrous to comprehend, but there was something about this one that seemed to enchant everyone. Heilel wanted to see what all the fuss was about . . . and maybe he was a little jealous, as well.

Until the arrival of the humans, *he* had been the Maker's favorite.

Heilel arrived quietly, hiding himself in the trees and the shadows. The air was thick with magick, he noted. He could see one of his brothers standing at the gates, ready to deter any of the wild creatures wandering this new world. Humans were too weak to fight them off, and they'd be extinct in no time if left to their own devices.

The guard was proof of the Maker's interest in humankind, Heilel thought as he turned away. Why protect them at all? Why not let them die or thrive on their own, as the Maker had done with so many others?

Today, he would find out. He knew humans liked water, and the Maker had built their bodies to be dependent on it.

That was where Heilel found them.

In the middle of the Garden, there was a river, and the humans had gathered around it. Heilel moved amongst the strange creatures, remaining out of sight. They were oblivious to his presence. Even the smaller ones, whose souls glowed a bit brighter. After the Maker finished making the first humans, He had gone on to make more. Now there were dozens of them. They bred quickly.

They were also *loud*, Heilel thought. But he found he wasn't annoyed by their noise. *Laughter*, one of his siblings had called it. The sound was infectious. Heilel had been to many of the Maker's worlds during his short existence and he'd never heard anything like it.

It didn't take him long to notice that one human laughed more than the others.

They called her Persephone. Her movements were as fluid as the water that sustained all of them, and the longer Heilel watched her, the less and less strange he found their ways. She didn't lounge around like so many of the others. She played with the children. She sang as she walked through the trees. She spent her time making things, like the circle of flowers she tied together and named a crown.

Heilel saw that he wasn't the only one watching her—male eyes trailed Persephone wherever she went. Before he knew it, the sun was descending. The humans retreated into the trees, where they separated into piles. Persephone went to do the same.

Heilel couldn't help himself. He followed her.

Persephone rested beside the two humans who had made her. Heilel sat at the base of the tree they'd settled under, still hiding himself from sight. Their eyes slid shut and they curled around each other like shells. Although Heilel had never witnessed this before, he knew they were sleeping. One of his sisters had told him about it. She'd also described something called dreams. Heilel sat near the slumbering humans and discovered he could see the things in their heads. His sharp ears noted the changes in their breathing and heartbeats as they physically reacted to those things. Heilel quickly realized they couldn't tell the difference between dreams and reality while they were asleep.

One human imagined breeding with the dark-eyed female whose scent had just changed. Nearby, nestled with her parents, the dark-eyed female dreamed of another. A girl she spent all her waking hours with. She imagined what it would be like to kiss her during one of their afternoons in the river. Her younger brother, a boy so young that his voice was high as a whistle, dreamed of taming one of the horses that ran through the Garden. A wild stallion with a coat white as the clouds he watched during the day.

Sitting there, rifling through their dreams one by one, Heilel had to admit it.

Humans were fascinating.

He stayed until the sun rose. He stayed until Persephone opened her eyes again. He stayed in the Garden for *days*.

It was much longer than he'd planned, and Heilel knew his presence would be missed. He might not be the Maker's favorite anymore, but he was still second best. He had duties to perform and other places to be. Heilel didn't care, though. He was too busy observing. Learning about *her*.

He discovered how Persephone had a natural affinity with the green, growing things the Maker had created. He began to recognize the melodies she hummed. He memorized the way she brushed her long, thick hair out of her eyes every time she bent over or looked out at the distance . . . which was often.

Persephone loved the Garden. She was devoted to her friends and her family. But the Maker had also given humans free will. Persephone was curious about the world, just as Heilel was about her. Whenever she looked toward the horizon, Persephone wondered if there was anything beyond it. Heilel found himself imagining her reaction to stories about the vast universe beyond this tiny place.

He decided to wait until she was alone, but that was a rare occurrence. Humans were social creatures. They preferred to stay in pairs, or small clusters. Then there was the matter of Persephone's mother, who loved the girl with a ferocity that Heilel found both annoying and intriguing. Demeter, she was called. She sought Persephone out constantly, fussing with her hair or eager to share an anecdote.

His chance finally came when Persephone went to the river for a drink. The others were distracted by a commotion amongst the children, whose wails were so powerful they echoed across the water. Heilel appeared before Persephone just as she straightened. Her eyes widened, and she wiped the drops from her chin.

"Who are you?" she asked.

"I am Heilel," he answered.

"You're an angel."

"Yes, I am."

"Have you come to guard the gates?"

"No."

"Then why are you here?"

"I came to observe your kind," Heilel said. He paused. "But I stayed to meet you."

Persephone studied him. Behind them, the chaos had died down. Soon someone would come or notice Heilel. After a few seconds, Persephone seemed to come to some sort of a decision. The human smiled sweetly at the angel. "Would you like to see the rest of the Garden?" she asked.

Heilel smiled back without thinking, and he resisted the urge to touch his mouth. There was wonder in his voice as he answered, "Very well."

Persephone took his hand. He stared down at their interlaced fingers as he allowed her to lead him up the riverbank. Persephone didn't notice. All her focus was on the other humans, who had started to turn or lift their heads. "I've made a new friend," she called. "Come meet him."

They welcomed Heilel warmly. They shared their food and taught him how to dance. That night, as the fires on the riverbank faded, Persephone's parents invited him to rest with them. Heilel accepted.

He decided not to mention that angels couldn't sleep.

The four of them went to lie beneath a tree. Although all the other humans were pressing together, Heilel hesitated to do the same with Persephone. He felt young and uncertain, two things Heilel had not experienced in a long, long time. He hadn't thought it was possible anymore. Heilel reminded himself that he was the Morning Star. The Maker's favored. He would not be undone by a species that was younger than the small feathers at the base of his wings.

Persephone made the decision for him by nestling her back against his chest, then pulling the angel's arm over her waist. Heilel felt himself stir at the feel of her warmth. Her scent.

Demeter got up without warning. She stepped over Persephone and lay down again, lodging herself between them. Heilel frowned and rolled over, putting his back to the humans. He was unsettled by the sensations creeping through him. Hoping it would pass, Heilel shifted his focus to the dreams around him. He spent another night watching them, and this time, he discovered that he could change things. All he had to do was imagine it, and the dream shifted to match the image he'd created. Had his siblings discovered this ability as well? Heilel resolved to ask one of them when he returned.

Then morning arrived, the humans awoke, and they extended another invitation to Heilel. Once again, he accepted. Persephone sat beside him while they ate, her knee touching his thigh. Heilel caught Demeter glancing toward their legs, and her nostrils flared.

That night wouldn't be the last time Persephone's mother inserted herself between them. As Heilel's stay in the Garden extended another day, then another, he observed how Demeter treated her daughter as though she were still a child. The older woman's mouth puckered every time Persephone did something that went against this. But Persephone never lost her patience. Heilel noticed how she smiled every time she saw her mother, and he knew enough about humans now to recognize love.

"What does it feel like?" he asked Persephone. "To love someone?"

She considered his question. They were high up in one of the trees, hidden from Demeter's relentless gaze. Dusk reached between the leaves and spilled across Persephone's face. Her eyes were soft, distant. Heilel knew she wasn't thinking of him, and the realization sent another unpleasant sensation through his body.

"Loving someone is feeling like you will never have enough time with them," Persephone said.

She turned her head to look at him, and then she smiled. Small indents appeared in her rosy cheeks. Heilel stared at Persephone, thinking that he'd never seen anything so beautiful. An urge rose up inside of him. Thinking of how the humans expressed their desire, Heilel's gaze lowered to Persephone's mouth. Her chest rose and fell more quickly, and he could hear her heartbeat. They leaned closer to each other. Closer. He could feel her breath on his lips.

"Persephone!"

Demeter's voice cut through the stillness like a sword. Persephone froze, staring into Heilel's eyes. For a moment, neither of them moved. Then Demeter's calls became more urgent. Persephone smiled again, the curve of her rosebud mouth tinged with regret . . . and a promise. Heilel watched as she pulled away, his mind dim with shock at the effect this human had on him.

They climbed back down and went to meet Demeter. It was time for the evening meal. Persephone kissed her mother and started toward the river, her expression brightening when several of the children appeared. They seized her hands and tugged at her, talking excitedly. Heilel started to follow. Demeter shifted, putting herself in his path. Her eyes were hard, and there was no sign of the welcome she'd shown him in the beginning.

"You don't belong here," the human said.

Heilel studied her. Demeter was already showing signs of degeneration. There were lines at the corners of her eyes, and grooves across her forehead. Pale streaks had begun to appear in her hair. She'd existed for a blink, a blip in time, and yet she was nearing the end of her life. But this human had given the world Persephone before she went, and for that, Heilel would always be grateful to her.

He had also spent a considerable portion of his existence training young angels, and it wasn't easy to get a rise out of him.

"You're right," Heilel said. "I am a guest here. And I appreciate your hospitality."

Dislike came off Demeter like a scent. She didn't answer. Heilel waited for another moment, and then turned to find Persephone. He could feel Demeter's eyes boring into the back of his head for the entire walk down to the river.

Demeter's coldness didn't make Heilel distance himself. Neither did the visits from his siblings, who had discovered where he'd been all this time and were growing concerned for their Morning Star. Heilel wasn't just the Maker's favorite—he was theirs, too. But their efforts at persuasion didn't work. Their pleas fell on deaf ears.

Heilel stayed so long in the Garden that its magick began to change him. He began to experience emotions. He started to have dreams of his own. Heilel was new to desire, but he understood what the dreams meant.

He wanted Persephone to love him.

So he courted her. He pursued her. He showed her his interest.

One night, while the moon was high and everyone slept around them, Heilel woke Persephone soundlessly. She untangled herself from Demeter with slow, careful movements. Once she was free, she took Heilel's hand and broke into a run. They slipped away, giddy as children, weaving through trees and shadow. Persephone started to hide from Heilel, evading him every time he managed to get close. Her soft laugh echoed in his ears.

Deep in the forest, he caught hold of her. Heilel tugged her to him, and the sound of Persephone's laughter faded.

His hands moved slowly down her body, and Persephone did the same to him, tipping her head back. Heilel's focus moved over her heart-shaped face. His eyes landed on her mouth and stopped. Intensified.

This time, there was no one to interrupt them as they tasted each other.

Their hearts quickened with passion and wonder. They kissed, touched, explored, and discovered what else the Maker had designed their bodies to do.

And there, in the heart of the Garden, an angel and a human consummated their love.

For the first time in the course of his existence, Heilel experienced joy. Pure, blazing joy. He held Persephone close to him that night, and the change in him felt irreversible. They joined together again, and again, and again. When the sun rose, Heilel was awake to greet it. Persephone slumbered in the crook of his arm as he watched colors seep across the sky, but Heilel was blind to Earth's splendor. His mind worked busily. He had found a new purpose. Her. This. Heilel looked down and traced the side of her face with his finger. Her name filled his mind like music. *Persephone.*

There were two things that stood between them. Demeter . . . and time.

As the days wore on, Heilel couldn't stop fixating on Persephone's death. His dreams became troubled, and they lingered with him during the daytime. Worry became obsession. He watched Persephone and thought about how her body had been designed to be temporary. Fleeting. Heilel was young by his kind's standards, but he had existed long enough to know how quickly a single human lifetime would go by.

So he made a plan.

Heilel would bring Persephone back to his world. To the Maker's world, where death didn't exist and she would live forever. There was just one glaring problem.

Humans were forbidden in their realm.

Only their souls could enter, and only when their physical beings had expired on Earth. Heilel could easily accompany Persephone's other form to his dimension, but spirits were unpredictable, and they found his presence unsettling. If Heilel lost hold of Persephone's soul, he might never find her again. He could doom her to eternity in another dimension—one full of darkness and monsters—or condemn her to wander Earth as a ghost. It was too risky, he decided.

The Maker had never given a reason for this rule, but then, Heilel had never questioned any of His commands before. Whatever the reason, this was the only way to save Persephone. Heilel had considered every angle, every possibility, and bringing her home was all that could ensure their future together. Magick always had loopholes, Heilel assured Persephone as he told her of his plan.

She agreed. Not because she was consumed by the prospect of death, as Heilel was, but because Persephone was obsessed with living. Seeing. The walls of the Garden had begun to chafe, and this was her chance to go beyond them.

They decided not to say goodbye to the others. Secretly, Heilel worried Demeter would resort to more than arguments and persuasion if she knew what they planned to do. Persephone couldn't bear the thought of seeing her parents in pain or hearing the children cry.

As morning spread over the horizon, the starcrossed lovers left the Garden together, taking to the sky. Convinced their love would persuade the Maker to change His rules.

There was no such thing as fear. Not then.

But when Heilel and Persephone arrived at the gates, they were firmly closed. A lone figure stood in front of them, and though he wore a helmet, Heilel recognized him immediately.

Michael was an Archangel. One of the Seven. He held a shield in one hand and a flaming sword in the other. An angel's weapon only lit when they intended to use it, and the sight of those blue, crackling lights made Heilel approach more slowly. Doubt had begun to creep in. His hand tightened on Persephone's waist, and she covered it with her own in a light, comforting touch. The only sound on the staircase was Persephone's footsteps against the precious stones. They drew to a halt in front of the other angel, their heads tilted back.

Michael was the largest of all the angels, and his wingspan was the length of three human men. Where Heilel was bright and golden, Michael was dark-skinned and black-haired. His features were blunt and strong. Unmoving, much like the angel himself. Heilel had never known his brother to disobey a command or break a rule.

"Michael," he said.

His brother looked back at him without any flicker of feeling. Michael was ancient, as far as angels went, and he was nearly as reticent as the Maker. He didn't bother with greetings, and he didn't try to soften the blow as he replied, "She cannot enter."

Heilel didn't move. "She's innocent."

"Her innocence is irrelevant. She shouldn't be here, and you have caused an equational disruption. Balance must be restored."

"And how do you intend to restore it?" Heilel hardly recognized the sound of his own voice. Suddenly it came to him, the name for what he was feeling. It was like a faint whisper at the edge of a dream. *Fear*.

Following his instincts, Heilel sent a distress signal to his other siblings. *Come to the gates. Help us.*

He'd barely finished the summons when Michael sifted. The Archangel reappeared at Persephone's side, and his arm rose. The flaming sword filled Heilel's vision. He drew his own weapon without thinking, and he wrenched Persephone out of the way with a panicked shout. *"No!"*

Too slow. Heilel watched with helpless horror as his brother's burning sword came down, and the edge cut through Persephone's side.

Blood splattered over the pearls of the gates, red as a sunset in the Garden.

Heilel caught hold of Persephone and lowered her to the steps, keeping his eyes on Michael. The smell of burnt flesh clung to the air. Heilel shielded his lover as he moved into a fighting stance.

His brother turned to him. The flames moved in Michael's eyes as he intoned, "The Maker has ordered your execution, as well."

Like the star he was named after, Heilel moved in a shining blur. Michael might have been older, but Heilel was one of Heaven's most talented soldiers. They were evenly matched, and neither showed signs of yielding or tiring. They sifted, struck, blocked, retreated. Their battle could have gone on for days.

But Heilel was distracted.

While he struggled to fend off Michael, his attention kept swinging back to Persephone, his beloved Persephone, whose blood had flown through the air like a Garden rainstorm. To his surprise, his brother Gabriel knelt at her side now, holding hands over the girl's wound. He was one of the few angels with the gift of healing. He must've heard Heilel's call.

A surge of hope went through him. Heilel renewed his efforts, swinging his sword at Michael's so fast that even he could barely see it. He slid away like a sound in the night and returned in a rush of golden rage. Like a lion defending his mate. Then he glanced over at Gabriel and Persephone again.

That was when Michael struck.

Heilel didn't react quickly enough, and the flaming sword went through him in much the same way it had wounded his beloved. The prince gave an agonized shout just before his knees hit the hard stones, but he managed to raise his blade again. Michael's next assault went through Heilel's entire frame like a ripple. He gritted his teeth and tried to sift, but blood flowed freely from his side, bright and blinding. His strength poured out with it. He tried to crawl toward Persephone instead.

Michael reappeared in front of him, blocking the way. Even now, his expression was unchanged, and there was no hint of mercy in his dark eyes. Heilel knew he'd been defeated. Wanting the last thing he saw in this world to be Persephone, to be someone he loved, he lowered his head and waited for the end.

A shadow fell over him. Heilel steeled himself for another burst of pain.

Then he heard a clash of swords.

Heilel's head jerked up, and he saw that his sister Ananiel fought Michael now. Her armor flashed in the incandescent light that shone from the pearls, and her short, cropped hair gleamed blue-black. Ananiel was small in stature, but what she lacked in height she made up for in skill and strength. She was holding her own against the larger warrior, her amber eyes gleaming, teeth bared in silent ferocity. She drove the Archangel away from the broken, bleeding lovers on the steps.

Heilel had only been watching their battle for a moment before his attention shifted, noting movement nearby. The gates were opening. A host of angels came through, all of them holding weapons aloft, decked in complete, divine warrior regalia. Others were sifting onto the steps. Raphael. Suriel. Zadkiel. Sarathiel. Heilel's gaze darted around, noting faces, determining who was fighting for him . . . and who had come in support of Michael. They'd taken one look at Ananiel and the Archangel and launched into a full-scale war. For centuries, the angels of Heaven had been tinder, and Heilel had just given them a spark.

He needed to help his comrades. He needed to join the soldiers finally taking a stand against the Archangels, the inner circle, the angels that had come first and never let them forget it. Heilel braced himself for pain and reached for his sword. It hurt far less than it should've. His wound had begun to close, Heilel realized. His gaze shot up from the gash in his side and met Gabriel's.

The healer nodded at him, and Heilel nodded back. "I owe you a debt," he said.

"Go. I will guard her," Gabriel replied. His hands hadn't left Persephone's body.

Heilel picked up his sword, cast one last look toward the woman he loved, and then threw himself into the fray. He didn't hesitate to cut down the angels he'd known for millennia. His kind weren't the nostalgic sort, and time had hardened them even more. They weren't like the humans. So Heilel faced the angels he'd fought beside for several lifetimes and snuffed them out like candles. They died in brief, blazing bursts of light. He could see Michael on the other side of the staircase, but there were dozens of angels between them. Something dark had entered Heilel's heart, and he intended to cause Michael as much pain as he'd inflicted upon Persephone.

But that day would not be today, Heilel realized grimly. As he finished beheading an angel whose name he didn't know, and the warrior's body disintegrated in a radiant blast, he glanced around. Earlier, he'd gotten word that a small party had reached the throne room. That the rebellion might actually succeed in overthrowing their Maker.

But now the tide of battle was turning against them.

Everywhere Heilel looked, his comrades were dead or flagging, surrounded or cornered. Blood glowed on the steps, on swords and armor, on faces and pearls. Heilel knew many, many of those flashes he'd seen from the corner of his eye hadn't just been angels fighting for the other side. He searched for Michael again. He might not live to see the sunset, but he'd live long enough to take the Archangel with him into the light.

Fingers bit into Heilel's shoulder. He turned, weapon raised, but he stayed his hand when Heilel realized it was Olorel standing behind him. His friend almost rivaled Michael in size, but his hair was the color of an orange from the Garden, and his eyes were gray as a stormy sky.

"We must retreat," Olorel said.

His voice was calm, but there was something in Olorel's eyes that Heilel had never seen before. He didn't try to argue or strategize. The time for that was past, and it was obvious that what remained of their rebellion couldn't stay here. The Maker had ordered Heilel's execution, and He wouldn't forgive the angels that had fought for his sake. Heilel had unwittingly signed their death warrants when he'd brought Persephone to the gates.

Persephone.

Heilel whirled to the place where she and Gabriel had been. Ananiel was still defending them, but she was injured, and she wouldn't last much longer against the onslaught. She was holding her side, and beams of light shone between her fingers.

Heilel turned back to Olorel, and his voice rang with command. "Bring Persephone back to Earth. The rest of us will follow."

Olorel nodded and blinked out of sight, then materialized beside Gabriel. He said something in the healer's ear. Gabriel's gaze darted to Heilel, and he must've agreed, because Olorel straightened, stepped back, and began to move his arms as if he were stirring the air. While Olorel gathered his power, his eyes already flaring with gold light, Heilel plunged back into the chaos to spread the word. Others took up his call. *Retreat. Retreat!*

Everyone on the staircase knew the exact moment Olorel opened a rift between worlds. It felt like electricity filled the air, and the sounds of battle were drowned out by a sound like wind or a planet-shaking roar. The rebels began to sift, trying to reach the tear. Some died the instant they lowered their guard. More lights flashed.

Heilel spun just in time to see Olorel scoop Persephone up and leap into the swirling chasm. She was still alive—Heilel saw her mouth form the shape of his name. Their eyes locked for one breath-less, agonizing moment.

Then the tear swallowed Persephone whole, and she was gone.

CHAPTER EIGHTEEN

The stillness felt as thick as smoke. When Lucifer set his fork down, the sound echoed off the high ceiling. Candles hissed and spat along the center of the table we sat at. Overhead, the chandelier flickered, and on both ends of the room, a fire crackled on beds of fresh heaptani. Its rich, sweet scent filled the room, making me think of floral perfume or vases of wildflowers.

We'd been only sitting here for a few minutes. After I had freed myself from Lucifer's past, reeling from what I'd seen, he suggested we head downstairs for breakfast. *There's more to the story*, he told me. I agreed only because I was curious. I'd come this far, might as well finish what I'd started.

We had parted ways briefly, so I could change, and now here we were. My food was half-eaten, rather than just being pushed around the plate. I'd switched out the sweaty tank top for a soft, long-sleeved shirt that was the color of Collith's eyes.

Before I could urge Lucifer to continue, one of the doors opened. Roger slipped through, his weathered face serious as ever. He crossed the room and stopped next to Lucifer's chair, and the devil turned his head. He listened to whatever the demon said. Roger's voice was too low for me to hear.

"Reschedule it," Lucifer replied instantly. He refocused on his plate and took another bite of food. "Reschedule all of it, actually. Clear my day."

Roger bowed and retreated. He gave me a kind, fleeting smile.

"You didn't need to do that," I told Lucifer hurriedly, my eyes darting toward the demon's retreating form. "I'm leaving right after we finish here."

"As I said, the story isn't done, Fortuna."

"Then finish it," I countered. But Lucifer just took another bite, the corners of his mouth curving in a faint smirk. I glared at him—I knew a stall tactic when I saw one. He thought he could keep me in this tower so long that I was stuck here until the next safe window. Tension crackled up and down the dining room table . . . but it wasn't all anger. There was an underlying current beneath, one made of whispers and images of bare skin.

"You say you're not evil," I said without preamble, setting my fork on the table with a harsh sound. "If that were true, how can you do the things you do? Take enjoyment from causing pain?"

Lucifer didn't flinch. He chewed his food slowly and then took a drink of water. As he set the glass back down he asked, "Are you saying you've never liked it? The fear you take from your prey?"

"They're not prey." My response was immediate. Automatic.

The devil raised his eyebrows. "Then what are they?"

This time, I paused before answering, and I hated myself for it. Because however much I wished I could be righteous and indignant, Lucifer was right. I did like it—seeing the terror in their eyes, tasting them, punishing them.

It also didn't escape me that I'd had this conversation before.

I pictured a small, white cell and a lanky figure sitting against one of the padded walls. Once upon a time, Gil had called our victims "morsels." I wondered if he felt differently now that he'd felt how they suffered. How they died.

Be the better monster. That's what I'd told him.

"What happened after that? After Olorel ripped a hole between dimensions?" I asked abruptly, changing the subject yet again. I was avoiding Lucifer's question, and we both knew it. But I also wanted to know the rest of his story.

To my relief, he didn't call me on it. Lucifer took another drink and answered, "I kept fighting. I couldn't abandon the siblings that had saved me. But we were too few, and they were too many. The tide of battle turned against us. I was wounded. As I lay bleeding, one of my brothers dragged me to the tear, where the others had already fled through."

Here, Lucifer stopped again. Recounting his past, even with all the time that had passed, seemed to have darkened his mood. He wiped his mouth with a napkin and moved his chair back, standing.

"During the Fall, I ended up in a realm you know of as Hell, and Persephone back in the realm where He put the humans," he concluded. The note of finality in his voice made it obvious. Lucifer held his hand out and tipped his head toward the doors. "Shall we?"

I pushed my chair out and stood without touching him. "I already told you. I'm leaving."

"The story isn't done, Fortuna."

I was getting tired of this game. I shrugged at Lucifer and started walking toward the doors. "You'll have to tell me the rest later, I guess. I'd like to go down to the ground floor now."

He followed without argument. He moved with such arrogance, I decided as I waited for him. Every step was that of a fae male, self-assured in his position and power. We stepped onto the elevator and I watched Lucifer navigate the screen. I'd seen Roger do it enough times to recognize that he had pressed the symbol for the library. "What do you think you're doing? You said you'd honor the bet," I snarled.

Lucifer didn't answer. In fact, no matter what I said, the devil kept his gaze firmly on the elevator doors. When they opened again, the library loomed before us. I didn't look at it. I was too busy murdering Lucifer with my eyes, and I was on the verge of demanding an explanation, again, when he turned to me.

"I offered to teach you once before," he said with that infuriating calm. "I'd like to extend that offer one more time."

"Why?" I snapped, my hands curled into fists.

He walked into the middle of the vast, well-lit room. The dummy was still where I'd left it. "Because if you truly intend to leave the safety of this tower, and you refuse to take my guards, then you must know how to protect yourself. Hell is not an evil world, but it isn't a kind one, either," Lucifer countered.

I stared at him. He looked steadily back at me. He didn't move from his place beside the practice dummy, and his offer floated between us. "I'm leaving today. I mean it," I insisted.

Lucifer knew a surrender when he heard it. In response, he took off his shirt and tossed it on the back of a chair. The ridges of his stomach gleamed in the light shining from a nearby sconce. My mouth went dry, but by the time Lucifer turned back to me, I'd gotten my expression back under control. I rolled up my sleeves and pulled off my shoes, then faced him.

We started with cardio to warm up our muscles. At first, it was strange doing something so mundane with the devil himself. But it quickly reminded me of all those hours in Adam's garage, and I felt myself starting to relax. This was comfortable. This was familiar.

Then we started on hand-to-hand combat.

I'd never thought Adam was a gentle teacher, but compared to Lucifer, he was Mary fucking Poppins. Every time I blocked a hit, a jolt of pain went through my bones. Lucifer was breathtakingly fast, and something told me that he was still holding back. I started to tire. I knew it was all in my head, and yet a familiar ache had begun in my side and breathing became harder. I got sloppy. I ducked Lucifer's swinging arm—air whispered over my face as his fist passed an inch above my head—and bounced back up. I spun around to face him again, but my pants were too long, and my heel caught on the soft hem.

There was a blur in the corner of my eye, and before I hit the floor, Lucifer caught me. He brought my body upright as if I were weightless . . . and didn't move away. His hands pressed against my back, our pelvises crushed together. At some point, I'd grabbed onto his shoulders, and I was looking into the devil's sea-blue eyes when

I felt his cock harden. It was as long and thick as I remembered from my dream. I watched those eyes slowly lower to my mouth, and I fought the urge to look at his. I could hear my heart like an anvil.

Give in. Give in. Give in.

Fight him. Fight him. Fight him.

I jumped back and aimed a kick at his groin.

Lucifer caught my ankle in a deft, arrogant movement. I dropped, yanked my leg back, and rolled, bouncing back up to face him. Every part of me cried out to close the distance between us again.

"I want to fuck you, Fortuna Sworn," the devil said, his voice silken and guttural at the same time. "When are you going to realize that it's inevitable?"

"How about never? Is never good for you?" I shot back, even as my body said something very different. Lucifer was trying to distract me, I realized once I'd put some space between us. I swiped some sweat off my forehead with the back of my arm and circled him, breathing hard. He wasn't even winded, of course. I faced my opponent in the starting position again and added, "Since we're here, you may as well finish your damn story."

Lucifer's stance was loose and casual, but there was nothing casual about the way he looked at me. We kept moving around each other. "Many of the things you face won't have eyes to gouge, or legs to kick, my lady. You don't know their pressure points or where their vital organs are. What will you do then?"

"Guess I'll just start stabbing and see if I hit anything important," I countered, trying to pay attention to how he moved, rather than the words coming out of his mouth. Everyone had their own technique and range when it came to fighting, and if I could nail down Lucifer's, it could give me an advantage.

"You've been studying in the best library my world has to offer," he remarked. Before I could respond, Lucifer's body blurred. He appeared right in front of me and swiped his leg under mine. I reacted just in time, and used the opening to get in a hit of my own. A cut opened on Lucifer's cheek as he continued, "These books cover every species in the city, how they communicate, what their dietary preferences are, even where you can find their nerve centers. What have you been reading, my lady?"

The question broke my concentration. My eyes met his, and I managed to block a strike. I bounded away, working to control a spike of adrenaline. *He knows I'm looking for something*, instinct whispered. To hide my expression, I pretended to be out of breath, bending over. A second later, I felt a slight shift in the air, and I moved just in time to avoid Lucifer's next attack.

"The Maker created the dimensions using a construct of magic and rules," he said suddenly, watching me spin out of reach again. "Equations that can't be changed or broken. Balance. And what Gabriel did—guiding Persephone's soul back to her body—caused an imbalance. That terrible thing I felt, just before her death, became the price she paid. Fear. Every time she touched someone, she knew theirs. Lived it, like it was her own. But eventually, Persephone learned how to control that."

My brows came together. I went still. "Wait. Are you saying she was the first Nightmare?"

"I am." He feigned a hit. I dodged it, but I was too slow, and Lucifer yanked me against him again. I felt his lips brush the soft skin of my ear as he murmured, "You're not ready for the First City, Lady Sworn. You have more skill than the average human, but not much more. Some of the things down there will eat you alive."

"Fuck you." I looped my arm around Lucifer's neck and grabbed my wrist with the other hand. Just as his hands landed on my waist, preparing to throw me, I shoved my heels against the floor and used all my body weight for momentum. The hold was meant to snap someone's neck or get them off their feet, at the very least. But Lucifer slipped free as if my arms were a flimsy scarf, and I was the one who fell. In a single movement, he rolled back to his feet and lashed out with a kick. It connected with my skull, and for a few seconds, I was seeing stars.

"Decades went by," Lucifer went on, ignoring how I staggered. He walked around me, and it felt like I was being stalked by a lion as I straightened. "Persephone didn't allow her grief to prevent her from living, and she went on to have children with another. But she never forgot me, and her love didn't fade. She befriended a Time Walker. A faerie called Nym. She was so desperate for answers—for a way back to me—that she broke his mind with her requests. She also broke the rules of the universe, and caused an imbalance by using what he saw to get here."

This was too much to process, too much new information while my head was still pounding. Nym had known Persephone? And she'd been the one to cause so much damage to him?

The pain subsided, and my feet settled more firmly on the floor. As I faced Lucifer, I wasn't focused on our sparring anymore. My mind raced. I had to tell Collith about Nym. I had to relieve him of the guilt I knew he felt about Nym's broken mind, because he was Collith and he felt guilty about everything.

There were so many other questions I wanted to ask. But then Lucifer was coming at me again, his blows landing like a hammer. I was going mostly off muscle memory. A minute ticked by. Normally my lungs would've been burning by now, my arms aching. I forgot to think about my body's limitations, though. It was subtle, what Lucifer was doing. He was guiding me. Correcting me. *Teaching* me, just like he'd promised. God, it hurt.

"But Persephone did it?" I managed when we finally broke away again. "She actually got to Hell?"

"She survived for three days." Even now, after all this time, the memory of Persephone's death made Lucifer's eyes darken. Then he fixed them on me, and I watched the shadows clear. "Would you like to join me on the roof, my lady?"

I blinked. The roof? Now?

Without waiting for a response, Lucifer walked over to the table and retrieved his shirt from the chair. He pulled it on as he went over to the elevator, and I scowled when I saw that he hadn't even broken a sweat. Still struggling to switch gears, I hurried to catch up with him. I felt like a mess compared to Lucifer's unruffled appearance. The elevator rose and brought us to the top of Hell.

More time had passed than I'd realized. After the doors opened,

I took one look up at the flickering sky, and noted the beasts flying through the dark. There were fewer of them now, which meant they were returning to their nests for a few hours. Or so Roger had explained it. The necrool, he called them. Once the winged carnivores were gone, other scavengers and predators came out, albeit the less threatening ones. That meant the demons and souls came out, too—they were what I was hoping to avoid. I'd take my chances with the necrool. Odds were, I wasn't worth their notice.

Lucifer and I reached the edge of the roof and stood there for a moment. I was about to peer down at the street below when he spoke again.

"As she lay dying, Persephone told me what else she'd learned. Before she came to Hell, she couldn't bear the thought of leaving her children without knowing how they'd fare, so Persephone turned to the Unseelie Court and made one more request to the young faerie. The Time Walker traveled far. He saw how powerful one of her descendants would become." His eyes met mine, and his voice was full of heavy meaning. "A power that could undo entire worlds."

"And you think he was talking about me?" I asked incredulously. But then the warnings from Gwyn and Mercy echoed in my ears, and a knot formed in my stomach. I shook my head. "Even if he was, why does it matter? Why have you been trying so hard to find me all these years?"

Lucifer leaned over and propped his elbows on the ledge. A breeze played with his hair, giving it a tousled look. His voice was soft, hardly louder than the crackle of the torches behind us. "Persephone told me about her descendant because she wanted me to stop it. To save you."

I frowned, studying Lucifer's profile. *She's promised to him.* That's what his witch had said to my parents. "Stopping the apocalypse is not why you wanted to find me, though," I said.

Silence.

And there we were, right back at the big question. The one Lucifer refused to answer.

Needing space to think, I walked a short distance from the edge and started pacing. "Let's see if I can fill in the gaps. You wanted to find me, but you didn't know how."

I imagined myself as Lucifer. Peering out at the world from his eyes, thinking the way he would. I believed the devil's love for Persephone was genuine. I also believed there was another reason he'd searched for her descendent so fervently. He claimed he didn't want a host . . .

I shook my head. I was getting off track. My brows furrowed as I put myself back in Lucifer's head. If his demons couldn't get results, and his other resources had run dry, he would've turned to magic outside his dimension. I already knew that Lucifer liked his witches.

"Enter Goody," I breathed, comprehension dawning. I stopped and faced Lucifer, slowly lifting my head. It all fit now. "You heard about a seer. You didn't know how to find me, but a vision or a prophecy would probably help you figure out where to start your search, at the very least. That's why you were so interested in Goody, and why you went through the charade of falling in love. She was the one who started all that 'promised to him' bullshit, wasn't she? By the way, what happened to her?"

More silence. Unsurprised, I returned to the ledge. A necrool shrieked overhead, swooping alarmingly close to the tower. Lucifer didn't react, but the fact he hadn't responded made me think my theories about Goody were right.

But there were other pieces of the story I was missing. Sometimes, the motive could only be found at the beginning, and Lucifer had led a long, long life. Getting kicked out of Heaven had just been the prologue. I refocused on him and asked, "What did you do after Persephone died?"

Another small gust of wind carried Lucifer's scent past me, but we were standing so close now that it brought some of his warmth, too. I prayed he didn't hear how I held my breath, trying to stop my body from reacting to his proximity.

"That was the first time I experienced true grief," Lucifer answered. His shoulder brushed mine, but he didn't seem to notice. "I felt powerless. Angry. I couldn't travel back to the Maker's realm, and I sought another way to strike at Him. To make Him feel the pain I felt. There was only one creation He truly loved."

"The humans," I said. Lucifer's silence confirmed that I was right.

"I can't travel between worlds, but I can still communicate across them. After the Fall, I taught myself the art of possession. I discovered that, other than our kind, there was only one form that could bear my presence long enough to suit my purposes—the creature you call a snake. I went back to the Garden, and I waited until I could speak to one of God's favorite humans alone. I seduced her. I persuaded her to eat one of the apples He'd forbidden."

Apparently seduction was a regular technique of the devil's, I noted silently. Eve, Goody, Fortuna . . . no wonder he was always calling me *my lady*. Lucifer probably couldn't keep all our names straight.

"Seriously? The Eve story is true?" I said out loud. None of my thoughts leaked into my voice.

Lucifer scowled. "Vapid little idiot. With those genes, it's no wonder the human species is destroying itself."

I didn't respond. I was still processing everything. It was strange to think that, technically, my kind were descended from humans. Nightmares were not truly Fallen. There was no more angel blood in my veins than there was in Emma's or Danny's.

As I kept mulling over what I'd just learned, Lucifer shifted even closer. His hand rested beside mine on the stone barrier. My guard shot up. My mental wards thickened.

"So this is your plan, huh?" I asked casually. I felt him looking at me, and my voice became mocking. "Poor Lucifer. So tragic. So misunderstood."

"That is not my name." The devil sighed and turned his face away. "Humans are consumed by good and bad, but the truth is, there is no such thing. I'm not trying to convince you of my innocence. What I do wish you'd believe is that you have nothing to fear from me."

"Then why am I here?" I asked. Now I was the one to turn. "Why hold my brother's soul hostage and force me to come to Hell? Those aren't the actions of someone who doesn't mean harm."

But Lucifer kept his gaze on the horizon. "Do you still plan to leave the tower?"

It was the same tone he'd used the other day, when I'd asked him what was behind that closed door. *Something you're not ready for*. Lucifer wanted me to think he was so honest and transparent, and yet he shut my questions down with the skill of a faerie. "I do," I bit out.

"What if I accompanied you? I'll take you wherever you want to go. To any part of the First City, or beyond. If you want me to step away, I will, no questions asked." Lucifer was looking at me now, and there was tension in the line of his shoulders. Red lightning flashed, revealing his expression in stark, fleeting detail.

Even without my power, I was a Nightmare, and I knew real fear when I saw it. My eyes flicked between his. "Why is it so important that I don't see your city on my own?"

"I can give you several reasons, my lady. First off, there are the Tanar'ri, an ancient demon race that comes from the Waste to gather souls and take them back. Souls that are never seen again. There's also the risk of being touched by someone with the Peeling, which is a sickness that affects nearly every species in Hell. Yes, it's exactly what it sounds like. Oh, and we mustn't forget the powerful bloodlines and courtiers vying for any scrap of power they can get in this city. You'd make a good bargaining chip, should your identity come to light. Then there are the millions of broken souls endlessly roaming—just one of them could kill you, and they don't need a reason. Some will do it just because they can.

"I don't want you to leave this tower alone because I am invested in your survival," Lucifer said bluntly. "And if you leave this tower without protection, I can't guarantee you will."

We stared at each other, and after a few seconds, I realized I believed him. Looking away, I pulled a strand of hair from the corner of my mouth. None of the things Lucifer had mentioned sounded like fun, but the Peeling in particular had gotten my attention. *Fuck*. I felt the familiar weight of defeat settle on me. I cleared my throat and said, "Fine. We leave in the morning. Or when everyone goes to bed, I don't know how this place works."

"We call it *ellarian urileth*," Lucifer said. On his lips, Enochian sounded like music. "In the angelic tongue it roughly translates to 'the brief surrender.'"

It's beautiful. I didn't say the thought out loud. I couldn't open myself to Lucifer in any way, no matter how harmless it seemed. I moved my hand away from his and stepped back from the ledge. "I'm tired."

It was still too early to sleep, and both of us knew it. But Lucifer just smiled and said he'd take me downstairs. A minute later, we arrived at the door to the guest suite. The devil didn't try anything, and he didn't linger. He bowed and said, "Until tomorrow, Fortuna. Don't worry, I'll stay out of your dreams."

I gave him a cold, thin smile. "Good luck keeping me out of yours."

When I saw the faintest light of unease in his eyes, triumph streaked through me. Before the devil could respond, I stepped back and closed the door.

A bone-chilling sound yanked me from my dreamless sleep.

As I snapped back to consciousness, it took my mind an extra beat to realize what I was hearing. Screaming. Male, hoarse screaming. I recognized Lucifer's voice immediately, even if I'd never heard him make that sound before. My instincts sharpened, and before my feet hit the floor, I was considering what I could use as a weapon. None of the furniture had legs I could break off, and the bathroom was devoid of anything pointy or sharp.

"No!" Lucifer shouted.

I abandoned my search for a weapon and ran to the door, pantsless.

Roger wasn't in the walkway when I emerged. The shouts hadn't sounded like they were coming from Lucifer's room. Was he in his office? I swung to the left, searching for someone to ask. There was an unfamiliar guard standing near the elevator, a demon species with slitted eyes, which kept darting upward. I couldn't sense the creature's fear, but I could see it plain as day as I hurried up to him. My uneasiness grew. "Take me to Lucifer, please," I said.

I expected the guard to argue, but he just opened the elevator doors and followed me inside, navigating the screen with twitchy, preternaturally fast movements. Since there was a good chance the guard didn't speak English, I didn't ask any of the questions searing my mind. But I did note that he hadn't drawn his weapon, which meant the tower wasn't under attack, at least. I let out a breath and focused on the line between the doors, wondering what could possibly have made Lucifer scream like that. Had something happened to one of his siblings? Had *he* been hurt, somehow?

And why did my heart quicken at the thought? Because I was thrilled by the possibility . . . or terrified?

The second I stepped out of the elevator, I saw that a small crowd had gathered outside Lucifer's office. Roger and Dagan stood in front of the door, blocking the way, and I heard snippets of a hushed argument as I drew nearer. Several guards noticed my approach and turned. Gazes dropped to my bare legs, and I was about to say something when I heard Lucifer cry out again. It was a thin, broken sound. My eyes darted to the door, then back to the guards, who were avoiding looking at me now. Why wasn't anyone going in? Why were they just standing here?

In the next moment, I had my answer. Just like the guard in the elevator, I could see the truth in their eyes.

They were scared.

Roger was the one to finally address my unspoken questions. "His Majesty has dreams sometimes, my lady. Terrible dreams."

"And?" I prompted. He'd stopped as if that was the end of the explanation. I raised my eyebrows and scanned the faces around me again. "Does he sprout claws and rip his guards apart? Does he breathe fire?"

No one answered.

Lucifer moaned.

"You're all being ridiculous," I muttered. I brushed past Roger and moved toward the doors, reaching for the handles.

"No, my lady, don't—"

The room was a shambles.

I walked over the threshold as if I weren't afraid. Firelight and lamplight cast everything in moving shadow and shades of red, yellow, orange. It looked like there had been a struggle in here. A chair was upturned and the corner of the rug was flipped. Across the space, Lucifer was on the floor. From where he was lying, he must've fallen asleep on the couch and fallen off. He was still caught in the throes of a nightmare, and he curled on his side, facing the crackling fire. *Strange*, I thought. How had the chair tipped over if Lucifer was sleeping so far away?

Dismissing this, I hurried over to him and knelt, reaching for his shoulder without hesitation. Lucifer's skin was cold, and for the first time since I'd met him, I saw a sheen of sweat on his brow. It also seeped through the material of his button-down shirt.

"Lucifer," I said firmly, shaking him. "Hey, wake up. You're dreaming."

Lucifer's eyes shot open. Distantly, I was aware that Roger and Dagan had entered the room, but my attention stayed on the pale, shaken king in front of me. Lucifer sat upright. His expression was pained, and it felt like a window had been opened into his soul. Lucifer never let that mask of his slip. Without thinking, I put my hand on his shoulder again. I was no stranger to a bad dream; I knew the power of a simple touch. It was a universal gesture that said, *You're not alone.*

Just as I'd hoped, it seemed to calm him. Lucifer reached up and grasped my forearm, startling me. His fingers trembled slightly. When I felt that, I couldn't bring myself to pull away.

"Leave us," Lucifer said, putting his head down.

The command was clearly meant for Roger and Dagan. The warrior obeyed instantly, bowing as he retreated, but Roger hesitated. His eyes darted in my direction, and in that instant, I knew he was defying his master out of concern for me. What had Lucifer done in the past to make them so wary?

It's okay, I mouthed, nodding at the demon in reassurance. Roger stood there for another second, then slowly moved into his back-ward walk, his hooves clopping along the floor. He pulled the doors shut behind him.

As a soft click wafted through the stillness, I turned back to Luci-fer. He was still on the floor, one arm resting on top of his knee. Light quivered along the curve of his spine and the edges of his bright, wild hair. He'd never seemed so human. So . . . young.

"What do you know," I murmured. "Even the devil has night terrors."

He kept his face lowered, and his voice was ragged as he asked, "What did you see?"

"Nothing." It was the truth. I still didn't have my powers, so there hadn't been any glimpses of what had frightened the creature who frightened everyone else. Studying Lucifer, I considered what usu-ally helped me after my own nights of tossing and turning. I stood up and held my hand out to him, inclining my head. "Come on."

Unlike me, Lucifer didn't hesitate. His fingers curled around mine, and then he was standing. Neither of us moved. I looked up at him and absorbed the gentle scent of sandalwood.

Lucifer bent. It was so sudden that I didn't have a chance to react. There was a brief sensation of soft lips brushing mine. Every thought fled my mind and I was incapable of speech. But Lucifer didn't close the space between our bodies; he didn't try to deepen the kiss. There was only that moment of contact, his fingertips spread-ing over my hips.

Feeling Lucifer's warmth reminded me there was only a thin shirt between us, because I'd bolted from the guest suite without getting dressed. Desire and confusion held me too tight for me to regain my composure. I stared up at Lucifer and tried to make myself say something sharp, or move away, at the very least.

To my surprise, Lucifer was the one to break the tension. He didn't take advantage of my confusion. The slight pressure of his hands vanished, and he stepped back, deeper into the shadows.

"I wish to be alone," he said. Not unkindly—just fact.

"Okay. Good night." I tried to hide my eagerness as I nodded and started walking toward the door. My lips were still tingling. I wasn't sure if the tightness in my chest was relief or something else. But the sound of Lucifer's voice stopped me.

"Lady Sworn."

"Yes?"

He turned his head, giving me a glimpse of his profile. "Thank you."

I paused before responding. I told myself to say something cruel or mocking. Lucifer was the enemy. I hated him. He didn't deserve kindness.

"You're welcome," I said softly.

The devil didn't say anything else, so I walked away again. Halfway to the door, I faltered—there was a piece of paper on the floor. It was crumpled into a ball, just another piece of the chaos. It blended in perfectly. I would've missed it entirely if it hadn't been near the door, all on its own, as if someone had dropped it on their way out. There was a glimpse of writing visible, and it didn't look like Lucifer's neat hand. I frowned and knelt down, glancing over my shoulder to make sure he hadn't noticed. Following a stray, insistent instinct, I closed my fingers around the paper ball and tried to hold it subtly as I left. But Roger was distracted as he accompanied me to the elevator. *Worried about his master*, I thought.

I waited until I'd gotten back to my room to open my hand. Leaning against the closed door, I unfurled the paper and read the scribbled words written in the center. Once. Twice. My heart beat so hard that I could feel it in my ears. I didn't recognize the handwriting, and my mind burst with a thousand new questions. What did this mean? Was it a warning . . . or a threat?

I read the note a third time, and I resisted the urge to clench my fist around it. It wouldn't matter, anyway. The message was seared onto my brain, as permanent as the brand on my back.

Three words. Ink so deep that it showed on the other side of the paper. Letters shaky with rage, or urgency, or fear. Maybe all three.

Don't trust him.

CHAPTER NINETEEN

"Do I need to hide my face?"

I was nervous, and the feeling leaked into my voice. I tried to disguise it by relaxing my shoulders and tugging at the waist of the dress I was wearing. A green, long-sleeved design with a thin belt and delicate buttons down the center. My heeled boots clicked against the stones. A long, dark coat warded off Hell's relentless chill.

"No. Don't ever hide your face, Fortuna." Lucifer's gaze felt like a caress, and I pretended not to notice. "As long as I am at your side, no harm will come to you."

Now that I could believe.

It felt strange to just walk past those frothy-mouthed dogs and out the front doors of the tower. I kept waiting for Lucifer to make some excuse, or for something to happen that would conveniently force us to turn back, but it seemed he was actually making good on his word. Today, Lucifer would show me his city and take me wherever I wanted, since I'd agreed to a protective unit.

Why, then, did this feel so much like . . . a date?

I told myself I was overthinking it, and focused on the landmarks and details around us. If Lucifer's guards followed, I didn't see them. They continued to stay out of sight as we made our way down the street.

We spent hours in the city. I didn't know where to start with my search, and Lucifer ended up showing me his favorite places. I figured it was a good way to familiarize myself with the area, anyway. Unsurprisingly, the King of Hell turned out to be an excellent guide. Wherever we went, he had facts or history to share. He seemed to know everything, not just about the city but its citizens, too.

There was one borough called Edallosa with stalls full of gems. There was the mining district where I had first awoken. Another section of First City seemed entirely dedicated to sex clubs and brothels.

Demons and souls filled the streets as if it were Mardi Gras. As one would expect in Hell, nothing was off limits, and there was no kink too bizarre or macabre. I was careful not to look at Lucifer as we passed the windows, doorways, and stalls of this particular neighborhood.

Then we crossed a bridge made of what looked like elephant bones, and it was jarring when we entered a section of the city that was quieter. Everyone spoke in low murmurs. Objects hung on strings in the stalls, flashing and tinkling. Feathers, bones, stones. The air was full of smoke and strange smells. Drugs, I realized quickly, watching a small bag of white powder pass between a soul and a demon. A small, reckless part of me was tempted to try one of the wares on display, and I passed quickly through this part of the First City, as well.

Bursts of music accompanied us wherever we went, spirits playing instruments on busy corners, a hat or bowl lying at their feet. Some of the instruments I recognized. Some I'd never seen before. But no matter how disjointed the melody, or how strange the words were, it was beautiful.

Lucifer must've noticed how intently I listened whenever we walked by, because he went silent each time, allowing me to hear every kind of music his world had to offer.

For dinner, he brought me to a square with streets that looked like cobblestone, and glowing lights strewn across them like the string lighting from my world. There was still nothing green, but there were bits of colored rock embedded in the doorframes and around the windows. The music that floated through the air here was playful, almost whimsical. Lucifer and I sat at a small, round table illuminated by candlelight. Our server placed something between us—a strange, spiky object that pulsed slightly—and it emanated one of the most pleasant scents I'd ever encountered. As I continued to breathe it in, I felt myself relax. I even ordered a dish that resembled a coral reef and took several bites of it.

As we ate, it was obvious that every single soul and creature here knew who Lucifer was. The other patrons stared in our direction, but they were subtle about it. I could feel the pressure of eyes on my skin, yet every time I looked up, no one was looking back.

We were still sitting there when another band of musicians arrived. There were four of them, each one of a different demon species. But their wings and talons and claws didn't prevent them from holding instruments. The music floated through the air, low and unrushed. There was something ancient and sensual about how the notes ran together. I sat there, hands in my lap, swaying.

Lucifer slid out of his chair. Our server hurried over, her expression alarmed, and he said something in Enochian, his tone reassuring. She backed away again, her double-lidded eyes darting between us nervously. The devil turned and bowed, his hand extending toward me. I'd had wine with my meal, and after an entire day of being at Lucifer's side, breathing in his scent, I'd forgotten how to hate him.

I stood and allowed him to take hold of me.

Wordlessly, he pulled me closer. I still didn't fight it. Instead, I pressed my hands to his warm chest, and we started to sway, moving in and out of the shadows. A staff member cleared our plates. Gargoyles looked down at us from the rooftops all around, but I barely spared them a glance. I tilted my head back to look up at Lucifer. Even though his expression was impossible to read, I noticed a light in his eyes. He was looking at me like I actually meant something to him.

I wondered what the devil saw when he looked into my eyes.

The thought unsettled me, and I felt a disturbance in my chest, as if there were a storm coming. The song ended and I pulled away.

As usual, Lucifer missed nothing.

He took me back to the tower. We didn't talk as much during the return journey, and it wasn't until we'd crossed the lobby and stepped back into the elevator that he spoke again.

"There's an event tomorrow night," he said, glancing at me. "I wasn't sure whether to tell you, since it doesn't seem like something you'd be interested in. Olorel can get . . . messy."

I turned to him, eyebrows raised. "Wait. You guys celebrate Olorel?"

"It holds a different meaning for us, but yes, we celebrate it. To an extent."

His tone made me search his expression. "What meaning does it hold for you?"

"It's a promise," Lucifer said briefly. "Would you like to come? Several of my siblings will be there, and they're not the most . . ."

He hesitated again, and seeing uncertainty in the devil's eyes was so rare that it stirred my curiosity. It also occurred to me that I might overhear something useful, or learn something from one of the guests. Our excursion into the city today, while interesting and potentially useful for later, hadn't yielded anything conducive to my mission.

"As long as you don't think any of them will murder me, I'll go. Why not?" I added, shrugging.

The corners of Lucifer's mouth tilted in amusement, and I knew it was because my response was so unenthusiastic. Everyone in this realm fell all over themselves to please him. It was no wonder he liked my rejections so much.

Moments later, the elevator halted and we got off. Lucifer accompanied me down the walkway, silent again. We faced each other in front of the guest suite. *Thank you*, I almost said. It was a gut reaction, because that's what you said after someone spent the day playing tour guide. But we'd made a deal. It was purely transactional, the time we had spent together. Lucifer had only tagged along to protect his precious Nightmare and probably stop me from seeing something I shouldn't.

"Good night," I said blandly, meeting his gaze only for a moment before I reached for the knob.

His murmur followed me inside. "Rest well, my lady."

I closed the door and immediately turned my focus to the room, determined not to think about Lucifer or the fact that I could feel myself doing exactly what I'd vowed I wouldn't—softening. Giving in.

The suite was empty. Narfu had been here recently, though, because the fire was bright and well-fed. I took pajamas from the closet without looking at what I'd chosen, and undressed roughly. I yanked the nightgown over my head and it settled on me like silk. It was shorter than I had expected, the hem stopping mid-thigh. Didn't matter, since I was just going to bed.

I soon discovered, however, that in spite of the busy day we'd had, I wasn't tired in the slightest. I tossed and turned for what felt like hours. I had no way of knowing how long it really was, of course, since they didn't believe in clocks here. Restlessness drove me from the bed. Going over to the curtains, I pulled one aside and peered across the atrium, looking toward the higher windows. I couldn't see into Lucifer's office, but light shone through the red drapes. Was he still working?

Acting on an impulse, I pulled a throw blanket off the bed, wrapped it around myself, and slipped out of the room.

A random guard brought me upstairs. While we were in the elevator, both of us staring ahead, a small voice slipped through the deliberate quiet I'd filled my head with. *What are you doing?*

My jaw clenched, and I tried to ignore it. But my reflection stared at me from the closed doors, and I saw the fear in my eyes. The answer to that tiny voice's question. *I don't know.*

I was relieved when the elevator stopped. I hurried onto the walkway without a word, leaving the guard and the truth behind. My bare feet made small sounds against the stones. I concentrated on that as I kept going.

I slowed when I saw the door to Lucifer's office was cracked. Roger's voice drifted through the stillness, soft and solemn.

"The true measure of a man is not found in the things he does, but in the things he refuses to do, Your Majesty."

There was a soft thud. "Good thing I'm not a man, then."

Silence met Lucifer's response. Roger said something else, but he spoke too softly and I couldn't make out the words. After another moment, he opened the door the rest of the way and stepped through. He stopped short at the sight of me, surprise flitting across his face. I didn't try to hide that I'd been eavesdropping.

"Should I come back later?" I asked.

The demon opened his mouth to reply at the same moment we both heard, "Let her in, Roger."

Lucifer's voice was low. Hard. There was a hint of misgiving in Roger's eyes as he moved aside, pushing the door open wider for me. He bowed as I passed. I touched his sleeve fleetingly, and he stood a little straighter.

I walked in expecting to see Lucifer by his desk, but he was nowhere in sight. Roger pulled the door shut with a soft *knick*. Firelight trembled over the rug and all the empty chairs. I turned, frowning, and a startled jolt went through me.

One of the bookshelves had been hiding a door, apparently. The room it opened into was smaller than Lucifer's office, but no less modern. The walls looked like they were covered in wooden panels, and standing in the center of the space was the strangest, most beautiful pool table I'd ever seen. The edges were covered in latticework, if it could be called that. But the design made me think of a spiderweb. Spindly lines that met and split in unusual patterns, creating shapes that seemed dangerous and otherworldly. The felt—black, instead of green—was lit by wall sconces.

Lucifer stood beside the table with a cue in his hand, his long fingers curled around the delicate, gleaming material that also looked like wood. A few buttons of his shirt had been undone. He looked like he'd just come from a meeting, and one that hadn't gone well, if his exchange with Roger was any indication.

As soon as I saw him, my instincts went on high alert. There was something different about Lucifer. This was not the patient, gentle host I'd known during my time in Hell. It was like something had fallen away, or he'd shed invisible constraints, and the lion was just beneath his skin. Prowling. Pacing.

Hungry.

"Shall we play?" Lucifer asked, his eyes gleaming. He held out the pool cue.

I shook my head, holding onto the blanket so tightly that I felt the bite of my nails. "I'm not in the mood."

The devil tilted his head, appraising me, and he rubbed his thumb over his bottom lip. The gesture drew my attention to his mouth. I quickly brought my gaze back to his. Lucifer seemed to reach some sort of decision, because he moved to place the cue back in its stand with the others. Strands of his hair caught the light as he turned and closed the distance between us. He began to circle me. I still didn't move. I couldn't think of an insult or any cutting remarks. That sandalwood scent teased my senses. I felt Lucifer draw closer.

"What are you in the mood for?" he whispered in my ear. Heat curled inside me.

I thought I hadn't known why I'd come here. But in that moment, I did know.

My feet moved without me telling them to. I'd finally backed away from Lucifer, but I had only gone deeper into the room. Moved farther into the shadows. Lucifer came with me, and I felt something collide with the backs of my thighs. The pool table. I looked up at Lucifer, breathing unevenly. I must've dropped the blanket, because I felt it pool around my feet. Cool air greeted my skin. It did nothing against the heat surging through me, which only worsened when Lucifer saw the nightgown I was wearing. Slowly, he trailed his fingertips down my chest, and they didn't stop. I closed my eyes, swallowing.

Then he brushed my clitoris through the silk. I rocked my pelvis into his hand, hating myself even as I did it. I would find the strength to resist him, I promised silently. *Just not yet.* His tongue traced the curve of my neck. *Not quite yet.* His hand slipped under my nightgown. A few more seconds, that's what I'd give myself . . .

Then Lucifer was leaning over me, pulling the front of the nightgown fully down, and my resistance completely melted away. We were like a spark and dry tinder. Lucifer's kiss was everything I'd dreamed of. Hard, erotic, and all-consuming. I groaned, bucking my hips and clutching handfuls of his thick hair. Lucifer bent over my exposed breasts, claiming them with his mouth, darting his tongue over my nipples. Feeling him suck on them ignited my core like a furnace. I was already slick with need. I started to grind against him, my hand trailing the length of his hard stomach, going down, down, down. Just as I found what I was looking for, Lucifer straightened and pressed his lips to mine again. I felt him sliding my nightgown up my hips, exactly how I had imagined so many times. My fingers wrapped around his rock-hard erection while my other hand lifted, reaching for the button on his slacks—

"How long do you think this will take?"

Lucifer went still.

My head swiveled in the direction the voice had come from. When I saw a figure in the doorway, I pushed myself off the pool table, away from Lucifer, and shoved my breasts back in my nightgown. Lucifer leaned against the spot I'd just vacated, his fingers curling around the edge of the table. His hair was still mussed, his buttons undone, yet somehow he looked in complete control.

"Samael, what are you doing here?" the devil said by way of greeting. Though his body language was relaxed, something about his stillness betrayed him. He wasn't as calm as he seemed.

"I've come for the party, of course. Can't one brother visit the other without a reason?" The newcomer stepped out of the shadows. He fixed his watery eyes on me. "And who is this?"

Lucifer made the introductions briskly. "Samael, this is Lady Fortuna Sworn. My lady, this is Samael, ruler of the Fourth City."

The stranger made me think of a reed. Everything about him was long and thin. His arms, his torso, his hips, his legs. Even his face was elongated. His hair was shoulder-length, parted in the middle and tucked behind his ears. He wore a three-piece black suit that looked like something from the Victorian era, and the striped material somehow enhanced his gangly legs.

Unease trickled down my spine as I studied him. I'd learned to trust that feeling.

"A pleasure," Samael said. His eyes were so dark they appeared black, pupilless.

I didn't answer.

"Roger? Will you ask the kitchen to make something for us?" Lucifer said, turning his head to the doorway, where the old demon now stood. Roger bowed and retreated, the sound of his hooves fading.

"I think I'll head to bed," I interjected quietly. All my instincts were urging me to get away from Samael as quickly as possible.

Lucifer bent and pressed a kiss against the back of my hand, moving so swiftly that he'd already straightened before I could debate whether to pull away. He smiled at me, a private smile that whispered of things to come. "I'll see you tomorrow."

I just nodded. I could feel Samael's eyes on me, but I didn't look at him again. Guilt snapped at my heels like a Hell Hound as I returned to my room.

To the guest suite, I corrected myself. This wasn't home, no matter how comfortable I'd become in the tower. I was going to find some damn rain in this dimension, which would end the spell and return my soul to my body. Until then, I needed to control my thoughts, and resist the comfort and luxury Lucifer had provided. And everything else he was offering.

When I got to the guest suite, though, I wasn't any calmer. Sandalwood clung to my skin and wafted pleasantly from the nightgown's soft material. I needed to wash his smell away.

I went into the bathroom and turned on the shower. The water was scalding, but even as my skin turned red and I scrubbed at it relentlessly, I couldn't get the feel of Lucifer's hands off me. *You don't really want him*, I told myself over and over. *Everything is a lie. It's just magic.*

By the time I turned the water off, I almost believed it.

It took me hours to fall asleep, and when I did, I dreamed of *him*. I woke up and immediately took another shower, scrubbing at my skin as if I could scrub Lucifer away, too. As I lingered beneath the hot water, my mind turned to the night ahead. I was already rethinking my decision to attend Olorel. Lucifer might try to finish what we'd started last night, and after the way I had practically melted, I wasn't sure I'd be able to resist him.

All my thoughts cut short when I reemerged from the bathroom and saw the gown draped across the foot of the bed. I slowed, knowing instantly who had sent it. My stomach gave a traitorous flutter. I approached and peered down at the devil's gift.

I'd worn beautiful dresses before, but something about this one made the breath catch in my throat. I drew close and skimmed my fingers down the red bodice. Its texture was like a cross between ribbons and feathers, somehow.

If I were really trying to push Lucifer away, I'd cut this gown up and send it back to him.

Feeling restless, I moved away from the bed and perched on the padded stool before the vanity. The face looking back at me was frowning. Fixing my eyes firmly downward, I reached for the silver brush. As I started running it through my damp hair, I eyed the intimidating variety of powders. Maybe I'd give it a shot tonight. I didn't possess a fraction of Laurie's skill when it came to creating beautiful masks, but I'd picked up a few things from him.

I didn't allow myself to wonder why I was trying so hard, or why I wanted to look good at all.

A while later, my hair drying around my shoulders in thick waves, I moved back over to the bed. As I dropped my towel, I glanced toward the glass wall automatically, but Narfu had drawn the curtains. Relaxing, I bent and picked up the gown. My eyebrows rose when I felt its weight.

God, this dress really was beautiful. I turned, holding it up to the firelight so I could see the intricate design better. Before my time at the Unseelie Court, I'd never been someone who gave a shit about clothes or presentation. But Laurie had shown me other uses for such things.

Giving in to a small rush of girlish excitement, I stepped into the skirt and shimmied it up my hips. Once I'd gotten every part in place, I stood in front of the mirror.

The bodice was stiff and tight, making my curves look more pronounced than usual. The material at the shoulders was shaped like flames, and the swirls curved over my collarbone and reached partway up the sides of my neck. The long sleeves were purple, and they clung to my arms like a second skin. In contrast, the skirt—a deep blue-green that made me think of the sea after the sun had gone down—flared dramatically, and it was somehow patterned and gossamer at the same time, allowing faint glimpses of my legs beneath. There was also a pair of heels on the floor, violently red and sharp enough to stab someone in the throat with.

At a party filled with demons and mad princes, shoes like that could come in handy.

I left the suite expecting to find Roger. He'd probably been given instructions to bring me to Lucifer, or take me downstairs.

Instead, I found the King of Hell.

He turned at the sound of my footsteps, and the sight of him made my breath catch, just for an instant. It should've been cheesy or clichéd, the devil dressed entirely in black. Unfortunately, there was nothing clichéd about how Lucifer looked. All of his striking features were heightened, somehow, by the dark suit. Even his vest and shirt were black. His thick, bright hair splayed over the collar, and his shoulders seemed more broad than usual.

"I am an immortal, and I speak dozens of languages," Lucifer said, his voice soft, "and yet I can't think of a single word to describe you, my lady."

I couldn't bring myself to mock him or roll my eyes. I took his proffered arm and kept my expression neutral. "Thank you. I . . . I like the dress."

Lucifer's eyes lit up, and he gave me a pleased smile. "I'm afraid I can't take all the credit for it. I gave your description to a seamstress in the city, and she did the rest. Seeing you now, however, I don't believe she was paid enough for her services. I'll have to rectify that."

Once again, we got onto the elevator together. But this time was different than all the others. Now, we'd tasted each other. I had given in to my desire for him, and it was pointless to pretend that I didn't feel it. I didn't look at Lucifer as we waited, not once. I was afraid to.

To my relief, our ride was short-lived. The elevator had barely moved before the doors were opening again. I wasn't sure where I expected the celebration to be—the lobby, maybe, or the library, or one of the many floors I still hadn't seen—but Lucifer led me to the atrium.

The moment we walked through the main set of doors, the waterfall appearing in front of us, I realized that I hadn't looked through the curtains in my room for hours. Since last night, the space had been transformed. Musicians played amongst the big rocks at the far end. Lanterns were strewn overhead on thick, coarse-looking ropes. Rugs adorned the flagstones.

And there were figures *everywhere*. Some looked human in appearance, but most of them were so strange that it took effort not to stare. I forced myself to study their clothes instead. Seeing their gowns and suits reminded me of the Unseelie Court, purely for the chaotic variety of styles and eras. But it was even stranger seeing the fashions from my world in Hell.

The party must've been underway for a while, and we were fashionably late. The moment we entered, a ripple of awareness spread through the crowd. I half-expected someone to dramatically announce Lucifer's arrival. Instead, he strode to the pool and stopped at the edge, where he faced his guests. I was still on his arm, and I felt dozens of eyes rake over me like hot coals. I resisted the urge to pull away and move out of sight. Without my power, I felt smaller. Vulnerable. I was a mouse in a den of vipers.

"We are here to acknowledge Olorel," Lucifer said, his voice ringing out strong and clear. "Centuries ago, I made you all a promise, and I still intend to keep it. But tonight, we dance, we drink, and we fucking remember. To Olorel."

"To Olorel," everyone chorused, raising their glasses. There was a dark undertone in their voices I didn't understand. Every expression I saw seemed solemn or tight. What promise was Lucifer talking about? I didn't plan on asking him, since his dismissal in the elevator made it clear he didn't want to discuss the real reason they acknowledged Olorel. Maybe he just didn't want *me* to know. I scanned the atrium again, looking for anyone who seemed weak or drunk. If I couldn't get any answers from the host, I'd find them elsewhere.

As soon as the toast was finished, three figures approached us. I recognized two of them—Samael, who I'd met in Lucifer's office, and his sister Mammon. Although her hair was different, she looked exactly like her depiction in the dining room portrait. Severe features, an austere nose, thin lips that seemed curved in the ghost of a smile. Her gown was black lace, and it pooled dramatically on the floor, clinging to every curve on the way down.

The third was one of the most beautiful people I'd ever seen. Her hair hung to her waist in raven waves. She had a heart-shaped face, thick dark eyebrows, and red lips. Her gown wasn't elaborate, or revealing in any way—it made me think of a slip. White, long, and thin. It should've washed out her creamy skin, but it only enhanced it. Almost as if she were glowing.

"Lady Sworn, I would like you to meet the Princess of the Third City, Lilith. She is one of the oldest souls in Hell, and the only mortal to ever rule here."

Lilith turned her green eyes to me, and it felt as if I'd been pinned, like a butterfly to a board.

"Sworn. I know that name," she murmured thoughtfully. Her voice made me think of honey. She searched my face, and then her own sharpened with realization. "Fortuna Sworn. Oh, the souls talk about you. Such passion. But some of them are angry. You have enemies here, child. Be on your guard."

This last part she said in a whisper, as if it was a secret between us. Before I could form a response, her jade eyes shifted, and I knew she'd forgotten me. Lilith drifted away without speaking again.

"You'll have to forgive Lily. She's a bit touched," Samael said. I turned back and found the prince's dark eyes on me.

That same uneasy feeling as before crept through my body. I lifted one shoulder in a shrug. "I didn't have a problem with her."

Mammon made an amused sound. My gaze swung toward the other royal, and the corners of those eerie lips tilted up. Where Lilith's voice was honey, Mammon's was poison as she said, "Did you know we can hear it when you try to deceive us? The truth is in your heartbeat. You're a good liar, better than most, I'd say. But the heart never lies."

"And this is my sister, Mammon," Lucifer said dryly.

I got the same instinct about her that I'd gotten from her brother. Old Fortuna would've said something clever, an insult that I'd pay for later. But there were people waiting for me. I had a home to get back to. I stared into Mammon's bottomless eyes and saw silver ones instead.

I want to be with you in any capacity you're willing to give me. I don't need all of you, and I'm not asking for it—I just want a small piece.

I refocused on Mammon, and my heartbeat was steadier. "It was nice to meet you," I said coolly.

The gleam in her eyes only brightened, as if I'd excited her.

"Enjoy the party," Lucifer told them.

I could feel Samael and Mammon watching as we walked away. I wanted to ask Lucifer about them, but I knew they'd hear it, or someone else would and tell the creepy siblings all about it. Something told me to avoid their notice as much as possible.

Lucifer continued to guide us through the room, making more introductions as we went. It seemed like everyone had a title. There were dukes, and counts, and governors, and knights. I even met a marquise.

Their reactions to me were different than I was used to. Without the influence of a Nightmare's power, I was just another pretty face. Some of the courtiers didn't try to hide their contempt, but I looked back at them, unbothered. Contempt was just another form of envy, and the people in this room had spent thousands of years fighting for Lucifer's favor, their positions, their status. Then I came along and had it all handed to me on a silver platter.

None of them were stupid enough to outright insult or threaten me, not with the king at my side, but I'd been to enough parties at the fae courts to recognize the games they played. Kind-sounding words came out of their mouths, but their true meaning was something else entirely.

I wondered if their envy was the reason for my extra security detail. Lucifer probably thought I hadn't noticed, but we were in a crowded room, and it was harder for Dagan and the other guards to keep their distance. They moved with us through the clusters of people and dancers, their expressions alert, eyes constantly roaming. Seeing that reminded me of Lyari, and a pang of homesickness hit me. With effort, I refocused on the conversation Lucifer and I were having with a duchess. She must've been one of the original angels, because there were no signs of scales, fangs, or a tail.

None of the more affluent people, I noted, were demons. Just as my world had its prejudices and fucked-up class systems, so did Hell, it seemed.

It happened gradually. The party had started as an elegant affair, but as the hours wore on, it became something else. Something darker. I glimpsed more of that white powder that I'd seen during my tour of the First City, and discovered that it wasn't snorted as I'd assumed—a horned female in a blue-green tulle tutu sprinkled it over her head. She closed her eyes and twirled as it floated back down, and the powder glistened like tiny falling stars.

The music shifted, too. At the start, it had been neutral background noise, comparable to a string quartet. But eventually the notes came faster, harder. There was an underlying feeling beneath the sound I spent several minutes trying to put my finger on. I half-listened to the cloven-footed demon Lucifer was speaking to, envisioning dark forests and beasts weaving through shadow.

"Dance with me."

I blinked, realizing the cloven-footed demon was gone and Lucifer was looking at me now, waiting for a response. For a moment, his face blurred, and I saw someone else standing there. Someone else who had once said those words. A figure with dark hair and solemn hazel eyes. What would Collith think if he could see me now? Wearing the devil's gown, a guest at one of the devil's parties.

I reminded myself that Collith wasn't here, and I'd come to Olorel with a purpose . . . even if dancing with my biggest enemy wasn't exactly necessary. And I hadn't had a chance to ask anyone a single question, considering Lucifer hadn't left my side once.

But was that for my protection, or his own?

Lucifer's fingers closed around mine, and I let him lead me into the throng of writhing, swaying bodies. Then he faced me, and I felt his fingertips brush my arms in a feather-light touch. The glow of the lanterns shone down on us, casting parts of his face in darkness. Other things moved in and out of the shadows. Feeling the telltale prickle of someone's intense focus, I glanced to my left. A pair of round, yellow eyes peered back. The demon was dancing nearby, and her body was a disorienting blend of humanoid and bird.

"Look at me." A soft command.

Surprisingly, I obeyed. A lock of his hair had come loose. It fell into his eye, making him seem younger. Almost boyish. Lucifer put his hand on my waist and pulled me closer, but his grip was gentle. I could easily move away.

I put my arms around his neck.

We immediately stood out from the dancers around us, and not in a good way. I was stiff at first. But Lucifer stayed relaxed, his movements languid. He didn't rush or pressure me. After a few minutes, the tension began to leave my limbs. The sensual rhythm wound through my veins. I'd barely had anything to drink, but I still felt buzzed.

Turning in place, I lifted my hands and stretched them toward the pretty lanterns above us. I moved in time to the beat. Lucifer reached up and laced our fingers together, causing his entire body to press against mine. My core tightened at the feel of his erection. Sighing, I tipped my head back and let it rest on his shoulder. I felt Lucifer's lips tickle my ear again as he murmured, "I want you."

I wanted him, too.

The music got louder. So did the revelers. I could hear cackling laughter and breathy moans. Flesh slapping against flesh. The air felt hotter, and sweat beaded my collarbone. Lucifer's palms skimmed down the length of me, grazing my breasts, and landed on my hips. My thoughts muddled. The music intensified again, and became faster, too. I moved my ass against Lucifer's hard cock. I imagined what it would feel like to have it inside me.

My eyes flew open.

Space, I needed space.

I spun around and pushed Lucifer away, shaking my head. I could feel everyone around us watching, listening to every word, but I didn't care. "I need a minute," I said hurriedly, then added, "by myself."

Lucifer must've seen something in my expression, because he didn't argue. "Very well. But I'm sending two guards with you. On that, I'm afraid, I can't bend."

I was so desperate to get out of that room that I didn't argue, either. "Fine."

Overhearing this, another courtier was already moving to get Lucifer's attention. I knew if I didn't bother coming back, he wouldn't be hurting for new date options. I heard her speaking to him in Enochian as I made my way out of the chaos. A staff member walked by with a tray of drinks. I snatched one of them, nodding my thanks, and headed for the closest doorway. Dagan and another guard followed me out. Others noted my departure, I saw as I left. Samael. The duchess. One of the servers, who drew my gaze because of her silver eyes—they reminded me of Laurie.

I couldn't trust any of them, I thought as I walked toward the elevator. Hoping I'd get any worthwhile information from tonight had been a fool's errand. Anyone in that room could be a spy, or have their own agenda, or just be bored out of their fucking mind and lie to me for the hell of it.

"Shit," I muttered, halting as something else occurred to me. Where could I even go? There were probably people in the library, and I did *not* feel like listening to whatever they might be doing amongst the shadowed bookshelves. The guest suite was always an option, but that window wasn't soundproof. The noise from the party would fill every corner of the room.

We were all standing in the elevator, which wasn't moving, since no one had given it a destination. Silently, Dagan stepped forward and made a selection on the screen. It was the symbol for the roof. I'd just assumed people were up there, as well. The thought of fresh air and a place without any courtiers made my chest feel looser. Relief. "Thank you," I said quietly.

Dagan still didn't speak, and neither did the other guard. They must've been feeling tense, too. The elevator shot upward, and my leg jiggled beneath the dress Lucifer had given me. The second the doors opened, I lifted my long skirt and ascended the stairs. Once I reached the top, I walked across the roof without looking back, heading for that stone circle with all the gargoyles. Weirdly enough, I found them comforting.

But I'd only gotten halfway there when I heard the scuff of a footstep. Dagan never made a sound when he walked, so I stopped and turned, expecting to see a guest from the party. My gut was tight with dread. When I saw it *was* Lucifer's guard, I let out a breath. My eyebrows drew together. I started to speak, and then . . . Dagan smiled.

It was one of the creepiest things I'd ever seen. His chin was dipped, his eyes rolled up to meet mine. I had witnessed Dagan's smile before, and it hadn't looked like that.

"Who are you?" I breathed. I was still holding my skirt, and when I felt a burst of pain, I registered that I'd clenched my fist so tight my nails had gone right through the gossamer material.

Dagan's features began to bubble and shift. Seeing this, my mouth went dry. The movements reminded me of Finn when he transitioned from his humanoid shape to the wolf, or even Sorcha, on the few occasions I'd seen the faerie change her face.

I started to back away, only to discover the second guard behind me. She bared her teeth, and then her features started transforming, too. My breathing came faster as I swung back around to face the other demon. Because that's what they were, I'd realized sometime in the last three seconds. If they'd come here to kill me, though, why hadn't either of them drawn their sword?

"Who sent you?" I asked. I sounded much calmer than I felt.

The demon was still in the midst of its shift. Clothing and weapons lay scattered on the ground, along with pieces of torn flesh. The squelching sounds from behind told me the female demon was doing the same. But there was no time to take advantage of their distraction.

Within seconds, I found myself staring at their true form.

The demon drew to its full height of seven or eight feet and stared back at me with round, black eyes. Its skin was milky white and gleamed in the firelight, almost as if it were . . . wet. It had two long slits where a nose should be, and rows of teeth that looked like a shark's. It was completely naked, and its arms dangled in front of it. Instead of five fingers, there were three long talons. This thing didn't need a sword to slice through me, because those claws would do it without any difficulty.

Before I could react, the monster tilted its head back and let out a bone-chilling sound, something that made me think of a primal, scale-covered beast. A creature that had adapted in the dark.

Survive. Assess. The inner command—my training kicking in—steadied me. I swallowed the terror clawing up my throat and shifted into a fighting stance. My skirt instantly hindered the motion. *Fucking dress.*

At the same moment I took stock of the swords on the ground, evaluating whether I could reach one in time, another sound came from the left. My head jerked.

Eyes stared back at me. Dozens of glowing eyes that belonged to creatures hiding in the pockets of darkness. Some shone with malice, and others with blatant hunger. Not friendly, then, I decided faintly. The reality of my situation was hitting me.

With one demon in front, one demon guarding the elevator behind, and all those others off to the left, the only direction to retreat was toward the edge of the roof.

I was surrounded.

CHAPTER TWENTY

As a rising chorus of snarls, clicks, and chitters filled the air, I made a decision. If this was how I died, I wouldn't go quietly. And I would take as many of these ugly bastards with me as possible.

I didn't have my powers, but I wasn't powerless. I went back into a fighting stance.

When the closest demon reached for me, I moved my body to the right. I kept my left foot planted, leg out like a tripwire. The demon fell forward and I slammed my elbow back into its gut. The instant it bowled over, I snapped my fist up into its face. There was a crunch and blood sprayed. Child's play. I was already facing the next demon, a species with a snot-drenched snout and a crouched, humanoid body covered in coarse hair. It squealed in pain as I drove my heel into its ballsack.

The others were swarming all around me now. Too many of them. I kept fighting, making my way over to the swords. A claw caught me on the jaw, and one of the creatures bit my shoulder. I shouted in pain, then jabbed the sword I'd finally retrieved and cut into the side of the demon's skull. Blood sprayed my face as I whirled, free again, and raised my head to face the next—

My eyes widened. I tilted my head back more, and more.

The demon's skin looked like stretched rawhide. It had a massive belly that hung over bowed legs, and beneath the gut, I could see its splintered, black toenails. The creature's face was like someone had punched it, right in the center, and the hole just never refilled. Holy fuck, this thing was big. Another tremor of terror shot through me, but it was short-lived. I was acting on instinct and adrenaline. I darted forward, sword raised.

I hadn't counted on its speed. Despite its incredible size, the demon moved in a blur. It clubbed me before I could make a single cut. I stood there, stunned, and it took all my strength to remain upright. I heard the sword clatter to the stones. While I battled the threat of unconsciousness, the behemoth shuffled to the side.

The horde parted again, making way for a single demon approaching the stone slab.

She had thorns all over her head and skin the color of a desert sunset. *The server from the party*, I thought. I recognized those silver eyes. She wore a band over her breasts and a long skirt, both made of the same coarse material. Our gazes met for an instant before she lifted her hand . . . and blew.

Something gritty and glittering hit me in the face. I blinked rapidly, still swaying.

Then the ground rushed up to meet me.

My vision went in and out of focus. It was the same feeling I'd gotten when one of the cherubim had smashed an egg-like thing against my head, back when they'd come for me at the hospital. The same stench, too. If I hadn't been so dazed, I would've gagged.

I couldn't fight as the demons surged forward and took hold of me. Claws and talons clamped down on every part of my body. Then I was in the air, being carried toward the circle of pillars, where I'd intended to go all along. As we went beneath the arches, torches flared to life in every direction. Horror burrowed in my stomach, even in my drugged state. There were so many demons here that it felt like a living sea of flame, hideous faces, and gleaming fangs.

I was still frozen with helpless terror when the demons began to lower me. As my body tipped, I glanced down. I caught a glimpse of candles and crystals. Someone had built a raised platform out of stones.

They were putting me on an altar, I realized with a dim rush of horror.

A scream lodged in my throat. I tried to look toward the elevator, but even as I did, I knew it was futile. No one was coming to my rescue. The noise from the party would've drowned out all the commotion we'd made. Lucifer thought I was safe with his guards. If I was going to survive, I needed to overcome this mental fog and fight for myself.

The spike-covered female appeared at the edge of my vision. Her voice was papery, as if she didn't use it very often. "No use in fighting. That was the ground scales of a salas demon," she said.

It took me a couple extra beats to speak. "Eat shit."

In response, the demon lifted a spellbook in her hands, and a jolt went through me. *That's* why I hadn't been killed yet—someone wanted me alive for whatever spell was about to happen. Desperation blazed through me. I decided to take a gamble. "You're w-working for S-Samael, aren't you?"

"You foul his name with your tongue," the demon said coldly, all but confirming it. She began to chant, the words guttural and complex. My head lolled as I tried to escape again. My eyes filled with black sky and winged statues, and a hazy frown pulled at my mouth.

Did that gargoyle just . . . move?

I stared upward, hardly aware of the demons around me now. I was too entranced by the ones above me, unfurling their wings. Cracking their necks.

Then they opened their eyes.

My reaction was halfway between awe and terror. They were eerie creatures, their skin covered in what looked like a layer of cracked, black stone, their eyes flaring neon-red. Like mine. The demons who'd just raised their weapons to kill me went still, their gazes slowly going upward. If my life hadn't been on the line, I might've laughed.

The gargoyles descended upon us with supernatural speed. The screaming began an instant later.

Watching the monsters battle each other, I was abruptly reminded how brutal this world was. Death was always a moment away.

I had to get off this rooftop.

The thorn demon was long gone, so there was no one to stop me as I dragged myself off the altar, light-headed and wheezing. It felt like my lungs had closed. *You don't need to breathe, it's all in your head,* I chanted slowly, silently. A demon went screaming over my head, thrown by a gargoyle's meaty arms, and it crashed into a pillar so hard that stone and dirt fell over me like dust. I waited for a beat, terrified that the demon would get up. It didn't move.

Definitely had to get off this rooftop.

I used my last scrap of strength to rise to my knees, and somehow I moved forward. In every direction, black ichor sprayed and the air trembled with roars. The ground was littered with body parts. For a moment I saw double of everything, then I squeezed my eyes shut and kept crawling, kept dragging, and the world righted itself.

Just as I reached the line of pillars, a clawed hand seized my ankle.

A scream exploded in my mind. I couldn't release it, though, and no one noticed as the demon pulled me toward the edge of the tower. Another one joined it. They wanted me alive, that much was obvious, but for how much longer? Was I meant to be a sacrifice or a subject? Either way, I couldn't let this happen. I couldn't let them take me. I tried to cling to the flagstones, the ledge, anything I could get my hands on as they dragged me away. I raised my gaze and saw one of the gargoyles put down another demon, snapping its jaw open with a single jerk. "Help me," I tried to say.

But the hallucinations had started.

I could hear Lilith's voice, those dulcet tones coming from far away. *Fortuna Sworn. Oh, the souls talk about you. Such passion.*

My vision went solid again, the fuzzy lines sharpening. I could see the lights of the First City below. I wasn't sure when I'd become airborne, and I knew I needed to be concerned about it. While I struggled to look up, trying to get a glimpse of what carried me,

Lilith started talking again. Her voice was more solemn. *But some of them are angry.*

It was a demon. It looked like a moving skeleton, the thin membrane of its wings catching the light. *You have enemies here, child,* Lilith whispered in my ear.

Her urgency beat at my mind. It slid through my veins like fire. Just before I slipped into a black void, I heard Lilith one more time. Saw her lovely eyes filled with warning.

Be on your guard.

The gargoyles arrived silently.

They dropped down from above, catching the demons by surprise. I'd started to regain consciousness and come back to myself, a little more with each passing second, but I still couldn't get my body to obey me. I was forced to watch again as another battle broke out. This time, it was in the sky.

And I didn't have wings.

Shrieking and screaming pierced the frozen darkness. I only glimpsed flashes of what was happening as I lay in a demon's talons like a glassy-eyed doll. A red-eyed gargoyle landed on a demon nearby, opening its jaws to bite down on the creature's entire head. Above me, an even bigger gargoyle tore a demon's wing clean off, and the creature bellowed in agonizing pain. In another flash, I saw one of my defenders—if that's what they really were—ripping into a demon's stomach and pulling out organs like a child gleefully rummaging through a toy box. It all had the feeling of a surreal dream.

In seconds, the dream changed into a nightmare. One of the gargoyles came at the demon I was flying with, and with me in its grasp, the creature couldn't defend itself. Chittering excitedly, the gargoyle latched on and began to tear out chunks of flesh. The demon's roar shook the world. Moments later, a scent stuffed itself up my nostrils, and I knew I was smelling its blood. It was sharp and fetid and horrible. *What do I do, what do I do?* I thought wildly, holding onto the beast's legs for dear life.

Just as I feared, the beat of the demon's wings faltered, and we plummeted.

The gargoyle was still ripping into the demon. Wet drops landed on my face and streamed past us. Even if I could've done something, I wasn't sure which monster to help. My thoughts moved sluggishly through the haze, trying to see outcomes and deduce whether the gargoyles had an objective of their own.

All at once, though, none of that mattered. Everything started happening in slow motion. Every noise or sound became muffled, as if someone had put their hand over a microphone. The demon went slack, and its claws opened. For an instant I saw the red horizon reflected in its wide, unseeing eyes.

Then I was falling.

It felt like arriving in Hell all over again. I tumbled through the air, and small, panicked sounds burst from my lips. I threw my arms out in a desperate attempt to stop the wild flips and turns, and the action made me realize I had control of my limbs again, not that it did me much good. I was heading straight for the hard, unforgiving ground, and in this world I was just another soul. I wouldn't survive it. There was no time for furious grief or frantic hope.

I closed my eyes and prepared to meet my end.

Something caught hold of me. Or, rather, I felt its arms slide beneath my body and fall with me. My wild momentum slowed, eventually stopping completely. I craned my neck and found myself peering into a gargoyle's whiskered, curious face. *Didn't even know they had whiskers*, I thought with numb shock. I instinctively wrapped my hands around the creature's arm, needing to hold onto something, and wondered if I was in as much danger now as I'd been with the demons. Did gargoyles possess the ability to speak?

Before I could attempt to ask, something huge and dark slammed into us from the side.

I heard the gargoyle scream as it dropped me, and just like that, I was falling again. *Fuck.* My body did another flip, and as the skyline rushed past, I saw the rapidly approaching ground. We'd gotten closer than I'd realized.

Pain ricocheted through me as I collided with the earth. It must've been at a slant, because suddenly I was rolling, over and over again, grunting and crying out. I waited to slam into a rock or fall off a cliff, but luckily, I just . . . stopped.

I'd reached the bottom of the slope.

Wind whistled in my ears. *Everything* hurt. I couldn't afford to rest, though, or tend to whatever injuries I might have. My eyes went to the sky. Nothing moved in the vast darkness, but that didn't mean it was empty. I pushed myself up, wincing, and scanned my new surroundings. Those red lights crackled and raced across the horizon. In the distance, there was a mountain range, if those oddly-shaped rocks could be called mountains. I frowned, staring harder. The effects of whatever that demon had blown into my face hadn't completely worn off yet. My vision was still blurry, my thoughts slower. The line of those mountains triggered a memory . . .

It was called the Maiden, I remembered suddenly, my stomach dropping. Because of how the line looked like a naked woman, her back arched, her long legs clamped shut.

I knew this place. Not because I'd been here before, but because I'd read about it in one of the books from Lucifer's library. The souls called this region the Lowlands. While it wasn't nearly as dangerous as the Waste, I was still royally screwed. I had no power, no weapons, and no way of knowing which direction would take me back to the First City. There weren't just hungry demons out here—there were deadly storms and other natural dangers, like patches of earth that looked like solid ground but were really vast gaps, sealed over by wind and time. Holding my side, I searched the sky again, nervous something would notice movement down on the ground.

Demons and gargoyles weren't the only things I was looking out for. I had to get back before the necrool awoke. I'd learned more about them during my tour with Lucifer, and they weren't a foe I was ready to take on. Especially not right now.

So I started walking.

It was agony. The fall had done more damage than I'd thought. I tried to tell myself the pain was just a remnant of my old life, my old body, but it felt pretty fucking real to me. I gritted my teeth and found the will to keep going, step by step. I imagined the necrool plucking me off the desert floor and going to one of their nests, where an enormous baby reptile would make a crunchy snack out of me. No thanks. I grimaced and pressed onward.

A chittering sound came from behind.

I froze, and my heart pounded in time with the seconds ticking past. *One. Two. Three.* In a rush of panic, I spun around. The wind blew in my ears, but I strained to listen for other sounds. Had I imagined it? Maybe this place played tricks on the mind . . .

My thoughts were cut short when something finally moved in the darkness.

It was the gargoyles. They crept forward on all fours, wings folded against their spines. There was something feline about the way they moved, and their eyes weren't glowing anymore. I spotted the one that had fought the demon I'd been flying with. The creature looked no worse for wear, despite the battering it had gotten.

One of them stretched to its full height, and it was almost as tall as the demon that had clubbed me earlier. My body tensed with the instinctive urge to run, but I fought it. That would be stupid; regardless of whether the gargoyles were on my side, they were still predators. Predators liked to chase. So I stayed rooted in place and looked back at them, but not directly—I pointed my gaze toward their barrel-shaped chests.

The one standing in front began to make that sound I'd heard before. A series of meaningless clicks and purrs. From the way it looked at me, it was clear the creature was trying to communicate something.

"I'm sorry, I don't know what you're saying," I croaked helplessly, shaking my head. At least I could talk again, I thought. I'd be able to scream while these things ripped me apart.

Happily, none of them seemed inclined to do that. As I kept

listening to them, still trying to discern whether they were friend or foe, the one in front started making shapes with its claws. It took a while for me to figure out what it was doing, since I could only see whenever the sky deigned to send a burst of light. The gargoyle's claws kept starting at the top, then going down, down, down, and ending in a flat line.

A tower, I realized.

They were going to bring me to our tower. They were taking me to Lucifer.

As soon as I grasped this, I felt a wildfire flare of relief, immediately followed by a drenching of shame. Here I was, free, and all I wanted was to return to my cage. I was no better than Narfu, or any other creature that found itself without chains, masters, or bars and yet still went back to what was familiar.

But at least with Lucifer, I wouldn't get eaten by a giant, winged beast or fall into a bottomless hole.

It was this thought that propelled me forward, hurrying after the gargoyles, who had set off the moment they saw recognition in my expression. The pain wasn't as bad now, and I hoped that meant I was healing, or finally making the disconnection between my old body and this new, terrifying reality.

The gargoyles matched my slow pace. They might move like cats, but in this moment, they were behaving like dogs. One of them even had its tongue lolling out of its mouth. I watched them race ahead and circle back, several of them always staying near me, muscles rippling beneath their uneven skin as they walked. In spite of the bloody battle these creatures had just engaged in, their demeanors were playful. They snapped their jaws at each other and exchanged what sounded like insults. Observing them made me feel lighter, and at one point, I even felt a smile tugging at my lips.

Then a structure appeared in the distance, and the smile vanished.

I could see its outline against the flickers. It made me think of a shepherd's hut, for some reason. Maybe it was the low roof or the small fence around the crooked front door. The gargoyles were bounding toward it, so it seemed that was our destination. My heart sank. Did they think this was the First City? Had I misunderstood what they were trying to tell me?

My unease only grew when we got closer and I saw a small fire burning outside the shelter. A figure sat beside it. I heard a voice extend a warm greeting to the gargoyles as they arrived, prancing and bouncing in circles. The picture they made could've been torn out of a book of fairy tales.

I approached more cautiously, and stopped a healthy distance away from the fire. The figure was male, tall, and emaciated. A walking stick rested in the dirt next to him. He'd been cooking recently, if an empty metal plate and a stained, empty spit were any indication. Steam rose from a dented cup in his hand that looked like it was made of tin.

Hearing my footsteps, the stranger turned his head and met my gaze. From what I could see, he had no tail, talons, or scales. He was a soul, then, since it seemed unlikely he was one of the original fallen angels. Crow's feet extended from the corners of his eyes. His gray hair was shaved close to his head, and his brown skin looked like leather. He wore a pilled, ragged-edged cloak.

By way of greeting the soul said, "They brought you here because they knew I could translate."

Translate? I thought, nonplussed. Out loud I said, "Okay. Could you ask that one what it was trying to tell me earlier?"

He followed my gaze toward the gargoyle, which was standing on its hind legs again, watching us with its bright, beady eyes. "Elo."

"What?"

"That's her name, my lady." He pointed to the others. "Salbrox. Givi. Tarek. Ircuk. That's it, really. That's all they wanted to say."

As he took another drink, I waved at the gargoyles awkwardly, uncertain how else to react. I was also anxious to ask about the First City and how to get there, but the gargoyles had saved me. The least I could do was be polite. I spoke under my breath so they wouldn't hear. "They brought me all the way here so I could . . . learn their names?"

"Gargoyles are simple creatures. They like you. They said their friend Narfu likes you, too." The solemn-faced stranger set his cup on the ground. "We should get going. The shedim come out at midnight, when the sky is at its darkest. They don't like me, but you would work them into a frenzy."

He was coming with us? "The shedim?" I repeated.

"Evil spirits. They have teeth and claws, and they're also very fast."

"I'm *so* glad I came here," I grumbled. "Hell is great."

Evidently the soul had no comment on this, because he just hefted his walking stick up and used it to pull himself off the ground. I stood, debated for a heartbeat, then followed him. For a while, neither of us spoke. I was focusing on the ground, paranoid I would fall or step on something. There were also twinges of discomfort with every step, and it took effort to keep up with the soul. For a dude with a walking stick, he was surprisingly fast. I encouraged myself with the fact that I was already improving. Little by little, the pain was easing.

I only let myself pause when a small, rodent-sized animal scurried past. Spotting it, the gargoyles raced ahead of us. They plunged into the dark without hesitation, and I shook my head wonderingly, envying them. The soul noticed and said, "This is their home. They know the terrain even better than I do."

"If this is their home, why do so many of them stay at the tower?" I questioned.

His walking stick hit a steady beat between us, the vibrations going through my feet. *Thump. Thump. Thump.* "Something must be drawing them there" was all he said.

My guide didn't seem worried about our voices carrying to anything that might be out here. Since we had a long walk ahead of us, I decided to voice the question that had been at the back of my mind throughout this entire ordeal. Ever since the moment I'd stared up at that thorny demon from a crude platform covered in half-melted candles. *You foul his name with your tongue.*

"Do you know why a demon prince would want me dead?" I asked.

"Do you know which demon prince, my lady? Be careful not to speak his name," the soul added quickly.

"He rules the Fourth City."

The soul pressed his lips together and went silent as he thought. Our shoes crunched over the hard earth. For a few seconds, it was the only sound between us. "I do know some history about the Prince of Solitude that most have probably forgotten. I've always found him a fascinating figure," the soul admitted. "Over the years, I paid attention to the rumors and stories. Some claim that he's not truly an original angel. Others have said he's never taken a mate or a wife because he transforms into a flesh-eating demon every *ellarian urileth*. For a while, there were whispers that he pined for his brother's lover."

While all of that was interesting, it didn't exactly answer my question. None of it was a motive for Samael wanting me dead. I pursed my own lips and focused on the ground, searching for any signs of danger while I kept trying to figure out why, exactly, Samael had been about to slaughter me on an altar of magic and fire.

We were nearing the First City now. I could see those dark towers off in the distance, lit up by red flashes. Once it struck me that we'd be parting ways soon, I realized something. I turned my head and mustered a weak smile as I said, "I don't know your name."

"I don't have one, my lady. Not anymore. Many of us don't remember our lives from before."

"Why not give yourself a new one, then?" I asked. Up ahead, the gargoyles started making their excited noises again, and a moment later, I heard the tiny squeal of something dying.

The soul gave me a look I couldn't decipher. "Most don't find it so easy to let go of who they used to be, my lady."

Lights appeared in the distance, distracting me from our conversation. We'd reached the outskirts of the city, but it wasn't the same area where I'd first awoken. Instead of the sea of shanties, there was a barbed wire fence on one side and straight-edged, nondescript buildings on the other. Almost like military barracks. There was movement behind the fence. It was a work yard of some kind, I discovered as we drew nearer. The squeak of wheels reached my ears a moment before I saw the square shapes of several trailers, or carts, more accurately. Then we got even closer, and I saw the source of the movement. It felt like a hand was squeezing my heart.

Souls. They had souls pulling the carts.

Lucifer hadn't let me see this during our tour, I thought darkly. I didn't even entertain the possibility that he hadn't known, because Lucifer knew everything that went on in his city. What else was he hiding?

"Best not to look, my lady," the soul beside me said. He guessed what my next question would be, because he added, "We do have our own justice system, believe it or not."

One of the souls was being whipped now. From the sounds of her screams, it was a woman. She crashed to her knees and raised her arms to protect herself. Her clothes were so ragged that most of her body was visible. The green-skinned demon only brought the whip down harder, and if I'd had my powers, I would've broken his mind with the most brutal hallucinations I could think of.

"You call that justice?" I asked tightly.

The soul beside me didn't answer.

The tower was within sight now. It was taller than everything else. As we neared the block where it stood, my guide halted and said, "This is where I leave you. I wouldn't want to catch the king's attention."

I faced the nameless soul. Just as I opened my mouth to thank him, something else occurred to me. "Wait. Before you go . . . can you tell me where it rains? Is there a certain region it happens in, maybe, or a time of year?" I pressed.

He bowed. "Rain doesn't exist in this world, my lady."

For a moment, I just looked at him, keeping my expression carefully blank. I didn't want this kind stranger to see how deeply his response cut.

Lucifer had already confirmed it was impossible for him to send me back. I could still try to look for a magic user in this world, to go on a wild goose chase for another spell that could put my soul back in my body . . . but now I realized how idiotic that hope was. If there were a way for a soul to return, swarms would be leaving Hell.

I was never going home.

"I see," I said finally. "Thank you, sir. I . . . I hope you remember your name."

He looked at me with the same expression from earlier, but now that I was so close to seeing Lucifer, I was eager to go inside. I smiled one more time, giving my new friend a small wave, and turned to ascend the rest of the steps. I heard the soft thud of a walking stick as he went on his way.

When I reached the top of the stairs, I heard the skitter of claws on stone and wings flapping against the air. The gargoyles were probably returning to the roof. It meant they weren't flying back to the Lowlands, at least not yet. Knowing they'd be nearby offered the same strange comfort I had felt back when I thought they were statues and I'd stood in the circle of pillars to ask them for advice or courage. I also owed them a thank-you for saving me from Samael's goons. With that spot of warm reassurance in my chest, I wrapped my hand around one of the door handles and pulled.

Locked.

I raised my fist and drew it back to knock. Before my knuckles could make contact, an eye-level opening appeared—a hidden door I hadn't known was there—and a demon's dark eyes glared at me.

"The tower is closed today." It was a guard I'd never seen before. Some of the demonic drug must've been lingering in my system, because I didn't react to the sight of its face, which distinctly resembled a hedgehog.

"I live here," I said, and hearing the words leave my mouth with such ease sent a jolt through me. I shook myself and continued, "My name is—"

But the guard had already started to pull the small door shut. I rushed to ram my hand inside. He swore at me in Enochian and I saw his hand move, probably reaching for a knife or a sword. I was about to blurt out my name when I heard a low, furious exchange. A new face appeared over Hedgehog Guy's shoulder.

Relief unfurled in my chest like a flower. I gave him a soft, weary smile. "Hi, Roger."

The old demon's eyes widened. "Let her in. For fuck's sake, man, let her in!"

The guard hurried to comply. I heard a sequence of turns and clicks. Moments later, the doors opened.

With a deep sigh, I walked inside the tower.

CHAPTER TWENTY-ONE

*T*hat strange, familiar calm had stolen over me.

Roger and I rode the elevator toward the top levels of the tower. None of the guards had come with us. Normally, I wouldn't have thought anything of this, except there was a strange tension in the air as we walked away from them. I caught the nervous looks on some of their faces. A moment later, the elevator doors closed.

Now I faced the glass wall, and I kept my eyes on the horizon. It was a view I'd seen almost every day since arriving in Hell. Except this time, I knew what waited beyond those craggy rocks. Now I'd experienced just how terrifying and deadly the beauty of this world was.

The moment we stepped off the elevator, the strained silence was gone, replaced by what sounded like an argument. Shouting echoed down the walkway—the doors to Lucifer's office were open, another anomaly. Roger and I had just started walking toward them when something shattered. The demon beside me stopped. I kept going, knowing I probably should be afraid, like Roger and all those guards downstairs. But everything inside me was just focused on those doors.

Then I heard his voice, and a quake went through me. Despite the noises of destruction, he spoke in calm, level tones. "I want her found, Dagan. I don't care what it takes. Burn all seven cities to the ground if you have to."

"I understand, my liege."

"Heilel."

I said his name softly, but it echoed through the room like a shout. The King of Hell stiffened. He turned toward the doorway, where I was standing. His eyes latched onto me as if I were a mirage in some bleak, endless desert. I waited for him to say something.

Instead, Heilel closed the distance between us in five long-legged strides, and every footstep felt like a heartbeat, pounding wild and fierce in my chest. I didn't move. I watched him and my breathing quickened. Without a word, Heilel picked me up and strode out of his office, passing Roger and several guards as if they weren't there.

Even when we were alone in the elevator, he still didn't speak. I didn't push Heilel away or fight his hold. I just looked up at him, tracing his perfect features with my eyes. Heat and urgency thrummed between us. The elevator stopped, releasing its usual chime, and then came the hushed sound of the doors sliding open. We went down the hall, never breaking eye contact.

The devil carried me into his bedroom and slammed the door shut with his heel.

I'd never been in here before, but I didn't care about that right now. Didn't care about anything other than him. I only had a vague sense of dark walls and a fire blazing in the hearth. Moving slowly, Heilel set me on my feet. I rested my hands on his chest, and he put his on my hips. It should've felt strange that neither of us had spoken yet, but it seemed like we were saying so much anyway. Things I still couldn't admit out loud. *I want you. Touch me. Take me, take me, take me.*

With the barest of touches, Heilel skimmed the length of my body with his palms. His fingertips brushed against my nipples and the material of my torn dress. Excitement was already rising in me, leaving a blazing path in its wake.

But Heilel's fingers went still, and he frowned. Cool air floated in the small space he'd put between us. "You're hurt."

I pulled him close again, shaking my head. "Just some scrapes and bruises."

As Heilel buried his fingers in my hair and bent his head, I braced myself for an unrestrained, world-ruining kiss. Instead, he pressed his forehead to mine. I watched his eyes slide shut. Gentle. Tender.

I didn't want tender; I was *starving*. It felt like I'd been starving for *weeks*, and not for anything in the kitchen.

With a growl, I crushed myself against Heilel and kissed him, hard, hot, demanding. His mouth opened, and the taste of him banished all my thoughts, along with every memory and reason why I should push him away. We were past that point, anyway. Something had shifted in me. I wasn't sure when it had happened, exactly— maybe when I'd thought I was about to die and I'd never see him again, or the moment I'd realized I was never leaving Hell—but the timing was irrelevant. We'd rung a bell that couldn't be unrung. Crossed a line that couldn't be redrawn.

We got rough. Urgent. I yanked off his clothes without giving a shit about popping a button or breaking a zipper. But even when he was completely naked, my nails raking over the warm, hard planes of his back, I couldn't get enough of him. He was pure addiction. His kiss, his cock, his hands. *Speaking of his hands* . . .

Heilel had reached down between us and slipped his wicked fingers beneath my dress. When he found me wet and clenching, he made a masculine sound that almost made me come right then. He pressed me into the wall, one hand around my throat while the other rubbed my clit, teased it, circled it. Mindless sounds filled the air. I knew I was making them, and that the guards in the hallway could probably hear, but I didn't care. I held onto Heilel's wrist with both of my hands, helpless against the waves of pleasure crashing through me.

I was just beginning to crest that invisible mountaintop when Heilel stopped.

Before I could protest, his mouth was on mine again and we were moving toward the bed. The backs of my legs bumped the frame. Heilel shifted his head, his mouth trailing along the curve of my neck. I turned around, letting his hands move over all of me. Suddenly I didn't feel my injuries anymore. Heilel caught hold of my sleeves on the way down, and I felt the puff of fabric skim past my waist, my legs. The dress fell to the floor and left me naked. I shivered.

Still behind me, Heilel smoothed his fingers over my shoulders, across my collarbone, and down to my breasts. He weighed them in his hands while his cock slid past the insides my thighs. This time, I didn't deny him. I didn't fight my desire for him. I tipped my head back and rested it on his shoulder, reaching up to tangle my fingers in his hair while I ground against him. He licked my neck, slowly, and something about him doing that made my toes curl. His fingers curved around my breasts, holding them firmly now, and the tip of his penis prodded at my opening. Prodded it, but didn't go any farther. I bit my lip to hold back a frustrated moan. I moved even faster.

"Say it," Heilel murmured.

I didn't need to ask what he meant. "I want you, okay? *I want you.*"

He turned me around, guided me onto the edge of the bed, and lifted both of my legs. A breath after that, Heilel lodged his hips between them and pushed inside of me.

I was wet with need, but he still entered slowly. The sound he made told me that he was savoring every second of it. A moan slipped past my lips as my core stretched to envelop him. I put my arms over my head, overcome by the ripples of pleasure moving through me.

I'd thought resisting the devil had been thrilling, but giving in to him was a feeling that had no word to describe it.

In a hard, sensual movement, Heilel drew his hips back and entered me again. Again. Again. There was nothing slow and gentle about the way he claimed my body now, and my hands fisted in the sheets. We fucked against the edge of the mattress for a minute, then he stopped to haul me farther onto the bed. On my back, in the center of the bed, he put one of my legs on his shoulder and thrust inside again.

Time ceased to exist. I didn't mark that first night with Heilel in seconds and minutes, but in gasps. Thrusts. Kisses. Expletives.

No one had gone as deep, and it should've hurt. He knew exactly where to touch, though. As if he already knew the secrets of my body and how to make it sing. I had never orgasmed from penetration before, and yet I soon felt the telltale prickle of heat and mounting ecstasy.

As I lost myself to the delicious building sensation, Heilel buried his cock deep within me one last time and held himself there. A moan wracked his entire body, and he was still groaning when I cried out, clenching around him, caught in the throes of my own release. Light. Colors. "Heilel," I breathed. "Oh, God, Heilel . . ."

Afterward, neither of us moved. Neither of us spoke.

Once our haze of desire had begun to fade, and it was possible to think again, Heilel pulled back slightly. He held my jaw lightly in the curve between his thumb and finger. I raised my gaze to his, and he peered down at me with an expression I couldn't read. All I knew was that it made my heart ache and soar at the same time.

"I didn't expect to love you," he said.

I stared into his eyes, searching them. Everything inside me wanted to believe him. "What did you expect?"

But he didn't answer.

"Now," Heilel said, easing his weight off me. He settled onto his side, resting on one elbow. His eyes met mine, and they were hard with purpose. "Who did this to you?"

I woke up alone in Heilel's bed.

The room was cold, and I saw immediately that the fire had almost gone out. It cast the rest of the room in near darkness. Unease crept over me. Maybe it was waking up in an unfamiliar place, or the way the shadows moved on the walls, like they knew they were dying. Like they were writhing in pain.

Had Heilel gone back to work? I started to wonder. My mind went back to the conversation we'd had shortly before I fell asleep. Just like that, I knew he wasn't in his office. It also explained the heavy feeling in my gut. Maybe part of me had known this would happen from the moment I'd told Heilel the truth about Samael.

I shoved the bedclothes off me and realized, belatedly, that I was completely naked. But I didn't want to put on the clothes I'd been wearing when Heilel had undressed me—they were still covered in dust from my trek through the Lowlands.

Walking on the tips of my feet, arms crossed over my chest, I hurried over to Heilel's walk-in closet. As I expected, his clothes were mostly business attire. I found a few sweaters, and even one pair of leather pants, but no robes. Eventually I pulled on one of his white button-ups. It was too big, of course. I rolled up the sleeves, found my shoes in the dark, and slipped out of the room.

There was no sign of anyone in the hallway, and all the critters that hid in the shadows left me alone. I went to the elevator and pressed the symbol that I knew would take me all the way down. Down into the darkness where the devil did his famous work.

Moments later, the doors slid open with a hushed sound. Apprehension quivered inside me as I forced myself forward. My shoes padded softly against the stone.

Dagan stood outside one of the cells. Unlike all the other guards I'd encountered during my time here, he wasn't staring straight ahead or ignoring me. Instead, he gave me a polite nod. I slowed as I drew closer, torn between the desire to see Heilel and the urge to run.

Dagan made the choice for me by moving aside. He opened the door as he went. A *whoosh* of air greeted me, and I could instantly smell the blood. My stomach clenched. I entered the cell—I could already tell it was bigger than the ones I'd seen—propelled by the need to find Heilel.

The first sound I heard was a whimper.

The first thing I saw was a hammer.

It hung from Heilel's hand, its bulky head pointed at the ground. Blood trailed down the long handle and dripped off the end. Thick, black blood. Heilel stood with his back to me, shirtless, and he didn't move at the sound of my footsteps. His head was bent, as if he'd stopped to take a breath or utter a prayer, neither of which were things the devil did. My eyes scanned the rest of the room, and I didn't let anything show in my expression.

He had his subjects arranged in a neat row, each prisoner hanging an equal distance from the ones on either side. At this point, the majority no longer had faces, but I still recognized some of them. Or rather, I recognized parts of them. Two had milky white skin. Another had teeth like a shark.

They were the creatures that had taken me last night. The creatures that were in league with Samael.

I wondered whether he would suffer the same fate, or if Heilel had something different in mind for his brother.

Hanging in the middle of all the others, the demon with the thorns in her head was very, very dead. I couldn't tell which part of her Heilel had removed first, but I would've placed a large bet that he'd done her thorns one at a time.

I turned my back on the gruesome scene and put my hand on their king's arm. "Let them die, Heilel. They've been punished."

His expression was detached. His grip on the hammer was white and unbreakable. Still moving slowly, I ran my fingertips down the length of his arm, traveling over every ridge and vein. I didn't flinch when I felt the warm, sticky handle of the hammer. I curled my fingers around it and gave it a single, gentle tug.

Heilel released it instantly.

It was way heavier than it looked, but Dagan was already there, waiting to take it from me. I handed it over without hesitation. When I pulled at Heilel, half-expecting him not to budge, he came silently. We left that bloody room and started back down the passageway. My instincts urged me to get out of this place as soon as possible.

But as we passed the door to Belanor's cell, I couldn't help myself. I stopped.

The previous Seelie King was still chained to the wall, but his wounds had started to heal. He was almost recognizable now. Our eyes met, and I saw the exact moment Belanor registered who I was. A slow, crooked smile touched his blood-crusted lips. It was a taunt. A dare.

Rage surged through my veins. I moved into the cell slowly, my hands clenched at my sides. I immediately noticed the table pushed against the wall—it hadn't been there before. Its uneven surface was stained and covered in glinting, wicked-looking tools. As Heilel appeared beside me, I looked at the tools, and I thought about it. I imagined picking them up, one by one, and figuring out what each one did. Using them to repay my old tormentor for everything he'd done to me. Not just the physical pain, but the scars Belanor had put in my mind, too.

He waited.

Heilel waited.

But I knew, no matter how tempting it was, killing Belanor would be a mercy. An eternity down here was the real punishment, and I wouldn't have another name on the list of lives I'd taken. Wouldn't have another stain on my soul.

I didn't say a word to Belanor. To either of them. I just kept going down the passageway.

Heilel came back to the bedroom with me. But when we got there, I still didn't speak. I went into the bathroom and locked the door, making it clear that he wasn't welcome inside. I hadn't gotten blood anywhere other than my hand, but I still felt the need to shower. I took off the shirt I'd borrowed and scrubbed every inch of my body beneath the hot water.

When I reemerged, wearing a towel around my body and another on my head, Heilel was still there. He sat at the end of the bed, his hands folded between his knees. There was a line between his brows. After a moment, he looked up and met my gaze.

"Please don't be scared of me," he said. Nothing else.

I walked toward him slowly. At the bed, I put a knee either side of him and sat, wrapping an arm around his neck. His palms rested on my waist, over the towel. I tugged the one off my head and set it down next to us, allowing my damp hair to fall free.

"You do scare me," I admitted, reaching down to skim my fingers over his tattoo. It made me miss my own, which were on my real body back home. "But mostly I'm scared of myself. I stood in front of Belanor down there, without a drop of power in my veins, and I wanted it. The screams. The fear. The pain.

"It turns out, it wasn't the Nightmare part of me that liked doing terrible things. It was just . . . me."

I waited for Heilel to say something encouraging, or comforting. Responses that I'd come to expect from the other males in my life. Instead, he buried his fingers in my hair, pulling me close. He gave me a hard, thorough kiss that made my core ache, in spite of everything I'd just seen. *I accept you*, his bruising lips said.

I couldn't say it back.

We broke apart, but neither of us pulled away. Our foreheads rested against each other. I didn't open my eyes. As my fingertips trailed down Heilel's bloodstained chest, I thought of the other words I couldn't say back. What he'd said to me last night. The memory, I knew, would haunt me until the day I died. I remembered the gold flecks in his eyes and how the light played on the flaxen strands of his hair.

I didn't expect to love you.

CHAPTER TWENTY-TWO

e spent the entire day in bed. And the next. And the next.

Heilel canceled his meetings. We ignored anyone who came to the door.

I had never felt so intoxicated by someone before. Like I could spend an eternity entangled with him, my mouth on his skin, his cock buried inside me. We learned how to play each other like instruments. We learned how to make each other moan, and cry out, and sigh. Once or twice, Heilel did things that made me forget my own name, much less that there was an entire world beyond the door.

Eventually, though, we did leave his room.

And thus began one of the strangest, most peaceful times of my entire life. The weeks blended together. They turned into months, and at some point, I stopped keeping track. The changes happened gradually. I began to sit in on Heilel's meetings. I met with his governors and courtiers. The staff called me *Your Majesty*. They bowed to me when I passed in the halls.

And every night, there was Heilel. Loving me. Worshipping me.

The only ones I avoided were his siblings, who still came to the tower sporadically. Roger or Dagan always sought me out to give a warning, and I'd slip away, spending the duration of their visits in the library or Heilel's room. Or our room, as it soon became, no matter how much the realization unsettled me. Technically, I didn't need to hide whenever Mammon or one of the others came. According to a vague remark from Roger, Heilel had made an example of Samael after what he'd done. But I could never forget Olorel, and what had happened when I'd lowered my guard around them. Sometimes, if I closed my eyes, I could still remember the cold altar against my back.

I didn't avoid *all* of Heilel's siblings, however.

One night, Lucifer flew me to the Second City to officially meet his brother, Asmodeus.

The journey was shorter than I thought it would be. Heilel soared high, and it felt like we nearly brushed the top of the sky. A strange haze surrounded us on all sides, and it wasn't quite like clouds, but it wasn't smoke or mist, either. A subtle scent clung to it that reminded me of sulfur. Dagan and several other guards followed us at a distance, as they always did, though it took me a while to realize it. I rarely caught sight of them through the darkness. It became a game, of sorts, seeing if I could spot the tip of a wing or hear something rustle nearby.

But then Heilel and I broke through the hazy wall, coming out on the other side of it. My eyes were immediately drawn downward, where I could see thousands of small, faint lights.

The Second City was a lot like the Hell I'd imagined before I'd actually seen it. There were fewer skyscrapers here, and the roads far below were cracked, the depths within glowing like molten lava. There were fewer machines here, as well. Instead, the main mode of transportation seemed to be lumpy-sided carts, all of them being pulled slowly along by gigantic, strange-looking creatures that somehow made me think of a cross between an elephant and a donkey. To my relief, Heilel never began our descent. Instead, he flew higher, and I quickly realized why.

Asmodeus lived on top of the crest that overlooked the entire city.

It was a jarring palace. It looked like it had been carved out of the rock, and if it hadn't been for the lights flickering in many of the windows—which were barely more than slits in the stone—I would have wondered if anything even lived there. Bat-like creatures nested in every crook and crevice, and darted through the open air all around.

As we approached, I saw that there were the same red flashes here as in the First City. But where I found the flickering horizon to be beautiful in Heilel's city, it seemed more sinister here. Like there was something hungry in that darkness. Something that had no good left in its heart.

We landed on a ledge, of sorts. A ledge that had been converted into a bizarre, eerie courtyard. This one was vastly different than the rooftop of Heilel's tower. It was endless, for one thing, spreading in both directions as far as the eye could see. There were no stone pillars or walls, no friendly gargoyles perched overhead.

Instead, there were statues. Dozens and dozens of statues.

It reminded me of a scene from a book. As I turned my head, a hollow wind stirred the ends of my hair, and the sound was eerie in the stillness. The statues looked like real creatures and souls that had been encased in stone. Some of them were even on their knees, as if they'd been begging when their flesh went solid and the light went out in their eyes, bright pupils becoming dull and gritty.

I quickly shifted my attention elsewhere. In front of us, a set of vast doors loomed. They were covered in carvings. I was unsurprised to discover these were twisted and bleak, depicting moments of torture or death. I was sensing a theme for the palace of the Second City, but I hadn't taken Asmodeus for the murderous type. This seemed off-brand for him.

Just as I started to wonder if we should knock, the doors parted. The hinges creaked like this really was a horror movie. Heilel moved forward without hesitation, so I did, too, despite how this place made my skin crawl.

The first thing I saw was the staircase. It filled most of the space, and like the walls, the steps were carved directly out of the rock. It wasn't the black, gleaming stuff Heilel's tower was made from. This was gray and dull. Lifeless.

Before I could take in more details, Asmodeus appeared in a

doorway on the left. He walked toward us, his bare feet slapping against the stone.

"Brother!" the Prince of the Second City exclaimed, opening his arms wide. He wore a black garment similar to a robe, but beneath the open flaps, there was nothing else. Asmodeus was naked.

His beauty was different from the fallen angel at my side—there was something wistful about it. Though his body was defined with muscle, he was thin, and his skin was as pale as the surface of a pearl. His dark hair looked like silk, and his high cheekbones accentuated the hollow shadows either side of his face.

Unaware of my scrutiny, Asmodeus embraced Heilel. The two of them lingered like that for a moment. The love between them was so obvious that I thought of my own brother, and a pang of longing went through me. Then Asmodeus pulled free from Heilel and turned. To my relief, he didn't attempt to hug me. Instead, he bent over my hand, and a lock of his hair brushed whisper-soft over my skin.

"My lady," he murmured. "Since the day of your arrival, I have longed for our paths to cross. The gargoyles have much to say about you."

There was genuine reverence in his voice, and it disarmed me. I didn't even think to pull my hand away as I replied, "I've been wanting to meet you, too, actually."

As he straightened, the demon prince gave me a warm smile, revealing subtle dimples. He started to say something, but Heilel beat him to it, making a gesture toward his brother's open robe. "Asmodeus, must I keep reminding you that not everyone has your proclivity for nudity?"

Asmodeus made a long-suffering sound and rolled his eyes at me, as if we were in complete agreement on this and Heilel was being totally unreasonable. I kept my opinions to myself, but my lips twitched while he dramatically closed the flaps of his robe and secured the ties around his narrow hips. "There. Now that we're appropriately *civilized*, shall we adjourn to the dining room?"

He tucked my hand into the crook of his arm and led me through a wide doorway to our right, saying, "You'll love what my chef has put together, I promise you. His skill with spices is unparalleled in all the seven cities. I believe we're just waiting on one more guest . . . ah, here he is now."

A fourth figure had entered the room behind us. I hadn't even heard him.

Every angel in the room could probably hear the way my pulse reacted. I instantly worked to slow it, control it. I gathered power around myself and imagined plates of armor, knowing even as I did that it was a childish gesture. Meant for my own comfort, and nothing more.

Because Samael hadn't come for me this time.

Heilel's eyes narrowed at Asmodeus. "I thought we were past these childish antics," he said.

"Just hear him out, brother." Asmodeus handed Heilel a glass full of amber liquid, then casually walked over to the table and stood behind one of the chairs. Not the head of the table, I noted. Even though Asmodeus ruled this city, it didn't change the family hierarchy. Heilel was the alpha here, regardless of the obvious affection they held for each other.

We were all reminded of that fact when he didn't move. Heilel held the glass Asmodeus had just handed him in a loose grip, keeping his blue eyes on the prince standing in the doorway. Samael stared back at his brother without flinching, and in that moment, I had to give it to him—the guy had some balls. If the devil looked at me like that, I'd probably shit myself.

Samael's voice was steady, too. "You have my word that I will never attempt to harm Lady Sworn again while she is in this dimension," he said.

Even I was tempted to believe him. I didn't, of course, and it was clear Heilel wasn't swayed, either. His demeanor was cold and remote as he replied, "Let's just eat."

Asmodeus was still standing by the table. The rest of us entered the dining room, which was another cavernous space. There were fireplaces carved into two of the walls, the flames so well-tended that I could hear the hiss and crackle from here. The other walls were covered with paintings. There were dozens, all varying in size and degrees of creepiness.

Our small party sat, slowly. Samael settled beside Asmodeus and I claimed the chair across from them, sitting to Heilel's left. As he went to the head of the table, Heilel's posture didn't give anything away, but I knew him now. Or knew him as well as anyone could know the Morning Star. After countless lifetimes of hiding his emotions, or eliminating them completely, Heilel practically had no tells.

No tells . . . except one.

Small, subtle, barely detectable, unless you were looking for it. The slightest shift in his shoulders, as if there were a pair of wings attached to his back, real wings, and the long feathers were stirring in agitation.

Countless lifetimes, and Heilel still couldn't forget what he had lost.

". . . have to forgive the decor, Lady Sworn," Asmodeus was saying. I refocused on him, and the prince leaned back as a staff member set the first course down. It looked like a plate of pink cotton candy. Around the table, the rest of us were also receiving our food. Asmodeus finished the wine in his hand and added, "I only recently took up my tenancy here, and preparations are still being made for the remodel."

"You haven't always ruled the Second City?" I asked, startled.

"God, no. Stheno and Euryale were here before. They ran this place for thousands of years, but Heilel just sent them away. They were becoming positively feral." Asmodeus gave a regretful shake of his head as he poured himself another glass of wine. I liked that he didn't make someone else to do it, like I'd seen courtiers do at Olorel.

Silverware clinked in the background while I mulled over what he'd said. Stheno and Euryale. I'd heard those names before, during one of the lessons from my parents. Sisters. But there were three of them, not two. What was the third one's name?

Heilel and Asmodeus were talking now. Samael said something, too, but even his voice was a thin sound in the distance. I reached for my wine glass, frowning, and then it came to me.

Medusa.

Holy shit. This was the palace of the Gorgons. Demons who could turn creatures to stone with their gaze. Famous for their volatile tempers and brutal nature.

Suddenly the courtyard made a lot more sense.

I thought of all those frozen expressions, twisted in horror and anguish. Had they died instantly? Or was part of them still trapped inside the stone somewhere, aware of every agonizing second that passed?

Suppressing a shudder, I took another drink of wine. Food held no appeal to me anymore. The three males around me had gone quiet, probably sensing an increase in my heart rate. Seeking a distraction, my gaze rose to the paintings on the walls. There was one bigger than the others, and it hung in the middle of everything. I recognized some of the figures in the image.

"The family portrait," I said, studying every face. "You're not in it, Asmodeus."

He eyed the painting, a bite of food bulging in one cheek. "Am I not? How strange."

"Why are Mammon's lips black?" I asked, ignoring his teasing.

Asmodeus cut into his meat. "Because she has the Kiss of Death. The artist took liberties, of course. They're such a melodramatic lot, the creative souls, but they certainly know how to make beautiful things."

His tone was wistful, but I barely noticed. My attention lingered on Mammon. I didn't feel repulsed, exactly, since I could hardly judge someone for having a strange, dark power. Maybe I felt unsettled by the fact that it had been given to someone who, according to rumor, liked to murder her lover before moving on to the next one. What if the Kiss of Death was her final, twisted gift to them?

"Why would the Maker give one of his angels that ability?" I asked, frowning at my wine. The question was rhetorical, mostly, but Asmodeus answered right away.

"Oh, she wasn't originally built with it. There is a transformation that every original angel goes through in Hell. It only occurs after our wings fall off. We call it . . . ack, what is the word in your tongue . . ." Asmodeus made a fast, frustrated gesture with his hand. He turned to his older brother and abruptly switched to Enochian—the only word I understood was Heilel's name. Heilel said something back, and Asmodeus's expression cleared. "Yes, that's it. We call it the Darkening."

It sounded a lot like what had happened to the Fallen in my world. It was how we'd split off into werewolves, and vampires, and all the other species that had gone into hiding.

"What happened to you?" I asked, raising my eyebrows at Asmodeus. "After your . . . Darkening?"

Asmodeus's eyes gleamed. "Would you like to guess? Shall we make a game of it?"

"Oh, God." I took another drink and shook my head. "I think I've had enough of games to last me a lifetime."

"Maybe the next one, then." Asmodeus smirked and ate another piece of meat. I watched a few drops of blood fall to his plate, and any lingering curiosity I'd had vanished. Maybe it was for the best that I would never know—I liked Asmodeus, and I wanted it to stay that way.

Heilel and Samael had sat silently throughout our exchange. When it was clear that we'd finished, Heilel asked our host about a demon species whose name I couldn't even pronounce if I tried. Apparently there was a herd of them at the edge of the Waste, causing problems along one of the trade routes. I listened, at first, but it was difficult to concentrate with Samael across the table. I held my wine glass with white fingers and wrestled with the fear response still happening within me. Every time I caught a waft of Samael's scent, I was back on that altar, my vision filling with flames, monstrous faces, and the glint of that rough-edged knife.

A foot touched mine under the table.

I glanced over at Heilel. His focus didn't waver from Asmodeus, and he didn't falter in what he was saying, but he didn't pull away or stop touching me. I thought of the night I'd woken him from a nightmare. The hand I'd put on his shoulder, and the silent message that had passed between us. *You're not alone.*

My insides calmed. The tension eased from my shoulders. When I sipped from my glass again, I could actually taste the wine.

The rest of the meal was tense but uneventful. After our plates had been cleared away, Asmodeus insisted on one more drink.

"You didn't get a chance to browse the collection," he told us, rising. "Say what you will about Sthenno and Euryale, but they were passionate about the arts. They spent centuries searching for materials and creators."

The four of us began to wander the room. Heilel stayed within touching distance, making a point of not leaving me alone with his brothers. I could see Samael from the corner of my eye. Although he didn't approach us, or even stand near us, it was obvious the prince wanted to say something.

"Maybe you should hear him out," I said, scanning the black-framed painting in front of us. It was a landscape, but not like any landscape I had seen before. Rather than meadows, mountains, or flowers, there were eerie rock formations, a red sky, and a scaly tail stretching casually out of the darkness. The tail alone looked the size of a small house, and I decided I had absolutely no desire to meet whatever was attached to it.

Heilel tossed the final dregs of his drink back, and his throat moved as he swallowed. He didn't look at me as he said, "Please don't try to repair things between me and Samael."

"Or what? Are you going to bend me over your knee as punishment?" I crooned, brushing my hip slowly against his. Trying to lighten the mood, or make him smile, at the very least.

"Punishment?" In a flash, Heilel pulled me against his chest. His breath of laughter stirred the hair at my temple. "We both know you would enjoy it far too much to constitute punishment."

His mouth traced the shell of my ear, sending shivers through me. I suppressed a smile and turned around, putting my hands over his heart. Maybe it was because he lived in another dimension, or because he was an original angel, but it was much faster than any heartbeat I'd felt before. It made me think of a hummingbird.

"Go talk to him," I said softly, giving his chest a gentle push. "People can surprise you sometimes."

Heilel's jaw flexed, and his eyes flicked between mine. Whatever he saw made him silence the refusal he'd been about to give. With a soft, swift kiss to the side of my head, the devil turned and moved toward the other end of the room. I watched him go, twisting the stem of my glass between my thumb and index finger.

Truthfully, I didn't give a shit about Heilel's relationship with his brother. What I was interested in was self-preservation, and as long as Samael blamed me for the rift between them, I would be an obstacle. A target. According to Heilel, if anyone was killed in this dimension, it would wipe their soul from existence. I didn't plan to go out like that, and I sure as hell didn't plan to die on an altar.

Another figure sidled up beside me. Even if I hadn't glimpsed his robe in my peripheral vision, Asmodeus's scent was becoming easy to recognize. He smelled like incense, maybe, or candles.

"He's different with you," Asmodeus mused, watching Heilel. "I think this is what my brother looks like when he's . . . happy."

The wonderment in his voice made me smile. But the smile froze on my face as a memory popped into my thoughts. It was that word, *happy*. I thought of the last time I'd truly felt joy, and I saw Matthew, his tiny face wreathed in smiles. His nose and ears red-tinted from the cold. Damon nearby, a snowball clutched in his glove. All of us surrounded by ice, and trees, and blue sky.

Home.

Heilel had either picked up on the shift in my mood, or he was eager to leave himself, because I felt his hand on my arm a moment before he said, "We should go. I'd prefer to avoid the necrool."

Asmodeus's eyebrows rose. "The necrool are little more than pests, and yet the King of Hell is adjusting his schedule to stay out of their way? Is someone getting *old*, Heilel?"

"Let's step outside, and I'll show you how old I am."

Even in Hell, males were so typical. Asmodeus's chest puffed, and the two of them started walking off, as if they were really about to scuffle. I bit my lip, secretly enjoying their interaction. Then I felt the prince behind me move closer, and my smile vanished. Samael's breath heated my ear. "Farewell, Lady Sworn."

"Goodbye, Samael," I said flatly. I wouldn't give him the satisfaction of sensing the fear that crept up my spine at his proximity. My gaze stayed on Asmodeus and Heilel.

"May I give my new sister an embrace?" Samael asked. I started to say *Fuck no*, but he was already reaching for me. I stood there, stiff as a board, as the prince pressed close and cupped the back of my head. Then he whispered, "You are nothing more than his pet. Remember that."

My first reaction was involuntary. My gut churned and it was like I'd been punched. I started to believe him . . . and then another voice crowded in. More familiar to me than a lullaby, and one I trusted infinitely more than this spineless asshole. I pictured Emma Miller's gentle smile and her soft features.

Never forget how strong you are. Or that you are loved.

As we pulled apart, I looked into Samael's eyes and gave him a small, crooked smile. "And you're nothing more than second best. The eternal runner-up. I won't bother advising you not to forget it, because something tells me you never do."

"Are you ready?" Heilel called, standing near the enormous doors. He was looking at us with an inscrutable expression, and I wondered if he'd heard any of our exchange. Heilel must've put his wings on while I was distracted, because they shone in the burnt glow of a nearby torch, folded and tucked against his back.

I drew back from Samael, and I didn't bother with parting words or taunting smiles. I'd poked the beast enough for one night. I'd also fucking won, and we both knew it. I turned my back on Samael and walked over to Asmodeus and Heilel.

"Thank you for having me," I said to the younger brother, allowing him to see my sincerity.

As if he knew how rare it was, Asmodeus smiled. "You are always welcome in my city, Lady Sworn."

With a grip lighter than the strange mist outside, he bent and skimmed his lips across the back of my hand. Then he straightened and nodded at the staff members waiting by the doors. They pulled on the massive handles. Once again, Asmodeus didn't attempt to hug me, and it only made me like him more. I pulled my hand out of his and went to Heilel, who put an arm around my waist and led me back into the sisters' eerie collection of the dead.

The doors started to close behind us, the hinges groaning like wounded giants. Heilel and I walked away, my boots making soft sounds against the rock. But just as Heilel spread his wings and started to reach for me, Asmodeus's voice cut through the courtyard.

"You asked about my Darkening. It was rude of me not to answer."

I turned toward him, staring past all those tormented statues. There was still a figure standing in the doorway, but it wasn't Asmodeus anymore. I recognized the newcomer immediately, and my jaw dropped.

It was the soul from the Lowlands.

Still wearing my Lowland guide's face, Asmodeus winked. "The gargoyles like me, too. They told me where to find you. I couldn't resist having a little fun while I escorted the infamous Fortuna Sworn back to my brother."

"You little—" I started, stepping forward.

He waggled his fingers, and the doors slammed shut.

Later, I would look back and think it was funny how quickly things could change.

When Heilel and I left the Second City, soaring high above the dangers of his world, I rested against him and felt calm. Safe. Almost . . . happy. Heilel and I had found a delicate balance, and our strange life together worked. We worked, as long as he didn't pull me over the line between us and I didn't try to see what was hidden on his side.

But that night, I had a nightmare.

It was the beginning of the end.

Maybe Samael's leering face had triggered it. Maybe it was seeing Asmodeus's features change. Whatever the reason, whatever the thing was that caused it, the damage was irreparable. A rupture opened inside of me and terror came pouring out.

I fell asleep in Heilel's arms . . . and woke up in Belanor's.

"Hello, darling," he said, peering down at me with a pleasant expression. "Sleep well?"

Manacles bit into my wrists as I tried to recoil. Belanor got out of the bed calmly, striding over to the chair where he liked to drink his tea. I watched him, my chest heaving and my breath coming in ragged, frantic gulps. I was back in that gilded room at the Seelie Court, weak as a human again, powerless against the terrible things Belanor had planned for me.

No sooner did I have the thought when Fende appeared on the other side of the bed, a giant, faceless hulk. He bent over and yanked me onto my stomach, a bright poker in his hand.

"No!" I screamed, clawing at anything I could grab onto. "*No!*"

A moment later, I could smell my own flesh burning, and then I could hear it, too. Like the sizzle and hiss of burgers on the grill. I pushed my face into the mattress and screamed.

Suddenly I was choking on sand. Suddenly I was surrounded by the dull roar of a crowd cheering for my death.

I lifted my head just as a new sound reached my ears. It was like thunder. Then the memory clicked into place, and I remembered I wasn't alone in this arena.

I whirled at the same moment Finn threw himself on top of me. I didn't even have a chance to say his name before the werewolf lowered his head and began to rip me apart.

The agony was indescribable, but somehow I found the strength to reach up in a feeble attempt to stop him, to plead, to remind him that I was Fortuna and he loved me and—

"*Fortuna!*"

My eyes snapped open, my mouth still gaping in a silent cry. Heilel's silhouette loomed over me, and his voice coaxed me the rest of the way out of the memory. I sat upright slowly, the hollow of my throat damp with perspiration. Heilel didn't press me to speak. He sat near enough that I could touch him, if I wanted, or lean back and rest against his chest. But I didn't move. I stared at the dying fire and saw Belanor's taunting smile the last time I'd been downstairs.

Without saying anything to Heilel, I yanked the bedclothes aside and got up.

The dream had shaken something loose in me. I felt strange as I left the room and strode down the walkway, completely ignoring the guards that hurried after me. Just as I reached the elevator, Heilel appeared at my side. He was dressed now, and there was a robe in his hand. He held it out wordlessly, and for the first time since waking, I took note of what I was wearing. Right. I'd fallen asleep in a thin, short nightgown. I took the robe and pulled it on, securing the ties, then stepped onto the elevator. Heilel did the same and pressed the symbol that would bring us underground.

Ding. I got out the second the doors opened, plunging down the creepy passageway without hesitation. My bare feet slapped against the stones. I didn't pause to think, or peer into any of the cells on either side of us. I knew exactly where to go. As if part of me had sensed I'd be coming back here, and that I would need to memorize the way.

One of the guards hurried to open the door for me. They'd put it together, apparently, or Heilel had warned them we'd be coming. I strode into the cell, and it felt like there was a low buzzing sound in my ears. Heilel said something to the guard before he followed me inside. I barely heard him; all my attention was on the far wall.

The faerie I'd dreamed about hung right where I'd left him. He'd been tortured recently, but not so recently that he was bleeding. His wounds had just started to close. His naked body dangled from the chains like a chicken on a spit, arms and wings spread wide. I knew for someone as proper as Belanor, the indignity of that alone must be torture. I committed the image to memory, knowing it would lull me to sleep for many nights to come.

To my surprise, Belanor didn't say anything, or give me that taunting smile. Heilel's demons had almost succeeded in breaking him, that much was obvious. If there was nothing left of his mind, it seemed pointless to do anything. The possibility sent a rush of sharp-edged fury through me. Standing there, glaring up at the faerie who had tortured me, I could finally admit the truth to myself.

I'd been thinking about doing this from the moment I first saw him in Hell.

I hated Belanor Dondarte. I hated him more than I'd ever hated anything. The feeling was all-consuming, like Gil's bloodlust. My gaze went to the table of torture tools, which was pushed against one of the walls. Feeling Heilel's eyes on me, I went over to it and looked over the selection carefully. After a minute, I chose a knife with the most jagged, painful-looking blade.

I returned to my place in front of Belanor, who continued to hang there without making a sound. My fingers curled around the hilt, and I was shaking.

"Remember," Heilel said suddenly, his voice harsh in the stark silence of the cell. "If you kill him here, in my dimension, that is the end. He will cease to exist."

I understood what he was trying to tell me. If I did this, I wouldn't just be killing Belanor—I'd be obliterating him from existence. There would be no other dimensions for him, no chance for his soul to wander. Heilel was giving me all of the information before I made a choice.

Exactly like last time, I just stood there. And looked, and looked, and looked. The longer I hesitated, the more I could hear Collith in my head, breaking through the rage and pain like a beam of light on a dark night. *Choose mercy, Fortuna.*

Fuck. My shoulders sagged. Belanor wasn't the only one I hated. Sometimes I hated Collith Sylvyre, too. Apparently it didn't change the fact that I also respected him, or that his opinion meant something to me. My hold loosened on the knife, and after another moment, I put it back on the table.

I was about to turn away when Belanor said, his voice halting and tight with pain, "I would do it all . . . over again."

I faced the faerie slowly, but I kept my eyes downward. I knew he was goading me. Belanor *wanted* to die after everything he'd endured in this cell. Killing him would be the real mercy.

Except . . . no one said it had to be a quick death.

This was Hell. Here, there were no rules. No such thing as good or bad. Right or wrong. I raised my gaze slowly. As I stared at the monster chained to the wall, it felt like I could hear the darkness calling my name. This time, I didn't turn away.

I answered it.

I picked up the knife again and stepped forward. I looked into Belanor's eyes, and I saw his defiance give way to fear as I brought my arm up. "Wait—" he started frantically.

Blood splattered my face.

CHAPTER TWENTY-THREE

A fire crackled in the grate.

I rested on my side, one hand tucked beneath my cheek. Heilel slept beside me, light flickering over half of his perfect face. His breathing was deep and even. There was no hint of fear in the air around us, no flavors in my mouth other than toothpaste. I kept expecting Heilel to have another nightmare, but ever since we'd started sharing a bed, they seemed to have stopped. I shifted on the pillow, seeking a drier spot—my hair was still damp from the shower I'd taken before bed.

The shower I'd needed to take because my entire body had been covered in Belanor's remains.

As I lay there, staring into the fire, my mind went back. Back to when I'd stood beneath that pounding stream, my head bent against the water. I'd watched gore run into the drain and felt nothing. It was like I had started to drift away.

Heilel was the one to bring me back.

"Fortuna," I'd heard him say.

The devil had such a beautiful voice, I thought to myself. The husky edges felt like a feather against my senses. I turned my head, water cascading down my spine. Heilel stood on the other side of the cloudy glass, respecting my privacy. I felt him studying me. After a moment, he must've come to a decision, because I saw him move in my peripheral vision. He hooked his thumbs into the band of his boxer briefs and slid them off.

Heat coiled in my core as Heilel stepped into the shower and pulled the door shut. I didn't move, and he stopped just short of the stream. A moment later, I felt a sponge move over me. When I remained still, not uttering a sound, Heilel continued. He washed my back first, then my neck. His strokes were so tender. He lowered himself to his knees, cleaning my thighs, my shins, even my feet.

Once he'd finished, Heilel stood and stepped away. The intensity of his expression felt like flames licking over my skin.

"What do you want?" he asked.

Now it was my turn to study him. I was still looking over my shoulder, one hand pressed against the wall. Heilel's sultry lips were slightly pursed, and there was a line between his golden brows, as if he'd found a problem he couldn't solve. After a moment, it hit me—Heilel was trying to comfort me. He just didn't know how.

It felt like there was a flower blooming inside my chest. The petals unfurled and pushed out all the bad feelings again. I finally turned around and took Heilel's hand, pulling him back through the water. My spine pressed against the cool wall. Heilel kept his eyes on mine, moving slowly, carefully. He took the backs of my thighs in his hands and lifted me effortlessly, then adjusted my legs so I was wrapped around his waist. We looked at each other, and for the millionth time, Heilel's beauty struck me. Every hard plane of his naked body was lined in shadow, making him look like a carving. His golden hair was wild from the water, the waves more prominent.

As I watched, a wet strand fell back over his eye. *Damn it*, I thought helplessly. Giving in to the need burning through me, I hooked my wrists behind Heilel's neck and bent my head, kissing him deeply. I was obsessed with his taste. Every part of me was fused to him, and I couldn't get close enough.

What began as a slow, tender kiss quickly heated into urgent hunger. Heilel held me tighter, pressing me even harder against the wall. My arms wound more fully around his neck as we consumed each other. His tongue drove me wild. I felt his arousal between my legs, long and thick. I clenched involuntarily, desperate for him, but he didn't shift or reach down.

"Heilel," I whispered against his mouth. A plea.

After that, he didn't make me wait any longer.

My sex was so wet that when Heilel entered me, his length slid inside with a single movement that banished every thought, if I'd had any left. My eyes fluttered shut of their own volition, and I gripped his broad shoulders. His question still hovered between us. *What do you want?*

I opened my eyes and looked into Heilel's. Water gleamed on his skin like diamonds. "I want you to fuck me until neither of us can stand," I said clearly.

That was all he needed to hear.

Heilel drew his hips back. His eyes bore into mine, and I saw a fierce light burning in those blue depths just before he rammed his entire length inside me. A gasp tore from my throat. My arms shot out, and I flattened my palms against the wall. Heilel was already filling me again, his erection sliding in and out as though our bodies had been made for each other. I moved with him, caught up in a rough rhythm that tore mindless, frantic cries from my throat. Over and over again, Heilel plunged so deep that I could feel him high inside my body, but it wasn't enough. I wanted him deeper, harder. I bit Heilel's shoulder, riding him as he thrust even faster.

He roared as he came inside me.

Watching Heilel climax, and feeling the tip of his cock scrape that secret place within my body, brought me to mine just a second later. I was still in the throes of it as Heilel's hips slowed, then stopped. He watched me with a masculine, satisfied smile. Even after I'd recovered, though, he didn't pull out or step away. I had my arms around his neck, and my eyes stayed closed. The only sound between us was the running water. I rested against the curve of Heilel's neck and inhaled his scent. We stayed like that for a minute, holding each other tightly.

When Heilel finally set me back down, my legs were shaking. I regained my balance and realized that I still had some of Belanor's blood on me. Heilel had already noticed, of course. He turned back to me, holding the sponge in his long fingers again. He silently proceeded to soap every inch of my body a second time, stopping now and then to caress a nipple or lick my neck. By the time he'd finished, I was craving him. Aching for him. Heilel knelt on the tiles and peered up at me.

"Still standing," he said huskily. "Now that won't do."

Seeing the devil on his knees was erotic enough. Then he leaned forward and buried his face between my legs as if my body was paradise. I gasped, and my stomach buckled. Heilel caught hold of me without pausing, and I braced myself on his shoulders.

Briefly, I thought of another shower, another male who had touched me like this . . . but then Heilel did something new with his tongue that made another gasp tear from my throat. I forgot about anyone else. There was only him.

Afterward, he toweled me dry and carried me into the bedroom. We made love again, then again, and the orgasms made me hazy. Heilel saw the way my eyes fluttered and pulled me close, his chest against my back.

Now here I was, feeling sleepless and strange. Heilel's breathing was deep and slow. I wanted to follow him into whatever dream he'd weaved, but there was something bothering me. And it was more than what had happened with Belanor.

Holding my breath, I reached over and opened the nightstand drawer. I lifted the cover of the book I'd been reading and found what I was looking for. Heilel didn't stir. I exhaled and slipped out of bed, walking over to the other side of the room on bare, silent feet.

Standing in the light of the fire, I opened my fingers, revealing a crumpled piece of paper. My eyes scanned those three words for the thousandth time. The harried handwriting. *Don't trust him.*

I tossed the paper into the flames and watched it burn.

I became listless.

Slaughtering Belanor had made something inside me crack. *He deserved it,* I thought over and over. But all the good feelings I'd been having had spilled out, leaving guilt, worry, and shame. At first, I hid it. I went through the motions of the life I'd built here, dressing, talking to Heilel's staff, reading in the library, resolving conflicts that came to the tower when Heilel wasn't there to do it himself. Every time I was blinded by a flash of memory—Belanor's guts spilling out of the violent slash I'd made—I tilted my chin and pasted on a hard mask. *He deserved it.*

Heilel still knew. Whenever we were in the same room together, I felt his eyes on me. He tried to start a conversation more than once, but I always changed the subject or didn't answer. I didn't want to talk about Belanor, or what I'd done and who I'd become during those long, dark, terrible hours beneath the tower.

I only felt like a semblance of my old self when Heilel was touching me. When he was inside of me. When he was devouring me. But then he always left, called away by some kingly duty or other, and I was alone with myself again. Forced to acknowledge the darkness in my heart.

After a few more days, I stopped pretending to be okay. Because I wasn't.

I got into bed and didn't get out.

The curtains kept every flicker of light away, and things like night and day stopped mattering.

Eventually, a sound reached my ears. Or at least, I thought it did. I returned to awareness gradually, like coming down from a bad trip. I wasn't sure how much time had passed, or whether I'd slept at all. If I did fall asleep, Heilel hadn't come to me in a dream, and there'd still been no sign of Oliver. With a hazy frown, I opened my eyes and waited for my vision to adjust. Something had pulled me out of my stupor. A noise of some kind, I remembered.

Narfu was in the room. It must've been the door I'd heard, or the soft pad of his footsteps. He wasn't cleaning, though. Instead, he plucked at my blankets, and tugged at folds and parts where the material had bunched. When there was nothing left for him to fix there, he started rearranging the canopy curtains secured to the bedposts.

In a slow, sleepy way, I realized what was happening. The demon was . . . fretting over me. Worrying about me like a mother hen over its egg. I gave Narfu a slow, sleepy smile. "Stop fussing. I'm fine."

To emphasize my point, I patted my chest, as if the heart living inside it wasn't breaking. Narfu stared at me for another moment. I didn't think lizards were capable of frowning, but as I gazed back, I swore that's what he was doing. Slowly, Narfu backed away and disappeared soundlessly through the door. The latch didn't even click as he closed it. I tugged the covers over my head, hoping I'd convinced him.

But the demon must not have believed me, because Heilel arrived a few minutes later.

He knelt on my side of the bed, where I was curled into myself. I didn't move at the sight of him, but I opened my eyes and met his gaze. For a few seconds, neither of us spoke. Heilel's ocean eyes were dark with worry. Seeing it made me want to sit up and try to go back to the way we were. But what if I left this bed, and that darkness within me spread?

"I want to do something for you," Heilel said finally, sliding his index finger down the slope of my nose.

"What do you mean?" I murmured.

Heilel hesitated. His brows drew together in a rare expression of uncertainty. I was so startled by the sight of it that I remained silent. At last he said, his words slow and halting, "I want . . . to make you happy. To give you something that will make you smile. What would do that?"

I didn't need to think about it. I sat upright and hugged my knees to my chest.

"I would love to see my family." I swallowed, feeling a prick of guilt that I'd barely thought about them during my time with Heilel. "Even if it's just for a few seconds. To look at them and know they're doing okay."

Heilel pulled away and crossed the room. He reached into the top drawer of the dresser and pulled something out. He returned to me gracefully, his scent surrounding the bed. Every atom in my body was zeroed in on the object in his hands.

"This is how I watch your world," Heilel said.

He held a mirror out to me. I grasped the handle carefully, knowing this was the key to seeing my family again. I held it up and stared at my own face. The mirror was eerily similar to the one Collith had given me, back when we'd first met.

The spell upon it must've been the same, because I thought of the people I loved—the ones I was pulling strength from every single day I was here—and my reflection blurred.

I expected to see Damon.

Instead, Emma filled the glass.

A flare of joy went through me, but within seconds, it sputtered and went out as I registered more details. My grip tightened on the mirror. *Something is wrong*, instinct hissed. Emma stood in the kitchen, as usual, but there was a strangeness about her posture. Her eyebrows were knitted together, her spine slightly bent.

As I watched, Emma's hand rose. She pressed it against her stomach. Fear burrowed in mine, and I felt Heilel's hand on the small of my back. His voice was full of concern. I didn't answer, didn't even hear because all my focus was on Emma. I knew she couldn't hear me, but my mouth parted instinctively, about to call her name anyway.

Then she started vomiting blood.

CHAPTER TWENTY-FOUR

*F*ar below where I stood, the First City writhed with fire-light and fear.

The gargoyles chittered above me. They must've sensed my mood, because none of them had dared to come near or try to communicate. I stood at the ledge with my arms crossed over my chest, my shoulders hunched. Wind howled in my ears, and the cold gusts brought a distant sound with them. There were games happening in the arena, which Roger had told me about—I could hear the dull roar of the crowd, even from here. My mood darkened even more at the thought of so many helpless souls getting ripped out of existence.

It had been an entire day since I'd seen Emma in the mirror. An entire day since I had confessed the truth to Heilel about having no way to get home, and begging him to help me. An entire day since he had denied me. *If I knew a way out of my world, don't you think I would've done it by now?* he'd asked.

What if it was too late, anyway? What if Emma hadn't survived? My stomach wrenched at the thought. I stared out at the dark sea of buildings and spires, wondering if there was anyone out there who possessed the magic I needed. I'd given up on my search so quickly.

If I'd fought harder, Emma might be okay right now. But I'd allowed myself to get distracted. To get *complacent.*

One of the gargoyles dropped to the ground, and the sound of its claws hitting the stones drew me out of my guilt. It was Givi, I noted as I turned. He crawled closer, and there was something odd about his gait. After a moment, I realized he was holding a small object. The creature stretched out his arm to me, and I carefully removed the object from his grasp.

It was a stone. It looked a lot like the ones that had been piled around me when I'd first got to Hell and had woken up in that big structure. The outside was dull and gray, almost mottled, like gargoyle skin. Its shape was lumpy and jagged.

I met Givi's wide, concerned eyes and smiled faintly. "Thank you. It's beautiful."

The small gargoyle made a sound that was halfway between a croon and a purr, then he flapped his enormous wings and lifted off the roof, flying up to rejoin the others. I looked out at the city again and recrossed my arms, still holding the rock. The rough surface scraped my skin, but I didn't care; its solid weight was strangely soothing. My fingers curled around it even tighter. The calls of the bloodthirsty spectators returned, fainter now, as if Givi's kindness had worked some sort of spell. I stood there for a few more minutes and tried not to think about all the people I'd let down with my weakness.

His voice came from behind, as it so often did. "I hope you don't plan to ignore me forever. It's going to be a very boring eternity for both of us."

The horizon flashed red, and just like that, I saw Emma again. I faced Heilel, and for once, the sight of him didn't send my thoughts scattering. I only had one thought now, and her face haunted me. Desperation surged through my veins like a thousand tiny needles. It showed in my voice as I said, "There *has* to be something you can do. You must know someone, just one person, in all of the seven cities, who can work the kind of magic I need. We can create rain, or summon it, I don't know. Or forget the rain, we could find a spell that—"

"I'm not a god, Fortuna. I'm not omniscient, nor do I have limitless magic at my disposal. There are still rules, no matter how much I may resent them."

I was shaking my head before he finished speaking. I didn't accept that. Any of it. Heilel just didn't want to let me go. There had to be a way, and he was refusing to tell me.

"Whatever this is," I made an abrupt gesture between us, "had to end at some point. It's not even *real*, Heilel. It's just magic."

He didn't reply. His blue eyes fixed on those distant flashes, and I wondered what he saw in the darkness. What haunted *him* whenever he stood on this rooftop. I didn't ask. It would feel like giving up, somehow, and I'd already given up on Emma too many times.

Still not saying a word, Heilel turned to me. His hands curved around my waist and he pressed our foreheads together. I started to pull away, but then his scent drifted past. Sandalwood. I breathed it in, wondering when that smell had become safety and comfort. Within seconds, the tension drained from my entire body. Heilel was breathing me in, too. I put my hand on his chest, searching for his heart. And there it was, fast but steady. A heart that had beat for an eternity and would keep on beating for several more. Once, I would've been infuriated by the thought.

"'In the very depths of Hell, do not demons love one another?'" Heilel whispered, fingering a strand of my hair.

Closing my eyes, I swallowed a sigh and looped my other arm around his neck. Our bodies touched. Our chests, our thighs . . . everything else. "What is that from?"

"A human named Anne Rice."

"You've read Anne Rice?"

Heilel pulled his head back. Feeling his eyes on me, I opened mine and met his gaze. "I've read everything from your world I could get my hands on," he said.

I started to respond, but the words stopped in my throat. I couldn't talk about books, or Anne Rice, or anything other than the world I needed to get back to. The people who needed to know that I hadn't abandoned them or forgotten them. I was still drawing on the power of the Shadow Court, and somewhere along the way, I'd stopped thinking about the consequences or effects this could be having on them. One person I loved may have already paid the ultimate price for my selfishness.

A soundless scream filled my head, and I pursed my lips to contain it. My hands were still on Heilel's chest, but I looked toward the horizon again. He watched the play of emotions across my face and I did nothing to hide them.

When he broke the silence again, there was something in the devil's voice I'd never heard before. "Come with me. I want to show you something," he said.

I shook my head. "I'm not in the mood for one of your field trips, Heilel."

"Not even to see what's behind the locked door?"

I went still. Heilel had gotten my attention, and he knew it. But now that he was finally willing to show me his big secret, I was wary. I didn't rush to agree as he'd probably expected. I remembered what he'd said the first time I'd asked about the door. *There's still fear in your eyes when you look at me, Lady Sworn. When that's changed, you'll be ready.*

"Why tonight?" I asked.

Heilel stepped back and let his hands fall, leaving the choice to me. I could follow, or not. As he walked away he said over his shoulder, "Because it's time."

Why? I wanted to ask again. It was convenient that he wanted to open up exactly when I needed to leave. I stayed where I was and glanced up at the gargoyles, wishing they could offer advice or warn me what to expect. None of them bothered to pretend they hadn't been eavesdropping. But Heilel was disappearing down the stairs, and it felt like his offer had an expiration date on it. Like it was now or never. And if I didn't find out what was behind that door, the mystery of it might drive me insane.

Swearing under my breath, I hurried after him. I caught up with

Heilel just as he reached the bottom of the steps. We got onto the elevator and rode it in silence. We stayed silent, even as the doors opened and we moved down the walkway. Heilel's posture was relaxed, his pace unhurried. When we arrived at the locked door and faced each other, his beautiful face was still calm.

"This is why I searched for you, Fortuna Sworn. This is why I fought so hard to bring you here."

With those ominous words, Heilel finally opened the door. He stepped back to let me pass. I stepped over the threshold, peering into the dimness eagerly.

The room was long and narrow, but it only took a second to find what Heilel had brought me here for. There was barely anything else in here, save for the fireplace, the old-looking settee covered in red velvet, and a plush, patterned rug on the floor. The object that held my attention was above the fireplace.

"What is this?" Feeling dazed, I walked toward it slowly, willing myself to wake up. Because this had to be another dream, another one of those relentless, endless terrors. But it didn't shimmer like a mirage or change into something else, no matter how close I got. My voice dropped to a whisper. "That isn't possible."

His voice floated through the still room. "It was foreseen. We were foreseen."

It was us. Me and Heilel.

The likeness was incredible. The artist had gotten every detail right, right down to the small birthmark beneath my eye. They'd gotten the subtle gleam of wickedness in Heilel's gaze. The hint of arrogance.

In the painting, Heilel and I were on the rooftop. The devil wore his wings, and they were spread wide. He carried me in his arms. Both of our faces were turned, as if there really had been someone else standing there, painting our portrait or taking a picture. In the background, tucked in the shadows, gargoyles peered out.

As I stared at their gray faces, I remembered a comment Roger had made recently. It was during one of our many walks to and from the elevator, after we'd passed a gargoyle bold enough to land on the railing. *They don't usually perch in the city. Something is drawing them there*, Roger had said.

Even Heilel had mentioned something, once. *They like you*, he'd remarked when I'd first arrived in Hell. At the time, I'd thought he was joking. There had been something strange in his voice. I hadn't known him well enough then, so I'd dismissed it as teasing. Now, as I reviewed my memories, I knew I'd been wrong.

Heilel had been looking at this painting for decades. He must've known the gargoyles would be a symbol, a confirmation that he had truly found the one he'd spent eternity searching for. But now I could feel his eyes on me, staring at my face instead of the canvas. I hadn't even heard his footsteps.

"Did you paint this?" I asked finally.

I still hadn't looked away from it, so I couldn't see Heilel's expression as he answered. "No. Goody Baldwin did."

I stopped breathing.

"Her vision was so powerful that she had a seizure." Heilel followed my gaze, and the faintest tinge of sadness entered his voice. "When she awoke, she started painting. She wouldn't stop, not even for rest or food. She painted until the final brush stroke, four days later, and then fell down dead."

"Charming story," I managed, my voice hoarse.

No wonder Goody had never written another entry.

For the past minute or so, my mind had been frozen in shock. Now it launched into movement and raced ahead, considering this revelation and all its ramifications. Was it just coincidence that Goody Baldwin's journal had sent me here, in the exact same way she'd arrived in Hell? Lyari had brought it to me, I knew that much. But did I ever ask where she'd gotten it? There were too many coincidences, and I didn't believe in those.

"I don't want to possess you, Fortuna," Heilel said, distracting me. "I never did."

So that's your angle, I thought. He wanted me to believe he'd done all this for love. Because a witch had painted us together and he'd been staring at her vision for all these years. But I wasn't falling for it. Heilel was ruthless and cunning. He hadn't pursued me across generations and dimensions out of some delusional infatuation.

"And all the dead Nightmares? How do you explain them?" I demanded.

"I used them," Heilel said bluntly. "I wore them until I couldn't anymore."

I stared at him, horrified, and he looked back without remorse. I imagined all the lives Heilel had taken. All the bloodlines he'd snuffed out. An entire species nearly decimated because of him. At last I said, my voice swollen with pain and betrayal, *"Why?"*

Heilel finally turned to the painting. He stared up at it, but there was a look in his eyes that made it obvious he was seeing something else. "I may loathe your world, but I've always been intrigued by it, as well," he murmured.

I made a sound of disbelief. "Are you telling me that you murdered dozens of my kind just so you could, what, experience life on Earth? Catch a few shows, eat at some high-end restaurants? Yeah, totally justifies it."

"Can you say you wouldn't have done the same, if you were in my position?"

I opened my mouth to tell him exactly that, but then I hesitated. I thought of Belanor. I thought of the other terrible things I'd done that, once, I never would've believed myself capable of. There was darkness inside all of us. How far would mine have spread if I'd spent an eternity without light?

It didn't change anything, though. No matter how tempted I was to pretend that it did. I met Heilel's gaze again and ignored a small, desperate whisper urging me to stay silent. "I have to go back."

"Do you love me, Fortuna?"

The directness of it made my heart quicken. Heilel's question hovered there between us, and when I started to think about the answer, a bubble of panic burst inside of me.

I kissed him instead.

Heilel didn't try to push me. He kissed me back, and his other hand slid up my waist. His fingertips gently skimmed my breast, then reached my throat, where he gripped it—firm yet gentle—steadying me as he devoured me, pressing his mouth harder and harder against mine. As I responded, my hands gripping his shirt-front, my eyes went up to that painting. The other Fortuna was so calm. So unafraid. As if she was exactly where she belonged.

But this was not where I belonged.

Damon. Matthew. Emma. Finn. Gil. Cyrus. Ariel. Nym. Seth. And then I thought of them . . . Collith and Laurie. I'd buried their memories deep at the back of my mind, put them in a box and closed the lid, then locked it tight. The box was open now. I allowed myself to remember them. To acknowledge how much I loved them. The thought of never seeing Collith and Laurie again sent a sharp sensation through me, as if there were a glass shard lodged in my chest.

We'd been living in a dream, Heilel and me. We'd been deluding ourselves, pretending to be other people so we could fit together. But it was always temporary. He would always be the one who had slaughtered my people, and I would be a means to whatever end he was planning. Secrets grew between us like thorns. Even if we cut them away and hoped that time would dull the edges, we were something ugly and painful.

I looked up at him, and sorrow clung to my heart.

"It's time to wake up, Heilel," I said.

He didn't give any response, and I didn't wait for one. I turned my back on him, on the painting, on the entire room, and I walked out without looking back.

Later, I wasn't surprised when I woke up in an empty bed.

I touched the sheets where Heilel had been, and they were cold. He'd returned long after I'd fallen asleep, and apparently he hadn't stayed. But I knew he'd been here, and that I hadn't dreamed the mattress shifting beside me—his sandalwood scent still lingered.

We hadn't spoken since I'd left that dim, creepy room with the painting. I'd spent a few hours training, trying to put all my anger

389

and frustration into the dummy, and Heilel had kept away. Things between us felt strange. Unfinished. But I'd used our time apart to think, and I had reached a decision.

I wasn't a prisoner here. Not anymore, at least. If I asked one of the guards to take me downstairs and out of the tower, they would. So that's exactly what I was going to do. If Heilel didn't have a way to send me home, and he refused to look for one, then I'd find it on my own. It was time to go back to my original plan, and scour the First City for magic. If there wasn't any here, I'd move on to the next city. And the next. It was long past time for me to go home, and I would do whatever it took. Even if that meant taking on the creatures Heilel had mentioned when he'd first talked me out of leaving.

This time, I reminded myself, I'd have gargoyles on my side. Not to mention whatever weapons the guards supplied me with, and the new skills I had learned from Heilel. I wasn't sure how long I'd be gone, or whether I would be coming back. I'd packed a bag before bed, which contained several changes of clothes and food I'd gotten from the kitchen.

All that remained was saying goodbye.

I'd already said my farewells to Narfu, and Saida, and a few of the others who lived in this tower and had crept into my heart. That only left Dagan, Roger, and . . . Heilel. As soon as his name echoed through my mind, I left the bed and got dressed. I wouldn't be able to fall back asleep, anyway. I chose clothing as close to hiking gear as I could get. Pants, boots, a long-sleeved shirt, and a coat with multiple pockets. Once I was ready, I swung the bag onto my shoulder and walked out. I didn't linger for a final look or hesitate at the door.

This time, Roger was in the walkway. "Do you know where Heilel is?" I asked, approaching.

He gave me a smile that seemed sad, somehow. "His Majesty is on the roof, my lady. He's waiting for you."

Waiting for me? I knew from experience that it would be futile to ask questions—Roger would just say something vague, or promise that Heilel would tell me everything. That never stopped the demon from asking questions of his own, though. As we stepped onto the elevator, I waited for Roger to mention my bag, but he just stood there. He didn't even hum, which was something he'd started doing around me recently. As if the demon had become so accustomed to my presence he wasn't even aware of the low, cheerful sound he was making. Now I almost missed the disjointed melody. What was going on? I frowned and tried not to fidget. The silence pressed in on all sides.

Seconds later, the doors opened. *Ding.* I peered out at the rooftop, and I spotted Heilel straightaway, his distant figure visible in the firelight. I was about to move forward when Roger spoke again, and I turned at the sound of his voice. "I would just like to say, my lady, that you are the loveliest creature I've ever met, and it was an honor to serve you."

As he gave me a deep bow, I studied him. Somewhere along the way, Heilel's adviser had become dear to me. His hands were tucked behind his back, as they always were, and his wrinkled face radiated sincerity. He wore the ragged, shapeless clothes he'd been wearing since the day we'd met, and those tufts of hair over his large ears were more chaotic than ever.

"Why does it feel like you're saying goodbye, Roger?" I asked finally.

"Because I am, my lady." The old demon smiled at me again, and the elevator doors slid shut.

I stood there for another moment, frowning. A gust of cool air stirred my hair, blowing it across my chin as I turned. Heilel stood in the center of the stone structure, the shapes of the gargoyles looming far above him. The devil wore his wings, and they were spread but relaxed, the metal edges curved all the way to the ground. He was dressed all in black again.

"Will you please tell me what's going on?" was the first thing I said once I drew close enough.

Heilel smiled, and it looked like the one I'd just seen from Roger. Wistful. A little sad. "Will you fly with me one last time, Fortuna?" he asked.

My heart pounded harder. Suddenly I understood what was happening. Why Roger and Heilel were acting like we would never see each other again.

He'd found a way. In spite of everything, all our back-and-forth, his own desires, and his claims that it was impossible, Heilel had figured out how to send me home.

He confirmed it when he said, "You won't need this," and slid the bag off my shoulder, setting it on the flagstones a short distance away.

A hundred more questions crowded in my skull, but I didn't speak. I couldn't. I allowed Heilel to pull me close and lift me into his arms. I relaxed in his hands as his wings began to flap—a habit, since we'd been flying many times now—and Heilel arched his head back. The air rushed past as we ascended into the inky expanse of sky. *Swoosh. Swoosh.* I watched how Heilel's muscles rippled beneath his golden skin while he brought us higher, higher. I wrapped my arms around his neck and forced my thoughts to settle, so I could commit every detail to memory. Heilel. The glint of red light on metal feathers. How warm and safe I felt, there at the top of the world, resting against the Dark Prince's warmth.

After a while, the First City was enshrouded in darkness. Without moon and stars above us, it felt like there was no beginning and no end to the world. Nothing else existed, save for me and Heilel. He still hadn't offered an explanation, and I'd lost the urge to press for one. I leaned my head against him and stared at the black horizon, unafraid of what it held.

We'd only been airborne for a few minutes when I heard a familiar chittering sound. I straightened and craned my neck to see behind us. After a moment, I saw the glow of red eyes. The gargoyles had followed us. They were making the sound that meant my name. I would've been alarmed, but there was no urgency in their voices . . . only sorrow.

It felt like someone had pinched my heart. They must've figured out that I was leaving.

Heilel kept going, his eyes fixed on something I couldn't see. We were still ascending, and he'd never brought me this far before. I waited for a sense of unease to take root.

Then something landed on my cheek. I touched it, startled, and my fingers came away wet. My eyes widened in disbelief. I stared at a small, gleaming droplet that clung to my skin, visible only because the sky was flashing now.

Rain.

I lowered my face and met Heilel's gaze. He'd been watching me, instead of the sky. As if he'd known exactly what to expect. Realization hit me like a bright, roaring truck.

He'd brought us to this spot deliberately.

My grip tightened on his shoulders. My heart was beating so hard it rivaled the thunder all around us. There was lightning, too, but Heilel didn't seem concerned about it. The gargoyles didn't, either. They were still flying around us, calling my name, shouting farewells in their strange, rasping voices.

Heilel still hadn't explained. I shook my head in denial, even as a glistening drop clung to my eyelash. "I thought rain didn't exist here. Both you and Asmodeus said it!" I shouted.

Another bittersweet smile curved his beautiful lips. "We lied. No time to talk about it, unfortunately. Spells like this tend to work fast."

What? Why would you lie about that? I started to ask, but the rain was coming down in torrents now. All at once, my confusion faded. It was sinking in that I was really going back. Right here, right now. I would never see Heilel again—not like this. Never touch him again.

He must've had the same thought. Before I could say anything else, Heilel bent his head, kissing me roughly. Consuming me. I kissed him back and matched his fierceness, digging my fingers into his hair. Losing myself to his taste, his hands, his tongue. My heart called out his name. *Heilel.*

Suddenly the insides of my eyelids lightened. *But there's no light in Hell.* I broke our kiss, startled. My skin prickled and tingled. I recognized magic when I felt it.

"Wait," I gasped. I didn't know who I was speaking to, but my voice was full of pleading. "I'm not ready yet!"

Heilel pressed his forehead to mine. "No one ever is," he murmured. "Have courage, dear heart."

I held him tighter, as if I could delay the spell just by holding on. But I was fading, little by little. Soon, Heilel's arms would be empty. He'd be alone again. I stared into his eyes, and water ran down my face, tears intermingling with rain. Words lodged in my throat. There was nothing I could say that he didn't already know, anyway. The light got brighter, and brighter, and brighter. There was a sound coming out of that blinding orb now. Collith's voice, I realized excitedly, even as I despaired about what I was leaving behind.

I tried to turn, to catch one final glimpse of Heilel.

But there was only the light now, and a high-pitched ringing sound. Then there was a soundless, blinding flash.

I was home.

CHAPTER TWENTY-FIVE

*R*eturning to my body felt like being engulfed in flames.

It was the sort of pain that blocked out all reason or thought. I cried out helplessly, my eyes flying open. I couldn't see through the haze of agony. Just when I was about to scream, pleading for someone to make it end, the excruciating, red-hot sensation faded. I blinked a few times, and suddenly I could see again. I caught a glimpse of my bedroom and the slanted ceiling just before my stomach lurched.

Gagging, I turned onto my side and vomited all over the floor.

"Thank God," a familiar voice breathed. Gentle hands held my hair back. "I'm here, baby. I'm here."

I moaned, slowly reaching up to wipe my mouth with the back of my sleeve. Collith didn't move. I sat up, and the room tipped. I grabbed onto the edge of the mattress and focused on Collith, who was sitting beside me on the bed. "Emma. Where's Emma?"

As I swayed, his hands flew out to catch me, and his fingers curved around my waist. Even through my T-shirt they were a welcome coolness, and my eyes fluttered shut. "You have a fever. You should get some rest," Collith murmured.

I forced my eyes back open and caught hold of his hand. "I'll get some rest later. Where is she, Collith?"

His mouth tightened. "At the hospital."

"Is she—"

"She's alive."

A small sound slipped out of me, something halfway between an exhale and a sob. Until that moment, I hadn't realized how scared I'd been. No, not scared . . . I'd been fucking *terrified*.

Another sound burst out of me, louder this time, and I covered my mouth. Without a word, Collith leaned over and picked me up. He set me on his lap and wrapped an arm around my waist. His other hand cupped the back of my head. When I didn't try to fight him, it was as though a hundred pounds slid off his shoulders. Collith rested his chin against my head and held me as I cried. But after a few seconds, it started to feel like I wasn't just crying about Emma. I didn't even know what I was crying about, really. Now that I'd started, I couldn't seem to stop.

Then Collith's cell phone rang into the silence. Hearing it jarred me, and reality sank in like a spell had been broken. My tears dried as my mind began to race. The others. My pack. They'd been keeping me alive all this time. Were they all right?

While Collith silenced his call, I touched the bonds with my mind. They glowed like Christmas lights. Beautiful, bright Christmas lights. In an instant I felt their essences, every single one of them. *Finn. Gil. Seth. Cyrus. Ariel. Nym.* I felt their love, their worry, their secret pain. Then I sensed their simultaneous surprise as my Court realized I was there, in their heads, alive and conscious.

The rush of joy was like all my happiest memories rolled into one moment. It was so overwhelming I could only manage to say back, *I can't wait to see you. Yes, I'm okay. I'm okay.*

That was the moment it started to sink in. I was back. I was home. All the tension left my body, and I practically sagged against Collith, holding onto him as though he was all that kept me upright.

"Will you take me to her?" I whispered against his chest.

Collith hesitated—he probably wanted me to rest, or at least wait until morning—but only for a moment. I felt him nod. "Of course."

Later, I wouldn't remember the drive to the hospital. But I'd remember Collith helping me down the stairs, my body weakened from the spell. It was the same weakness I'd experienced when I'd first got to Hell. I'd remember him putting me in the passenger seat and getting behind the wheel, cranking the heat to the highest setting. It was only then I realized that I was shivering. I'd remember the edges of my vision going hazy, and then . . . nothing.

The next thing I knew, the name of the hospital loomed over us in glowing letters.

Collith had obviously been here before, because he led the way without hesitation. There was a human sitting at the front desk, but he walked right past her. I steeled myself for her to stop us, say something about visiting hours, but her eyes moved over me as if I weren't there. Collith must've been using the powers he'd taken from Laurie.

For the first time since I'd learned the truth about Collith's abilities, thinking about it didn't hurt. Instead, I just leaned into him and allowed him to steer me into an elevator.

Emma's room was on the third floor.

Collith stopped outside the doorway. He reached up and skimmed my bottom lip with his thumb. "I'll be right back. You should be nourishing your body right now, so I thought we'd start with some water."

I just nodded, my mind on the person lying a few feet away. Collith pulled back slowly, then turned and left, his long shadow stretching across the tiled floor. I watched him for a moment, wondering if he would call Laurie. As far as I knew, the Seelie King didn't know I was back.

And you're stalling, that inner voice of mine said.

Emma was alone when I went in, a small figure in the hospital bed. There was an empty chair next to her, and it reminded me too much of the chair that had been in Damon's bedroom. Another clang of pain went through me, and I put my hand on the armrest as I stared at Emma. Would our family ever be together again? It seemed that whenever one of us woke up, another one fell.

She was hooked up to so many tubes and machines that it was impossible to tell where they ended and Emma began. Even in the short time she'd been here, the veins in her eyelids had become more pronounced, her cheeks more sunken, her skin paler.

Blinking rapidly, I sank into the chair. I reached for Emma's hand and cradled it in mine. Her skin felt like clouds, I observed distantly. Why did that thought make me want to cry again? Letting go of her, I pulled away and sat with my knees clutched to my chest, like a child in the womb. I began to watch the monitors, calming myself with every steady heartbeat they recorded.

I'd been there for less than a minute when Lyari appeared in the chair next to me. I jumped a little, giving her a look of surprise. Had Collith let her know I was here? A second later, I dismissed the thought. None of it mattered, not even the fact that I hadn't seen Lyari since the night we'd performed the spell.

My friend looked better than she had when I'd left for Hell, but not by much. She was still too thin, and there was a blankness in her eyes that hurt to look at. Lyari was controlled, yes, but she radiated strength and ferocity. As those empty eyes did a quick scan of my person, assessing me for injuries, she didn't bother with a greeting.

"What happened?" Lyari said. Even though she'd spoken softly, her voice felt harsh in the small, quiet room.

I knew, somehow, that she wasn't asking about Emma. She meant Hell, and Lucifer, and all the rest of it. My eyes went back to monitoring Emma's heartbeat, and some of the tension drained from me. It was still strong and even. Lyari's question hovered in the stillness, and it felt impossible to answer in just a handful of words. What happened? When I thought of my time in the underworld, there were hundreds of terror-filled memories I could've picked from. Instead, I only had one thought.

Him.

I remembered Heilel fucking me. Heilel making love to me. Heilel bathing me. Heilel showing me his soul.

I met Lyari's gaze and told her the terrible truth in my heart. My voice was hoarse and broken.

"I think I fell in love with the devil."

Emma's heart monitor beeped into the silence.

I'd been at her side for hours. Lyari was long gone, off on another secret mission. She didn't offer to stay and I didn't ask. I hadn't wanted to talk much after my confession to her, and Collith came back a few minutes later, bottle of water in hand. He was asleep in the other chair now, apparently worn out from forcing me to play more games of Connect Four. He'd brought the box when he returned with the water, which explained why he'd been gone so long.

As I studied Collith's sleeping face, I felt myself starting to drift away. The sound of a nurse's voice startled me awake. It was harder than it should've been to open my eyes. I still felt weak. As the nurse's footsteps faded, I touched my forehead, irritated to find that I was still feverish.

There was no more danger, I reminded myself. Heilel hadn't said it in so many words, but I doubted he was still intending to hunt me. He'd let me go. I folded my arms on the end of Emma's bed and leaned down on them, allowing my eyes to drift shut again. We were in a busy hospital. A few minutes couldn't hurt . . .

"Open your eyes, Fortuna," someone said.

I knew that voice, I observed dimly. It couldn't actually be who I thought it was. It was just someone that sounded like him, or it was my drowsy brain blending dream and reality. I lifted my head expecting to see the walls of Emma's hospital room.

But I was in the dreamscape.

I stood on the path, facing the sea. I barely registered that glitter in the distance, though. I'd spotted a figure in the corner of my eye, and for a split second, I thought it was Oliver. Then I turned my head and realized who I was looking at. The sight of him sent an electric current through my body.

Heilel stood beneath the tree.

This is a dream. It has to be. I walked over to him, slow with confusion. A moment later, I felt Heilel's fingers bury themselves in my hair, his thumbs resting on my cheekbones. I put my hands on his chest. He felt so warm and solid. My voice was breathless as I asked, "Is this real? You're actually here? I thought . . ."

"You thought you'd never see me again?" he finished, resting his forehead against mine.

I breathed in his scent. But after a few seconds, thoughts began to creep in, and the bright rush of joy faded. *Not right*, the voice inside me whispered. Something didn't feel right. I moved back, forcing Heilel to let go of me. The imprint of his fingers lingered on my cheeks as I asked, "Seriously, what is this? Where's Oliver?"

"This, Lady Sworn, is the moment I've been dreaming about for centuries." Heilel paused, and his eyes were dark with regret. "I'm coming back to your world, and I intend to finish what I started that day in the Garden."

My only reaction was a confused frown. It felt like I was missing something, and my mind worked quickly, trying to think of some detail or clue that I might've overlooked. "You can't," I said finally. "You don't have a host. I still won't do that for you, Heilel, no matter how much things have changed between us. I will *never* say yes."

"I won't need a host," Heilel replied. He was still looking at me with that infuriating expression, and suddenly I wanted to punch it off his face.

"Why don't you need a host?" I said, my voice sharpening. "How are you here right now, and what the fuck is happening? Where is Oliver?"

"You'll understand everything in a moment. I promise."

"What are—"

Roots exploded from the ground and closed around me, forming a makeshift cage. I slammed down on all fours, screaming, and the roots continued to crackle and thicken. When they went silent, I lifted my head. In an instant, I saw there was no way out.

I crawled over to the roots and peered through them. Heilel hadn't moved, and the fact he hadn't even lifted a finger to beat me was infuriating.

"How are you doing this?" I snarled, yanking at the wooden bars. When that proved ineffective, I shifted and raised my legs to kick at them.

Heilel knelt in front of me, his hand dangling off his knee. "That's one of the things I love about you. Your fire."

I stopped struggling and stared at him in disbelief. "You don't love me. Caring about someone means you don't want to hurt them, you asshole!"

He arched a brow. "And what makes you think I want to hurt you, Fortuna?"

I made a sound that was meant to be a laugh. "I get it now. You're just insane. All those centuries stuck in the dark fucked you up. I don't know how I didn't pick up on it, though. Either you're an incredible actor or I was an incredible moron. I'm pretty sure it was the latter."

I'd barely finished speaking when movement over Heilel's shoulder drew my gaze. I felt myself begin to frown. There was something behind him. Keeping low, creeping closer. When I realized what I was looking at, my stomach dropped.

Oliver was crouched in the grass.

There was a knife in his hand, and he was about to bring it down and plunge it into the devil's back. *Don't do it*, I wanted to scream at him. Not for Heilel's sake . . . but for Oliver's.

Heilel spun so fast that I didn't even see it.

He looked at Oliver and raised his arm. It was positioned in such a way that I knew, in a burst of terrible intuition, that he was about to decapitate my best friend.

Before I could scream, beg, or bargain, Heilel's hand froze. Oliver had frozen, too. The two of them stared at each other. It was almost as if they'd met before. To make the picture even stranger, Oliver's winged doppelgänger stood near them, encased in stone.

"Now you," the devil said, "are *fascinating*."

Oliver's lip curled and his eyes blazed like heavenly fire. "Let her go, or I'll obliterate this place with both of us still inside."

"I shall make you a bargain, strange creature," Heilel replied, completely unperturbed by the threat. I saw him lean forward, and he put his mouth beside Oliver's ear. Heilel said something else, but the words were too low for me to hear. Ice formed in my veins. What could Heilel possibly have to offer Oliver?

"Don't listen to him, Ollie," I called urgently, renewing my efforts to break the wooden bars. "You can't trust a single word he says!"

Neither of them seemed to hear. Heilel was still speaking, and something he said made my best friend glance at me. His eyes were full of longing. Before I could tell Oliver not to do anything stupid, he refocused on Heilel and, after another beat of hesitation, gave a single nod.

I knew, then, what the devil had promised him.

Heilel put his hand on Oliver's shoulder. He leaned forward and spoke again. I kept wrenching at the bars of my makeshift cage, trembling with adrenaline and rage. When Heilel was done, he stepped away from Oliver and looked at me. I froze, staring back at him, and I was holding the roots so tightly that pain vibrated through my hands. But then his gaze shifted. I followed it, twisting around to look out a different side of the cage. Confusion swirled through me.

A door had appeared.

It stood there, held up by nothing, and it reminded me of one of the memories I'd found in the dreamscape. That memory hadn't ended well, I recalled with a sinking stomach. There was nothing ominous about the door itself, and yet every instinct I had was screaming that I didn't want to open it . . . or anyone else to, either.

I spun back around, learning forward to peer through the bars. Heilel had already walked away from Oliver, and his blue eyes were intent on the door. Something about his expression made me think of what he'd said earlier.

This is the moment I've been dreaming about for centuries.

Horror filled my throat, brought on by a surging sense that

something terrible was about to happen. "Heilel," I said hoarsely. "Heilel, wait. Just wait."

He walked past me. I said his name again, louder this time, with a frantic edge. I yanked the roots. Heilel didn't even look back. It was like he couldn't hear me at all. Was he in a trance? At the exact moment I opened my mouth, he wrapped his long fingers around that round, old knob, and twisted it.

Slowly, the door creaked open.

My mouth went dry. On the other side, I could see a familiar hospital room. Emma was still unconscious in the bed, and there I was, fast asleep in a chair. It was jarring to see myself, my real self, and I lost precious seconds staring. I blinked, recovering, but it was too late.

Before I could try to stop Heilel, he stepped through. The door swung shut behind him with a resounding slam that made me flinch.

And then it vanished.

CHAPTER TWENTY-SIX

*S*omeone was shouting. Someone was saying my name.

There was no time to speak to Oliver, or process what had just happened with Heilel, because the door had barely closed before everything was rushing away. I felt a world-tilting sensation, my head spinning, and then the blur of darkness and color became solid again. Within seconds, I was back in Emma's room, still in the chair beside her. Someone else was here, and they were speaking to me, but the words were a meaningless hum. Thankfully, I recognized his scent.

Collith. Collith was the one who'd woken me.

"What happened?" he bellowed, shaking me. I blinked groggily, my head jerking back and forth. I grabbed onto him, words of panic rising to my lips. It was then I noticed the scorched footprints leading away from Emma's bed. Big, bare feet that had left such deep indents in the floor the cracks spread far beyond them. Whatever I'd been about to say faded.

Heilel was free. Heilel was *here*.

Collith's fingers bit into my shoulders, bringing my gaze back to him. His eyes were wilder than I'd ever seen them, and that was the moment I realized how bad this was. What had I done?

His voice was rough with urgency. "Did you give him permission?" he demanded.

"No," I whispered, holding his arms in a white-knuckled grip. My heart was a hammer as I thought about every word I'd said, every interaction we'd had. I shook my head adamantly. "No, I didn't."

What had changed? How had Heilel gotten through?

Collith kept searching my eyes, my face, and his lips were thin with tension. He thought Heilel was inside me, I realized dimly. He thought I was a host. But it was even worse than that. So much worse.

My mind was slow with horror, desperate to explain this. To find the signs that I'd missed. As I struggled, a memory resurfaced.

You're the one who lets him out! It was one of the first things Nym had ever said to me. He had gone into my future and he'd seen the path I was on. He'd tried to warn me, just as he'd tried to warn me of so much else. But Nym's mind no longer worked as it should have. His messages always seemed to get lost in the haze and the jumble.

I was too dazed to explain all of this to Collith, and I was still trying to figure out when I'd made the fatal mistake. My mind rewound. The last time I'd seen Heilel, we were in the skies of Hell. The spell couldn't have affected him, not when Savannah hadn't performed the rites on Heilel and he wasn't connected to my Court. What happened after that, then? I had returned to my body, and the first thing I'd done was visit Emma. I was talking to Lyari before I fell asleep.

In my mind's eye, I saw the two of us sitting there, light from the hallway slanting over the floor. I struggled to remember everything we'd said—I had just returned from Hell, and I was still pretty disoriented when Lyari came to the hospital—but there was one part I remembered vividly.

I think I fell in love with the devil.

Wait. My frown deepened. Lyari had been here. I'd only been back for a few hours, and I hadn't even told my pack where I was going. How had she known? I raised my gaze to Collith's. "Did you tell anyone you were taking me here?"

A line formed between his brows, but Collith didn't ask any of the questions I knew were rushing through his head. "No."

"Will you stay with Emma? There's someone I need to talk to, and you're the only one strong enough to keep her safe. The only one I trust to . . ." I stopped and swallowed. It was just hitting me, the reality of how much danger my family was in. How much danger I'd *put* them in. Even if Heilel had no further use for me, we would see each other again, and I still had a part to play in all this. Nym had seen that, too.

"I'll guard her with my life, Fortuna," Collith said, cutting my thoughts short. I refocused on him. His hazel eyes held mine, steady and unflinching.

I trust him. The realization came quietly, but it felt right. True in a way so few things were. I kissed Collith's cheek, and then I walked to the door. The keys to the car were on a small table. I picked them up and paused on the threshold, unable to stop myself from glancing back. But the sight of Collith instantly calmed me. He'd already settled in the chair next to Emma, his posture relaxed, as if he was prepared to be there for a long time. His dark head was tipped toward the window, probably listening to every sound out there, too.

There was a warm feeling in my chest as I left.

Once I'd found the car and gotten in, closing the door behind me, I thought about where to go. In the end, I went back home. I probably should've summoned Lyari to a place we wouldn't be interrupted, but I wanted to shower. I could smell myself, and it was a wonder Collith hadn't recoiled from me. His fae senses would've made my stench even worse for him. If Laurie had been here, he would've informed me that not only did I reek, I needed to make an appointment at a nail salon immediately. I didn't even need to close my eyes to picture the scornful look Laurie had given my hands before. More than once.

Morning hovered on the horizon during my short drive. It was that in-between time, not quite night anymore, but not yet dawn. The trees were still bare, but the snow had gotten to that half-melted, dirty stage. The blue-black tone of the world softened those parts, though. For a few brief, beauty-filled minutes, I sank into the silence and thought about absolutely nothing.

Gil was leaning against the barn when I pulled in. The end of his cigarette glowed like a tiny sun. I got out of the car and closed the door quietly, conscious that people with sensitive hearing might be sleeping inside. "What are you doing here?" I asked.

"Just looking out," Gil said, pulling me in for a brief, rough hug. "The kid is inside with Cyrus and Ariel. Damon wanted to be at the hospital with Emma, and his boyfriend had to work."

Damon was at the hospital? He must've got there just as I'd left. Now that I thought about it, I had gone through the lobby in a rush. I'd wanted to get this conversation over with and return to the hospital as soon as possible. Damon was probably there sleeping in one of the chairs, or getting coffee. It was a good thing he was with Emma, I decided. Not just for her sake, but his own.

I had no idea how this confrontation would go.

Just as I started to feel prickles of apprehension, I realized I was staring out at the trees. I'd been looking for a glimpse of bright, golden eyes or a tall figure striding out of the shadows. Finn was still out on his hunt, obviously. If he'd been home, he would've come outside right away. I longed to feel his warm presence beside me or at least know he was nearby.

Gil was still leaning against the wall. I studied him for a moment, thinking how strange it was that I hadn't known this person my entire life. His features were as familiar to me as Damon's or Emma's. The long, sharp nose. The thin lips that were always smirking or smoking. The bleached hair, which had grown out these last few months. "I need something," I said, hesitant.

Hollows appeared in the vampire's cheeks as he took a drag from his cigarette. Plumes of smoke left his mouth as he said, "I've already given you my favorite throw blanket. Don't think I didn't notice that you haven't given it back."

"The blanket is mine now and you'll never see it again. But that's not what I was going to ask you."

The vampire heaved a long-suffering sigh. "All right, I'm listening."

"That's exactly what I need you to do, actually. To listen." I faltered. It felt strange, almost unnatural, to ask for help. To ask someone else to be there for me. I swallowed and added, "Vamp hearing is as good as a faerie's, right? So I'm hoping you'll stand here and tune in when I summon Lyari. If she does show, I might eventually need some backup."

By the time I was done, Gil's features had sharpened, and all traces of humor had vanished. I waited for his fangs to elongate, a sure sign that he was losing control. But it didn't happen. Seconds ticked past, thick with tension. Then, all at once, the bomb inside Gil abruptly defused. He threw his cigarette butt down and stomped out whatever sparks were left. Without looking at me he said, "I'll listen, then."

I nodded at Gil in silent gratitude, hoping he saw it from the corner of his eye, and finally turned toward the door. I knew he probably had a dozen questions now. I'd have to explain later.

Later, after I confronted Lyari Paynore about why she'd betrayed me and everyone I loved.

As I crossed the garage and headed for the stairwell, I tried to shift all my focus onto what I wanted to say. If this went south, it would undoubtedly be because I said something stupid. My lips were moving silently when I got to the top of the stairs and found the door locked. I put the key in and listened for any sounds. There was only silence. Seth must've gone back to his place, and I wasn't entirely certain whether or not Nym still lived here. I was probably the only one home.

The door swung open at the slightest push. It opened on well-oiled hinges—Finn was always doing tasks around the property, on the rare occasions he actually had the hands to do them—and a quiet, empty space greeted me. I hung up my coat and took off my shoes, glancing around. The loft felt strange without Emma. She hadn't been gone long, I knew that, but it felt like she was the heart of this place. Her terrible perfume was usually lingering on the air. There were always baked goods on the countertops, food bubbling on the stove, and fresh coffee in the pot. All of that was gone now, the heartbeat silenced.

Focus, Fortuna. I nodded and let out a breath. A beat too late, I realized Gil had probably heard it. Now he knew how nervous I was. Silently kicking myself, I walked around and turned on more lights. When that was done, I started moving toward the kitchen, thinking of a dozen other things I needed to do now that I was home. But I'd only taken a few steps when I recognized that I was stalling. Avoiding.

I stopped in the center of the room and said it.

"Lyari."

For once, my Right Hand appeared right away. "Are you all right?" she asked. "Is Emma—"

"How did you know where to find me, when I went to see Emma in the hospital? No one knew I was back yet," I cut in. Lyari went quiet, and the longer the silence stretched, the heavier I felt. I'd been hoping I was wrong. Part of me still wanted to bury my head in the sand, but I forced myself to continue. "Where do you go every time you disappear, Lyari? Why have you been missing some of my summons?"

"He told me where to find you," she said. Taken aback by the speed of her answer, since I'd been prepared for another silence, I said nothing. But it turned out, Lyari didn't need me to push her anymore. Disgust seeped into her voice as she went on. "He knew which hospital Emma had been brought to, even the room number she was in. He ordered me to use your trust. Get you to talk, especially about your feelings for him."

"I had to say the words, didn't I? I had to admit it to myself, in order to make him corporeal." I waited, but Lyari had apparently fallen silent again. And now, finally, I voiced the question I'd been wanting to ask all along. *"Why?"*

She still didn't answer. There was a slight hunch to her shoulders, though, and she kept her face turned away. I allowed the quiet to hover between us as I studied her. Absorbing every detail. Acknowledging the feeling in my gut.

"What does he have on you?" I asked. Lyari's head jerked around, and her startled eyes met mine. She remained silent. Understanding again, I gave her a sad, small smile. "I know you, Lyari. You wouldn't betray me, not by choice."

"I thought you'd . . ." Her mouth worked, and somehow I knew what she was trying to say. Lyari thought I'd believe the worst of her. Hate her. I wondered if it was because she'd known of the prejudice I used to hold against her kind. Or maybe it was a result of how she'd been treated by her own people for so many years.

It occurred to me that we were still standing in the middle of the room, facing each other as if we were on a battlefield. Hoping to ease the tension, I walked over to one of the barstools and sank onto it. I hadn't missed that Lyari never answered my question about the missed summons and her disappearances.

With my hands folded between my knees, I lifted my head and met her gaze. I forced myself to voice the next question, even though I didn't want to ask and I knew she didn't want to answer. "He hurts you, doesn't he?"

Lyari swallowed. "His witches do. It's why I didn't answer your summons the night you killed Logan Boon."

The shame in her eyes told me what she still couldn't say. I knew, then, that Lucifer had been using her to keep tabs on me. On us. It was how he'd figured out where Damon was.

Using Collith had just been a distraction. A red herring.

As we stood there, both of us silent now, something else occurred to me. I raised my head. "Goody Baldwin's journal. I've always wondered how you wound up with it. Did Lucifer . . . ?"

She nodded, her mouth tight. "He planned all of it. In order for you to arrive in Hell, you had to want to go there. He predicted every move you made after that. Agreeing to his deal. Using the spell you'd found in the journal. Making you think you were stuck in Hell forever. He knew you wouldn't ever give in to him if you believed there was a way out. That you were going back."

Hearing this, my mind flashed back to the last conversation I'd had with Lucifer in Hell. He had literally confirmed what Lyari was telling me now.

I thought rain didn't exist here, I remembered saying. My voice had been full of such wonder. Poor little fool.

That night, Lucifer had looked right at me and said, *We lied.*

I had all the missing pieces now. Suddenly it was easy, finishing the puzzle I'd been trying to solve for so long. Lucifer had always been twelve steps ahead of me. Even sending me home had been part of his plan, but he'd only enacted it after he failed to manipulate an admission of love himself. Lyari had been a failsafe, a backup in case I proved to be less malleable than he hoped.

It was so intricate. So careful. If it weren't so terrifying and manipulative, I would admire the devil for how well he'd played the game. Behind every random event or conversation, there was Lucifer, manipulating strings from the shadows.

But he'd hurt someone I cared about. Any chance at admiration, or redemption, was long gone. I refocused on the person he'd harmed this time, determined to lessen some of the damage left in his wake.

"Lucifer is good at desire. He figures out what we want most, and he uses that to get what *he* wants. So all I need to do is answer the question. *What does Lyari want most?*" I felt my expression soften with pity. "A cure."

The warrior's jaw worked. She didn't try to deny it. "After Viessa banished me, I began the search for a solution immediately. I couldn't wait for a miracle. How was I to know you'd form the Shadow Court after I signed the contract?"

"Contract?" I repeated.

Lyari nodded again. "I thought it was part of her spell. The witch I found. I placed my hand in the heart of the flames."

Lost in thought, I stared at the floor and frowned. It was all too coincidental, the fact that a witch had handed Lyari's soul over to Lucifer just when he needed leverage on me most. I raised my gaze back to Lyari's and asked, "Did you ever learn her name? The witch who oversaw your contract?"

"Iris." Lyari didn't hesitate. "She said her name was Iris."

I closed my eyes. Iris, the witch from the Seelie Court and Belanor's old lover. I'd basically killed him right in front of her—gleefully. More weight settled on my shoulders as I realized I was responsible for yet another person's pain. Iris never would've targeted Lyari if she hadn't been connected to me. The witch probably could've sent anyone to spy on us. But she'd chosen to torment someone I loved.

Pain seeped into my voice as I said, "I told you I'd find a way to save you, Lyari. And even if I hadn't, would it be so terrible, becoming a goblin? You've met Seth. He's a good person."

"If I don't have my honor, what else is there? My name?" she countered. "Bloodline Paynore is the laughingstock of the Unseelie Court."

I was about to respond when Lyari stiffened. Her eyes went distant, and I recognized that look—anyone with supernatural hearing had some version of it. Lyari was listening.

She confirmed it a moment later. "Someone is downstairs," the faerie murmured.

Before I could respond, there was a knock at the door. I stayed where I was and glanced at Lyari, wondering if she recognized the scent. She nodded to give me the all-clear, but her expression was strange. As soon as I opened the door, I realized why.

"Thuridan? What are you doing here?"

His gray eyes instantly moved past me. "I was looking for Lyari."

I stayed between them, appraising the faerie Jassin had taken such a personal interest in. Lyari and I had never been able to find out why, and the mystery still bothered me. Thuridan was bigger than I remembered. He stood in the doorway, his muscular frame nearly filling it. He must've come from the Unseelie Court, because his ginger hair was raked back and he wore his Guardian armor. He also bore the Guardian weapon of choice, a sword that looked like rough-edged glass.

"You're afraid," I observed. I didn't even need to be a Nightmare to see it—agitation came off him in waves and his hands were clenched at his sides.

"Stay out of my head, filth," Thuridan snarled. I just looked back at him calmly. Thuridan frowned at me for a moment, as if I'd done something strange. His focus quickly returned to the beautiful faerie standing at my side, and I watched a change come over him. It was subtle, but it was there. Some of that softness slipped into his voice as he asked, "Is there somewhere we can speak privately?"

My gaze darted between them, noting the familiarity in how they looked at each other. *Well, well,* I thought. It was obvious they'd been spending some time together. But how much, exactly? Did Lyari know why the devil was after Thuridan? She opened her mouth to respond to him, but a new sound tore through the loft, making all of us freeze.

Nym was moaning.

I was the first to recover. I whirled away from Lyari and Thuridan to hurry down the hall. Nym's door was cracked, and I pushed it open without hesitation. "Nym? Are you okay?"

The faerie stood near the window, but he was bent over, his head clutched between his hands. He wasn't wearing a shirt, and he was so underweight that it felt like I could see every bone beneath his thin, pale skin.

"Nym?" I ventured again, reaching for him hesitantly.

Just before my fingers made contact with his back, Nym spoke. He didn't look up at me as he mumbled, "The Dark Prince is outside."

My hand froze. Heilel was here? Now?

All thoughts of comfort vanished. Without another word to Nym, I whirled and ran toward my room, intending to get the Glock. Lyari must've been listening from the living room, because she'd drawn her sword. Thuridan stood beside her, and he met my fleeting look with contempt. It didn't fool me, though.

Fear came off Thuridan Sarwraek like a downpour of rain.

"Modern weapons won't work on him," Lyari reminded me as I flew past.

I swore, halting. My mind worked quickly, running through a list of what *would* work on that immortal asshole. But we didn't even know what he'd come back as. Was Lucifer a Fallen creature, like the rest of us, or was he something more? Would holy water affect him?

I could only think of one thing that might have a chance of slowing the devil down. I started moving again, and went into my room at a calmer pace. I reemerged a minute later.

When Lyari saw what I was carrying, her features tightened. "This is the Dark Prince, Fortuna. You've been training for less than a year."

"Wow, thanks for the vote of confidence." I went to the row of hooks beside the door. I set the sword down and reached for my coat, shrugging it on. I wrapped my fingers around the sword's hilt, lifting it again, and faced Lyari. "I may not be a warrior, but I am a Nightmare. And a fucking badass one. If it comes down to a fight, I might be the only one of us that can actually take him. The sword is just a distraction."

I pulled up my hood, gazed at Lyari for another moment, then turned and left. I jogged down the stairwell and tried to loosen my muscles as I went. I wasn't going to use the sword, not if I could help it, but I knew this could go wrong in about ninety different ways. Just before I pushed the outer door open, I stopped and took a long, shaky breath. I caught myself wishing Collith and Laurie were here. Heilel knew how much they meant to me, though. I needed to keep them far away.

It was raining when I stepped outside. Raining, just like the last time Heilel and I were together. Only, then, I'd been in his arms, and I'd actually believed he loved me.

Apparently God had a pretty twisted sense of humor.

"Over there," Gil said, startling me. I glanced at him. The vampire wasn't leaning against the wall anymore. He stood still, his head turned.

Following Gil's gaze, I turned toward the driveway. Surprise shot through me. Not just at the sight of Heilel—he stood at the edge of the lawn, his hands shoved in the pockets of an elegant coat—but also the fence that hadn't been there before. I was guessing Damon or Cyrus had put it up to stop Matthew from wandering into the road. My nephew loved playing in the yard.

Thinking of Matthew pushed out some of the fear, and my grip tightened on the sword.

"Summon them, Fortuna," Gil said just as I was about to start walking.

I darted another glance at him. His expression was probably how I'd looked the first time I met the devil. That day felt like a hundred years ago now. I reached up to rake my damp hair back and asked, "Summon who?"

"Everyone."

Gil didn't take his eyes off the figure in the distance, but I could still sense his urgency. I hesitated. Anyone that came with me would be putting their life on the line, and I refused to lose a single member of my Court. Even before Savannah had performed the binding spell, the thought of it had been devastating.

Now it was unimaginable.

Don't hate me, Gil. I turned slowly, putting my back to Heilel so I could focus solely on my friend. It took Gil an extra beat to notice. I waited until his gaze met mine to say, "I want you to go inside with everyone else, and stay there. We put a protection spell down a few months ago, and it could still be active. Keep our family in the boundaries. Keep them safe."

After I'd fallen silent, Gil looked at me with no emotion in his pale, pointed features—he knew I wasn't making a request. I felt his mind working. Considering. He wanted to defy my command and stay at my side. Would he force us to cross this line? And if he did, who would we be on the other side of it?

"I'll listen, then," Gil said finally. It was the same thing he'd said earlier, word for word. This time, there was no confusion in his eyes. No hesitation. It was a promise in a language only we understood.

If I stood here a second longer, I would slip up and Gil might see how scared I was. With a calm nod in his direction, I set the sword on my shoulder and turned away. I walked toward the road alone. My left hand flexed of its own volition, as if part of me were still trying to reach for Finn's fur. I clenched it into a fist and forced it to be still.

Just as the sun crested the horizon, its brightness hidden behind hordes of roiling clouds, I raised my gaze to the figure waiting for me. When those blue eyes met mine, it felt like I was going to my death. The sound of the gravel had never been so loud. It crunched under my sneakers as I closed the distance between me and Heaven's most infamous fallen angel, gathering my power to me with every step. I skimmed my mind along the bonds like fingertips on harp strings, taking comfort from them. Memorizing where they were, so I could reach my Court quickly if the need arose. No matter how this ended, I would protect our family.

I drew to a slow halt. Without the noise of the gravel, I realized how silent it was. Even the birds had retreated, as if they sensed something evil was here. The light that streamed over the naked, twisted treetops was dim and hesitant. Rain still pattered onto the ground.

The devil and I stood on opposite sides of the fence. Neither of us spoke. I stared at the water clinging to Heilel's eyelashes and noticed how full his lips were in the silvery light. In that moment, I hated beauty. I hated that it had no rules, and even the cruelest people could still look like an angel.

"How?" I said finally.

Heilel's expression didn't change. He knew what I meant, of course. What I was really asking. How had he known what I could do, even when I hadn't? How had I made him corporeal?

"The knowledge was lost throughout the generations. Persephone's abilities formed when fear was born, but that was only its activator. Its switch. If a Nightmare is powerful enough, she can bring her dreams to life. She just has to believe it can be done, or feel something strongly enough that a part of her believes. Emotions like terror, rage, or . . ." He stopped.

"Love," I finished for him, my voice even softer now. I searched Heilel's face, and in that moment, I swore I felt another crack run through my heart. "You *were* telling the truth about possessing me. You didn't want my body—you wanted one of your very own. You used me."

"Yes, I did."

I waited for him to go on, but Heilel didn't lie or make excuses. I wasn't even angry at him, really—it had been my choice to fall for him. My choice to tell Lyari about it.

416

"That's why you tortured Collith when he went to Hell. You wanted to learn about me. To figure out the best way to worm into my heart," I said tonelessly. This might've seemed random to Heilel, but it had always bothered me, the fact that Collith had ended up in a cell. Hell was a miserable place, but the ones being held beneath the tower were there for a purpose. Part of me had known, I supposed, that it was Collith's connection to me that had gotten him an afterlife sentence worse than death.

For once, Heilel misinterpreted my silence. "I feel compelled to tell you that it wasn't his fault. Truly. I broke him. Half of the words that came out of his mouth were meaningless. The half I did understand, I found . . . captivating. The faerie spoke of a dark, beautiful creature. A queen that loved fiercely and lived recklessly. By the time we actually met, I was half in love with you myself." His voice softened. "I didn't want to hurt you, Fortuna."

His little speech didn't move me, and I looked back at the devil with utter contempt. "Don't flatter yourself. Life is full of disappointments and I just added you to the list. Now that you have your precious body, what do you plan to do with it?"

As usual, Heilel took my rejection in stride. He gave me a faint, sad smile. "I plan to go inside and secure Thuridan of the Sarwraek bloodline," he answered matter-of-factly. "I received word that he was here."

Out of all the things I'd expected him to say, this wasn't it. My eyebrows knitted together, and I looked at Heilel with a bewildered frown. "Thuridan? Why?"

"That's a story for another time."

His tone made it clear this topic was a dead end. I twisted my lips thoughtfully, then nodded. "It's a solid plan. There's just one problem."

"Oh?"

"Yeah." I lifted my sword. "I can't let you do it."

"I won't fight you, Fortuna. You expect me to be evil, to be some monstrous thing. You need me to be the embodiment of hate and greed, because it kills you to be responsible for your own

417

shortcomings. Tell me, if I were to be vanquished, would you breathe easier? Or would you find a bottle to crawl into, to hide from the nightmares of what you've done? I've made peace with who I am and who I have to become. Can you say the same? Go on, tell yourself another lie."

Heilel raised his eyebrows, expecting me to fall right into his trap. But I'd learned my lesson when it came to engaging in psychological warfare with the devil.

"Either shut up and fight, or get the fuck off my property," I said.

He sighed, and the sound was heavy with disappointment. "It didn't have to be this way, Fortuna."

I smiled bitterly. "Don't kid yourself, baby. It was always going to end this way."

He just kept standing there with that sad look on his face. I waited for Heilel to say something like *Ladies first* or *I'd be happy to break the ice.* Things he'd said to me before. But he must've been impatient to get inside, because he launched at me without warning. I barely managed to react in time. I shouted in pain as the clash of our swords reverberated through my entire body. Heilel swung around, coming at me again, and I barely managed to block him. He was toying with me, I thought dimly. Proving that I was nothing more than a fly in his web. Some small creature.

But I refused to back down. I met him blow for blow, fighting with every shred of strength I had in me. I didn't even consider using my abilities, as I'd originally planned. I could hardly form a coherent thought, much less multitask and get into Lucifer's head at the same time.

This was different from the day we'd fought in his tower. Every clash felt like a blow to my heart, my soul. I could see from the tightness in Heilel's jaw and the shadow in his eyes that it was hurting him, too. As we kept fighting, I heard his voice as I'd heard it the night I gave in to him. *I didn't expect to love you.*

"Enough of this," he said abruptly.

My sword swiped through empty air, and I'd put so much strength behind it that I staggered. Heilel didn't even notice. He swung away and strode over to the fence. Before I could speak, he pulled one of the posts out of the ground—plucked it, like the embedded wood was nothing more than a weed—and turned back to me. He closed the space between us in a blur. I had an instant to register the sight of the devil's blue eyes before a star-bright burst went off inside my mind.

He'd stabbed me with the stake.

As pain roared through my stomach, I realized, dimly, how much he'd been holding back. I sank to the ground, looking down at myself even though part of me didn't want to. There was something . . . confusing, about seeing a hole in my own body. Like my mind was fighting to accept it, even as I thought, *Holy shit, there's a hole in my stomach.*

Somehow, I ended up on my back. The white sky filled my vision, and rain hit my cheeks, my eyes. I squinted against it just as Heilel leaned over me. He wrapped one hand around my throat and used his other to drive the stake deeper into my gut. "And now I will give you a gift," he said through his teeth.

I resisted the urge to scrabble at his hold. He had me, and I knew it. I glared up at him and snarled, "Death isn't a gift. Not if I have to spend all of eternity with *you.*"

"Death? You think so little of me? No, the truth about who killed your parents, my darling. It's been locked away all this time. Have you ever asked yourself when the dreams started? Those cozy ones with you and your pretty friend?"

"Fuck you and your riddles," I spat, wrapping both my hands around the base of the fence post. Defying him, I leaned upward and shoved my face into Heilel's. Agony screamed through my body.

His eyes burned. "I—"

Uttering a warrior's cry, Lyari was suddenly there, moving in a blur of bright glass and swinging hair. But her sword sliced through empty air; Heilel was already gone. He reappeared a few yards away, his gaze seeking mine again. I was still on the ground, bleeding out on the damp, cold grass. Once again, Lyari went for him, displaying a breathtaking speed I'd never seen her use before.

Even Heilel was taken off guard, and his arm blurred as he lifted his own sword. Lyari didn't give him a chance to sift. She was already coming at him, her blade singing. The sound became another violent clash as their swords met. Then it happened again, and again, their feet scraping over wet gravel as they fought.

The devil may have had the advantage of age and experience, but all of that was nothing against Lyari's explosive, incandescent rage. I did nothing to stop her, because there was something about her expression I recognized. It was the same face I saw in the mirror when I thought about the crossroads, or Belanor. Something had been taken from Lyari, and in this moment she was reclaiming it. I knew she could very well lose this battle, and yet being aware of the risk still didn't compel me to intervene. Some battles were inevitable. Some battles had to be fought, regardless of how they might end.

It only took a couple minutes for Heilel to finally lose his patience. "Stand *down*," he snapped, blocking Lyari again.

But Lyari didn't stop. Their swords continued to flash and clang. "You. Do. Not. Control. Me," she bellowed.

They moved so fast that I couldn't watch the fight anymore. Their arms were blurs, their weapons striking with such speed that I kept waiting for them to shatter. My eyes finally caught hold of the fighters again when their swords crossed and both stopped there, Lyari looking at Heilel with steel in her expression. She would never relent.

He leaned his face close to hers and said, "I release you from your contract. I have no further use for you, anyway."

Lyari reacted as if he'd yanked something out of her, or maybe shoved something back in. Her sword clattered to the ground, and she staggered, just barely managing to regain her balance at the last second. Heilel turned like he'd already forgotten her existence. He showed no signs of exertion as he sheathed his sword, then looked over at me. I was still on the ground, several yards away. His battle with Lyari had brought Heilel partway down the ditch.

Unable to move, I just lay there and stared at him. His mouth opened, and he was on the verge of speaking, but then he paused. Something about his expression made me go still, too. I stopped breathing. My eyes searched his. Hope broke through the shadows around my heart like beams of light.

Was there actually something good inside him? Did love matter to the devil more than whatever plan he had for Thuridan Sarwraek?

Wishful thinking, a voice in my head whispered.

It was proven right when, a moment later, he bowed and said, "Goodbye, Lady Sworn. If you change your mind about joining me, you know how to find me."

"Goodbye, Lucifer." I said his name with soft venom, and before he turned away, I could've sworn I saw remorse in his eyes. Then he sifted, and the devil darkened some other place with his presence.

The instant he was gone, my attention shifted to Lyari. She didn't seem to have any injuries. She was on her phone, pacing back and forth across the driveway. I heard her say my name, and I would've bet my life that Collith was on the other end. Not that I'd have a life to bet with much longer—I was still impaled by a fence post, and I was bleeding out all over the brown grass.

A new sound reached me through the pain. I lifted my head, which had gotten heavier, suddenly. The edges of my vision flickered, but I still saw the figure coming toward me. Or rather, saw his head of bleached hair.

"Gil, no," I protested, my voice weak. "The smell . . ."

The vampire didn't even bother acknowledging me. He dropped to the ground in a graceful tangle of long limbs, and once Gil had scooted close enough, he crossed his legs. He carefully moved my head into his lap and said, "I don't know much about stab wounds, but I did go through a *Grey's Anatomy* phase. I'm pretty sure you're supposed to keep the stake in and lie still. Oh, if you tell anyone about the *Grey's Anatomy* thing, I'll eat you."

He waited for one of my usual comebacks. That was what we did, me and Gil. Even if we'd gotten more tender after the bonding spell, we spoke to each other in insults and sarcasm. I opened my mouth to do exactly that, but . . . I couldn't. I felt like a rag wrung dry. I didn't want to ignore it anymore, how terrified I was of Gil's bloodlust. I didn't want to pretend that I wasn't constantly worried.

So far, all pretending had gotten us was fear, shame, and blood. So much goddamn blood.

"It doesn't bother you anymore?" I asked softly.

Gil knew what I meant, I could tell. But he dismissed my concern. He even made a flapping gesture with his hand. "Of course not. We've all got jobs, you see. Miss Uppity is getting a healer. Cyrus and Ariel are with the kid and the grumpy fellow—Thuridan, sorry—and they're tucked into the protection spell like a baby in a swaddle. Seth is out looking for the wolf, because we all know he's your favorite, and you'd feel better if he was here. So your only job," Gil concluded, "is to lie very still, and try not to die."

"What changed?" I pressed, looking at him intently. Gil sobered. He looked down at me, his dark brows drawn together. I couldn't tell what he was thinking, even with the bond, and the realization was startling. Maybe Gil still had some secrets of his own, just like I did. We were connected, but we could still choose how much of ourselves we shared.

"It was the spell," Gil admitted. "Since the witch tied us all together, it's been . . . easier. I feel more like myself. I don't get a whiff of blood and turn into a rabid animal."

I was about to respond when a bright, copper head appeared in my peripheral vision. *Cyrus.* I couldn't summon the strength to give him the warm greeting he deserved, but there was no time, anyway. In his usual quiet way, the dragon told us, "The protection spell was breached. Thuridan is gone, and he didn't go quietly—there are signs of a struggle. Ariel said there's also magic lingering in the loft, so they must've done a silencing spell, and a transporting spell, too. That's how they got him out so fast."

Lyari made a strangled sound and sifted. She was going after him. She wanted to save Thuridan.

I knew she wouldn't find him. Lucifer probably had countless Fallen at his disposal scattered throughout the world. He'd provided the distraction while one of his followers got to Thuridan and spirited him away. How had the devil known Thuridan would come here, though? Was it pure happenstance? Or was there some fucked up fate thing at work, bringing me and Lucifer together again and again?

I'd have to think about that later, I told myself faintly. "Gil?" I said, his name barely audible.

Luckily, my friend was a vampire, and he could hear everything. "Yeah?"

"I'm going to faint soon," I told him.

"I've got you. I'm not going anywhere."

A moment later, the wind shifted. Even though I was trying to be strong, I couldn't hold back a shiver. Shit, it was cold. Gil said something at the same moment the air carried a scent past us, and I stiffened—it was the undeniable musk of wolf. I turned my head and saw something move in the trees. My heart lifted with hope.

"Finn? Is that you?" I tried to call. If he answered, I didn't hear it.

Once again, the darkness claimed me.

CHAPTER TWENTY-SEVEN

I regained consciousness a few minutes later.

I knew it had only been a few minutes, because while enough time had passed for someone to carry me upstairs, there was still a fence post lodged between my ribs. Zara was leaning over the bed. After Viessa's coup, she'd continued to be the healer for the Unseelie Court, but apparently she was loyal to Collith, too, if she was here. She touched my abdomen with her cool hands, her brows drawn together in concentration. By all appearances, we were alone.

"Would you like to know something funny?" the faerie said.

It took me a second to realize she was talking to me. She hadn't looked up from my wound. "Sure," I replied weakly.

She peered closer at the base of the post. "When the Dark Prince stabbed you, he struck a spot without any vital organs or arteries. You would've been completely fine if you'd just stayed still. But you kept struggling, so you caused massive damage. I'm surprised you're still alive, actually."

"We have very different definitions of 'funny,'" I remarked. Then Zara wrapped her hand around the piece of wood and my mouth clamped shut.

"Well, I think we can both agree there isn't anything amusing about this next part. The stake needs to come out. I'll count to three, all right? One . . ." She yanked it out.

My entire body jerked, and agony blazed through me. "Son of a *bitch*. You fucking liar! You said you would count to three!"

Zara rolled her eyes and set the stake aside. "It was either a little pain or a lot of death. Which do you prefer?"

I was about to offer up a snappy comeback when the world tilted. I grabbed a fistful of blanket as if that would keep me anchored. The door opened while I was still swaying. Collith came in first, followed by Laurie. Both of them wore coats, as if they'd come straight from outside. Zara completely ignored them and got to work.

I hadn't seen the Seelie King since the night I'd left for Hell, and I felt a burst of happiness at the sight of him. But my worried gaze went immediately to Collith, who'd moved to sit on my other side.

"Gil is with Emma," he said the instant we made eye contact. Some of the stiffness left my shoulders, and Zara made a pleased sound, continuing her administrations. Her hands were hovering over the wound, and though I couldn't see anything happening, I knew she was pouring her energy into the ruined tissue. Weaving it back together. Closing the gaps. By the end, there would be barely any sign of trauma at all. Maybe a faint scar, but I liked scars. They were the marks of a survivor.

Laurie met my gaze from across the room. He stood beside the window now, his arms loosely crossed. Gray daylight slanted over him, making him seem like a distant, untouchable creature. "The vampire gave us an account of what happened out there," he told me. "Everything you said. And Collith has made me aware of last night's events, as well."

Good, I thought, holding back a wince as Zara did something that sent a lightning bolt of pain through me. I really didn't feel like reliving it all, or telling Laurie about what an idiot I'd been.

Out loud all I said was, "Lucifer said he was coming back to finish what he started. Why do you think it was so important he have his own body?"

425

Laurie gave me a tight smile. "I doubt he's here to play tourist."

"We've both sent our spies out to see if they can learn anything," Collith added. I looked at him and mustered a faint smile. He was trying to offer reassurance in whatever way he could, but we both knew I'd fucked up. Like Laurie said, there was a reason Lucifer had come here. If Nym's drawings were any indication, stopping him was worth dying for.

"Do either of you know why he took Thuridan?" I asked. The hard part of Zara's healing seemed to be over, because she straightened slightly, returning to the chair she'd dragged over to me. Her eyes remained shut, her eyebrows drawn together in concentration. The hands she held over my body were steady.

Laurie turned his head back toward the window. He looked out at the trees and murmured, "No, but we intend to find out."

Collith leaned forward, bringing my attention back to him. "Last night, before Lucifer appeared, you were dreaming. Next thing I knew, Lucifer was in the room with us. He stood there and looked at you, and then he walked out. What was your dream about?"

Last night. Why did that already feel like so long ago? I really didn't want to talk about it, but they had a right to know. With Zara's hands still hovering over me, I told them everything I could remember about the confrontation in the dreamscape. Toward the end of my account, she finally lowered her arms and settled fully in the chair. Her eyes still hadn't opened.

"Then Oliver showed up," I concluded. "Lucifer heard him coming, and they just . . . stared at each other. Eventually Lucifer whispered something, and whatever he said convinced Oliver to let him go. A door appeared, or Lucifer summoned it, I don't know. He walked right through, and I woke up. You know the rest."

"What else?" Collith pressed. "Something else must've happened for him to gain a foothold in our world. We need to understand, if we're going to have any chance of sending him back where he came from."

His confusion seemed genuine. He still didn't know, I realized. I may not have told them about my confession to Lyari, but even after everything Gil had heard outside, Collith hadn't put it together. He was no fool, so it could only mean he didn't want to see the truth. He didn't want to accept that I'd fallen in love with the creature who'd spent decades torturing him.

Looking at Collith now, I wondered if he had regained more of his memories from that time. Or maybe his reaction was just instinctive. I knew better than anyone how your soul could remember terrible things, even if your mind couldn't.

Laurie, I suspected, had known the truth before he came into this room. It explained the rigid line of his shoulders, and how he couldn't seem to look at me. Oh, Laurie was very aware of what I'd done.

"I let him in," I said simply, looking at the Seelie King as I spoke. I hoped he could hear what I was really saying. Hear the words hidden underneath. *I'm sorry.*

But Laurie didn't move. I turned back to Collith. He was frowning. "What do you mean?"

"My patient needs to rest," Zara interjected. I was so relieved that I almost shot her a look of gratitude. She gave me a knowing look of her own, as if she knew, anyway.

I'd always liked Zara, but that was the moment I started thinking of her as a friend.

Without giving them a chance to argue, the healer ushered the powerful fae males out as if they were unruly toddlers. Laurie gave her an affronted look, and I half-expected him to swat at her hands. Collith, of course, was more composed in his reaction. He did allow a flicker of annoyance to show in his eyes just before they vanished through the doorway.

Once they were gone, I had a fleeting, curious thought about whether they'd stay here or go back to the Seelie Court. *Actually,* I thought faintly, *I don't even know where Collith is living right now.*

Everything had been so chaotic since I'd gotten back. But wherever my faerie kings went, something told me it wouldn't be too far away. I sank down in my bed, letting out a ragged breath. God, so much had happened. Things I hadn't even begun to process. While I didn't love getting stabbed, I did appreciate this moment to myself. I needed to *think*.

As I lay there, I realized the loft was completely silent. The rain had stopped, and the birds still hadn't returned after the Dark Prince's visit. Any other day, I would run from the quiet. Right now it was a relief. My bleary gaze went to the window. It was still morning, the day only just begun, and I felt like I could sleep for days. I decided to give in to the urge. I'd need my strength to fight Lucifer. I may have lost today, but our war had just begun.

I'd only been lying there a few seconds when a sound crept through the stillness.

My closet door creaked open.

I sat up, frowning. I looked toward the closet and waited, wondering if there was a draft somewhere. Or if Finn had oiled the front door hinges a little too well. Nothing else moved, and the silence was so profound I could hear a distant ringing. I was about to lower myself back down, and finally drift off to sleep, when the closet door moved again.

Something pale came out of the darkness.

Something living and vaguely human-shaped, crawling on all fours. I saw a flash of elbows and knees. Panic exploded in my chest, but there was no time to react. The thing moved fast as a spider, and I watched with wide-eyed horror as it stopped at the foot of the bed and straightened.

I saw the gun first, pointed right at me. *Odd choice for a monster,* I thought with dim shock. Then whatever held the weapon shifted closer. Light fell across its face.

"Bella?" I blurted. In a rush of relief and confusion, I realized that I hadn't recognized her because she was wearing an animal carcass. I pressed my hand against my thundering chest. "What are you *doing* here?"

"Slipped inside while you were all distracted with those pretty boys," the human said. Her hand wobbled, and her other hand shot up to steady it. She held onto the gun with both hands now, drawing my attention back to it. Then Bella asked, "Do you like my disguise?"

My gaze dropped to the fur she was wearing around her shoulders.

There were bits of dried flesh and hardened blood along its edges, but I knew that fur. I'd buried my fingers in it a hundred times. *Finn.* A dull roar started in my ears, and I heard myself say calmly, "Where did you get that?"

"I've been watching this place for weeks. Months, actually. At first, I couldn't get close enough because of the wolf. It was always around, damn it!" Hysterical laughter clung to Bella's voice. She stopped and swiped roughly at her nose, making a visible effort to recompose herself. Once again, she adjusted her grip on the gun and continued, "Then I found one of the gooey messes it leaves behind, and this pelt was right there, just looking up at me. I got an idea. Ian liked to hunt, see, and he told me things about disguising your scent. It was easy after that. The wolf left me alone, and the others walked right by, too. I listened and watched every chance I could. I learned all about you and the rest of the demons living here."

Oh my God. I stared at Bella as her words triggered a memory. Just before I passed out, I'd smelled a wolf. But Finn still wasn't back from his hunt. That meant I'd been smelling Bella O'Connell while she was hiding somewhere, staying out of sight until I was vulnerable.

My mind went into survival mode. Everything Dad taught me, all the lessons from Adam. I glanced down at the gun, intending to reexamine Bella's hold on it. I'd been taught how to disarm an attacker in multiple ways. It was the first time I'd really stared at Bella's hands—before, I'd been absorbed by the gun. As the seconds ticked by, a distant part of me knew this was my opening. Bella's pause was a chance to ask a question and keep her talking. But my gaze was still glued to the woman's hands. I'd forgotten my plan to get the gun away from her.

Bella's fingertips were black.

I looked up slowly, my stomach tight with certainty. "You're the one who put the hex on Gretchen," I said.

Bella's mascara-lined eyes darkened. "She brought it on herself! I told her my suspicions about you, and she gave me this pitiful look. Like I was delusional."

Part of me had always assumed I was responsible, in some way, for what had happened to Gretchen that day. She'd been afflicted with magic, and magic tended to follow me wherever I went. But there was no time to acknowledge how I felt about that fact. At the moment, I was facing a human on the verge of a psychotic break, or a human who was in the midst of one, and she was pointing a gun at me.

"I don't think you're delusional, but I am confused," I said, trying to seem unruffled. "Why are you so convinced I killed Ian?"

"Because she told me you did," Bella replied instantly. A glazed look had entered her eyes now. I knew that look. Dread made my insides sink.

"Who?"

"The woman." Bella frowned, as if I'd confused her. It was the same expression I'd seen on Gretchen's face. In that moment, I knew for sure.

Bella O'Connell had been bespelled.

"Did the woman tell you her name?" I asked.

Bella was looking through me now. Her voice softened with remembrance. "She came to our house. She said she was a witch, and she could help me get revenge on the person responsible for my husband's death. I didn't believe her, but then she made the furniture float. She gave me a spell and said I could make you do anything I wanted. But I told that bitch Gretchen to kill you instead. That way I got to watch, she'd have to live with the guilt afterward, and I wouldn't get in trouble with all that DNA stuff Ian used to talk about. It was perfect."

"Her name, Bella." I dared to speak a little sharper, hoping it would get through to her. "What was the woman's name?"

She wagged her head as if she were trying to shake something free, or out. One of her hands rose to hold her temple. "Fuck, I don't remember, okay? No, wait. It was a flower. Yeah, that's it. Some kind of flower."

I felt like I'd been punched in the gut. So Iris had struck again. She must've learned the truth about Ian during my torture at the Seelie

Court. A lot of that time was blank or hazy, since I'd been delirious for half of it. Who knew what else they'd gotten out of me?

I'd made myself a terrible enemy the day I'd pissed off Belanor's pet witch.

Another train of thought that would have to wait. Bella hadn't lowered the gun and I was still sitting in bed. The vulnerable position put me at a disadvantage. Moving slowly, as if Bella were a wild animal, I slid my legs to the floor and stood. I held my hands out and faced her, speaking in a low, even tone. "Bella, listen to me. That woman you spoke to? She isn't a good person. She's just trying to—"

"I don't care what kind of person she is," Bella snarled, her fury snapping back like a whip. "I care about the *truth*. Did you or did you not kill my Ian?"

Technically, Laurie had killed him. He'd only done it because I was afraid of Ian, but Bella didn't need to know that.

"No," I said, meeting her gaze. I didn't flinch or look away.

Slowly, her jaw locked into place. She didn't buy it. *Okay, back to Plan A.* Getting the gun away. I had one shot to do this right. Wanting another look at how her hands were positioned, my eyes flicked down.

This time, Bella noticed, and she stiffened. Immediately, I knew I'd made a grave miscalculation. A stupid, stupid mistake. I'd forgotten how much terror lived inside Bella O'Connell. When she saw that I was about to attack, her hand tensed around the gun.

I was slow to react—my energy had been depleted after getting stabbed—and I felt time shift as I watched her finger close on the trigger. There was a flash and a thundering sound.

I felt an instant of hot, searing pain before the light came back.

This time, I went tumbling into it.

CHAPTER TWENTY-EIGHT

*H*eaven wasn't a place of gilded streets or looming mansions. Instead, it was a beautiful dream.

After Bella O'Connell shot me, I opened my eyes expecting to be back in Hell—I didn't even let myself hope for anything else. Fallen or not, I was a killer. The blood of innocents stained my soul. But instead of a dark tower or red horizons, I saw familiar rolling hills and green leaves quivering above me.

The dreamscape.

I'd arrived beneath our tree, mine and Oliver's. A moment after I noticed this, I spotted him farther down the path. Sunlight bounced off his bright head and his arms hung loosely at his sides. He was walking toward me, but his face was turned toward the horizon. His eyes squinted against the fading sun.

I hadn't seen Oliver since Lucifer had broken free. Since the devil had whispered something mysterious in his ear and then shattered my entire world. As I watched my best friend close the distance between us, something about his expression made me decide not to bring it up yet. There would be plenty of time to talk about Lucifer later.

I knew, somehow, that I wasn't here for a few hours, or a slightly longer visit. I'd seen that gun go off in Bella's hand. I'd felt a flare of agonizing pain. Zara had been nearby, so there was a small chance of survival, but I wasn't optimistic.

My instincts turned out to be right. I couldn't be sure how much time had passed on Earth, but days went by in the dreamscape. It didn't matter. That's what I told myself, over and over. I said it to myself now as a storm raged over the sea, making the sky flash and the walls groan.

I stood in front of the kitchen sink and stared out at the rain, trying not to think of *him*. Because thinking about Lucifer hurt, and when I hurt, I started to forget that nothing mattered. Goosebumps raced over my skin, and I rubbed my arms. A damp chill clung to the air, a relentless cold that hadn't eased over the course of the day. I couldn't seem to get warm, no matter how many layers I put on.

Behind me, the door to the cottage opened. A gust of cold wind howled through the room before Oliver kicked it back shut. I stayed where I was, shivering, and listened to the sound of his boots against the floorboards as he went over to the fireplace. There was a hollow clatter as Oliver set down the logs he'd brought. He didn't speak, but this wasn't unusual.

Ever since I'd been back, Oliver had been quiet, distracted. I kept trying to resurrect the magic of the old days—going for swims, reading to each other in dapples of sunlight, lying beneath the stars—but it seemed like every time we did something together, Oliver eventually slipped away with an excuse. At first, I worried that he was in pain again, fighting some mental battle against Lucifer or one of the other countless nightmares Oliver had always protected me from. But there were none of the outward signs of discomfort, and I couldn't shake the feeling that he was keeping something else from me.

So now, as Oliver resuscitated the fire, stoking the fresh flames with a poker, I said nothing. After a minute or two, he got up and put the poker back on its stand. I sensed him staring. I looked over my shoulder to confirm it, and raised my eyebrows. "Do you need something, Ollie?"

His eyes were hard. "Enough of this. You need to go back."

I faced the gray downpour again, pressing my crossed arms even harder against my middle. "What do you mean?"

"I think you're keeping yourself here," Oliver said. Footsteps sounded behind me, and then I felt his warmth at my back. His voice softened as he added, "But you're no coward, Fortuna Sworn."

One of the logs shifted and sent a flare of light through the space. When I didn't answer, Oliver moved to stand beside me. I glanced at him sidelong and noted the mud splattered on his clothes. "Where have you been?"

"I told you before I left. I was out chopping wood."

I shook my head. "No, before that. You leave for hours. All day long, every day. What are you doing out there?"

Lightning flashed, making Oliver's skin look pale and smooth, his freckles stark. His expression was resolute, as if he'd made a decision while he was out there chopping wood. "It won't work, Fortuna. We need to talk about this," he said.

A sigh filled my chest. He was right. There were a lot of things we needed to talk about, but neither of us had tried these past few days. Apparently that time was now. I faced Oliver fully, my arms still crossed. As I tipped my head back, I made a decision of my own.

"Fine. I'll try to wake up . . . on one condition." I met Oliver's gaze. "Tell me what he said to you."

His jaw clenched, but he didn't look surprised. He'd known this conversation was coming, too. Oliver's focus shifted to the window, and his gaze was dark with remembrance. "He urged me to be what I'm meant to be."

I frowned. "What does that even mean?"

"Whatever he meant, it doesn't matter. Taking advice from the devil would be like . . ." Oliver trailed off as it occurred to him that I'd done a lot more than take the devil's advice. The corners of his mouth deepened, but he didn't reveal any other signs of jealousy or tell me how much I'd fucked up. I knew that, anyway. Maybe this was my punishment. I looked back out the window, swallowing down a rush of guilt.

What had I unleashed on the world?

"I already tried," I said abruptly. I turned my head and met Oliver's gaze again. There was nothing I could do about the choices I'd made before, but I could make changes now.

Starting with the lies rotting between me and my best friend.

His eyes flicked between mine. "Tried what?"

"Waking up. Something is wrong. Maybe there's no body for me to go back to." My voice was cool. Detached. As if I couldn't care less, one way or the other, whether I'd see my family again.

Oliver started to reply, but before he could utter a word, a sound shuddered through the entire cottage. I jumped so hard that it sent my heart into a panic, and my head jerked toward the door. Forgetting the storm, the cold, all of it, I looked up at Oliver with wide eyes. "What was that?" I breathed.

It had sounded like . . . knocking.

Oliver's expression was grim. He went to the closet and took out two old semiautomatic rifles. He came back to me and held one out. I took it without thinking, and then my other instincts took over. I heard Dad's voice in my head as I racked the charging handle back, then checked the chamber for clear. "You asked me what I've been doing," Oliver said, watching me.

I knew my expression was bewildered as I looked at the gun in my hands and back at him. "You've been . . . building guns?"

"No, I've been building fences. The guns are just from our weapons stash."

"Fences? Why?"

Oliver faced the door, his eyes going flat and hard again. He raised his rifle and put his finger on the trigger. "To keep them away."

"Keep *what*—"

The door *exploded*. The wall on the opposite side of the cottage also shattered, wood, plaster, and glass flying everywhere. Luckily, Oliver and I were standing off to the side, closer to the fireplace. None of the debris hit us. Not that I would've noticed if it had.

All my focus was on the face peering through the gap in the door.

Ian O'Connell smiled when he saw me. He was wearing his uniform, and the buttons gleamed wetly as he stepped over the threshold. I held my gun tighter and backed away, struggling to breathe. Ian was bigger than I remembered, his head nearly touching the top of the doorway. His boots squeaked and left small pools of rainwater on the floor. I could hear my heartbeat like bombs going off in my head. From the corner of my eye, I noticed Oliver's arm tensing. He was about to shoot.

But I beat him to it.

Stepping into Ian's path, I tightened my grip on the gun and emptied the clip into his face.

Once the bullets stopped, silence filled the cottage from corner to corner. Even the storm had abated, as if the sky itself were holding its breath. I didn't lower the rifle. It seemed like Ian fell in slow motion, and when he finally hit the floor, my ears started ringing. Oliver said something, his voice nearby, but he may as well have been a thousand miles away. There was blood everywhere. My face, my hands, the gun, the floor. I'd been standing closer to Ian than I realized. On feet that didn't feel like mine, I walked over to him. Some distant, irrational part of my brain worried that it wasn't over. That he wasn't really dead.

No, he's definitely dead, I thought a moment later. I stared down at Ian's body—or what was left of it—and for a few seconds, the past and the present overlapped. The walls and floors flickered, showing glimpses of a yellow-tinted crossroads and dark trees. With slow, methodical movements, I turned and set the gun down on the table. It made a dull thud against the wood.

Something about the sound was jarring. Pain rushed through me, sharp as the lash of a whip. When I'd killed the demon I made the deal with, it had been wearing its true face. But it was Ian who'd come that night. Ian who had leered at me during the worst moments of my life. Killing this version of him, even in a dream, felt like I'd ripped something open inside of me.

Whirling, I grabbed the front of Oliver's shirt and arched my head back. "Make me forget," I said desperately.

His hands flew out to grasp my waist, steadying me and stopping me at the same time. "What?"

"Make me forget." I buried my fingers in Oliver's hair and pressed close, claiming his shocked mouth with my own. Oliver recovered instantly, and he made a sound at the back of his throat as he tasted me, deeply, his palms moving up my arms.

Then he grasped my wrists and pulled them down, separating us. He kept his fingers interlaced with mine, as if he was restraining me. "You're grieving right now, Fortuna."

"So?" I stared up at him, and even though I still had enough pride not to beg, I felt the pleading in my eyes. The silent imploring. *Just say yes. Just kiss me.*

"So I'm not going to take advantage of that."

"If anything, I'm taking advantage of you," I argued.

But Oliver just shook his head. "Let's take a beat, Fortuna. I need to fix the holes in this place so we don't freeze tonight. If you're still awake when I'm done, we can make some popcorn and watch a movie. Okay?"

"Okay." My voice was hollow. I didn't feel the sting of rejection or embarrassment; I was just tired. Deeply, suddenly tired, as if the adrenaline had burned through my veins and left nothing but smoke and scorch marks.

I fought it, though. I went to the couch instead of the bed, intending to keep Oliver company while he worked. Later, I wouldn't remember drifting off or Oliver draping a blanket over me. It felt like I'd just closed my eyes when his lips brushed my temple. He murmured against my skin, "Go to sleep, Fortuna. I may not be as strong as I once was, but I can still protect you from your bad dreams. I'll be right here when you wake up."

I must have believed him, because the tightness left my chest and I sank deeper into the couch cushions, letting out a long, low breath. Darkness claimed me, and for once, nothing awaited on the other side of it except oblivion. Beautiful oblivion.

But . . . Oliver lied. The next time I opened my eyes, he wasn't there.

I wasn't in the dreamscape at all.

At first, I thought I was having another out-of-body experience.

It had happened to me once before, when Gwyn drowned me in dirty cave water and I became a spectator to my own death. This wasn't the same, though, because I quickly realized that I was inside Finn's head. I felt him all around, so strongly that I could practically smell his comforting scent. It was like . . . pine cones, edged in frost. As it lingered, a pang of longing went through me.

Finn. I miss you, I thought.

He gave no indication that he'd heard. He didn't know I was here, and I quickly realized why. Finn's mind was so consumed by a memory that it played like a movie in both our heads.

The werewolf had just been returning from his hunt. He crossed the lawn on two legs, still aching from the shift. Gil came out of the barn as if he'd been waiting for him. Finn immediately halted, his nails falling out, the flesh of his fingertips pulsing and bubbling as claws sprouted in their place.

Gil got in his face, his fangs bared. *Where have you been, dickhead? She's been asking for you.*

In an instant, Finn forgot how much he didn't like the vampire I'd brought into our family. He stared into Gil's eyes, going still, his hearing directed toward the loft. *She's back?*

Been back for days now. You'd know that if you hadn't left. Now you may never get the chance to say goodbye. Gil's voice had gone flat and cold.

Finn looked at him slowly. *What do you mean, goodbye?*

Gil told him everything. He'd barely finished when Finn pushed past him and went into the barn. The werewolf fought the urge to run every step of the way. He followed my scent—it was fresh, and Finn felt some of his pain ease at its familiarity—all the way to my room. He completely ignored everyone he passed, but he was aware of each person in the loft and where they were. Finn slipped through the door that would take him to me. His bright eyes went right to the bed.

Only then did he slow down, his heart beginning to return to its normal rhythm. He leaned against the opposite wall and stared at my prone body, noting every detail. The bandages around my middle. The metallic smell of blood. The pale cast to my skin.

Since then, Finn had barely left my side.

The memory of Gil had haunted him all that time. Even now, tonight, when he was no longer alone in his head and I'd been in some kind of coma for days. As our mental movie came to an end, I focused and realized I could see the world through Finn's eyes. I felt a startled jolt. The werewolf was kneeling in front of the fireplace, his head turned toward everyone. And it really was everyone.

My Shadow Court. They were scattered throughout the living room, and a sense of solemnity hovered in the air. Cyrus. Ariel. Nym. Gil. Seth. Finn. Lyari, Collith, and Laurie were here, too, along with Damon and Adam. Emma must still be in the hospital.

All of them were focused on Zara.

The healer stood near Finn, on the other side of the fire. She lifted her head, and her expression was grim. "She's weak. Even with her connection to all of you, she isn't responding like she should," Zara said.

"Hard to fight for your life with a broken heart." Lyari didn't lift her gaze from the floor, but Finn could still see that her eyes were full of self-loathing. He was puzzled. *He doesn't know*, I thought. None of the others knew that Lyari had been Lucifer's spy.

"What do you mean by that?" Collith asked, his voice sharp.

But my Right Hand was done. We all watched her jaw clench, and she leaned back as if she was trying to retreat. She wouldn't give away my secret, I realized. She would never betray me again.

"She loved him," Gil said suddenly. "We all felt it. Her joy. She fell for his act. She thought it was real. And then he turned out to be a lying, evil bastard. He took Fortuna's hope, and now she's fighting to survive. Would you try all that hard, if you didn't have your hope?"

I watched my Court absorb this revelation with varying reactions. Anger. Confusion. Pity. *Don't feel too sorry for me*, I wished I could tell them. I'd known exactly what Lucifer was, and I'd fallen for him anyway.

Then Laurie glanced out the window and noted the fading sky. However the Seelie King felt about my forbidden romance with Lucifer, he kept it hidden behind a beautiful mask of indifference. "It's time," he remarked.

Still tucked away at the back of Finn's head, I felt myself frown. *Time for what?*

My wolf didn't answer. He really couldn't hear me, and it seemed like confirmation of Zara's warning—I was weak. Weak but alive, I reminded myself. The thought wasn't comforting. I couldn't shake the feeling, down in my gut, that I was losing the battle for my life.

"I'll stay with Lady Sworn," Zara said. Collith nodded his thanks, and she stood, striding gracefully into my room.

One by one, everyone else went to the stairwell. Finn brought up the rear, as he so often did. He paused in the doorway and scanned the loft, listening for any sounds that didn't belong. I could get a vague sense of his thoughts, which is how I knew he was worrying about my vulnerable body, lying in that room nearby.

But whatever awaited downstairs was important, too, because he tore himself away. Finn descended the rest of the stairs, crossed the dim garage, and joined the others outside. The moment he looked up, I saw what awaited on the other side of the driveway, just barely out of sight from the road.

Bella O'Connell was tied to a tree.

How long has she been out here? I wondered, bewildered by this turn of events. Why wasn't she in jail, or dead?

My Court formed a half-circle around the tree Ian O'Connell's widow was secured to. She was gagged and sobbing, snot running down the stained material muffling her every sound.

Suddenly I understood why Danny wasn't here. His love for my brother was undeniable, and he was clearly more open-minded than most humans. But at the end of the day, he was still a cop.

440

And my family was up to no good tonight.

They took turns addressing Bella. It was the bond magic, I thought as I watched them. They were so connected that they could anticipate when someone else was about to speak, and what they were going to say.

"You harmed our queen. As long as you're alive, you're a threat to her," Ariel said.

"But she wouldn't want us to take a life. Especially not for her sake," Gil added. "I don't understand it, myself."

"Our queen does have a tender heart. She's a fascinating creature." This from Laurie.

Each time one of them spoke, the circle closed in around Bella a little more. It was almost like they were hunting her. Playing with her. Even the most gentle of us, Cyrus and Nym, peered at Bella with a glint in their eye. The scene made me think of the Unseelie Court.

I wanted us to be different, I tried to say to my family. *We aren't like them.*

But my Court was made of faeries, a goblin, a vampire, and a werewolf. We were Fallen. We could pick ourselves back up as many times as we had to, but we would always be formed out of chaos and sin. The light . . . and the dark.

Everyone was standing shoulder to shoulder now. All of them except Collith and Laurie, who stood in front of Bella. Collith bent down and said something in Bella's ear. He'd been so gentle with me lately that I'd forgotten about this side of him—the fae side. Collith had darkness in him, too. Whatever he whispered made Bella's eyes widen.

"No," she said. "No!"

Just as Bella started to struggle against the ropes, my connection to Finn weakened. My view of the scene went in and out of focus, and then I felt a rushing sensation.

The last sound I heard was Bella's hoarse, terrified scream.

The rumble of thunder woke me.

I sat up, rubbing my eyes with the heels of my hands, struggling to adapt. The walls of the cottage looked back at me. Rain lashed against the windows. It was so strange the dreamscape was reality, and reality had become my dreams. But *was* the scene I'd witnessed between Bella and the Shadow Court reality?

Now that I was more alert, I registered the fact I was in bed. I'd definitely fallen asleep on the couch, I remembered. Oliver must've carried me here. I glanced toward the living room, where the fire burned strong and bright. Most nights, I could see a single foot dangling off the armrest, or the top of a golden head. Oliver had been sleeping there at his own insistence. The couch was empty now, and judging from the look of that fire, he'd never gone to sleep.

Yellow light spilled through the doorway that led to the attic. Since it was pouring rain outside, Oliver had to be up there. I left the sweat-dampened bed and climbed the stairs, my fingers trailing along the slanted wall.

I reached the top, and faltered. A flash of memory screamed through my mind, from the night Oliver's shadow attacked me—a hand grabbing my leg. Smoke pouring out of a stab wound. White ropes. A baseball bat. I hovered on the threshold and scanned the room, as if I was searching for any sign of the creature. But Oliver's shadow was outside, encased in stone, unable to hurt either of us ever again. To reassure myself of this, I went over to the round window at the opposite end of the space and peered down. There it was, off in the distance, a hulking shape that still emanated menace.

A thud came from behind, and I turned. Oliver was in the corner, flipping through a stack of old paintings.

"What are you doing?" I asked, watching him.

"Just pulling out some old pieces that I won't mind painting over. I'm having trouble making new canvases, so I'll have to use the ones I already have." He gave me a quick, distracted smile.

This was a new development. Chewing my lower lip, I sat on the stool that we used every time Oliver wanted to paint me. Over the years, I'd spent countless hours sitting here. No matter how much things changed between us, I was his favorite thing to paint. The curves of the stool were as familiar to me as the lines in my palm, and they had an oddly calming effect. I felt some of the tension leave my body.

Lightning flashed outside, drawing my gaze back to the window. "I think I'm dying, Ollie," I murmured.

"You're not dying." His response was instant. Automatic. "Just give it time. You'll figure it out, Fortuna."

"I've been here for days. If I'd just been injured when Bella shot me, Zara would've healed me," I insisted.

Oliver paused in his flipping and met my gaze. "If you were dead, I would know it."

The way he stated this reminded me of another night, another memory. As though what he was saying truly was so simple, or just a non-negotiable fact. *If you died, Fortuna, I'd follow you into whatever afterlife there is. The rest doesn't really matter, does it?*

All of a sudden, the room felt too warm. I got up from the stool to help Oliver in his search. I went to the opposite corner he was in, since it seemed unlikely he'd been over here yet. There were so many. Some were in vibrant color while others had been done with only black paint. Most had extraordinary detail, and a few had obviously been painted in fits of fury or passion. But there was one thing all the paintings had in common.

They told the story of our life together. All the way from the beginning, and even before that. It didn't take long before I became so absorbed in looking at them that I forgot I'd been trying to help Oliver.

Halfway through one of the stacks, I paused.

"I've never seen this one before." My voice was soft.

Oliver went still. After a moment, he crossed the attic and maneuvered into the narrow space where I stood. He studied the painting I'd stopped on, his expression unreadable. "I did that when we were seventeen, I think. Maybe eighteen."

It was a portrait of me. Hardly noteworthy, since the attic was full of them, but this one was different.

In the painting, I was sitting on the beach, down at the bottom of the cliffs. My legs were tucked beneath me, and I was naked, as Oliver and I so often were when we went swimming. The ridges of my spine stood out against the darkening sky. So did the peaks of my nipples.

I wasn't facing the horizon. Instead, my face was turned to the side, as if someone had called my name farther upshore. A strong gust of wind had blown my hair back, and it was wild from my time in the sea, all tangles and curls.

The viewer could only see half my expression, but the curve of my mouth hinted at contentment.

It was a beautiful, wistful painting. The feeling it invoked in me was different than how I'd reacted to Nym's most recent portrait, the drawing of Warrior Fortuna, decked out in full armor and a sword held aloft. This was something . . . softer. Quieter.

"You always portray the best possible versions of me," I said quietly, tracing the corner of the canvas with my finger. I could feel Oliver's eyes on my face.

"No. I just paint what I see," he replied.

I turned toward Oliver again, only this time, he was just a breath away. My heart hammered, and I felt a pulse of desire between my legs. With a slow, barely perceptible shift, I moved closer. Close enough that, when I lifted my face, our lips almost touched.

I didn't kiss him, though. My hands rose to Oliver's waist, then slipped beneath his sweater. My knuckles brushed against his smooth, warm skin. Slowly, I unbuttoned Oliver's jeans, staring in his eyes as I did it. He didn't speak. The whisper of a zipper floated between us. He didn't move. I reached into Oliver's briefs, wrapped my hand around his cock, and pulled it out.

Now a sound did escape him, and I heard it, deep in his throat. Encouraged, I stroked his length, just once, and Oliver's eyes closed. Lightning flashed again, casting a pale glow over his expression. If I were a painter, I thought, that was the portrait I'd do of him.

"Tell me you don't want me," I murmured, my fingers stilling. "Say it, and I'll stop."

He opened his eyes, and his voice was nearly a growl as he answered, "I can't."

I stopped holding back, and I didn't hesitate—in the next breath, I was kissing him. Claiming his tongue, tasting him in the way I'd been wanting to since that night in the tent. I felt his hands move up my sides, and my oversized T-shirt rose with them, caught beneath Oliver's paint-stained palms.

I wasn't wearing anything under the shirt, and Oliver's eyes darkened when he discovered this. I knew, then, that he was done hesitating, too.

He bent, scooped me up, and lowered me to the floor. He tugged the T-shirt over my head, tossing it aside, and I returned the favor. His pants joined the pile. His briefs. Oliver lodged himself between my legs, and a sound escaped my parted lips. He went still, probably thinking my intake of breath was pain. But it was excitement. A lurch of realization that we had no reason, absolutely none, to stop what was happening between us.

When Oliver saw that, he gave me a slow, masculine grin. He bent his head. His tongue traced circles around one of my nipples, then his mouth closed around it and sucked, hard. His hand claimed my other breast, squeezing and kneading it. Exhaling in pleasure, I arched my back and wrapped my legs around Oliver's waist. I felt his erection press against me. A burst of need went off like a firework almost at the same time another clap of thunder shook the walls.

My sex was throbbing as I pushed Oliver onto his back and swung my leg to his other side, trapping him beneath me. Oliver rested his head against the floor and gazed up at me with bright, hungry eyes. He ran his hands along my thighs as I bent down to reclaim his mouth. Our kiss was deep and rough. I could've made out with him for hours, but I was aching with need.

Tonight, Oliver and I would finally do the one thing we never had.

Breaking our kiss, I moved down his body, brushing my lips over Oliver's chin, his throat, his chest, where I could feel his wild heartbeat. Physical proof of what I already knew: that Oliver loved me. That he'd never stopped loving me, just as I'd never stopped loving him.

The glow in my belly got brighter. I continued going downward, reacquainting myself with every inch of Oliver's body. He was tan from all those hours outside, building fences to keep us safe. His chest, stomach, and thighs were hard muscle. Interestingly, Oliver had more hair than I remembered. It trailed down his ridged abdomen. I followed it with my mouth, and I finally arrived at his cock.

It was just as perfect as the one from my memories. I arched my back and lowered my face, giving Oliver a view of my ass as I licked the underside of his shaft, and then, using the very tip of my tongue, circled the sensitive head.

Oliver sat up, the muscles in his stomach bunching. Without a word, he took hold of me, turned, and pinned me to the floor. In seconds, I found one of my legs bent and tucked against Oliver's waist, and I held onto his shoulders with splayed fingers. Oliver's hips slid between my thighs in a sensual movement. Once again, I felt his erection brush at that most sensitive part of me. I clenched and unclenched, and I made a low, impatient sound. But when I saw the look in Oliver's eyes, my frantic need softened into warm anticipation.

"I've wanted this for so long," he breathed.

I moved my pelvis against his, resting my temple tenderly on the edge of his jaw. His wonderful, wild scent filled my senses. "I know. Me, too. Please don't make me wait any more."

Oliver positioned himself. As the V in his lower half tensed, readying to plunge, he gazed down at me with wonder, and pure male need. Another hot, near-unbearable surge went straight to my center. I forced myself to remain still.

Then, mercifully, Oliver moved his hips.

His cock still had my saliva on it, and my sex was wet—he slid in effortlessly, his entire length filling my insides in an instant. I groaned, and Oliver swore.

"*Fuck,*" I exhaled, dragging the word out. Oliver crossed my wrists over my head, and his other hand held my leg in place. As he began to move, he bent and kissed me again, releasing his hold. My nails dragged down his back and I was moaning, breathing Oliver's name against his mouth. We moved in perfect unison, as if we'd connected mind-to-mind. I was lost in him, consumed by the heat and light spreading through my entire body. He was part of me, pounding into me, and he still didn't feel close enough. I wanted more, harder, deeper. As if Oliver heard the thought, or sensed the need in my moans, he obliged. His grip on me tightened and he shifted, then thrusted again, getting so deep that I nearly came.

Then I felt it.

Our souls met, tangled together, and burned. A connection forged, and it felt like magic. Real magic.

Oliver's subconscious sizzled through me and melded with mine. I saw an image of myself. Seven years old, kneeling on a cold basement floor. A small boy knelt at my side—Damon. Our eyes were squeezed shut and our lips moved. Then, suddenly, I wasn't observing the scene.

I was in it.

"Monster, monster, come out to play. Monster, monster, I've been waiting all day," we whisper together. We want to scare ourselves, and practice manipulating each other's fear. That's why we started playing the game. We want to make our parents proud and become the strongest Nightmares who ever lived.

My eyes are still closed, and the basement is so quiet that I can hear my own heart. I begin to wonder where a beast like the one we're chanting about might live. What it might sound like. My heart begins to quicken.

Behind my eyelids, I hear something in the darkness. A sound from some forgotten place where nothing can die.

A monster emerges.

My eyes fly open. Across the basement, there's a place where no light reaches, not even the bulb that dangles from the ceiling on a string. A growl ripples through the stillness.

Red eyes lock on mine.

In an instant, I know—it's coming after me. I'm the one it wants.

I grab Damon's hand and bolt for the stairs. The monster snarls. I sense it emerging from the shadows as we get to the top. I slam the door shut and lock it. I back away slowly, panting, still holding onto Damon. He says my name, a note of protest in his voice, and I let him tug his hand free. Then something slams into the door. I jump, yelping, and panic takes over.

"Come on!" I shout to my brother.

I run for the back door. Damon runs after me, shrieking. He thinks we're still playing the game. I yank the knob so hard that the whole door ricochets off the chock, then swings back and hits my shoulder. I don't care, I don't falter. I'm sprinting for the big tree out back, the one with the thick leaves and easy-to-climb branches. Nothing bad can reach me up there.

Damon is right on my heels as I scrabble up the trunk. "Run, Tuna, run!" he cries.

Halfway to the top, I wrench around, looking over my shoulder. I scream so loudly that it pierces the autumn air. The monster is there, at the bottom of the tree, those red eyes peering up at me. I have the wild fear that it might have wings, and suddenly, it does. They stretch wide and catch the glow beaming down from a nearby streetlight. My mouth is dry with terror.

Beside me, Damon giggles.

Something about the sound makes my racing heart slow. He can't see the creature chasing us, I realize, staring at him. His small face is wreathed in delight. Maybe this means I'm imagining it. I risk another glance toward the ground.

Before my eyes, the monster disintegrates and blows away, as if it's ashes on the wind.

I almost sob in relief. A game. It was just a game.

Then I experienced what could only be Oliver's memories. But . . . it didn't make sense. These sensations and fragments couldn't belong to my best friend. They belonged to something primal and cold. I could feel its mind, its instincts and urges. Hunger. Fury. *Hate.*

More images were coming now. Confusion whirled through me.

The monster is free again. Made again. It rips out of the darkness. It wants to hunt, and kill, and eat.

It doesn't know where it is or what any of the shapes around it mean. The monster does recognize one thing, though—prey.

It finds the male first. The monster's claws swipe through his prey like knives. It likes the sound of screams. It enjoys the smell and the taste of blood. With a roar of triumph, the monster lowers its great head to feast.

But wait. There's another one.

The monster can hear fleeing footsteps. It abandons its first victim and explodes down the hall, where it catches hold of the female. This one puts up more of a fight. She doesn't scream as much. The monster feels the sharp sting of pain, and realizes its prey has a claw of its own. Snarling, it swipes at her with more speed than before, driven by the instinct to survive. She gasps and hits the wall, sliding down, the whites of her eyes glowing in the dim.

Once again, the monster is about to feast when it is interrupted—it hears a second sound. The rustle is so faint that the monster is uncertain, and it goes down the hall more slowly than before. It stands on its hind legs and pushes the door open. The hinges creak.

A slant of light falls over her. The monster cocks its head, but it doesn't move closer. It just stays on the threshold, staring. The girl stirs again, her brow creasing.

By the time she opens her eyes, the monster is gone. Back down the hall, rushing past its uneaten meals. The monster wants to get out of this small space. It wants to avoid being seen. But it's not quite fast enough, and she appears in the doorway of her room.

The girl glimpses the monster, just for a moment. And for that single breath of time, it can feel her gaze like a ray of warmth in a land of eternal winter.

Then it's gone again, fleeing this tiny creature as if she were the bigger predator. The monster slips outside. It looks toward the stars, and it's never seen these before, either. Those red eyes flare with certainty now. The monster knows that is where it belongs.

Just as it spreads its wings, the monster feels the world close in on itself. The monster feels like its entire body is torn apart. It returns to the darkness.

The monster doesn't expect to awaken again, but it does. It rises and sees that it's in a cave. One end of the cavern is cast into darkness, and the other is a circle of brightness. The creature can hear the roar of the sea, and feel the water's cool spray, even from the shadows. It feels a stir of curiosity, and moves toward the light.

At the same moment the light began to brighten, I blinked and realized I was back in my own body. And then I registered what I'd just experienced. Witnessed.

Horror burrowed deep into my stomach, tearing through tendons and organs until the pain was unbearable. I didn't want to believe it. But then I remembered Lucifer's words after he'd stabbed me.

And now I will give you a gift, he'd said. *The truth about who killed your parents. It's been locked away all this time.*

Locked away inside me. Trapped in the dreamscape. Wearing a freckled face over the winged, dark monstrosity it truly was, like a wolf in sheep's clothing.

At some point, Oliver had stopped thrusting. He wasn't even inside me anymore. Instead, he hovered over me, his freckled face the palest I'd ever seen it. I lay beneath him, still naked, my entire body trembling. Salt exploded in my mouth, startling me. I hadn't even realized tears were streaking down my face. I stared at Oliver and didn't think to wipe them away.

"My parents. It was you." I said it with disbelief. With denial. With irrevocable, crushing certainty.

He didn't deny it.

My stomach gave a violent lurch. Clapping a hand over my mouth, I shot upright and bolted for the stairs. Heat rocketed up my throat. I hurtled down to the main floor and wrenched the front door open.

I got two steps outside before I emptied the contents of my stomach.

I aimed for the ground, but I was so close to the cottage that some of my mess splattered on the stones. Wearing jeans he must've hastily pulled on, Oliver appeared in my peripheral vision. He didn't say anything, and he didn't try to help me—he just dropped a blanket over my shoulders, covering my nakedness. I dug my nails into the doorframe, swaying. This wasn't happening. This couldn't be happening. It was a burglar that had killed them, or a strung-out werewolf. Not him. Not Ollie.

I pushed off the doorframe and stumbled down the path. I didn't know where I was going, didn't know if I might get struck by lightning, but right now I would welcome it. My mind grappled for a

450

chance at sweet oblivion. Thunder sounded in the distance, and the grass stirred from relentless, angry gusts.

At the point in the path where it drew parallel with Oliver's frozen shadow, something made me stop. I stared blankly at the creature's unseeing, hate-filled eyes, then turned my head slowly, looking toward the figure standing farther down the path.

Oliver looked back at me with an expression on his face I'd seen once before, and another memory tore through the ruins of my smoking mind.

I don't deserve you, I'd said to Oliver once. It felt like a lifetime ago. He had looked at me with that expression I couldn't name, a fleeting shadow crossing his face.

Guilt. I hadn't known it then, but it was guilt.

The same guilt that was in his eyes now. He'd known, damn him. He had always known the truth. I gripped my head with both hands and bent down, pressing my forehead against my knees. This couldn't be happening. This wasn't real. My best friend couldn't have been the one who shredded Mom and Dad to ribbons. No, no, no.

Seeing that I was on the verge of a breakdown, Oliver reached for me. His face was even whiter now. "Fortuna, I—"

I recoiled. *"Don't touch me."*

He blanched, freezing where he stood. "I'm sorry. I'm so sorry."

His voice made me think of a child in the dark. He had never sounded like that before. But all I saw was a monster. A monster with Oliver's sad eyes.

Another wave of nausea rocked through me. I shook my head, once, twice, as if I were arguing with someone. It took all my focus to keep the vomit down. I bent over and closed my eyes,

Behind us, there came a great cracking sound. I shot upright and turned, my heart leaping into my throat. I half-expected to see Lucifer standing there, his hair whipping in the wind, his lips curved in that infuriating, amused smile he reserved just for me.

When I realized that Lucifer wasn't the source of the sound, there was no time for relief. Because the statue was moving. The part of Oliver that I'd transformed into stone had been dormant all these months, but whatever I'd done tonight had awoken it. It raised its head, and as I watched, the thing's shape began to change. Before, it had just looked like a severe-faced Oliver, except with wings. Slowly, it became something much, much bigger. Something vaguely . . . familiar.

The moment I recognized it, I bent over and vomited into the grass again.

It was the monster I remembered from my childhood.

The same monster I used to imagine chasing me and Damon. The same monster I saw at the end of the hallway moments after I found my parents' mauled bodies.

My throat was so dry that I couldn't even scream. It came closer, and closer, and closer. I couldn't move. I was on the verge of hyperventilating, but I couldn't even do that, because I'd forgotten how to draw air in and out. It felt like I was standing in two places at once—the past, where the bloody bodies of my parents were, and the present, where my worst nightmare had become reality. A whimper lodged somewhere inside me. But . . . nothing happened. It had gone right past.

It was then I realized the truth.

The monster hadn't come for me. Not this time.

Oliver's shadow self unfurled its wings. It bent over and wrapped them around Oliver, who was still on the ground. The two of them merged into one being, becoming something new. Something different from the thing that killed my parents.

Something far, far deadlier.

The shadow was gone now. Oliver straightened slowly. Black veins crawled up the column of his throat, and as his eyes met mine, wide with panic, I watched them go dark. His beautiful pupils filled with inky pools. Within seconds, they were completely black, and there was nothing left of the boy I'd loved.

Before I could speak, the winged creature turned away as if he'd heard something. I followed his gaze, and when I realized what was about to happen, it felt like time slowed.

The door was back.

It was the exact same one Lucifer had opened.

Light poured out of it, blinding me. I held up my hand to protect my eyes, numb and dazed. Wings beat at the air like a drum, but I was slow to comprehend the sound. I lowered my hand and registered there was something big and dark coming this way. Then it hurtled past.

Oliver shot through the illuminated doorway with a mindless, world-shattering roar.

CHAPTER TWENTY-NINE

*O*liver's second birth was just as violent as the first.

The instant I opened my eyes, and comprehended that I was alive, I saw a body on the floor.

It felt like my stomach fell out and my heart stopped working. A tiny cry escaped me, and I rolled out of bed, discovering too late that I couldn't stand. I didn't care. I half-dragged myself, half-crawled to the person lying in the middle of the rug, blood soaking the thick wool. I could see, from the light spilling through the open door, that the figure was male. My mind flipped through the possibilities in dazed horror. *Damon. Finn. Gil. Cyrus. Adam. Nym. Danny. Collith. Laurie.*

I didn't know what to do with my hands. They fluttered over the prone form like mad birds, useless and desperate. *Calm down. Hush. See who it is.*

Hardly daring to breathe, I turned the body over. Heavy. It was heavy. This couldn't be Nym, then. Just as I lowered my gaze and started to look more closely, my courage failed me. I let out a ragged sob and sat back on my heels, hands tightening into helpless, enraged fists.

At the worst possible moment, I heard Oliver's voice. *Close your eyes. Picture the worst possible outcome. Be cruel to yourself. Spare no pain.*

Do this again, and again, and again. Until one day, you find yourself immune to it, and the fear no longer controls you.

I felt my face twist in an expression somewhere between rage and anguish. *Fuck you, Oliver.* In defiance, I forced myself to look down.

A sob caught in my throat when I found myself staring at Finn.

The only indication that he was still living was the faint wheezing that escaped his lips. I put both my hands on the werewolf's chest, stupidly thinking that I had to stop the bleeding. Why wasn't he healing? My lips felt stiff and cold as I said, with increasing hysteria, "Collith. Laurelis. *Collith. Laurelis.*"

Both of them materialized within two seconds of each other. Collith took one look at Finn and said, "I'll get Zara."

He sifted without waiting for a response. Laurie stayed, but he didn't say anything. There was something about his expression I didn't like, so I gave Finn my complete attention, even as the sight of him made my stomach churn. He'd been ripped apart.

Just like my parents.

Laurie must've heard a noise I couldn't, because he quickly strode to the door. He pulled it partway shut, hiding whoever was on the other side. All the commotion had woken the rest of my family, no doubt. Laurie's voice was low and level as he sent them away.

My touch had roused Finn—he blinked up at me confusedly. Desperate to comfort him, I forced myself to speak, but I barely heard what came out of my own mouth. It was all terrified, nonsensical babbling. "Just hold on, Finn. Collith is getting a healer, okay? So I just need you to hold on a little longer."

I was still talking when Finn lost consciousness.

Panic roared through me as his face went slack. We were losing him. There had to be something I could do. Finn was part of my Court now. We shared a bond even deeper than the one we'd already had—a bond of magic.

Hope surged through me. We had lent each other strength before, hadn't we? Why couldn't I give it to him now?

From the corner of my eye, I saw Gil's narrow frame in the doorway. He must've left Adam's when he felt my distress. There was no time to greet him or explain what had happened. I closed my eyes, concentrating harder on the magic that connected all of us. I spent precious seconds waiting for my instincts to kick in. For some kind of knowledge to come to me. But nothing happened.

There hadn't been any kind of manual or guidebook to the innate workings of this spell, so I did everything I could think of. I mentally grasped the bond and imagined Finn's wound closing. I chanted under my breath. "Heal. Heal. Heal. *Live*, Finn."

The threads from my wolf's side of the bond didn't respond. They were glowing more weakly now. Then they started to flicker in my mind.

A frustrated sound burst from me. I sat back on my heels and bit back a scream. "*Fuck*. I can't do it."

Laurie knelt on the other side of Finn, his hand dangling off one knee. "Do what?"

"Heal him." I made a sharp gesture toward Finn. "Or make him heal himself, I don't know. I'm still new at this!"

"Even magic has its limits, Fortuna," Laurie said, his voice gentle.

For some reason, his calm tone only agitated me more. My mind raced. I tried to think of everything I knew about bonds and magical ties. I reviewed my own experiences with them. My thoughts halted on a memory.

There was something Collith had done, once, when I'd been mated to him. It seemed possible to replicate it with Finn . . .

At first, my gut instinct was to reject the idea. It wasn't enough. I wanted to *save* Finn. But what if it was all I could do for him?

Zara wasn't here yet. If she hadn't arrived by now, she probably wouldn't come in time. Savannah couldn't sift, and even if Laurie found her in the next five seconds, she wouldn't reach us soon enough, either. I closed my eyes again and forced myself to take several deep, ragged breaths. *Oh, God.* I was really going to do this. I was really accepting that Finn was slipping through our hands.

But I couldn't let him be in pain. Not while there was something I could try to ease it.

My hands crept forward again. I rested them on Finn's arm, then curled my fingers around it as I blocked out the rest of the world. The bonds of the Shadow Court lit up inside me, and I reached for the one that belonged to my wolf, thinking only of how much I loved him.

The feeling was so powerful that I could see it, suddenly, twining through Finn's bond and everyone else's, too. A soft light that only added to the brightness of the threads. I concentrated on my desire to ease Finn's pain, and the memory of how Collith had once used our old bond.

This time, whatever I did worked.

When I opened my eyes again, I was in a fishing boat.

It bobbed in the middle of a small lake, which was perfectly round and lined with thick trees. Sunlight glimmered on the water. There were only two cabins visible, both with long docks that reached out from a distant shore. I slowly turned on the bench, and it felt like my heart was holding its breath.

Finn sat next to me.

He squinted in the bright light, and there was a fishing pole in his hand. And even though everything about the werewolf was familiar and dear, right down to the subtle crow's feet at the corners of his eyes, this was a version of my friend I'd never seen before. He filled out the plaid shirt he wore, and there were fewer lines on his face. The way he held himself was different, too. I stared at him for another moment, then finally put my finger on it—he wasn't looking for any threats. My Finn always had his guard up.

"Where are we?" he asked, though I could tell from his expression that he knew. Full of wondering, Finn's gold eyes moved around as if everything was about to disappear.

Then I remembered that it was.

"Your favorite place," I said softly, hiding a pang of agony. "I'm using our bond."

Finn looked out at the lake again. His expression was as calm as ever, and he held the fishing pole loosely. "I used to take my family here. My father owned a small cabin across the way. It's gone now, but I remember being on the water. Sitting in this rusty fishing boat and listening to the loons while we cast our lines."

457

Finn's voice sounded different, somehow, as he recounted the memory. Not as if he were younger, exactly, but less . . . burdened. Like none of the terrible things that followed those days on the water had happened.

Some of those terrible things wouldn't have happened to Finn if he hadn't stayed in my life. What if I'd done the right thing, the smart thing, and sent him away once he was free of Astrid? Guilt swelled in my throat and made it difficult to say the things I wanted to say. The things I needed to say.

What-ifs were useless. There was no time for useless.

I shoved the guilt down and refocused on Finn, clearing my throat. I was about to speak into the stillness when he said, "I'm dying, aren't I?"

He said it so simply. Pain lodged in my chest. I wanted to lie, to say anything other than the truth, but it was more for my sake than his. Finn wasn't afraid.

"Yes," I answered quietly. "It won't be much longer now."

Finn smiled. Even though we only had seconds left together, I couldn't help but stare at the rare sight. "Okay, then," he said. He nodded, almost to himself, and then he repeated, "Okay."

Tears blinded me. Frantic not to miss a single moment with him, I swiped at my eyes roughly. My voice was ragged as I said, "I'm sorry, Finn. I'm so sorry I didn't save you."

Setting the fishing pole down, the werewolf set his elbows on his knees and turned his face toward the horizon. His eyes slid shut, and his lips curved in a soft smile I'd never seen before. "You have nothing to be sorry for," he said. "You gave me purpose again. And they've been waiting for me—it's time I get back to them."

I couldn't respond. The look on Finn's face sent a surge of pain through my chest, and for a few seconds I had to move my face away so he wouldn't see. I told myself to be brave. Strong. Selfless. All the awful clichés that you only resort to when you have nothing left.

When I finally turned back to Finn, the words *I love you* crowding in my throat, the boat was empty. He was gone. My grip tightened on the edge. Water lapped in the silence and the shadow of a bird darted over the place where Finn had been sitting. I felt him die. I felt the magic between us fade and fall away. I'd expected it to be some shattering, dramatic agony or explosion, but the spell ended quietly. The part of my soul that Finn had occupied was just . . . empty. Like the boat still bobbing on the water.

I opened my eyes and absorbed the familiar sensation of being in shock. This couldn't be happening. This was just another night terror.

"He's gone, Fortuna." Laurie's voice floated across the room. He was standing near the window now, and I wondered how long I'd been sitting there.

"Shut up." I wouldn't look at him. Wouldn't look away from Finn's peaceful face. My splayed fingers, which had been shaking in a death grip, curled into a fist on top of my knee. "He's resting. A healer is coming. He just needs to hold on . . . hold on a little longer . . ."

Laurie didn't answer. I wouldn't have heard him if he had. My focus was trained on Finn, still hoping, somehow, that he would start healing and open his eyes. My wolf stayed silent. He was always silent, but there was something terrible about his stillness this time.

The realization came slowly, almost like falling asleep. One moment, I was sitting there, desperately waiting for the sound of Zara's footsteps, staring at Finn's wounds in wild hope. The next moment a tiny voice inside me whispered, *He's dead.* The thought was almost startling, and I looked over at Finn's face, frowning.

That was when I noticed other details beyond the torn skin and sticky blood. I saw how chalky Finn's dark skin had gotten. I realized how he'd stopped moving, even the subtle rise and fall I'd felt beneath my palms earlier. *Oh,* I thought. Then again, more faintly, *Oh.*

This was real. This was happening.

I lifted my head as though it weighed a thousand pounds. Collith had returned at some point, and he stood beside Laurie. Both of them watched me silently, but their expressions couldn't have been more different. Tension bracketed Collith's mouth, and his dark brows were drawn together. Laurie looked . . . dangerous. His eyes were overly bright and fae. His body was preternaturally still, like a predator's on high alert.

Surprisingly, Collith was the one to speak first. "What happened?" he asked.

All at once, I saw the scene how they must have. What remained of Finn. The obvious evidence that whatever had killed him wasn't human. The new set of footprints on the floor, just like the ones Lucifer had left behind in Emma's hospital room.

When I saw that, hysterical laughter rose up inside me. It got stuck in my throat. I wasn't entirely sure I even knew *how* to answer Collith's question. I'd talked about Oliver to both of them at least once over the past year, but I had no idea how to tell these powerful, tense faeries that my imaginary friend had fucked me, then used me to get out of his prison. They had no idea that he was the thing from my past come to life. That *I'd* brought to life.

"Breathe, Fortuna," Laurie commanded suddenly.

I blinked at him, realizing half a beat later that my lungs were on fire. Right. Air was good. Inhaling in a burst, I nodded at Laurie to express my gratitude, then continued to think about Collith's question. *What happened?*

I tried to go back and remember every moment leading up to this one, but my mind flinched away from reliving it. As Collith and Laurie kept waiting for an answer, I thought of what Lucifer had whispered in my best friend's ear.

"Oliver became what he was meant to be," I said, my voice hollow.

Before either of them could respond, I shifted, which caused my hand to land in the puddle of Finn's blood. My stomach heaved, and for several seconds, it took all my concentration not to throw up everywhere. I bent over, which brought me closer to the blood, and the world tilted. I shifted again to get away from the smell, eyes squeezed shut. I counted and breathed.

To my relief, the storm inside me abated. Just as I started to sit upright, I felt something hot and wet drip off the edge of my jaw.

"Sorry," I said, wiping it away. But there was already another tear racing to take its place. I wiped that one away, too, and repeated, "Sorry."

Why was I apologizing? I frowned again, shaking my head. *Focus, Fortuna.* Collith had asked me something. I couldn't seem to scrape any more thoughts together. I was hearing a high-pitched ringing sound now, and I still hadn't pushed myself up.

Boots appeared in front of me. Then strong arms scooped me up, and my head and shoulder rested against a hard chest. *But the blood,* I tried to say. Even talking felt like too much right now, though. Collith moved to sit on the couch with me still in his lap, and I didn't fight him. His white shirt was already covered in red stains.

As the seconds ticked by, the ringing stopped. Silence crowded in, and I couldn't decide which was worse. My mind had finally started working again, but for a few minutes, it was only capable of reviewing the most basic facts. Oliver was real. Oliver had gotten out of the dreamscape.

And then he'd ripped my best friend open.

There was a sensation on the edge of my subconscious, like a bubble struggling to the surface. It was a memory. No, a voice. *You're the one who lets him out.* That's what Nym had said to me, once.

The Time Walker had been trying to warn me, in his own broken way. When Heilel had escaped, I'd assumed Nym was talking about him. I may have set two very bad things loose in the world, but the devil hadn't murdered Finn. The devil hadn't killed my parents. Oliver was the one I'd loved the most.

"I don't understand," I said dully. Hearing my own voice felt strange after so much silence. I didn't lift my head from Collith's chest as I wondered, more to myself than anyone else, "How did he get out? After all this time?"

"Intimacy blurs lines," Collith answered. There was heavy meaning in the way he said this, and if I hadn't been so numb with shock, I probably would've flinched.

Collith knew. Of course he knew.

Though I hadn't technically done anything wrong by having sex with Oliver, shame formed in my stomach, hard and tight as a fist. I

461

should've known better. I should've seen it. But I'd been so blinded by my feelings, by my desperation for a distraction, that I'd looked right past the truth. It was so obvious that only someone in denial would miss it. I blinked rapidly, my heart ramming against my chest like a pair of frantic fists, beating at a door. *Let me out, let me out!*

I had all the pages now. The grim story of Fortuna Sworn.

When I was a child, my brother and I had made up a game. To practice using our powers, we claimed. We decided there was a creature that no one else could see, and it liked to gobble up little children if it could catch them. The grown-ups couldn't protect us, so we had to save ourselves and defeat the monster with our abilities. If that didn't work, we fought with invisible swords or hid places where the creature could never find us.

It frustrated our parents to no end when it came time for dinner and we were tucked away in a cupboard, or huddled in the shadowed space beneath the basement stairs. Frustrated and terrified them, sometimes, if we continued to ignore their calls. More than once, it was sensing Mom's fear that made Damon and I abandon our game and crawl into the open, giving her guilty hugs and shame-faced apologies.

One afternoon, as Damon and I scrambled up a tree in a wild race for our lives, I actually pictured the beast we were pretending to be so afraid of.

And once the image formed in my head, I couldn't get rid of it.

We reached the top of the tree. I barely registered the open sky all around us or the feel of the wind on my skin. Beside me, Damon's scrawny chest heaved, his eyes bright with the thrill of it. But I didn't return his smile. My fingers dug into the bark of the branch I clung onto, and as I peered down through the branches, staring at the leafy ground far below, I imagined a noise. An echo of what I thought the creature might sound like.

That same night, I started having nightmares about a great winged monster that shook the world with its roar.

I began denying Damon every time he asked to play, but it didn't stop the dreams. Fear had taken root inside of me, and darkness only made it thrive. As the days went on, I started avoiding the basement and closing my closet door—places where a monster might lie in wait. The more I tried to ignore my mounting paranoia, the stronger it became.

Because of that game, that fear, one of my nightmares made a giant tree sprout to life in the middle of my bedroom.

It was the same tree I'd been climbing when I first pictured the creature. It was also irrefutable proof of my growing power. My parents had done the binding spell after that, but it hadn't been enough. Not against the strength of a child's fear, when their imaginations are most powerful, their hold on reality as thin as the veil between worlds.

I'd had one more dream. One more nightmare. One more terror. A terror that had never truly left me, so deep and endless that removing it would be tearing out something that had become vital. My power had cost our family the ultimate price.

Cost us everything.

I'd been so consumed by finding the memories hidden inside my head that I hadn't really considered why I'd hidden them in the first place, but now it was crystal-clear—guilt. Searing, all-consuming guilt. The shadow I'd seen that night had been a monster of my own creation. There were no terrible men who'd broken into our house, no out-of-control werewolf who'd been drawn to our power. All the theories I had considered over the years had gone up in smoke, leaving just the ashes of truth behind.

"It's my fault they're dead," I said. Saying it out loud felt like ripping something off. Suddenly I wasn't numb anymore. Now I was bleeding all over the place and there was *pain*. So much pain that I couldn't even tell where it was coming from. It was everywhere.

Collith's arms tightened. He must've put the pieces together, too, because his response was immediate. "You were a child, Fortuna."

I didn't accept his comfort. I finally straightened and leaned away, turning my face toward the bedroom doors. Every single one was tightly shut, maybe even locked, but that wouldn't be enough. Part of my mind was still in the past, and when I looked at those doors, all I could think was how thin that wood would be against Oliver's strength. "I should warn the others. He could come back."

"I can tell them, if you want. If that's easier," Collith added, his tone neutral. I nodded, and then he said, "Fortuna."

Collith waited for me to look at him, but I stared down at my hands. I splayed my fingers wider and flexed them, watching how they bent and straightened. I needed to focus on something. Needed to get through the next second, and the next one, until I wasn't on the verge of shattering. "Yes?" I asked faintly.

"You need to cry."

"I do?"

"Yes," Collith said firmly.

I looked at him with wide, tormented eyes. There was a faint voice at the back of my head, urging me to pick up the pieces of myself and get back to being the protector my family needed.

But then I let out a sound I'd never made before. Hearing it, Collith's fingers buried in the hair at the base of my scalp, and he pulled our faces closer. I felt his forehead press against mine, and that was the moment I just . . . broke.

I cried until my eyes were stinging and swollen. I felt like Alice in Wonderland, filling the space up with my pain. At the end of it, when I had gone small and quiet, I finally said the thing I knew everyone else would think once they learned the truth about what I'd done.

"I'm a monster," I whispered. I stared at the wall blankly. I was still curled against Collith, my temple resting on his chest.

Collith began to rock me gently, pressing his cheek to the top of my head. "You're not," he murmured. "I swear to you, you're not."

I didn't answer. Minutes later, the weight of his cheek disappeared, and I felt him look up. The smell of springtime drifted past. Something in me stirred. *Laurie is here.*

His silken voice floated over me, meant solely for Collith. "Dracula is outside."

Collith's response rumbled against my ear. "I'll speak with him. Can you stay with her?"

Laurie must've nodded, because I felt Collith stand up. He gently handed me off to the other faerie. Collith's coolness retreated, and Laurie's warmth replaced it. I was silent as the Seelie King's arms slid around my back and beneath my knees.

They were treating me like I was helpless. I wanted to tell them I wasn't, that I was fine, but the words wouldn't come. How much more could I endure? How much more pain could I bear?

To my relief, Laurie didn't try to give me any quotes, or talk about how brave I was. He just held me. His comfort was different from Collith's, I thought in a detached way. He didn't make soft sounds, or sway me. But his grip was fierce, almost as fierce as he was. It made me feel infinitely safe. A few minutes ticked by, and I felt that slow creep of falling asleep. *Oliver won't be there*, I realized blearily. The thought didn't hurt me because I was so far away.

"Look," Laurie said. "The sun is coming up."

The sound of his voice yanked me back to awareness. I wasn't really interested in observing the sunrise, not when Finn couldn't be here to see it. Not when his body was lying just a few feet away. But I looked anyway, mostly to humor Laurie. Bright, yellow ribbons streamed through the window over the kitchen sink, and the window farther down the hall. All at once, I heard Finn's voice as if he sat right beside me. *Good morning, my lady.* I became half-convinced that if I turned my head, I'd see him there, sipping out of the white coffee mug he'd always used.

I looked away from the light and tucked my face into the crook of my arm.

"Close the curtain," I mumbled. "Please."

There was a pause, probably because Laurie was fighting the urge to argue. But he eventually set me down, his movements gentle in spite of the displeasure that permeated the air. I listened to the faerie's soft footsteps as he moved to comply. I knew what he really wanted was to open those curtains wider and tell me to get up. Something held Laurie back, though. He pulled one curtain shut, then the other. He did the same at the other window and entombed the room in darkness.

Once he was finished, I sensed him coming to stand in front of me. "Fortuna," he started.

"Don't." I rolled over and put my back to him. "Not right now. Okay?"

Another pause. "Okay," Laurie said.

If he was disappointed in me, I really didn't give a shit. And if he said anything else before he left, I didn't hear that, either. I was already somewhere else. Not the dreamscape—I never wanted to see that place again. No, I was somewhere in the middle of countless tall, green trees. Somewhere with sun-tipped water and birdsong echoing across a vast, blue sky. There was a fishing pole in my hand, and I was back on the boat.

This time, it wasn't empty.

CHAPTER THIRTY

A day passed.

It was one of those days that felt endless and like a blink at the same time. I drifted in and out of consciousness. My face still felt puffy. I only left my bed long enough to use the bathroom, and once, to force down a glass of water. As I drank, I was careful not to look toward the stain on the floorboards.

It all had the listless monotony of a day I'd lived before. We were old friends, grief and I. At least I knew what to expect during its long visits. I crawled back into bed and tugged the covers over me, ignoring the noises beyond my bedroom door. None of it mattered. Nothing did.

Hunger pangs woke me the next time. Dusk shone through a crack in the curtains, casting a burnt glow over the entire space, as though everything were quietly burning. My skin felt hot, too, but the light wasn't completely to blame.

Collith was asleep in the bed. He held me as he dreamed, one arm draped over my hip while the other cushioned my head. I had hazy memories of Laurie being here, too. He'd spent several hours in the chair beside the window. The chair was vacant now, unsurprisingly.

I lay there and stared at the dust motes floating around it. Then, to keep the thoughts away, I started to count them.

I needed to get out of this room.

I slid out from beneath Collith's arm and crossed the room on the pads of my feet. The idea of food was unappealing, but fresh air seemed bearable. I slipped through the door and crept into the silent loft. The clock over the stove said it was only 5:30, but someone was sleeping on the couch. No, two people. I looked around, noting the other figures scattered throughout the sun-dappled room.

For the first time since Finn had died, the ache inside me eased, just a little.

It was all of them. My Shadow Court.

Cyrus and Ariel were asleep on the couch, her head resting against his shoulder. Seth was on the floor, curled around a throw pillow. Gil rested with his back against one side of the fireplace. There was a poker in his hand. Vampires were nocturnal creatures, and they didn't often sleep. The fact that he hadn't stirred when I opened the door spoke volumes—they must've stayed up all night, or they were drained from being tethered to me. Still, every single one of them had stayed.

Our wolf was gone, but we were still a pack.

Swallowing, I searched the room again. Besides Finn, there was one person missing. But I could feel him nearby, the bond between us relaxed and glowing. He was awake, his mind busy with thoughts and images I couldn't quite make out. Curiosity shone through the fog in my own head. Slowly, I turned away from the people slumbering in the glow of the dying fire.

I went to the room at the end of the hall.

Sunlight slanted over the floorboards at my feet, and a bird called into the stillness. The door was ajar. I pushed it open and the hinges let out a thin whine. Nym was on the bed, drawing in a sketchpad I'd bought for him. To my faint surprise, he was wearing jeans and a T-shirt. Emma's doing, most likely. His long, bare toes peeked out from beneath the pant legs. Even with the clothes, and his pointed ears covered by his wild hair, Nym still didn't seem human. There was something too old about his eyes.

I studied him for a moment. Nym looked even thinner than usual, and his movements seemed slower. Faeries didn't need to eat, technically, but it did make them stronger. How long had it been since he'd eaten? Or was I seeing another effect—another consequence—of the Court bond? Guilt swelled in my throat.

When Nym didn't say anything, I moved toward the bed. I hesitated before sinking down beside him, the soft mattress dipping with my weight. Silence resettled like gently-falling snow, covering everything. I squinted at the fading sky and listened to the sound of Nym's charcoal scratching across paper. The sun was nearly gone. It had been an entire day, I thought. I'd survived one day without Finn existing on this planet.

No. I couldn't think about that right now.

I turned to Nym desperately. But whatever I'd been about to say faded on my tongue as I caught sight of the wall behind him. My wide eyes darted around, taking it all in.

The drawings had multiplied while I'd been gone.

For the past few months, almost every time I'd seen one of Nym's pieces, I'd dismissed it. They were nonsensical. A random blend of shading and lines. But all this time, they'd been part of a larger drawing. A big picture. Nym had been creating a mural, or a timeline. He couldn't use his voice, so he'd told his story the only way he knew how.

It began with Persephone. She was as beautiful as the painting I'd seen, her hair long and bright, her eyes dark and imploring. She stood in front of Nym, clasping his hands. Lucifer's voice echoed through my memory. *She befriended a Time Walker. A faerie called Nym. She was so desperate for answers—for a way back to me—that she broke his mind with her requests.*

But even after Persephone's part ended, there were more drawings. Many more. Nym must've done some traveling of his own, or he'd gone at Collith's request, because the rest were about me. In one scene, I was sitting on my throne in the Unseelie Court. That twisted, eerie crown rested on my head. When I thought about that day, every detail was still vivid. There was one detail, though, I didn't remember.

There were two Nyms.

One stood in the crowd, peering up at me, and the other hid behind a pillar. He watched my coronation from the shadows. I knew he'd go back and tell Collith about what he'd seen, and create a domino effect of events that started with a mating ceremony in the woods to now. Here. Grieving in this bedroom, staring at a wall covered with the past . . . and the future.

The final image was familiar, since another version of it hung in my bedroom. It was me, wearing full armor and holding a sword. A supernatural army stood at my back. Future Fortuna glared at something in the distance, and I didn't need to be a witch or a time traveler to know who I was looking at.

Nym must've seen these moments. He must've been there. And if he could see these moments, he could probably change them.

An idea flared in my mind like a firework.

My hand was a fist in the blanket. It was the only outward indication of the tension trembling in my stomach. The rest of me still felt numb, or dead, as if Finn had taken something with him when he left. A part of my soul, probably. Maybe that's why I didn't even think about it.

I looked at Nym and said, "I need you to go back in time. I need you to save Finn."

The faerie didn't pause in his drawing. His expression didn't even change. His bony elbow went around and around, and the fringe of his dark lashes cast a shadow on his cheek as he kept his focus downward. "I have one more journey to make. It's not time yet," he said. His tone was dismissive.

"I don't know what that means, Nym. I know it's asking a lot, I have no right, but we can't survive this. We can't survive losing Finn. We have to *fix* it." As I uttered the words, I knew I was repeating the same mistakes. Doing exactly to Nym what I had done to Cyrus.

Finally looking up from his paper, the faerie patted my hand soothingly. He didn't know that I had given up on hope or that it felt like my heart had been carved out with a dull spoon. "The end of one thing is always the beginning of something else, my lady," Nym said.

I pulled my hand away. I didn't want comfort or vague platitudes. I wanted Finn.

Swallowing the sharp words lodged in my throat, I looked at all those drawings again. Now that I knew the truth, it was all I could see. Heilel. Persephone. Me. All of us bound together by time and pain and magic. It made me wonder whether free will existed at all, or if we were all on a set path there was no deviating from.

"Forget it," I said finally, getting to my feet.

Nym's eyebrows drew together, and now he seemed perturbed. "My lady—"

"Never mind, Nym." I bent and kissed his cheek. "Really. No one else should get hurt. I'm just not thinking straight."

Moving with purpose now, I stood and went over to the door. This time, Nym didn't go back to his drawing. I felt his eyes on me until I stepped out of sight. He'd sensed, no doubt, that I was lying through my teeth.

The truth was I was thinking very clearly.

I was thinking clearly enough to move as silently as I could through the loft, using the skills I'd picked up from spending so much time with werewolves and faeries. I was thinking clearly enough to lift a coat off one of the hooks, and open the door so carefully that none of the supernatural creatures in the living room woke. I was thinking clearly enough to remember the way down the stairs and outside without turning on a single light.

And I was thinking clearly enough to know exactly how I'd find Lucifer.

I couldn't drive, though. Turning on an engine would wake up the entire house. Halfway down the driveway, I turned left and picked my way over frozen clumps of tall grass. There was a crossroads one mile south, on the other side of the woods. It was more public than

I'd like, but I didn't want to return to the other one, anyway. My skin crawled at the thought.

"Where are you going?"

His voice was calm, but a sense of tension had disturbed the peaceful stillness.

I faced Laurie across a field. Dressed entirely in black, the Seelie King cut a striking figure against all the whiteness around us. The ends of his hair lifted in a cold gust. It hung free tonight, the perfect strands shining like moonlight on a glassy lake.

"To make a deal," I answered finally. "I'm getting Finn's soul back. There must be something I can trade for it."

Laurie's eyes darkened. In that moment, it felt like the air thickened, as if the sky was gathering to shoot a bolt of lightning at me. My instincts shifted uneasily, power recognizing power. "For once in your life, think with your head instead of your heart, Fortuna," he said.

"You're one to talk." I tried to smile. I'd forgotten how, though. My gaze moved past Laurie, looking toward the trees. They were the same trees I'd seen Finn's fluffy tail vanish into a hundred times. My voice was tight with pain as I said, "He would do it for me."

"Without a doubt," Laurie said bluntly. "But didn't you see the look on his face? He was relieved. He was *glad* to go. He wouldn't want you to put yourself in this position again, and especially not for him."

Laurie's words made me pause, just as he'd intended. I'd only been thinking of getting Finn back. I hadn't given any thought to what came afterward. Now I imagined Finn here, alive, and the image hurt. A flash of someone hollow-cheeked and silent. Collith had never been the same after I'd brought him back. But returning to Earth was better than an eternity in Hell, wasn't it?

Then it occurred to me . . . what if I ripped him from a different place?

Finn had been good, through and through. Lucifer had once told me that we end up where we think we should. All Finn had wanted was his family. What if he'd actually found his way back to them?

Damn it. Laurie was right.

As the weight of resignation settled on my shoulders, it hit me all over again. The realization that I'd never see Finn again. Unbidden, my mind filled with the memory of his last moments. Not the dream I'd distracted him with, but the terrible sight of him on the floor. Or what was left of him.

I clenched my jaw. "He deserved so much better."

"What he deserves is peace, and if you do this for him, he'll never have it."

I turned my face toward the horizon. The sun was gone now, and something about being surrounded by twilight jarred my memory. Suddenly I remembered the dream I'd had while I was in that coma. I had been so distracted by Finn's death that I'd completely forgotten someone else's. I refocused on Laurie, my stomach hard and tight.

"What did you do to Bella O'Connell?" I asked.

"Do you mean that screechy human with the awful cowboy boots? Alive, unfortunately. Your witch did a spell. Bella O'Connell is safe at home, tucked in her bed. If you ever cross paths again, she'll have no idea who you are. If I'd had my way, she'd be decomposing in a shallow grave, but I was outvoted." Laurie's tone was disgruntled.

Good, I thought. That was good. One loose end I wouldn't have to worry about.

A few seconds went by. Laurie said my name. I met his gaze slowly, noting the concern in his eyes. But I couldn't bring myself to care. A new plan was forming in my head, and no matter how much part of me wanted to recoil from it, I couldn't.

"There's going to be a wake," I said dully, turning away from Laurie. "I'll text you the details when I have them."

He responded, but I didn't hear it. A single thought pounded in my head like a drum, making the long walk feel like a death march.

If there was no going back, all that remained was forward. And I knew what I had to do next.

April arrived with a rainstorm and a funeral.

It still felt like winter, but the days were warmer, transforming the frozen soil to cold mud. Even so, my breath still sent plumes of air into the morning. Car doors slammed behind me, the sound stark, like someone clapping their hands in an empty room. We were all here, I noted distantly.

Well, everyone except for one.

Even Adam and Danny had come to Denver today. As we made our way into the church, mountains visible in the distance, I tugged at the bottom of my gray dress. It was too short, but it was also the only one I owned that didn't seem like it should be worn by a faerie queen. I'd wanted to look nice for him. For Finn.

It felt wrong to hold the service here, to bury him in a cemetery full of strangers. For a while I had considered cremation. But Finn didn't belong in a container, alive or dead, and there was still a small chance of finding where his family was buried. I'd sent a text to Cora, and the young alpha had promised to look into it. Astrid might've known something, and maybe she'd passed that knowledge on to someone in her pack.

In the end, I'd decided to put him next to my parents.

Finn was family, after all, and I thought Mom and Dad would've loved him if they'd had the chance to know him. Maybe they were getting that chance now.

Collith and Laurie stood to my left. Gil stood to my right. His face was clean-shaven, his hair gelled and combed. When we'd first gotten to the church, I had been on the verge of breaking. Then I took one look at his face, and I poured glue into the cracks that formed me. A person I loved was gone, but there was someone else who still needed my strength. Or whatever was left of it.

That strength felt dangerously precarious after the service came to an end and I watched Finn's casket get carried out. *My fault*, I kept thinking. *My fault.*

We made our way through the cemetery, and once we reached Finn's plot, the pastor opened his bible again. "For they quickly pass, and we fly away . . ." the human recited.

I barely heard him, because it felt like the earth was shifting beneath me. Like I would never know solid ground again. Collith and Laurie stood even closer than they had in the church, as if they sensed it.

Gil had wondered, once, if we were all following some grand plan. Treading an inevitable path that had been laid out for us. But if that was the case, I couldn't see the purpose in this. What possible benefit could there be to losing such a kind, beautiful creature?

The only one that could answer me was locked away behind high, bloodstained gates, and He wasn't talking to anyone.

Halfway through the pastor's reading, the rain stopped. I'd been listening to it like white noise, and hearing it cut short drew me out of my stupor. I lifted my head and refocused on the pastor's voice. I still couldn't seem to focus, though. Breathing felt hard, and with every heartbeat, a dull ache shot through my chest.

Cyrus stood on the other side of Gil, and he caught my eye. Just like Finn used to, the dragon sent a soft, subtle glow of encouragement down the bond. I couldn't muster a smile, but I didn't feel quite as empty now.

Then Ariel added her warmth, and the ground finally stopped shifting. I was able to listen to Finn's benediction and actually hear the words. I let out a long, low breath, and from the corner of my eye, I saw some of the tension leave Collith and Laurie. They'd probably been monitoring my heartbeat. Listening to its struggle. Thanks to my Court, it felt a little stronger now.

After the service ended, our small gathering turned and walked back toward the parking lot. Matthew started fussing, and Damon cupped the back of his son's head. Danny made a soothing sound and reached up to scratch the small boy's back.

Up ahead, there was a large oak tree on the right side of the path, but my gaze immediately went to the figure standing beneath it. I hadn't seen Lyari, or heard from her, since she'd left the day after Finn's death. This time, it wasn't Lucifer keeping her away—it was shame. I could see it in the stiff way she held herself, and how she avoided making eye contact with anyone.

"I'll meet you at the car," I told Emma, who'd been walking behind Danny. She touched my elbow in acknowledgement and followed the others, her frail shoulders hunched against the damp chill.

Once she was gone, I faced Collith and Laurie. Something about their expressions told me they were leaving. None of us said anything. We didn't need to. I knew they'd come if I needed them, and they knew I wouldn't be too proud to ask. Not anymore.

Still silent, Collith stepped forward and pressed a soft kiss to my forehead. His scent reached me, even through the smell of rain, and it had an instant calming effect. The feeling of his cold lips lingered on my skin as he sifted.

Laurie was next. He moved closer, and the edges of his fur-lined black coat brushed against me. I arched my head back to see his face. With such an overcast sky, his eyes looked more gray than silver. A cold gust of wind made tendrils of hair frame his pale face. Laurie skimmed the ball of his thumb along my jawline and gave me a quick, faint wink. He vanished a moment later, and I felt something in my hand. I knew, without looking, that it was a black rose.

I tucked it into my pocket.

Lyari watched me approach expressionlessly. I reached her side and turned, realizing she had a perfect vantage point of the burial plot. In an instant, I knew the faerie had been here the entire service. She may not have been kind to my wolf, or even trusted him, but she'd come for his funeral. For someone like Lyari Paynore, who saw significance in every gesture or choice, that meant something.

"We're all heading to Cyrus's. You're welcome to join us," I said. "Ariel thought we could do a toast, and maybe talk about our favorite memories of Finn, or whatever."

Lyari followed my gaze. The diggers had already started, though we were too far away to hear the dirt hit Finn's casket. She must've seen something in my face, or heard it in my voice, because her eyes darkened as she said, "The Dark Prince is to blame, my lady. Wherever he goes, pain and chaos follow."

My jaw worked at the mention of Lucifer. I'd been so absorbed with thoughts of Finn that I'd barely considered what to do about him. But grieving my friend would have to come later. I kept my gaze on the glint of sunlight off the car roofs as I asked, "Did you ever learn anything about Thuridan?"

"I've reached out to every contact I have, including those who live amongst the mortals. There are no records that mention Thuridan of bloodline Sarwraek. It's as if he didn't exist before he was ten." She paused. "Before he was taken, I tried speaking with him directly, as you instructed, but . . ."

"You couldn't," I finished.

Silence met me. Lyari was wearing her Guardian face, and once again I understood why she'd withdrawn. I didn't force her to admit anything. I knew, better than anyone, how terrifying love could be to acknowledge. Love made you vulnerable. Love blinded you. Love could literally fucking kill you.

Brakes squealed in the distance. I glanced toward the parking lot and saw that Emma was the only one left. The car ran steadily in the misty stillness, its headlights shining bright. Everyone else would be getting to Cyrus's soon, and suddenly the thought felt exhausting. I swallowed a sigh and turned back to Lyari. "Keep looking, please. Thuridan is important to him, and we need to know why."

She nodded. I waited for the warrior to sift, but she stood there, looking at me with a rare gleam of uncertainty in her eyes. I didn't know what else I could say to reassure her of my forgiveness. Especially not now, when I felt like an empty room or a dry riverbed. Barren. Cold.

In the end, I didn't say anything. I nodded my goodbye, then turned away and walked down the rest of the path. Emma was sitting on the driver's side, so I opened the other door. Music floated from the speakers. Before I got in, something made me pause and glance back toward that oak tree. The space below its long, twisted branches was empty now.

As I stood there, it started to rain again. I watched the silvery glints rush past the tree at a slant. Pinpricks of cold sank through my dress, jarring me again. I folded myself into the car and pulled the door shut.

Emma didn't ask me if I was all right, or whether I was hungry. She just changed gears and started driving. She hummed along to whatever song was playing while I looked out the window. While more naked trees blurred past, I kept thinking about love, and pain, and how much more pain waited ahead of me.

It felt like only a minute had passed when I spotted a familiar mailbox—the names LAVENDER, SWORN, and MILLER were painstakingly painted on the side, and scratched beneath these it simply read, NYM—and gravel crunched under the tires as Emma turned onto our driveway.

I finally tore my gaze from the window and watched Cyrus's house loom closer. Closer. I knew my family was inside, waiting to talk and mourn together. Emma navigated the car into its usual parking spot and killed the engine. From the corner of my eye, I saw her look at me. She was probably waiting to speak to me. But I was still looking at the house, and after a few seconds, I felt the dull weight of certainty.

I couldn't do this. Not right now.

Without a word to Emma, I pulled the handle and left. My heels walked unevenly over the gravel as I headed for the barn. I opened the door, and another strong gust of wind nearly flattened me as I slipped into the darkness.

"I've got her," I heard Damon say. I trudged up the stairwell, and my brother stayed close behind. "Fortuna? Are you okay?"

I didn't answer. I just kept climbing the stairs. It felt like I was floating above my own body, looking down at everything. The other Fortuna walked into the loft, her expression hollow and drawn. She left the door open behind her. A stream of light reached inside and spilled across the floor. Damon appeared a moment later. He must've handed Matthew off to someone else, because his arms were empty. Other Fortuna sat at the kitchen table, and after a moment, Damon sank down next to her. The chair creaked beneath his weight.

That single sound made me snap back into myself. I blinked and focused on him.

Before I could apologize, Damon said, "Collith told me everything."

I met his gaze, and I knew I should probably feel panicked. I was consumed by the plan I'd made, though. Nothing else really mattered. "That's a pretty vague statement. A lot has happened," I replied.

"Okay, then. He told me about Oliver."

Hearing my brother say his name out loud felt like a zap. For so long, Oliver had been my secret. I'd learned to hide our dreamscape from the rest of the world, because they didn't understand. The concern in their eyes had taught me to be ashamed of him.

They'd turned out to be right.

"As if you needed another reason to hate me, huh?" I asked. I waited for Damon to agree, but he was silent. A bitter smile touched my lips. "Fine, if you won't say it, I will. I'm the reason our parents are dead."

"I don't blame you, Fortuna," Damon said instantly. I didn't believe him. When I remained silent, my brother watched me with a worried shadow in his eyes. "What are you thinking?"

I stared at the wall across from us, my index finger tapping softly against the table. "I'm thinking the world is a place where the good die and the wicked live."

Damon's voice was soft. "What are you going to do?"

"Find Oliver," I said without hesitation.

"And then?"

Instead of answering, my mind went back. Back to the beginning.

Oliver had arrived during one of the bleakest, darkest times of my life. I remembered how I'd rush to bed every night, eager to see the goofy, gangly-limbed boy who fought so valiantly to keep my bad dreams away. I remembered how warm and solid his hand always felt, wrapped so tightly around mine as we leaped off the edge of the world and plunged into the warm, glittering waters below. He'd been my knight in shining armor. My best friend. My first love.

I thought I had reached my limits. I thought I had known pain. Now I knew everything I'd been through had been preparing me for this.

I lifted my head to meet Damon's worried gaze. "And then I'm going to kill him."

END OF BOOK FIVE

CONTENT WARNING

Please be aware this novel contains scenes or themes of decapitation, profanity, violence, sex, death, and murder.